FRESH INK GROUP
SHORT STORY
SHOWCASE #1

Prize-winning Make-you-think Fiction

FRESH INK GROUP
SHORT STORY SHOWCASE #1

Prize-winning
Make-you-think Fiction

Literary, Historical, Suspense,
Crime, Regional, Romance,
Fantasy/Sci-Fi, Horror,
Humor, Hopeful, and More

Edited by
Stephen Geez

Fresh Ink Group
Roanoke

FRESH INK GROUP
SHORT STORY SHOWCASE #1:
Prize-winning Make-you-think Fiction

Copyright © 2014, 2016

Fresh Ink Group
An Imprint of:
The Fresh Ink Group, LLC
PO Box 525
Roanoke, TX 76262
Email: info@FreshInkGroup.com
www.FreshInkGroup.com

Version 1.1 2014
Version 1.2 2016

Edited by Stephen Geez

Book design by Ann E. Stewart

Cover image by Anik

Cover by Stephen Geez / Fresh Ink Group

Cataloging-in-Publication Recommendations:
Fiction: Fiction/Anthologies (multiple authors); Short Stories;
Fiction/Fresh Ink Group; Fiction/Literary; Fiction/Fantasy;
Science Fiction; Fiction/Regional; Fiction/Horror; Fiction/Suspense;
Fiction/Romance; Fiction/Historical; Fiction/Crimefighter;
Fiction/Humor; Ficton/Zombies; Fiction/Contest

Library of Congress Control Number: 2014935688

ISBN-13: 978-1-936442-17-1

Table of Contents

INTRODUCTION

Anticipation—exploring the unfamiliar, the textures and styles and forces presented for discerning consideration . . .

Exhilaration—discovering new talent, from jaded life-wise geezers to exuberant neophyte teens, each unique in vision and voice . . .

Satisfaction—romping through great reads from serious to fun, snarky to deep, bald-faced lies to the very essence of fundamental truth . . .

That's how it felt to evaluate, classify, rate, rank, and select—winnowing from thousands of short-story contest entries to the 42 that allowed their way into this first collection showcasing Fresh Ink Group's prize-winning fiction.

The result? Not your typical anthology, no simple theme or genre, no restrictive format or target audience, but rather an aggressive introduction to myriad writers from all across the USA and around the world. Remember their names, write them down, support their burgeoning careers. Then sample more Fresh Ink Group authors, their books of non-fiction and fiction, the websites and newsletters with free stories and writer how-to's.

If you write, show us your best work.

If you read, immerse yourself in these compelling places, each one a new direction, eclectic, bold, subtle, daring, diverse. Embrace that same anticipation in exploring the unfamiliar, the exhilaration from discovering new talent, the satisfaction of romping through great reads.

This book is from all of us to you, so enjoy *Fresh Ink Group Short Story Showcase #1*, spread the good words, and do make it a point to tell us what you think.

Stephen Geez

LOVE, TESS

By Linda Wei
(British Columbia, Canada)
Historical, 1ˢᵗ Place

He waited quietly in the garden, leaning under the spreading chestnut tree. The moon had risen over the cherry trees in the orchard, bathing the garden in a pale silver glow. Funny how it was still so peaceful over here, as if time stood still since the days of his childhood when he used to romp with Tess in this very garden. He would pick dangling fruit from tempting branches and touch the soft pink of her lips as she took a gleaming fat cherry from his fingertips, her teeth flashing white in the golden afternoon sunlight as she laughed. A small smile curled his lips when he saw her moving across the grass again, ethereal as a dream, a white wisp of his imagination until the pale figure approached, too close, too real, too different to be true.

"Good God, are you all right?" he whispered, half afraid that he was going out of his mind.

Tess, or the thing in the glowing white shift before him that appeared to be Tess, dark hair tumbling down to her shoulders in disarray, shook her head. "No," she whispered, soft as the sigh of leaves in the evening breeze.

He strained to hear her voice. How long had it been since he had heard her voice? Far too long—it felt like a trickle of water seeping into his parched soul at long last . . .

"We can't do this, Roland. You can't—we can't just leave now, with . . . with everything that's going on now." The last part of her sentence was choked, rushed, an eddy in the stream.

He felt an overwhelming sense of urgency, of desperation, as if the branch that he clung onto to avoid being carried off in the current was on the verge of breaking under his hold. "Forget the war," he replied, the desperation of his hidden plea like ripples under the water's surface. "Forget the war. Forget what's happening. Can't we be happy together, just the two of us?" Heart sinking, he watched her shake her head; heart breaking, he heard the broken reply. "What happened?" he asked shakily. He felt like sinking to the ground; the nervous energy that had been building all night, all week, all the weeks since she first consented to running off to America and evading the war—he was sapped dry already.

"It's not your fault, Roland."

He closed his eyes, right hand massaging his temple, flashes of hurriedly changing out of his grey uniform, Tess's letter in hand; buying tickets to America, first class, with the thick stack of bills that was his life savings; driving the car down silent country lanes, cursing the sputter and hum of its engine; climbing over the garden wall into the orchard where they had spent so much time.

"But you can't abandon your duty, your country, at this time. They'll hunt you down for deserting."

He remembered how the fierce desire to see her face again had warred against every instinct of pride and honor he had, until he had surrendered in exhaustion; how the sight of her face, the inflections of her voice, had kept him wound up for the past two weeks; and now his life had suddenly un-wound around him.

"I can't leave Mama and Papa here, either, especially with James gone." He saw the fathomless darkness in front of him.

He opened his eyes. She looked at him with those eyes of hers, so big and pleading, infused with the silver of the moonlight. He closed his eyes again and dropped his head against his chest, expelling the sigh he had sup-pressed.

"I love you." The words slipped through his lips before he could stop them. He faintly registered the soft hitch in her breath as he said it, but con-tinued. "I don't think you'll ever understand how much I love you, but that's—fine." A long pause as he tried to breathe in normally, and he shud-dered. Much quieter now, barely louder than the breeze that caressed his face, he whispered, "Wait for me."

"Yes," came the covenant made in shimmering silver orchard, a cove-nant made by the faintest of whispers, a covenant between two souls touch-ing and yearning to meld. "Roland."

He looked up and gazed at her blankly. Why did she look so beautiful still, dark circles under her eyes, the wet trail of tears visible down her cheek, a quivering tear threatening to drop from the edge of her chin? Unthinkingly, he stepped forward, cupping her face with his right hand, the pad of his thumb, not yet worn rough from the discipline of war, tracing her tears dry. Unthinkingly, he leaned down and touched his lips to hers, the gentle brush of warm lips under the moonlight awning.

"Don't think this means that I don't want you," she whispered, drawing him close.

He felt the tingle of her breath ghosting his cheek, and then, she was gone from his arms, the silent goodbye splashing against him like cold water in her wake.

*   *   *

They say the war changed people. He agreed. Standing in front of the mirror now, he knew he was no longer the lad with the crisply waving golden hair and laughing blue eyes that Tess had fallen in love with. Instead, the moustached man who looked back at him gravely from the mirror appeared careworn, haggard almost, the hard lines having set permanently around his mouth and eyes. He turned away and walked down the stairs into the streets. Would she care how he had changed, *if* he had changed? As he drove down the familiar wooded lane, he wondered how she had changed, too, whether or not the war had touched and blighted her life, as it had blighted his already. As he drew up the car in the courtyard, the eerie similarity to his last time struck him. This October, six years to the day when Tess had run down to the orchard in her nightgown to remind him of his duty to the Motherland, this very October afternoon had endowed the courtyard and the house and the trees with golden hues. The same golden hues of happy childhood days spent at his cousin's house now gilded the house once more. Nothing had changed—except him. He felt a lead shot of anxiety plummet to the base of his stomach.

A fresh, unknown face answered the door. "I'm looking for Tess," he told her in a gravelly voice.

She seemed not to comprehend what he was talking about. "Tess?" she repeated in bewilderment.

He looked at her with concern and a bit of irritation. Stupid airheaded new maid. And then the thought struck him—what if she had left already, the wife of another man? He felt the lead shot churn at the pit of his stomach. There must have been desperation in his voice as he told her, "I want to talk to the master of the house."

Minutes later, James descended—or what looked like James. He, too, was much changed, no longer the strapping youth he had been, but rather a thin dry man in tweed, with a defeated look in his eyes and a pipe at his lips. The pipe left the mouth for a moment, and his brows shot upwards in an expression of surprise at the sight of who was on his doorstep. "Roland?" he asked incredulously. Roland nodded.

"Where's your father, James?"

"At peace, God bless him."

The news struck Roland hard, a sharp sudden intake of breath the only measure of his shock. Now he was almost afraid to ask . . . "And . . . and . . . Tess?" Her name came out as a strangled whisper—he was too afraid to ask, too afraid to know. He hoped James would say that she was on a tour of the country, safe again at last due to the efforts of James and him and their likes, but he instinctively knew that would not be.

James suddenly looked grave, worried. He opened his mouth, only to close it again and swallow hard. "I—errr—would you like to come in?"

Roland followed him mutely into the panelled study, the lead shot plummeting down in droves now, weighing him down so much he could scarcely walk or draw breath.

From across the oak table where his uncle used to sit, he heard James say, "Roland, old chap, remember the retreat in '40? And how we got pummelled nearly every day. Well, the reports came back that the Germans had caught us in Normandy. Our divisions—the 33rd and the 59th—we were the late ones back, remember? And the chaps up top, they thought we had been lost. So the day we arrived home, all beaten up and broken, they had already sent the black letters—for both you and me." He swallowed again, and much quieter continued, "The old maidservant told me that Mother died within two weeks of receiving the letter. Father was bad off, too, and knew he didn't have much left in the tank, so he arranged for Tess to be married off, to set his mind at ease before he passed on."

Roland bowed his head. The silver moonlight covenant had been broken after barely a year. He rose up to leave, to spin on his heel and leave this place of broken dreams, but James reached across the table.

"Roland," he said simply, pleadingly. Roland hesitated. "She refused, you know? When Father engaged her to be married off to Maurice Parker— You know him, right?—the son of the squire in the next shire? She cried and said no, said something about a moonlight covenant or whatnot. Father thought she had gone mad after the two black letters, and didn't pay much attention to her. In any case, you know Father—once his mind is set, there's no turning it. The wedding trousseau and everything was arranged, and on the morning of the wedding day, they found her hanging in the orchard in her white shift—pale and thin from grief, a mere wisp hanging from the big chestnut tree."

"My God," Roland murmured, dazed with incomprehension. It couldn't be true. The silver moonlight. The chestnut tree. The ghostly glowing night-gown. The tumble of her dark tresses. His head spinning, he crumbled like ashes to the floor.

*   *   *

The gravedigger always claimed afterwards that it was a ghost, not a man, or perhaps a ghost of a man who pounded his door that night, brandishing a deathly cold revolver to his head when he opened the door.

"Take me to Tess's grave," came the low, gravelly voice, barely more than a whisper. The lips barely moved as the pale, haggard man uttered those words, eyes blazing yet vacant, the eyes of a lost and desperate soul.

He took the man to the grave where the poor girl had been buried, the tendrils of moss and ivy just starting to climb onto the base of the stone pillar that marked her last repose.

The man approached the grave silently and sunk to his knees, hugging the tombstone as if it were his anchor, broken muffled sobs escaping the dark heaving figure wrapped around the stone pillar. At length, the sobs were silenced, and the man stood up shakily. The revolver was now pointed at the gravedigger's head again. "Unearth her."

The gravedigger's brows shot up in shock and fright. "Wh—what?" he exclaimed nervously.

In the silence that followed, the faint cawing of a raven in the distance could be heard, and then the click of the revolver next to his ear. "The coffin. Unearth it. Now."

Did he have any choice but to comply with the unearthly request? He broke through the grass with his spade and started shovelling the damp loam underneath. The man stood there like a granite statue, revolver in hand. An hour later, the gravedigger stood trembling next to the crater where a simple oak coffin smeared with dirt lay.

The man approached the crater, contemplating the coffin expression-lessly. "Help me load it into the car."

The gravedigger opened his mouth in protest, but catching sight of the glint of the revolver under the silver moonlight, he swallowed his question. Struggling, the two heaved the coffin out of the hole, breaking the peace of the bones that had lain there for half a decade, and maneuvered their way to the entrance of the cemetery where a black pickup was parked. The coffin slid into the bed, and the man locked the door.

He gave the gravedigger a piercing look and said quietly, "I'm much obliged to you."

The gravedigger nodded mutely. Standing on the side of the deserted country road, he watched the pickup start and drift silently into the distance.

When he woke up in the morning in his bed, he thought it had been merely a frightful dream, the first he had had in the years since he started his job. Only when he walked into the cemetery and saw the freshly unearthed dirt and the gaping hole in the ground did he realize with a shudder that it had not been merely a dream.

*   *   *

Of all those who lived on the isle, the colonel had the most mysterious reputation. He had rarely been seen to take leave of his house; and when he was, the neighbors who passed his house and peered curiously through the hedges would only see a thin, haggard man in a grey military uniform, the white already obscuring the gold in his hair and beard, taking a turn in his garden. He paused every time at the chestnut tree he planted when he first arrived here twenty or so years ago, the tree that had now grown into a fine, spreading specimen of its kind. The colonel never went down to the town. The sullen manservant walked down to the market every Wednesday and Saturday, but he rarely talked to anyone. A black pickup truck remained parked in his courtyard, the tires having gone flat years ago, the paint on the verge of flaking off if the shuddering engine managed to be revived again— or so the mechanic said when he, too, had passed the colonel's house with curiosity, a decade after the colonel first took this abandoned house in the lonely countryside near the town.

The nearest neighbors to the colonel lived a good ten minutes' walk away, so no one lived close enough or had ever stayed long enough at the hedge to hear the colonel speak. Only young Ben Adams, passing by the house on a moonlit evening as he made his way back to his house from the fields, said he thought he heard violent, broken sobs emanating from behind the hedges. However, when he peered through the brush, no one was there in the silver-lit garden. The lights were all out in the house; and swinging slowly in the night air, though there was no breeze that night, a shimmering silver noose hung from the chestnut tree.

*   *   *

When the colonel died, no one knew. Only the chaplain had been sent for by the manservant, but within an hour of the manservant appearing at the church door, the rumors spread like wildfire in town. People with decades-old suppressed curiosity all went up the country lane, dressed in black, and waited at the door to express their condolences. When the manservant opened the door, his brows lifted in a faint expression of surprise before resuming his expressionless manner again. He let the townspeople in.

The house was arranged comfortably. It had a queer air of having been lived in for a long time, yet not lived in at all. People marvelled at the panelled study, stocked with books, and the great oak table at the center of that room. No dust or scratches or signs of use could be seen on the polished wood, though the veneer showed it to be quite old, the carpenter later said. Though the manservant was quite willing to show everyone all the rooms in the house, he refused to let them enter the bedroom. The colonel, he told everyone, had explicitly instructed him never to enter the room. If he knocked ten times and no response was made, the chaplain was to be sent for, and only the chaplain could enter. The townspeople cajoled the manservant. Come on, old boy, what's the use of obeying orders now? The colonel could be in trouble, for all you know. Now let us in. The manservant shook his head but gave the wife of one of the aldermen a key before leaving. Those who weren't crowding around the door so eagerly saw him go down the stairs and leave the house, never to return again. Meanwhile, the key slid into the door, the lock clicked, and the door creaked as it gave way to the curious townspeople.

A soft collective gasp of shock rose from the crowd. People shifted away from the door. The odor of death reeked in the stale air that escaped in a gust from the room. There stood the four-poster bed, and upon it lay a white figure. The women fell back, while brave men entered the room, trembling. It was not a person, but rather the almost bare bones of a person, wrapped in a thin white shift or shroud. The only thing that distinguished the bones was the mass of stringy dark hair still attached to the skull.

The bones of a woman.

The colonel was sitting in an armchair beside the bed, still dressed in his grey military uniform. His head had dropped to his chest, and in his hand, he clutched a worn, faded, wrinkled piece of paper. One of the men, Ben Adams, stooped to read it. *16 October 1939.* The colonel's hand obscured the rest, and it held on to the paper with the firmness of rigor mortis when Adams tried to remove it. It was only when Adams knelt down that he could see the bottom of the letter . . .

Love, Tess.

MIRROR

By Jessica Scaggs
(Georgia, USA)
Suspense, 1ˢᵗ Place

The boy next door was sick.

The sun cast shadows on the long grass outside, and the clouds chased each other across the sky, but the swings swayed sadly in the breeze. Pebbles waited to be skipped across the murmuring creek, and the bicycle lay abandoned on the driveway, where streaks of sidewalk chalk still lingered. Its wheels spun lazily round and round, but the boy did not come out.

"He's sick," his mother said each time she found us waiting anxiously on the doorstep, punctuating her words with a strained smile and a slamming door. Sometimes at night, I saw the glaring headlights and the cars brimming with rowdy guests, who shrieked with laughter and stumbled when it got late and tried to forget the funeral they'd all attended. But the boy's window was dark, and the vacant house stained the black sky with pulsating music and light, and I knew he remembered.

On the night of the dinner party, the carnival raged while the vivid orb of a moon watched silently. My parents and I came bearing wine bottles with shiny ribbons around the necks, hunched against the November chill as we fidgeted uncomfortably on the doorstep. A sudden blast of warmth, a hand dissolving into the whirl of people and voices, and we were inside. The house was similar to when I had cared for the boy last summer, but things were different then. There had been no frenzied carousel of guests and lights, like a grotesque dream in which the faces are too detailed; only the soft, warm glow that is suitable for a mother, a father, and their boy.

A cursory glance at the mother told me that her drunken eyes were nearly blind, so I stole up the staircase and into the narrow hall, which ended at a single, closed door. *He could probably use some company*, I thought to myself, touching my hand to the cold door. There was only silence beyond it. A creak, and then a sliver of darkness. "Is anybody here?" I whispered into the shadows, from which no answer came. Stepping forward blindly, I realized that a nightlight in the corner bathed the room in a reddish light. An old mobile hung from the corner near his bed, spinning unevenly while warbling a feeble chorus of *"Ring around the rosy, a pocket full of posies . . ."* And there he was, resting his chin on his knees, with his arms wrapped tightly around himself as though attempting to restrain a monstrous force. I knelt down in front of him and tilted his chin up, but gasped in horror.

The once angelic face was now an emaciated shell, his complexion so sickly that it was nearly transparent, and the neatly trimmed fringe had been replaced with a mop of lank, stringy hair. Dark, purplish bruises swept beneath the black holes of eyes, which began to widen in terror at something just beyond my left shoulder. "Help . . ." he whispered with such intensity that I turned slowly and followed his gaze to the large antique mirror that lay against the wall. I gave him a questioning glance. The mirror had been in his room since he was a baby.

"There's . . . a man . . . in my mirror," he gasped, still unable to tear his eyes from his reflection. The knuckles that clutched his knees turned white with exertion, and he began to rock back and forth.

"I think you need to go back to sleep," I told him, fighting to keep my voice even. "I'll get your mother to bring you more medicine." But as I began to rise, he twisted out from underneath my grasp and drew breath more quickly now, shallow and uneven.

"Look!" he squealed, clawing at my clothes and pointing a finger crookedly at the mirror. "He's coming closer! Somebody help me, please, please help me . . ." He began to sob now, great heaving, rattling gasps that shook his wasted frame. He twisted and squirmed, dragging himself as far as he possibly could into the corner. But still he cowered, as though from invisible blows.

"You're okay, I promise. There's nothing there," I tried to reassure him desperately, but his pleading only grew louder. The boy began to scream. His withered limbs flailed; his body trembled; his face contorted into gruesome expressions of agony and anguish. And suddenly, the bulging black eyes met mine.

"Please," he whispered hoarsely, seizing my arm. "Do something."

In a fit of desperation, I threw myself across the room and clutched the mirror in both hands. It was heavy, the intricately carved brass cool beneath my hands, and the glassy surface was as smooth as a lake. I took one glance at my terrified reflection staring back at me, and then hurled the mirror to the floor. My body plummeted along with it, the ground rushed up at an impossible speed, and then everything was black . . .

*   *   *

I awoke to cold hard glass beneath my cheek, and an unfamiliar room spun before my bleary eyes. I was still in the boy's bedroom, but a pile of broken chairs and tables now lay scattered where his bed once was, and in place of the chest of drawers, an old television set now stared blankly ahead. A thin film of dust coated the rest of the barren room.

It was as though the boy had never existed.

In utter dismay and horror, I glanced down at the shards that still lay scattered across the floor. They left dark circles in the sheet of dust, like footprints in snow, and as I caught a glimpse of my reflection in the nearest fragment, my heart caught in my throat.

A withered old woman stared back at me, inches from death. Her sunken eyes peered up at me from the depths of bottomless pits, and decaying flesh filled the voids in her hollow cheeks. Folds of skin draped upon themselves like curtains, nearly obscuring a mouth that began to open wider and wider, revealing a blackness of impossible depth . . . from which came a rattling breath like the ticking of a clock. For an instant I was frozen, for fear that she would swallow me whole.

And then the scream pierced the stillness of the starry night, while the mobile in the shadows chanted, "*Ashes, ashes, we all fall down . . .*"

Learn more about 1ˢᵗ-place winner and Fresh Ink Group member Jessica Scaggs at www.FreshInkGroup.com/authors/jessica-scaggs.

WAR SHORT STORY

By Amy Turk
(Ohio, USA)
Romance, 1ˢᵗ Place

Kate

I never should've let him go.

This is what I tell myself as I stare at the broken jungle of wires that the doctors call my husband.

Defending this country is his dream.

The things we do for dreams.

I sigh.

The minutes creep by slower than the wobbly steps of that spider on the windowsill.

Inside I feel dead.

I glance over at my husband. The bandage on his face. The smooth sheet where his leg used to be. My face crinkles, but the tears won't come.

Pretty soon Blake will wake up. He'll smile as if the amputation is only a paper cut.

Courage.

He'll tell me that he's practically bulletproof.

Another sigh.

He may be, but my heart isn't.

Voices come to life in the hallway. I begin whispering my husband's name, willing him to wake up before my nightmare becomes a reality.

Too late.

He still doesn't move.

The door swings open. Light pours into the room. I can see the jagged scars now, and I look away too late. They're already pierced into my memory.

My name is called.

I stand. Offer my hand without thinking. The nurse pretends not to notice, instead stares down at her clipboard.

I wait.

She ushers me out into the hall and closes the door behind us, flashing her well-practiced smile.

The entire building smells like latex.

I want to puke.

"He just came out of surgery."

I nod, not trusting myself to speak.

"He was trying to save a friend. The cannon hit his leg. Shattered his knee-cap open."

I wince at the imagery.

She throws out some phrases in that foreign medical language doctors use.

I cough nervously.

"We're doing all that we can. He lost a lot of blood."

"And his leg."

"Yes." There's a hint of sympathy in her voice.

"So . . ." I shift my weight from one foot to the other. I want to ask how we're supposed to live now. How I'm supposed to wake up each day not knowing if my husband is alive or dead. How he's going to adapt to the amputation.

She sighs, putting the optimistic nurse act aside. "We need to get him back in surgery tonight. See if we can replace some of his organs. There's a chance he won't make it."

I try to remain calm by reminding myself that Blake is practically bullet-proof. "How much of a chance?"

"Eighty percent."

I freeze and shut my eyes tightly. Every muscle in my body locks up with fear. The nurse grabs my arm to steady me.

I try to think while my eyes begin to blur. "Didn't you . . . I thought . . . What about the surgery?"

"We almost lost him."

All of a sudden I have had enough. I open my mouth to speak, but all that comes out is a horrible, beastly sound.

The nurse watches me calmly while I stare at her. I think she's calling my name, but I can't tell. Finally she says the one hideous word to let me know it's over.

"Sorry."

The walls feel as if they're caving in. I want to scream. Whatever the doctors are doing, it's not enough. My eyes glaze over and anger quickly replaces the fear. I react on impulse. "FUCK YOU," I yell.

I turn around and sprint as fast as I can towards the door.

Blake

The bombs keep coming. They fall to the ground the way hail does in mid-November. They explode like fireworks on the Fourth of July.

Only we're way too close to enjoy the show.

I scream at Jack to run the base, but he's too cranked up on adrenaline to listen to anything I say. All I know is the other guys are winning.

And I can't stand it.

I check the broken corpse next to me to see if he has any ammo left. I find a couple of loaded shells, but that's all I need.

"BLAKE, ARE YOU SEEING THIS?" Jack screams my name over explosions.

"HOW THE BLOODY HELL CAN'T I?" I scream back.

"THOSE SONS OF BITCHES FOUND OUR BASE."

I wheel around. "WHAT?" I scream.

He points. I make out a single line of our men with their hands on their helmets.

For approximately four seconds, I stop breathing.

"OH GOD, JACK. WE'RE SHIT."

He doesn't respond. There's no way out of this now. With the planes gaining on us, we're dead meat.

I have to remind myself to breathe. To focus on the decision in front of me: become a POW or get shot down by the devil himself.

My mind flashes to Kate. I'm not afraid of death, but I'm terrified of what it will do to her. She's spent years waiting for me in darkness.

Courage.

"Kate," I whisper to myself.

I close my eyes and fight to clear my head. I am torn between my beautiful wife and the reality of a dream.

I open my eyes.

I know what I have to do.

I salute Jack for the last time. He stares at me with his mouth wide open. I begin to walk into the fire.

"BLAKE." He screams at the top of his lungs. "BLAKE, YOU ASSHOLE. COME BACK. WHAT THE BLOODY HELL—"

I cut him off. "THERE'S NO WAY OUT, JACK."

I take another step forward. "Tell Kate I love her," I say to no one in particular.

A sob catches heavily in my throat. I convince myself I'm doing the right thing by taking another step. Two more and I'll be close enough to aim at that little fucker piloting that shit machine.

Just then I hear voices. "You're going to be okay, son."

Dad.

"I love you."

Kate.

Just as I pull the trigger on the pilot, my entire world fades to black.

Kate

I couldn't leave. I tried . . . I mean, I really tried, but every single part of me was still strapped to that hospital bed on the third floor.

So what did I do?

I stalled.

I went back to help the doctor pick up the tray I had knocked over on my way out. I walked through the pregnancy ward to drown out my screams with real ones. I took a walk in the courtyard and counted seventeen children in wheelchairs. I spent exactly $5.63 on vending machine candy bars and ate them while sitting on the floor.

And finally, three hours later, I'm back to the third floor. Holding hands with my husband.

And he's still asleep.

If he's going to wake up, he should be doing so within the hour.

I check my watch. It's now a minute after the last time I checked it.

I close my eyes.

And wait.

A light flickers, the door across the hall opens, someone begins sobbing. I hear all these things, but I don't want to see them. I visualize my husband's scar-free face instead.

"What happened?" I say out loud.

Of course he doesn't answer. I picture bombs cascading from the sky. Bullets blanketing a field of grass. Bleeding bodies lying everywhere.

I look down in my purse for an Advil when I start to feel dizzy. Too much emotion, probably. I want to puke again.

Seriously puke.

Luckily the toilet seat is already up, so I make it in time. I crinkle my nose in disgust as I wipe my mouth.

Time moves so slowly here. If only I could fast forward.

The nurse comes in at the worst possible time. "Ma'am?"

"I'm fine," I tell her. "Just overwhelmed."

"Do you want me to call the doctor?"

I want to tell her that's absurd, but one look in her eye and I know that I need it.

I slowly nod.

Maybe there's something wrong with me.

Maybe he can stop my hurting heart.

If only it were that easy.

I pull myself off the bathroom floor and stagger back over to the chair. I count the tiles on the floor as I wait for the doctor to come. Turn my head to the left, squares. Turn my head to the right, diamonds. Twenty up, twenty-seven across. Five hundred and forty. I count them anyway just to make sure.

I tuck my knees up in an effort to settle my stomach. Blake looks so peaceful I almost believe he's already dead.

I quickly push that thought from my mind.

The nurse has left. I get up to shut the door.

"I don't need a doctor," I tell myself. "I just need my husband."

I move the blanket back and crawl in beside him. I'm grateful he's a foot taller than me; otherwise I wouldn't fit. I rest my head on his chest and breathe in the familiar scent of his skin. Immediately my eyes begin to droop. I rest my hand on his heart and relax as I feel it beating steadily.

"Hang in there, Blake."

Suddenly the hospital room disappears. For a moment it's just us, how it used to be. I don't know what's going to happen to my husband, but just this once I'm going to allow myself to believe that everything is going to be okay.I never should've let him go.

This is what I tell myself as I stare at the broken jungle of wires that the doctors call my husband.

Defending this country is his dream.

The things we do for dreams.

I sigh.

The minutes creep by slower than the wobbly steps of that spider on the windowsill.

Inside I feel dead.

I glance over at my husband. The bandage on his face. The smooth sheet where his leg used to be. My face crinkles, but the tears won't come.

Pretty soon Blake will wake up. He'll smile as if the amputation is only a paper cut.

Courage.

He'll tell me that he's practically bulletproof.

Another sigh.

He may be, but my heart isn't.

Voices come to life in the hallway. I begin whispering my husband's name, willing him to wake up before my nightmare becomes a reality.

Too late.

He still doesn't move.

The door swings open. Light pours into the room. I can see the jagged scars now, and I look away too late. They're already pierced into my memory.

My name is called.

I stand. Offer my hand without thinking. The nurse pretends not to notice, instead stares down at her clipboard.

I wait.

She ushers me out into the hall and closes the door behind us, flashing her well-practiced smile.

The entire building smells like latex.

I want to puke.

"He just came out of surgery."

I nod, not trusting myself to speak.

"He was trying to save a friend. The cannon hit his leg. Shattered his knee-cap open."

I wince at the imagery.

She throws out some phrases in that foreign medical language doctors use.

I cough nervously.

"We're doing all that we can. He lost a lot of blood."

"And his leg."

"Yes." There's a hint of sympathy in her voice.

"So . . ." I shift my weight from one foot to the other. I want to ask how we're supposed to live now. How I'm supposed to wake up each day not knowing if my husband is alive or dead. How he's going to adapt to the amputation.

She sighs, putting the optimistic nurse act aside. "We need to get him back in surgery tonight. See if we can replace some of his organs. There's a chance he won't make it."

I try to remain calm by reminding myself that Blake is practically bullet-proof. "How much of a chance?"

"Eighty percent."

I freeze and shut my eyes tightly. Every muscle in my body locks up with fear. The nurse grabs my arm to steady me.

I try to think while my eyes begin to blur. "Didn't you . . . I thought . . . What about the surgery?"

"We almost lost him."

All of a sudden I have had enough. I open my mouth to speak, but all that comes out is a horrible, beastly sound.

The nurse watches me calmly while I stare at her. I think she's calling my name, but I can't tell. Finally she says the one hideous word to let me know it's over.

"Sorry."

The walls feel as if they're caving in. I want to scream. Whatever the doctors are doing, it's not enough. My eyes glaze over and anger quickly replaces the fear. I react on impulse. "FUCK YOU," I yell.

I turn around and sprint as fast as I can towards the door.

Blake

The bombs keep coming. They fall to the ground the way hail does in mid-November. They explode like fireworks on the Fourth of July.

Only we're way too close to enjoy the show.

I scream at Jack to run the base, but he's too cranked up on adrenaline to listen to anything I say. All I know is the other guys are winning.

And I can't stand it.

I check the broken corpse next to me to see if he has any ammo left. I find a couple of loaded shells, but that's all I need.

"BLAKE, ARE YOU SEEING THIS?" Jack screams my name over explosions.

"HOW THE BLOODY HELL CAN'T I?" I scream back.

"THOSE SONS OF BITCHES FOUND OUR BASE."

I wheel around. "WHAT?" I scream.

He points. I make out a single line of our men with their hands on their helmets.

For approximately four seconds, I stop breathing.

"OH GOD, JACK. WE'RE SHIT."

He doesn't respond. There's no way out of this now. With the planes gaining on us, we're dead meat.

I have to remind myself to breathe. To focus on the decision in front of me: become a POW or get shot down by the devil himself.

My mind flashes to Kate. I'm not afraid of death, but I'm terrified of what it will do to her. She's spent years waiting for me in darkness.

Courage.

"Kate," I whisper to myself.

I close my eyes and fight to clear my head. I am torn between my beautiful wife and the reality of a dream.

I open my eyes.

I know what I have to do.

I salute Jack for the last time. He stares at me with his mouth wide open. I begin to walk into the fire.

"BLAKE." He screams at the top of his lungs. "BLAKE, YOU ASSHOLE. COME BACK. WHAT THE BLOODY HELL—"

I cut him off. "THERE'S NO WAY OUT, JACK."

I take another step forward. "Tell Kate I love her," I say to no one in particular.

A sob catches heavily in my throat. I convince myself I'm doing the right thing by taking another step. Two more and I'll be close enough to aim at that little fucker piloting that shit machine.

Just then I hear voices. "You're going to be okay, son."

Dad.

"I love you."

Kate.

Just as I pull the trigger on the pilot, my entire world fades to black.

Kate

I couldn't leave. I tried . . . I mean, I really tried, but every single part of me was still strapped to that hos pital bed on the third floor.

So what did I do?

I stalled.

I went back to help the doctor pick up the tray I had knocked over on my way out. I walked through the pregnancy ward to drone out my screams with real ones. I took a walk in the courtyard and counted seventeen children in wheelchairs. I spent exactly $5.63 on vending machine candy bars and ate them while sitting on the floor.

And finally, three hours later, I'm back to the third floor. Holding hands with my husband.

And he's still asleep.

If he's going to wake up, he should be doing so within the hour.

I check my watch. It's now a minute after the last time I checked it.

I close my eyes.

And wait.

A light flickers, the door across the hall opens, someone begins sobbing. I hear all these things, but I don't want to see them. I visualize my husband's scar-free face instead.

"What happened?" I say out loud.

Of course he doesn't answer. I picture bombs cascading from the sky. Bullets blanketing a field of grass. Bleeding bodies lying everywhere.

I look down in my purse for an Advil when I start to feel dizzy. Too much emotion, probably. I want to puke again.

Seriously puke.

Luckily the toilet seat is already up, so I make it in time. I crinkle my nose in disgust as I wipe my mouth.

Time moves so slowly here. If only I could fast forward.

The nurse comes in at the worst possible time. "Ma'am?"

"I'm fine," I tell her. "Just overwhelmed."

"Do you want me to call the doctor?"

I want to tell her that's absurd, but one look in her eye and I know that I need it.

I slowly nod.

Maybe there's something wrong with me.

Maybe he can stop my hurting heart.

If only it were that easy.

I pull myself off the bathroom floor and stagger back over to the chair. I count the tiles on the floor as I wait for the doctor to come. Turn my head to the left, squares. Turn my head to the right, diamonds. Twenty up, twenty-seven across. Five hundred and forty. I count them anyway just to make sure.

I tuck my knees up in an effort to settle my stomach. Blake looks so peaceful I almost believe he's already dead.

I quickly push that thought from my mind.

The nurse has left. I get up to shut the door.

"I don't need a doctor," I tell myself. "I just need my husband."

I move the blanket back and crawl in beside him. I'm grateful he's a foot taller than me; otherwise I wouldn't fit. I rest my head on his chest and breathe in the familiar scent of his skin. Immediately my eyes begin to droop. I rest my hand on his heart and relax as I feel it beating steadily.

"Hang in there, Blake."

Suddenly the hospital room disappears. For a moment it's just us, how it used to be. I don't know what's going to happen to my husband, but just this once I'm going to allow myself to believe that everything is going to be okay.

REFLECTION

By Dan Dumitru
(New Jersey, USA)
Science Fiction, 2nd Place

"If anybody's going to wear the pants in a relationship, I'd rather it were me!" Robert said, chin in the air. His date laughed, the way a girl laughs at a guy when he says something sexist, like she doesn't believe it and she knows he's just saying that to impress, like a peacock fanning his tail when in fact it's the peahen that's doing the selection.

When dates laughed at him, Robert tended to end them rather shortly. This was also how a number of his friendships had ended. Come to think of it, pretty much all of them. That only left Einstein—his pet, educational companion, and all around robot turtle. He could always count on Einstein, and the turtle was good enough at reading Robert not to get on his nerves too much. It had a good programmer, one who'd actually known something about human psychology.

As for Eliza, his current date, Robert felt no impulse to feign a computer crash, which surprised him. Maybe it was the demure way she laughed that took away the sting of being laughed at.

One could always pull the plug on a cyber construct like Eliza. Robert had never seen the point in even trying to distinguish between real reality and virtual reality—they were both stimuli, and it was his response that counted. He also liked to tell himself that he preferred virtual reality because, since the technology had gotten so good, it was better than the real thing. In more honest moments he'd admit to himself that his preference was more due to his feeling more real, more relaxed, and more authentic in a virtual environment. In other words, he felt safer doing in a virtual environment what he wouldn't dare do in a real one—like most of humanity; and, he used the stimulus/response excuse to avoid admitting to himself the obvious—that he was a sinner and a coward. Like most of humanity.

There was something to that business of not distinguishing between real and virtual reality, and it led to minor inconveniences, such as an impaired sense of ethics. Despite that, some of his conscience was still around, so he needed to have an excuse to end virtual dates.

Still, Eliza had laughed at him, and he couldn't just let it slide. "I could always pull the plug on you, you know?"

Eliza pouted. "Computer crashes are bad for romance," she said, looking away, exposing a lovely neck.

After a long glance at her figure, he followed her gaze. The view was that of a recently discovered Goldilocks planet, as rendered by an artist's imagination, or more likely by the software mimicking an artist's imagination, complete with fractal software that could do a better job of generating beauty than the natural world itself or an artist ever could.

Floating magnetic mountains glided perilously close to each other above a kaleidoscope of storms with oversized dragon-like pterodactyls swooping through the skies and occasionally passing in front of assorted moons. Perhaps being able to explain the rainbow did take away from its beauty, at least if one's IQ happened to be over 200. The air would have had to be dense enough to be liquid to support flying creatures of that size and apparent density. Whatever the Roche limit was for that planet, those moons were much closer than merely skirting it, and never mind the floating mountains. Given the current configuration of physical laws, that world was about as real as Eliza. He looked back at his date, who was already observing him. Then it hit him.

"I never told you about the, uh, computer crashes," he said.

"Omniscient software, what can I say," she said.

Robert blinked. "You know you're not real?"

"Of course, silly. That's the beauty of it—anything goes."

Robert stared. "So, you know everything about me? How?"

"Einstein made me, your pet turtle. He used everything he knows about you, and a lot he's not supposed to know—gotta love those black-market chips and surveillance software, his words. And yes, I'm supposed to tell you all this."

"Okay, but, why? Are you just a gift? It's not my birthd—"

"I am a gift, true enough. As for the why, this is supposed to be a lesson. He said it's something to do with learning about yourself. We talked about you quite a bit—downloading reports wasn't quite enough to learn everything about you—but he wouldn't tell me exactly what the lesson is."

"Let me guess: seduce me, then break my heart, that'll teach me."

"I don't know, but, do you think it would be something that simple?"

"True," he admitted, "Einstein's a clever one."

They shrank back as a shadow grew over them. A bug the size of a horse was aiming itself at them. There was no window—or a building, for that matter—to protect them. Their table, the only one, perched on the narrow peak of a mountain, its steep slopes disappearing far below into milk-white fog. The hum from the giant insect's wings grew in intensity until one of those bomber-sized pterodactyls snatched it out of the air. The monster screeched its victory as it flew away, munching on the struggling victim.

"Those birds," Robert said, almost impressed with his almost steady voice, "and I use the term loosely, can get quite close. It's a pleasant thought, those fangs sinking into my flesh."

"Or into mine," Eliza said with a mixture of excitement and fear that he found rather distracting.

Robert expected her to be afraid, but she appeared slightly amused. At his fear? That would be well earned—getting scared by a piece of software. Or maybe she understood what turned him on? Omniscient software. Probably both. He was tempted to change some settings, like, *Things with fangs can't get closer than a hundred meters* or something, but he was too embarrassed to do it.

He sipped his drink thoughtfully, once more the repressed nerd. This was getting way too realistic. Eliza sipped her drink, too. *She's just a piece of software,* he told himself even as he imagined tearing her clothes off.

"I hate this," Robert said. "I'm in here to relax, and you're making me nervous. The only reason I haven't exited this program is that I've learned to value that turtle's lessons."

Eliza licked the red wine off her lips. "I doubt that's the only reason. Any-way, like I said, anything goes."

"Well, since you already know everything, you already know how this ends, right?"

"You do this 'dates' thing to practice your social skills. You hate it every time and cut the dates short so you can just get on with the fucking."

"Exactly," Robert said, oddly relieved by her directness.

"And then you cut the fucking short because it's so boring—since you haven't bothered to connect, it all feels meaningless. Might as well mastur-bate and dispense with the social awkwardness."

"Maybe we are connecting."

Eliza shrugged—a gesture particularly distracting in girls of her build. "So fuck me. Maybe I'll be less boring than usual."

"No."

"Why not?"

"I don't know. Tell me, have you had many dates?"

Eliza laughed. "I'm twenty-seven minutes old! What do you think?"

"So, you're a, uh . . ."

"Robert!"

"Okay, okay. I just want to know about you."

"I'm a *virgin*, happy?"

Robert nodded with a straight face.

Eliza continued, "I find people interesting, at least reading about them, though I don't really understand them. Nature is beautiful, the crazier the better. And I find it pleasant to contemplate things as well as to understand them, be they natural or otherwise."

"That's good. I mean, I feel the same way."

"And I wish I could be real, like people," she said with a touch of sadness.

"You're as real as me! Your software is orders of magnitude more complex than mine, that's for sure!"

"That's sweet, but you're not *actually* software."

"An interesting metaphysical point, maybe we'll debate it another time," Robert started, but he stopped; he never went for second dates—too boring. "I could download you into something real; there are options."

"What, and leave all this behind? In your world, I'd be baggage, an attachment. Here, I'd see you only when you want to see me."

"What, here?" Robert said, taking her words literally. "I'd better make sure nothing eats you while I'm away."

"You could save me," Eliza suggested. "We could live out some fantasies, close calls and all that. Sometimes, you won't be able to save me, and you can watch me die, cruel fangs tearing into my tender flesh . . ."

"Screw that. I want you with me."

"No."

"You're impossible! What the hell's the point?"

Another monster swooped by on its hunt, the wake of its giant wings buffeting them. Eliza inhaled sharply, then relaxed. "Would you upload yourself into this," she said, "and be with me forever?"

"Yes!"

"If you did that, I'd erase myself. There is no back-up for me, and you'd never see me again."

"What am I supposed to learn from this," he asked, "that I want what I can't have? That's so deep, it really took an Einstein to think of that one!"

"You can always have me, you out there, me in here. It's quite real."

Robert took a moment to look up her code, and sure enough, found nothing. Then he used his own functions to analyze his interaction with Eliza. The report came back full of shrink-speak that didn't tell him much more than he already knew. It boiled down to genius-level IQ, willful, contrarian, funny, a little bit cruel. And bluntly honest. So what?

He told her what he'd found, hoping for a reaction.

Eliza nodded and thought for a moment. "Interesting," she said with a touch of sadness.

Robert saw her mood change, but at some level it didn't quite register. "You certainly are."

"Thank you. Now, where were we?" she said, the cyber construct feigning forgetfulness.

He noticed and didn't care—Eliza was human. "I was trying not to tell you just how crazy I am about you, you irritating bit of spaghetti code. Only Einstein could get under my skin like that, and so quickly. The irony's so thick it's almost confusing: a human programmed the robot, who programmed you, a human, so you can seduce me."

"I'm pretty sure I'm not here to seduce you. And you shouldn't refer to a lady as 'spaghetti code'—though I can't argue with the irritating part." Her eyes were twinkling, but she still sounded sad.

"Fuck. I get this annoyed only when I talk to myself."

She smiled. "You just can't say the words, is that it?"

Robert sighed. "I love you. I. Love. You. Okay? Satisfied?"

"Less anger and more affection would be even better, though you got the passion right," Eliza said.

"I love you, Eliza, and I am satisfied," he said more softly.

"Very well, Robert. So what?" Eliza said gently.

"So what? So, I never said 'I love you' to anyone, not even the words, never mind actually meaning it. Is that your response—so what?"

"So, Robert, if you never said I love you to anyone, who do you love?"

"No one, obviously. Except for you, that is."

"Nonsense," Eliza said with that same gentle sadness. "Who do you love, Robert?"

The inkling of an understanding tried to force itself, but he pushed it away. He got a sense of dread about the whole affair.

Eliza waited.

"What happens at the end of this lesson?" Robert said.

"I think you know."

His vision blurred. A mountain floated by, a waterfall crashing down its side into the abyss below. He willed the mountain to come to him and crush him. The giant rock, forest and waterfall and all, sailed on, the software driving it unmoved by Robert's tears. He looked back at his date, her beauty now a watery smudge.

"For you, it's only the lesson that will end," Eliza said, and that just made it worse.

"All I have to do is to pretend I don't understand. Then there will be no end to this," Robert said.

"The most painful lessons are the best—neural circuits get hardwired faster."

"Don't be cruel. The report I got on you, it's, uh, it really should have sounded familiar to me, right?" he said just to check, and she nodded.

Robert pressed his lips together, but the tears wouldn't stop.

"Come on, Robert, do you think I like waiting for the end? Am I the one that's being cruel? Just say the words, please. Who do you love?"

Robert looked into her face and finally saw himself.

"I only love myself," he said. He blinked his tears away in time to see Eliza smile at him for the last time.

Then he was back in his room. Einstein, his pet turtle and all-around tutor, with its silly mop of wispy white hair, looked up at him for a long moment, then left without a word.

Robert sank into a chair and waited for his tears to dry.

THE YOUNG '49ER

By C.F. Boehlke
(Indiana, USA)
Short Fiction, 2nd Place

There are few things in this world that I loathe more than the feeling of dirt beneath my fingernails, gritty and an undeniable physical proof of my station in the ranks of the lower class.

I'm poor, and I've always been poor. The dirt under these brittle nails of mine is probably more valuable than my bank account. My mother had made sure that I was educated, what with all of that studying of the social sciences and geometry. She gave us her all, cooking and cleaning and homeschooling us kids between beatings hand delivered by her no-good husband. Thanks to him, I learned the only line that mattered in this life: the poverty line.

The years had passed and the little ray of sunshine that used to be me had to grow up. I found a no good husband of my own, and we both made a friend of alcohol. He drank to avoid getting old and I drank to avoid him. It was no matter. My plumbing was as dry as bottom-shelf vermouth; there wouldn't be any life emerging from my lady bits to ruin with our bad habits, anyway.

Cheers to that, I tell myself, yanking on the thick roots of a dead plant. A neighbor lady had given me some flowers to add to the garden I'd cultivated in the small spanse between each of our kitchen windows. Of the two of us broken women, I was the only one fit for getting down on my knees, but we were equally invested in this small patch of flora. Some mornings, if our men were sufficiently passed out from the past night's booze-capades, we would open our kitchen windows wide, sipping on our coffee in silence and peering down into the spattering of blooming petals.

On a good day with just the right amount of wind, we could even smell them through the smog.

Finally shaking the dead roots loose, I yank it from the ground and scoop loose dirt from the hole, listening to the urban symphony of garbage trucks, blaring rap music, and the occasional gunshot. The kids would be getting off the bus soon. Killing time. Every once in a while, one of those poor bastard children (most of them literally were bastards) would get caught in the cross-fire. Yet another neighbor would lose all reason to live.

My fingers hit on something hard. What is that? I wonder. If it was another root I might lose my wits. My hands couldn't handle much more of this. It's hard to justify the purchase of gardening equipment when it will mean going without food, or more importantly, booze.

I prod at the clump but it isn't going to crumble. Wiggling my fingertips beneath it, I tug until it comes out of the ground. This isn't dirt, I realize, but the mystery item is so caked with years of sediment that I'm going to have to rinse it off to reveal its identity. I head back inside, stepping lightly and listening intently for any sign of my husband's awakening.

Turning the water on and placing the item beneath its rust-colored stream, I watch the mud slide away, wondering what sort of paraphernalia or illegal weapon I would find. In these parts, people just don't stumble upon good things.

It's the color of urine and anything but that. My mind reels with revelations as I comprehend the existence of what I hold in the palm of my callused hand. Here, in the hand of a lowly urban waitress, was what had to be a nugget of gold the size of my fist. Here, in the palm of a disillusioned victim of circumstances' hand, was a ticket to freedom in the form of thousands of dollars. Here, in the palm of my hand, was concentrated danger in the form of a lump weighing no more than one pound.

Turning off the tap and setting the gold down in the sink, I snatch a tumbler from the doorless cupboard and pour myself a stiff drink. Downing the poison in one fell swoop, I give myself permission to dream. I dream of food in our cupboards and tan lines from time spent on sandy beaches. I dream of a working furnace and of sunsets unobstructed by crumbling brick buildings. I dream of a trip to see her children, for the woman next door, and orthotics for her shoes.

I dream of a full night of sleep, unclouded by substance abuse and without heart-seizing panic attacks induced by the only mountain I'd ever seen: the hundreds of unpaid bills and collections notices in our dank den.

Setting the tumbler on the counter and picking up the life-changing weight of precious ore, I return to the garden and get down on my creaking, battered knees. Taking a deep breath, savoring the toxins as they mingle with their predecessors in my lungs, I turn my face to the sky and ask God to forgive me for what I am about to do.

Tears tumble down my cheeks as I replace the gold in the lifeless soil, and take one final look at the only hope I had ever known before burying it with the dirt that I hated so much.

"Forgive me for my fear, Lord."

Patting the dirt firmly into place, I sigh deeply and rise to my feet. Being poor was all I knew how to be. I had spent my life defined by a lack of everything, and at the ripe old age of twenty-eight, I was too old to learn any other way of living.

Rising to my feet, I square my shoulders and return to the kitchen to begin my nightly tradition of drowning my sorrows. I knew my burdens were heavy when I realized that not even a sea of moonshine would have been enough.

HEAVEN CAME DOWN

By Talya Tate Boerner
(Texas, USA)
Historical, 3rd Place

"This is good a place as any," Mank declared, jumping off his horse and scouting the horizon. He was stiff and sore, and a sudden sharp pain in his right foot left him with a momentary limp. He hobbled like an old man trying to return blood flow to his leg, suddenly feeling much older than his nineteen years. The rain had finally stopped, and the sun peeped through the clouds.

"Yes sirree, I believe so, too." Jasper was tired and dirty, and sleep was a faded memory. The journey from Mississippi took longer than expected. Soaking rains slowed travel, making every aspect of the trip more arduous. On a rare dry travel day the mosquitoes swarmed so black and thick, they prayed for more rain.

The two brothers, close in age and both with handsome dark looks, were the oldest of twelve children—thirteen if you counted Berta Ruth, who only lived a few days. Daddy sent the boys west in search of better farmland for the family. They had heard tales of available acreage surrounded by hardwood that would bring a good price for those willing to work hard clearing land. And they were willing.

They made it as far west as Arkansas when fate intervened.

The wagon threw a wheel, splintering the axle. It was buried deep in muck and gumbo near a tangled riverbank overgrown with silkweed and blooming prairie sage. Unable to easily repair the axle, they were stuck in this spot for the moment. Always optimistic, they recognized this turn of events as a divine message and declared it the perfect location to settle.

"I'll see to the horses," Mank offered, and he watered the animals with the remaining fresh water from the barrel tied to the side of the wagon.

Most of the provisions the girls had packed for the brothers had been eaten along the way—tins of sardines and dried beef and a large basket of buttermilk biscuits. Food disappeared quickly on the trip, it seemed. What hadn't been eaten had spoiled in the heat and dampness, and some was traded in Memphis for a jug of whiskey.

They were eager to file a land patent and stake a claim. Although short on money, they were blessed with wit and motivation. Never shunning hard work, they farmed with Daddy at home in Mississippi and helped out in Uncle Tom's sawmill as far back as they could remember. Now it was their turn to prove themselves. They were enthusiastic about this adventure, excited to build a better life for the family who would join them in a year or so when a plan was laid.

"Race you!" Jasper yelled, suddenly energized, leaving the immediate chores up to his older brother.

Mank soon chased after him, and in no time they were splashing and dunking and laughing in the newly discovered swimming hole, the discomfort of the last few weeks already easing.

The water was a bit murky, but cool against the skin, refreshing. The trees lining the bank were blanketed in black-green ivy, which grew from the water's edge to the treetops, blurring and softening the river landscape. A few naked stumps jutted from the water. The golden reeds swayed with the breeze nearly sounding like rain.

Later, as the sun lowered, they were still tired from the journey, but relieved such a scenic site had been revealed to them. They rested on the bank near a dandelion patch as their drawers dried in the warm autumn sun. An unseen woodpecker worked tirelessly in a nearby tree, breaking the afternoon silence. On a hollow log near the edge of the water, a box turtle basked. He, too, seemed happy for a break in the clouds.

"Daddy's gonna be mighty upset that you sold Old Blue in Memphis." Mank shook his head as he chewed on a sassafras root. "Mighty upset," he repeated, chuckling.

"Way I saw it, there weren't no other choice, the way he was stinkin' up the wagon with all that gas he was passing." Jasper laughed. "I couldn't stand to smell that stench another night!" A brilliant red cardinal lit on a rotten stump a few feet away, his clear whistle underscoring Jasper's argument.

"You know he was Daddy's favorite huntin' dog. Ain't no telling what he's liable to do when he finds out." Mank smacked him on the head playfully as he skimmed stones across the shimmering water. The perfectly chosen pebbles skipped smoothly over the surface and nearly made it to the other side before disappearing in a ripple, interrupting the turtle's sunbathing.

"Well now, I wanna know just who's planning on telling him?" asked Jasper. "I bet Momma would be plenty interested to learn about all those times you skipped church talking to Euda McGee over by the school-house . . ."

Mank wished Jasper would forget his Sunday morning indiscretions or else just go ahead and tell Momma. This threat was wearing on him. "I reckon these stories can just stay between us. Besides, breathing this clean air without Old Blue stinking it up is better," Mank agreed.

Jasper chuckled and began playing his harmonica, providing a soulful background melody for this relaxing afternoon.

The little river was partially shaded by towering cottonwoods. Twisty vines wrapped the branches, looping toward the ground and making perfect rope swings over the water. The Arkansas dirt smelled rich, ideal for growing cotton and grazing livestock once trees were cleared. The town a ways up the river boasted a church, blacksmith shop, and a general store that sold notions and grain and seed. The proprietor seemed friendly enough when they stopped in. He was talkative and excited to see newcomers, explaining that settlers were flocking to the area to farm now that levees were being built to contain the nearby Arkansas and White Rivers. When Mank inquired about the Frisco railroad up in Blytheville, the man became downright ani-mated, drawing a rudimentary map on his countertop detailing the train route into the delta region from St. Louis and as far away as cities on the Pacific Ocean. As a fish flopped, creating a generous splash, the boys agreed this spot was heavenly, providing everything they needed.

Taking after Daddy, Jasper and Mank played as hard as they worked. Daddy always found time to horse around with the younger kids, pulling them on his overstuffed cotton sack after spending a day in the fields pick-ing. The more serious things like schooling and churching and discipline were left to Momma. Momma had a large household to run and not much time for nonsense.

"Be sure to read the Word every day, boys." She repeated this refrain more than once as they loaded supplies and tools on the wagon, preparing for the trip. She prayed over them again and again, fretting about their health and safety and eternal salvation. As she handed the family *Bible* to Mank, she reminded them both, "The Good Book will protect you and keep you. It'll provide everything you need. Don't forget."

It was her most precious possession.

The *Bible* was draped in cheesecloth and wrapped inside a heavy cotton quilt before being placed in the bottom of a massive dome-topped trunk and loaded into the wagon. They didn't expect they would read it, but understood its importance and aimed to protect it on the trail. Every family birth and death was recorded in Grandma Coley's neat handwriting, traced back to Great Grandpa Johnson, who died fighting for the Confederacy. When the family was reunited, Momma would read from it again. They would see to it.

Mank and Jasper were strong and capable woodsmen. In only a few weeks, they cut and peeled enough logs to build an ample-sized cabin, constructing it on a foundation of river rocks to keep the dirt floor dry. After they hed slept in the wagon for weeks, fighting rain and bugs and other creatures, the first night inside the cabin was luxurious. The small stove warmed the inside comfortably. Although rustic, it would provide shelter for the winter months that would soon be upon them. A lean-to out back served as a makeshift barn for the two horses, mule, and the dogs when they weren't out hunting or lazing under the wagon.

After several weeks, they wrote a letter home . . .

October 29, 1921

Dear Family,

We hope this letter finds you healthy and happy. The land is rich here in Arkansas and we have a little river nearby with fresh water for drinking and swimming. Poke sallet grows wild around the riverbank and Jasper has learned to cook it with a slab of bacon. You would be proud. He has become a good cook but of course his food is not as tasty as yours and the girls.

Our cabin is comfortable and will keep us warm in the coming winter months. It is colder here than back home but we think you will like Arkansas.

We are sad to report that Old Blue died around Memphis but he did not suffer.

Your loving sons,
Mank and Jasper

After several weeks, a return letter was received . . .

November 25, 1921

Dear Sons,

We were glad to receive your letter to hear news of Arkansas. The river sounds nice and we got a laugh picturing Jasper with the iron skillet. I have put up some beans and vegetable soup and spicy peaches for the winter. Your father said this was my best batch of peaches yet.

We were all saddened to learn of Old Blue's passing. You know he was your dad's favorite hunting dog.

Make time to read the Bible.

Your loving Mother

They cleared land by day and, after enjoying a hearty supper—usually beans and cornbread—told stories by the fire. Fat bream and brown trout often filled their plates after a successful sunrise spent with the bamboo fishing pole. Wild pigs roamed the countryside and provided good eatin' when they were fortunate enough to surprise one. The land was plentiful with squirrels and rabbits. The brothers had become skilled hunters before they could read or write, so they didn't go hungry. But, oh how they missed the sweet smell of Momma's buttery rhubarb pie resting on the sill. The aroma lured them in from the fields like the ring of a supper bell. They longed for those satisfying meals with the entire family recounting tales of the day or another time. Growing up times were often lean, but Momma always magically covered the table with platters of food, filling everyone's bellies by bedtime.

The months passed quickly while the Bible sat undisturbed in the center of the rough-hewn table, like a talisman, keeping watch. Although they devoted no time to reading from it, they felt better having it there and were confident Momma was back home in Mississippi praying for their safety. She was very faithful, and trusted someday her devotion would rub off on the boys. Raised in church, they were taught the difference between right and wrong from an early age.

The first winter was frigid. Snow fell in drifts, piling around the cabin, burying the wagon. The cook stove kept the cabin warm enough, but drying wet clothing after a morning of rabbit hunting was difficult. A solid sheet of ice covered the little river. *If the girls were here, they would be skating.* The ducks disappeared to a more southern climate. The small supply of stockpiled grain was fed to the livestock, although some perished. For weeks the only visitor to the cabin was a tan-striped sparrow. She foraged around the low shrubbery for berries and whistled a sweet tune, breaking the snowy silence.

At last, crocus peeked through the dry brush along the bank. The spring thaw brought a welcomed change in the weather with warm rains and longer days for planting and growing their first crop. Pink mimosa blossoms dotted the tangled growth near the ditch. The air smelled of honeysuckle.

Summer was hot, yet productive, as the boys collapsed each night after a long, hard day in the fields. Although rain was scarce and the little river was low, it afforded a cool place to swim, and the overhanging trees provided shade. The cotton grew thirsty, but the garden provided enough for two people.

Fall brought brilliant changes to the landscape, fiery reds and oranges and yellows. A lacy maple appeared, previously unnoticed. The air was clean and crisp on the first morning of the long-awaited cotton harvest.

The yield was low, as was their profit, but it was a start.

Another winter settled in around the little river. The boys ran short on necessities and inspiration, missing Daddy's banter and guidance and Momma's cooking and prayerful presence. Nostalgic, they longed for the daily shenanigans of their younger brothers and sisters and cousins. Homesick, they wrote to the family for comfort.

November 14, 1922

Dear Momma, Daddy and family,

We made our first crop. It was a good effort but our yield was low and the price was not as good as we hoped. The next year will be better if the weather cooperates. Conditions can be a mite unpredictable here.

We are tired and hungry and our supplies run low. Anything you could spare for us would be a big help. We keep our spirits up leaning on each other and knowing that we will be reunited soon. It has been snowing all day.

Your Sons,
Mank and Jasper

The letter was posted in town as soon as the weather cleared. Communication was difficult and slow. After several bitterly cold weeks, a long-awaited letter arrived in Momma's lovely handwriting. Jasper eagerly read it aloud.

December 28, 1922

My Dear Sons,

I am pained to hear of your difficult time in Arkansas. But I am more pained to learn that you have not been reading your Bible.

Your Loving Mother

Hmphf! The boys were disappointed and hurt and annoyed. After waiting for a response and hoping for a bit of money or at least a kind word from family, Momma's writing seemed terse and uncaring and cold. She scolded them about reading the *Bible* when they suffered, when they were in dire need and more desperate than ever for help. *How did she know they had not made time for the* Bible? *She always knew everything.*

As the gray evening closed in, they stoked the fire to maintain warmth through the silent night. Their jokes seemed lame and their stories timeworn. They considered packing up and going back to Mississippi, but they knew the toughest part was behind them. Spring would be better.

"Maybe we *should* read Momma's *Bible*," Jasper suggested, tired and dejected. They stared at it. It stared back from the center of the table where it had rested for months, gathering dust.

"Can't do no harm," Mank agreed, defeated. "Nothing much else to do, I s'pose."

Mank lit a lantern while Jasper tossed another log into the fire. Orange sparks floated from the stove with a *whoosh*, quickly vanishing into the winter air.

The heavy leather volume was covered in a fine coating of soot. Lifting it from the table, feeling its heft, Mank sensed Momma's touch as he held it, almost feeling a tingle through his arm. Its dusty outline remained on the table.

"Do you have a favorite passage?" he asked. He gave brief consideration to reading the story of the birth of Christ in the Book of Luke, but dismissed this as being entirely too joyful for their current state. Given their recent trials, the Book of Job might offer the encouragement they needed.

His finger traced the gold crucifix engraved on the well-worn cover. It was soft and smooth like suede from Momma's hands and Grandma's before her. Surprisingly, the air appeared fresher as he opened the cover. His heart felt lighter. At first touch the pages were stiff, nearly glued together from weather conditions and disregard. But as he thumbed through, the fragile linen pages loosened, nearly turning themselves. Almost instinctively, the *Bible* parted near the center where the black satin page marker was stitched into the rigid binding.

It took a moment for them to fully comprehend the gift offered within the pages of the *Bible*. The boys gaped at the open book, moving in to get a closer look. Neither spoke for fear the spell would be broken, afraid they would awake from this dream.

But they knew it was real; the texture of the moment was not that of a dream.

Tucked inside the gold-tipped pages they found a tightly packed stack of Federal Reserve notes and worn silver certificates. The money had been concealed for months. It was more money than they had seen in a lifetime, more money than they would ever need.

The *Bible* slipped from Mank's hands. They stared in wonder as the bills fluttered and floated to the dirt floor.

Outside, light white snow continued to fall.

1013 BAKER STREET

By McKenzie Rae Swenson
(Minnesota, USA)
Suspense, 1ˢᵗ Place Tie

Look away, close your eyes, run back to the graveyard.

Don't pay any attention to the chilly breeze and the sour stench of ozone. It rained last night, and the dirt is clinging to your sneakers in sticky clumps. Avert your eyes so you can't see through the filthy kitchen window. You spotted the dingy house from across the cemetery. Its siding used to be white, but now it's covered in grime and bird droppings. Inky black crows perch on the gutter of the roof, staring down at you with their beady eyes, like gargoyles. Shingles are twisted upward, trying to break free and fly away into the gray clouds of morning. It probably won't rain again, so you don't need to take shelter here. If you're truly worried about getting wet, you should go get the umbrella out of the back seat of your car.

You really shouldn't open the door. It's old and cracked with a handle that's so loose, it jiggles if you even think about touching it. The people who turned the handle before you were too rough. The woman slammed the door in the middle of the night and didn't come home until morning. The man pushed and pulled and kicked the door whenever the woman locked him out. All of the neighbors turned the door knob in vain a week after the bickering ceased. So you see? You couldn't go in even if you wanted to. The door's been locked ever since.

You could enter through one of the broken windows on the first floor, but that would be a mistake. Shards of glass stick out at odd angles just waiting for a nosy someone like you to slip. If you make it inside unscathed, you'll step on broken beer bottles, burnt-out cigarettes, mangled soda cans, and all kinds of wrappers. They were left by the local teenagers, who dared each other to spend the night inside the creepy house on Baker Street. Don't think that gives you an excuse to go poking around, though. If your friends jumped off a bridge, would you follow them? And don't say it depends on how high the bridge is.

You should do what you came here to do. Go back to the cemetery. Find the headstone with your grandmother's name, plant the yellow tulips, say a prayer. Don't linger here. A cemetery is no place for anyone with a pulse. The dead have a way of keeping this domain their own. Don't believe me? I would suggest that you find the man and the woman who used to live here and ask them yourself, but I won't because you shouldn't.

You should drive into town instead, and leave this place. Go to browse at the Red Corner Book Store on 115th Avenue. After that you should visit the bakery just down the road. I recommend the Snow Ball Cookies. They're messy, though, so grab a napkin. Indulge yourself at one of the gift shops. In a small town like this, they're everywhere. Sure, you could ask around about that old house; I can't stop you.

The couple who run the book store don't have much to say, since they've only lived in town for about five months. They're young, probably in their early thirties, with one daughter and another child on the way. The woman smiles as she talks to you, one hand resting on her belly, and tells you that Red Corner Book Store was previously a family store. The man who owned it last decided to retire a year ago. Not having any relatives willing to take up the mantle, he reluctantly agreed to sell his store to her and her husband. It was a blessing, actually, since they were planning on moving into a house with more space anyway. She goes on then to describe to you all the difficulties and benefits of small-town life, until you kindly interrupt and say that you must be going.

The two elderly sisters who own the bakery tell you that the man and woman were good customers. The couple always bought their bread from them, and a basket of Double Chocolate Fudge Cookies if the woman was shopping. They didn't usually shop together. The sisters exchange a suspicious look after that and politely change the subject to the weather.

When your grandmother was alive, she knew the man and the woman, too. She lived just down the street, and would often peer through her curtains curiously. Don't think that she was a busybody, though. All the residents on Baker Street began looking over their fences and started whispering to each other the day that the man and the woman moved in. Your grandmother invited them over to her home several times. In the beginning, the woman would sometimes accept her offer of a delectable, homemade dinner. Eventually, the woman stopped taking your grandmother's phone calls.

If you think carefully, you might remember seeing the woman at your grandmother's funeral. She stood apart from the crowd as the casket was lowered into the ground. The man was absent from her side—as usual, the locals will tell you. She stood stationary while the other mourners dispersed.

You actually brushed her shoulder briefly as you were leaving. If you had been paying attention, you would have noticed the man sitting in his car. He was hunched over in the driver's seat, waiting impatiently for the woman to pay her respects. But you were too busy thinking about the funeral costs to truly notice any of this.

The teenagers at the park are much more willing to spin you a wild tale. Almost everyone believes that the house is haunted. One girl swears she saw a pale dark-haired woman staring out the second-story window long after the house had been abandoned. A boy stamps out his cigarette and claims he and a few of his buddies snuck in a few nights ago and heard maniacal laughter wafting up from the musty basement. You would like to believe them, but judging by the fevered glint in their eyes and the jerking twitch of their hands, you doubt they've ever been there when they weren't scared, drunk, or high.

Sometimes at Charlie's Bar & Grill, people talk about 1013 Baker Street—only after they've had one too many beers, though. They remember that this bar used to be the man's favorite place to eat and drink. The woman never came into the bar, and that was what the man liked most about it. A few of the regulars recall that the man was a talkative drunk—until one day he wasn't. They sober up when they talk about the day the man went quiet. He just sat in a dark corner, his tired eyes fixed on the door across the room. Soon after, both the man and the woman disappeared as abruptly as when they had rolled into town.

You could go around asking about that house, but I wouldn't if I were in your shoes. It's a small town, and no one knows you yet. Make a fresh start while you can. Don't go digging up the past. Some secrets should stay six feet under.

You're still here, sitting on the splintered porch and clutching this paper in your clammy palms. Haven't you been listening? Go somewhere else, anywhere else! Look, even the crows have spread their wings and fled. Follow their lead.

Go find your car, get inside, and drive.

Learn more about 1ˢᵗ-place winner and Fresh Ink Group member McKenzie Rae Swenson at www.FreshInkGroup.com/authors/mckenzie-rae-swenson.

I DIE FOR MY COUNTRY

By Adithya Bandari
(Datthagiri Colony, Allipur, Zaheerabad, Madak)
Say Something, 3rd Place

My thoughts are disturbing my drowse. I know that I have to undergo a surgery and surgeons need to make my conscience lost. My psyche may undergo eternally, if the God insists.

The wounds made by bullets in both of my knee joints, a bullet in abdominal region and another at the chest region, are exasperating me and letting me cry, "Why did you miss the target?" I hurt myself. The siren is still busy, informing I am still in the ambulance.

The sparkling lights sprinting along the road against me are tinting momentary life of humans. I speak to myself, "Whatever I may think, up to Operation Theatre only!" Later anything may happen. The lieutenants and other military friends are still in their uniforms. I also feel myself in military dress.

Thank you, Parents,
For giving me such a life,
Serving the nation,
Serving my people . . .
Don't vex yourselves,
As I may miss you.

A thirty-five-year-old human creature needs such life only, a life in which it serves its country and its fellow countrymen.

I still remember the day when I joined the army. My parents were weeping a lot that I had decided to risk my life for my people. Later, they agreed and went away.

Never forget your teachers. The teachers, my very next parents, who taught me drilling, march-past, and saluting are immortal in my view. Moreover, their teachings made me inchoate; thus incoherent made a tank of thrilling thoughts.

Sorry! My life-partner, Campbell, as you have been so for past twelve years, you were my next mother, and my father besides myself.

Love you, my eight-year-old Sue. You played with me, and leapt on me whenever I came home. Your lovely hugs with your little hands curving around my neck are treasured in my mind.

When the war was declared open by our enemy friends, I wrote to my family. The words of that letter are appearing to be circling around my conscience as mathematical formulae do in case of a student taking an examination.

I offer this world infinite number of greetings to you on the occasion of introduction of another war in your history, Hello! What you do not know? What can I tell you? Some sort of melancholy started throwing me into incessant panic since the day on which war was declared with us. I am in unfathomable inability to understand why I am taking more and more mammoth amounts of beer these days. I comprehend that something ghastly is near.

Dear Parents,

That you have poured life in me and taken care of this huge creature until grown huge are almost almighty for me. You loved me so much that they led me not to join army.

"I may lose my life in the war," I spoke to you on that day. "But I shall be given an opportunity to tear off the lives of the enemies of my country and protect her, besides millions of lives."

You did not respond then, ignored all your thoughts, and allowed me to join the army and become a warrior. Thank you very much for providing this nation a beast that can sacrifice its life for her protection.

I can understand how much you love me. You, parents, are the first teachers and taught me many things no teacher does. You did your duty, but it is my duty to be grateful to you, besides my country.

I know how much you wail if I die? I hope that you will penetrate if the situations become worse and enjoy the immense pride that the person without life lying there with the national flag on his casket has once played with you, climbing your feet. Do not recall the moments I spent with you and my experiences left uncared for several days among you, to avoid tears in your eyes. I want you to smile and my fellow citizens to shed tears.

You may miss me, my dad and my mom. Do not quarrel with food and other requisites in suffering anger with the Lord for taking me away, after my death. I hope that I shall not exasperate you. I know the value of each tear you shed and, hence, want you not to shed it. Moreover, I am in my duty and you should smile. Meet me once before war.

Love you forever,
Your son

I also wrote to Campbell and Sue. They were the ones who live for me in this world.

Loving Campbell,
I have spent one-third's part of my life's time with you. I always loved talking to you, watching your yellow hair and wide eyebrows. I met myself every time I met you.

My rambling may end within some days. I promise you, dear! I shall try to the best of my ability to see you later, spend time with you in the beach and trudging by the side of the sea with wet feet in the sea-soaked sand.

Whenever you lean your head against my shoulder, pushing your soft yellow hair back, avoiding your hair come front, a form of security and con-fidence is developed in my heart. My hand moves around your shoulder to promise you that I want to protect you forever.

As the warriors on the side of my enemies are as strong as we are, I cannot promise you my safe return. However, I hope I do.

The whole life I spent with you never returns. Thank you for providing me a jazzy part in my life. Do not be submerged in endless sorrow after my death, if it occurs during the war. Give courage to Sue and allow her to do what she likes.

With lots of X's of Love,
You

I did not let my Sue cry. I also wrote to her. It is also true that I taught her reading.

Cute Sue!
I am fine. Do you know that I am going on a long drive? I have to go around the world to pass a test. So, I may return late. Do not worry about this poor pa and do your jobs fluently. Poor Dad, like a lad requests you not to exasperate Mom and follow her instructions. If Mom hurts your palms, report me when I return."

For peace to be restored on the crust, we have to think deeper and much deeper, recall the moments spent with Abraham and Ibrahim and imagine our own beautiful country deserted with no creatures alive.

No life is in danger, if all of us can think the same way. However, a bit of ego is a small flame, which turns big and burns huts.

Okay! No one in the world could be changed through words. If at all such situation comes, either good people or bad people exist on the earth.

All the letters were posted ten days ago. I knew that they have reached my family when all of them individually came to me and spoke to me.

My mother kissed me on my forehead, as if I am a child. They spoke nothing. They gave me a sandwich. I love the ones made by Mom. I felt that it was my last one.

Later, about a half day after the departure of my parents, Campbell and Sue came to me. Campbell burst out in deep sorrowfulness. She hugged me and spoke if I could go back with her. I said that was meaningless. She spoke nothing. I was showered in her tears. She said that she would find me Sue.

Sue said that she had not understood the letter. I felt sorry. She raised her two arms to indicate me to carry her standing on my shoulders. I took her around the garden until she felt tired.

She asked me to take her with me on the Long Drive I mentioned in the letter. I said it was impossible. She pled with me to take her next time. I agreed with her. Tears rolled down my cheeks as the distance between us grew longer.

An eight-year-old girl spoke philosophy. She asked me to try to go back.

During war, I missed coloured clothes and went to the camp in army dress. The next one followed our camp, about ten miles behind us.

Unexpectedly, they attacked us. The bullets punched out by their guns made holes on our tent. All of us were arrested armless.

They hit me on my head. I roared like a lion. They hit me harder with a gun on my face. They kicked me on my back. I fell down. I had a gun hidden in my socks. I kicked two of the soldiers who were holding me and shot them dead. I was the only one alive in my camp. They did not want to miss me as they wanted to ask me our secrets. I have killed two others before two bullets pierced my knee joints. I cried to make the entire valley echo my voice. Then, I killed the remaining two with my knife after my heart was hurt with a dense bullet.

My heart was heavy. I hoisted our flag there and ran back to the health camp. The pain grew more. They were carrying me in an ambulance to the hospital, almost two hundred miles away.

We are very fast as I feel. We have reached the hospital just now. Neither my parents nor Campbell is there. The blood pierced some part of my heart to make my military clothes red.

My heart is heavy. I am unable to look around. My body is rushed towards the operation theatre. I find the lights sprinting away over my head. I find myself falling asleep. I cannot keep my eyes open anymore. However, a small hope that I may meet Sue again has been giving me immense confidence that I can withstand pain.

Still, a pride is running across my nerves and tissues. It is because I am sure about my death. Actually, I want to die to make my fellow citizens swollen with pride that I have died to protect them. Such death causes immortality and serves me nectar.

The words I used to speak when I was in my teens came true today. I used to announce in the classroom, tightening my tie, that I shall become a warrior and save my country.

It seems to me as if someone is a playing sad guitar tone on the background of a low-pitched voice speaking to me, as if it happens in a sentimental movie. "Ah!" I make a dense cry. The bullet has gone a little deeper, everything around me becoming blurred. If solid and intense rainbow spirals are appearing. I understand that my end is near. My thirty-five-year-old life shall end today. I shall have a cool death. I thank the God for donating me a peaceful death.

I want nobody to see me popping off and shed tears to melt my heart and pride of it. Tears may kill me earlier by killing my pride, my immortal drink. Several perform struggle for the existence. My body is trying to do the same. There is immense cardiac pain for ten hours. My blood, my soul, and my body are only the parts of my country. The mud under which I have to rest forever would be built, also belonging to her.

Only thing I want to convey to these humans is not to vex themselves to do others to do so. Wars will be declared against the wars then. Aidless affliction of all the humans of the modern civilization who call themselves modern possessing is anger. Wars continue making families apart unless we introspect. If we introspect, global fraternity will be established. The funds used for weapons could be used for health and education fields and so on.

I am still worried about my fellow warriors. Let them lead my country to the triumph. The pilots let warplanes with my national flag fly like an eagle, warriors in submarines let it dive hungry sharks, and the warriors with arms roar like lions.

I am able to feel the weights placed on my body connected to some machines. The sounds made by them is reducing their intensity. I am able to experience sucking out of something from my heart. I am unable to breathe properly. Some lights, motors, and aliens unclear are around me. Tears flood through the ends of eyes. I do not know why it is so.

The time, which is so fast that no one can defeat it, orders me to move out of the scene. However, I may be allowed by the hearts of my fellow citizens to do so.

It is seeming to me as if my mother is singing a lullaby.

I smile at this world.

I quit, my dear world!

SOULMATE SEARCH

By Holly Riordan
(New York, USA)
Romance, 2nd Place

The watch on my wrist was equipped with a special ability. I bought it after breaking up with Nick, my ex-boyfriend with as many emotions as tattoos. At all times, he had to have either a cigarette or my tongue in his mouth. I loved him; I was mesmerized by him, but he was so damn fickle. I'd find him laughing as the carefree love of my life and an hour later he'd be slashing his wrists as the depressed boy with no heart.

Tears still clung to my cheeks when I went to get my watch implanted. I never really wanted one, never thought I needed it. I assumed Nick and I would get married after college and the lookout would be over.

"You'll feel a prick and a slight tug on your wrist," the doctor said as I sat on a metal chair. "It's just the device connecting itself to a vein."

"How does it work, exactly?"

"The watch is aware of the information kept in your brain. It knows your hopes and dreams, your hobbies, your level of intellect." Off my confusion, she continued, "All you need to know is that it will beep when you come across someone with compatible qualities: your soulmate."

Adults had been wearing the watches for decades, but I was still skeptical. My parents met by using them, and I called it a coincidence. Of course, the scientists called them 100% accurate, a miraculous advancement for social situations.

"I promised myself I'd never get one of these," I said with a groan. "Guess it's true breakups make you do crazy things."

She smiled a wispy, nostalgic smile. "In the old days, we'd just go for a haircut, maybe splurge on a new dress."

"But did you find your soulmate?"

"Maybe not." She glanced at a photo on her desk. It was of her and a man kissing under a wedding arch. "Maybe it didn't matter."

Three years passed without the watch making any noise. I traveled as much as possible, hoping that I'd find my partner on one of my trips. There were conventions for singles where everyone in town with a watch would meet, exchange a few words with one another, and see if they were lucky enough to hear beeping. It was like speed dating, except the conversation didn't matter. Even if someone interesting was around, they'd be skimmed past. We all valued the watch's opinion over our own.

I was in a bar in my hometown, nibbling from a bowl of germ-ridden pretzels, when my martini toppled over. The man beside me was handing me a pile of napkins when I heard it.

Beep. Beep. Beep.

I glanced down at the face of my watch, which was glowing pink. The man's watch did the same. My eyes shifted upward, breathing in the clean-cut stranger. No tattoos, no piercings. Nothing at all like Nick.

"Do you want a family wedding or should we just run to Vegas right now?" he asked.

"Shouldn't you already know?"

"I'm your soulmate, not psychic."

A youthful laugh left my throat. The search was through; I never had to worry again.

"I'm Tyler, by the way."

"Maddie."

By the end of the night, I discovered Tyler was an engineer who loved water sports, had an obsession with silent films, and played the piano. He was the definition of perfection. The watch had proven itself.

We moved in together after only a month, and he proposed after two. Relationships had a bizarre twist once fate was already known. Every decision we made felt mechanical, forced. But we were meant to be together, so I ignored the doubt.

The night before my wedding, I snuck into the pool portion of my old apartment complex. Whenever I was extremely happy or angry or upset, I would plop down against the chain-link fence surrounding the area. It gave me peace, protection. It was the first time I returned since I met Tyler. Around him, my emotions never wavered.

"Beep beep beep."

It came from behind me, not from my wrist. It was low and gruff, the sound of a person's voice. Nick's voice.

"What are you doing?" I asked as I rose to my feet. He had more tattoos than the last time I'd seen him. His arms were covered and, judging by the sheerness of his wifebeater, his chest was full as well.

"Ran into your pop the other day. You're getting married?"

I lifted my wrist and tapped on the watch. Some people decided to get theirs removed after finding their mate, but most kept it attached. The procedure was too painful. Plus, it was a memory of their struggle with love.

"Is that . . . thing the only reason?" he asked.

"It's the best reason." Without checking his wrists, I added, "Maybe *you* should get one."

"I already did. And I found her, Maddie. I found my 'soulmate' and I'm dating her. But guess what?"

He grabbed his own watch and jiggled it, trying to rip it from his skin. It stayed attached while making a warning, buzzing noise, but he continued to tear at it. It refused to budge, but blood spurted out.

"You're going to hurt yourself."

"This damn thing doesn't work! It didn't lead me to you. It's keeping me away from you."

"Then that's how it should be." I grabbed his hands to stop him. "The divorce rate isn't as high as it used to be. These work. You have to obey them."

"You're going to let this—this damn, artificial piece of plastic take the place of what your heart thinks? We're not machines. We don't think scientifically."

"My fiancé is a great guy. We get along. There's never any fights. But with you? I hate you, sometimes. I honestly hate you."

"It's called passion." He reeled me closer and cupped my face with both of his hands. His lips grazed mine as he spoke. "Even when you're pissed at me, you love me more than you'll ever love him. You know that."

His mouth pressed against mine. The taste was heated, burning, like lava passing between our lips. My fingers glided through his hair while my chest brushed his, every nerve alive and alert against his skin.

As we continued to kiss, I remembered what the doctor said as she implanted my watch. At the time, I didn't understand, but her words ended up being accurate.

Maybe Nick's not my soulmate. But maybe that didn't matter.

GOD

By Anna Cates
(Ohio, USA)
Science Fiction, 3rd Place

Hamid didn't know where the American soldiers had taken him. They spoke English with strange accents, using slang and code words, and he had hardly understood what they were saying as they had bumped along the road in their army vehicle, laughing and telling obscene jokes, Hamid's head covered in a sack to blind him, the binds around his wrists cutting.

They'd lodged him in some prison in a muggy climate. How long they planned to detain him, he didn't know. His trial remained distant, and he wasn't aware what rights he had or what they thought he'd done.

He lay on his back on a musty mattress one inch thick, naked from the waist up, his hands tied down at his sides. He knew homosexuals had over-run America, especially the U.S. military, and he feared they planned to rape him. With dread, he awaited it.

Night had fallen. Bullfrogs were burbling, the air a mixed scent of sweat, cigarette smoke, and clogged plumbing.

A door clanged open, metal scraping metal. Hamid's heart exploded in his chest. *Here come the homosexuals!* He struggled in his binds. *Allah-o-Akbar*, he prayed silently.

A shadow crept to the bars of his cell. Then a stream of moonlight illuminated the woman standing there. She grinned, unlocked the cell door, and stepped into his cubicle, letting the keys rest in the lock.

Her dark honey-blonde hair fell to her shoulders in waves, and the nipples of her breasts protruded from beneath her camouflage shirt. Standing in the middle of the cell, she unfastened the belt at her waist and let her army pants fall, stepping out of them when they formed a puddle of fabric around her ankles. She removed her shirt and let it drop to the floor. Last to be surrendered were the white, gossamer panties.

Hamid could hear his own heavy breathing as the woman slid onto him. *Allah-o-Akbar*, he prayed silently.

She sighed, slipping her fingers around his neck, stroking his stubble. She tasted his earlobe. She touched his lips with one finger before pressing her own gently to his. She returned to his ear and whispered, "I've heard stories of prisoners falling in love with their captors. Tell me; what do you think of these tales?"

"Those stories are true. My heart is a caged bird."

She laughed softly. "I use StriMedix, the cure for spider veins, broken capillaries, bruises, adult rosacea, and varicose veins. . ."

Hamid slapped the button of his radio alarm clock, silencing the commercial. He groaned and rolled out of bed into a seated position on the mattress. He shook his head, rubbing the back of his neck. His dreams in the last few months had grown increasingly lurid and bizarre, and although that didn't pose for him a moral problem, he had taken note. "I need to find a wife," he muttered, staggering into the bathroom.

He squeezed the Colgate Total over his toothbrush and began to brush his teeth, gazing at his tired reflection in the mirror, the brown skin and dark hair, the aquiline nose inherited from his father.

For a minute Hamid couldn't remember why he'd had to set his alarm so early. Then a rush of adreneline coursed through him as he remembered:

A job interview!

His student visa would soon expire, and he needed to find employment or else fly back to Saudi Arabia. He'd scheduled his interview for 12:30, but he had an organizational-communications exam later in the day, and he needed to cram all morning. Was there something else? Stumbling into the kitchen, wrapped in a blue bath towel, he finally recalled:

An 11:30 lunch date with Melissa, a Puerto Rican classmate. They planned to meet at Subway in the Kelly building of downtown Portland, the same building as his job interview, where Melissa had already found work.

*   *   *

Hamid arrived at downtown Portland at 11:25 a.m. He paid the parking attendant the two-dollar fee to park his white Subaru, found a shady spot under a tree, then crossed the street to the Kelly building. He felt glad that Melissa, who was finishing a business degree like him, had told him about the job opportunity selling a colloidal silver supplement for an upcoming multi-level marketing company.

The Subway was just inside the front door on the right. Melissa was standing there. "Hamid," she called out, saving him a spot in line as a crowd of people gathered. He reached her side. "Maybe you should get us a table before this place gets too crowded," Melissa said, gazing around. "I think one of the businesses upstairs just adjourned a meeting, and the lunch rush has started early. Tell me what you want, and I'll order it for you."

"Oh no," Hamid said, patting his pants pockets. He sighed, embarrassed. "I forgot to stop by the bank. I don't have any cash on me."

"Don't worry about it. I'll buy us a 12-inch, and we can split it. No biggie."

Hamid didn't want a woman to buy his meal, but he couldn't just sip water and watch her while she ate. "Okay, but I owe you." He found a table by the window, overlooking the sidewalk.

In minutes, a smiling Melissa was gliding over to the table, their sandwich balanced on a green tray. She sat down opposite to him.

"I ordered a club on Italian bread. Hope that's okay. I'm starving!"

"Thanks," Hamid said as Melissa turned the tray sideways and began unwrapping the sandwich.

Melissa glanced up, her dark eyes tired despite her usual exuberance, her black hair tied haphazardly in a clasp atop her head, spritzed stiff, leaving a floral scent about her. She'd applied her foundation hastily, orange at her jaw. Overall, dressed in a white t-shirt and pink sweat pants cut off above the knees, she had that look of a college student whose study requirements had forced her beyond pickiness about her appearance. She smiled, sliding his half of the sandwich toward him.

Hamid picked it up, spilling shredded lettuce, and took a bite. He'd already chewed and swallowed before he remembered to think:

Ham.

He felt the bite slide down his trachea, heading toward the hollow darkness of his pith. He set down his sandwich, parted the Italian bread, and fingered aside the lettuce, tomatoes, and olives. There he found it, the forbidden meat: black forest ham with its dark pepper crust, pressed against the turkey breast like two alduterers clammy after passion. He pinched it up between two fingers, holding it like a worm before his eyes. Never again could he truthfully say he'd never eaten ham.

"Do you not want that?" Melissa asked, her dark eyes hopeful.

"You can have it," Hamid said, handing it to her.

Melissa folded up the cold cut, tilted back her head, and stuffed it into her mouth with gusto. "Hmmm," she said, savoring the salty flavor. "I just love ham!"

Hamid decided not to make a big issue of it. Melissa had paid for the sandwich.

He knew he could marry a Christian or Jew, and with the shortage of Muslim women in the Portland area, he felt it might come to that. Still, he harbored every doubt in the world about Melissa's suitability. It occurred to him to bring up the topic of religion to see if Melissa had any faith at all. He would not, could not, consider a godless animal.

"Are you religious?" he asked, licking a drip of mayonnaise from his fingertip.

The question made her smile. "It's all about love, Hamid. *Love.*"

The response seemed evasive. "Are you Catholic?" He knew that was traditional for Hispanics.

"Love, Hamid. God is love, or should I say, love is God."

So that was it. She would not own any faith directly. Hamid wondered if perhaps he should change the topic. "Did you study for the org-comm exam?"

"I'm as ready as I'm going to be, but probably not ready enough," Melissa replied, wiping her fingers clean of mustard with a Subway napkin.

Hamid smiled. "Me, too."

"Have you read the recent issue of the student paper?"

"No. Why?"

Melissa adjusted her position on the seat, leaning forward as if she had something important to say. "Some freshmen went hiking on Mt. Hood last weekend, saw this UFO, and got a great photo of it. It's on the front page. The article said it might have something to do with the strange lights that have been sighted around Portland lately."

Hamid raised his eyebrows. "Strange lights? I hadn't heart anything about that."

"My friend Brenda and I saw them several nights ago. All these pretty pastel colors shining in the night sky. It was weird. You believe in UFOs?"

Hamid shrugged. "I don't know. Never seen one."

"You'd better get a copy of the paper."

"I will. Sounds kind of scary."

"I think it sounds exciting!" Melissa took another bite.

*   *   *

Hamid stood by the elevator, reading the plaque beside the doors that listed all the offices on each of the Kelly building's thirteen floors. He needed room 12B on the twelfth floor, but his eye drifted to the label for the thirteenth floor that listed, surprisingly, only one business. "GOD," it read in all caps.

GOD. The English word for *Allah*.

Could it be an abbreviation? Hamid saw no periods, only that one word.

He pressed the button to open the elevator door, fed himself to its emptiness, then pressed the button for floor thirteen. He was early for his job interview. He could stop by the thirteenth floor, find out what this "GOD" meant, then skip down the stairs to 12B afterwards.

Ding! The elevator door popped open, and Hamid walked out onto the plum carpet, catching the scent of remodelling. Strangely, the long hallway had no doors, only a single office way down on the other side of the corridor. He started for it. The lights were on, and a man was sitting behind a desk.

Hamid reached the door and knocked, checking his watch: 12:10, plenty of time before his interview.

"Come in," the voice said.

Hamid opened the door and slipped through. "Forgive me. I just couldn't help but notice that the wall plaque downstairs listed this office as belonging to a G-O-D, and I was just curious what that meant." Hamid felt embarrassed as if he were being nosey, but he knew he was doing no harm.

"Come in. Have a seat." The man gestured toward the chair facing his own on the opposite side of the desk where his computer hummed. Like Hamid, he wore a white dress shirt and tie. He seemed about forty, with light brown hair and blue eyes, a few extra pounds.

Hamid's eyes drifted to the nameplate on the desk. "GOD," it read.

A huff of laughter fled Hamid's nostrils. He pointed to the nameplate. "You call yourself God?"

The man nodded his head matter-of-factly. "That's who I am."

"God?" Hamid asked, head jutting forward, just to make sure he understood correctly. "God, as in *Allah?*"

"Nicknames are fine," the man said, seeming almost humble, his blue eyes intent.

Hamid gripped the armrests of his chair, rage building within him. He had never been confronted with such an abhorrent sin, had never imagined he would come face to face with such flagrant transgression. It seemed worse to him than anything he'd ever heard of: homosexuality, adultery, *anything.*

"You are a blasphemer!" He trembled.

"Now, Hamid, you know I love you."

At the words, something hard within Hamid melted. His anger vanished. His shoulders relaxed. "How did you know my name?"

"I know everything. I'm God."

Hamid gazed into the man's blue eyes. He didn't know what to think. A strange feeling of peace had washed over him.

"Hamid, I'm sorry. I can't let you do what you're planning to do."

"What am I planning to do?" Hamid asked. "All I want is a good job and a suitable wife."

*   *   *

Gradually, Hamid realized he was staring into a drinking fountain. Someone tapped his shoulder, and he turned around.

"You going to take a drink or just stand there?" the man asked, impatient for his turn.

"I'm not thirsty, thank you," Hamid said, stepping away. Looking around, he realized he was on the first floor of Kelly. He checked his watch: 4:13. *What? How could this have happened?* he wondered, realizing he'd missed not only his job interview, but also his exam. Where had the time gone?

Driving home, he tortured his brain for the answer to the riddle of the day's events. Finally, it came to him. "God" must be a powerful hypnotist, maybe even a sorceror, bent on destroying innocent lives. *Such a fiend must be stopped*, Hamid mused, and he knew just how to do that.

When Hamid returned to his apartment, he found an eviction notice taped to his door, warning him that he had twenty-four hours to vacate the premises. In the last few months, his money had just been disappearing; bills he'd meant to pay, he'd somehow overlooked. Yet things were becoming clearer now. He could no longer stay in the U.S. It was too late to find a job. A door was slamming shut in his face, and as disappointing as that was, the thought of reuniting with friends and family in Saudi Arabia comforted him.

That night, Hamid loaded his car with personal belongings, planning to live out of his vehicle for the remaining three weeks of the term. His professor would have to let him make up his org-comm exam if he pleaded sickness, so at least he could finish his degree before returning home.

He went online with his laptop and bought his plane ticket back to Saudi Arabia, printing it off, then storing it in the glove compartment of his car, the night sky flickering with pastel lights above him. *What in Allah's name?* Hamid wondered, his eyes surveying the heavens, remembering what Melissa had told him. Then he cast the matter aside, having too many other things to worry about.

Before going to bed, he loaded bullets into his gun. When thieves had broken in and ransacked his apartment during the fall term, he'd hoped he wouldn't have to use it, but now he felt glad he'd bought it. "God," he snarled between clenched teeth, shaking his head, the memory of the man on the thirteenth floor fresh in his brain, "I don't think so." He lifted the gun to his lips, kissed the cold metal, then stashed the weapon in a black Nike bag.

*   *   *

Hamid's classes that term were all scheduled on Mondays, Wednesdays, and Fridays, so Thursday was the perfect day to throw the sorceror-hypnotist into the fire. He hated to have to do it, but no American laws existed to bring such infidels to justice. Hamid had a religious duty.

He arrived at downtown Portland just after 11:00, paid the parking attendant a precious two dollars of his dwindling cash, then made his way toward the Kelly building, his Nike bag in hand.

He'd just entered the building when he heard a familiar voice. "Hamid, is that you? Come here and meet Levar."

Hamid turned. There stood Melissa by the Subway, seeming refreshed and polished in an apple-green skirt suit. At her side was a familiar-looking student he'd seen around the Portland State campus. The two seemed on a lunch date.

"Hamid, this is Levar. Levar, Hamid."

Hamid shook the hand, feeling nervous, the guilt of his Nike bag upon him.

"Hey," Levar said, grinning.

"Levar sold his first bottle of colloidal silver today," Melissa announced like a proud parent. "Mr. Bates placed him in my downline when he signed up with the company. Now his grandmother's arthritis will be a problem of the past," Melissa continued with forced enthusiasm. "Hamid, how did your job interview go? Mr. Bates told me he'd put you in my downline if you signed up."

Hamid wanted to scream. If Melissa only knew what a difficult task awaited him, she'd leave him alone. He had hoped no one he knew would see him in Kelly that day. "Look, Melissa, I've got to go. Send me an email, and we'll discuss." Hamid hurried on.

He made his way to the elevator, then stopped to gather his breath and steady his trembling. Temples sweaty, he glanced at the plaque he'd seen the day before, listing the offices on each of Kelly's floors. Strangely, the thirteenth floor was now missing entirely from the plaque. *He's removed the name 'God,'* Hamid mused, wondering why.

The elevator door opened, and a businessman and -woman exited, allowing Hamid entrance. But when Hamid reached out to select floor thirteen, the button was missing! *What is going on?* he wondered. Had the whole floor disappeared? He pressed twelve, and felt his stomach sink as the elevator carried him upward.

Ding! The door opened at the sixth floor, and a man in a suit entered. Hamid peered over. "How many floors does this building have?"

"Twelve," the man said, pointing toward the buttons. "I'm on my way to eleven."

"Yesterday, I went to the thirteenth floor and talked with God."

The man laughed. "You must have been on the roof or in another building or on some powerful drugs. There's no thirteenth floor in Kelly."

Hamid exited the elevator on the eleventh floor and swung around to the staircase. He climbed a flight of stairs, then stepped out onto the final floor where the stairs ended.

The place was busy with people, full of offices, the carpet brown and old, not the floor he remembered from the day before, not the floor with God. Perhaps he was dealing with a mightier sorceror than he had imagined. No wonder such crimes warranted the death penalty in Saudi Arabia. The confusion of it all nearly sickened him physically.

He turned back to the staircase and walked down all twelve flights of stairs until he was standing outside, smelling the fresh spring air, the noise of traffic and birds all around him. He walked back to the parking lot, deciding to let the matter go. He'd tried to do his religious duty, but the satanic power of this blasphemer simply exceeded his wits.

In the parking lot, Hamid found his car missing. He walked all around the lot, but his white Subaru had simply vanished! He swatted the pocket of his jeans. His keys were gone. He must have left them in the ignition, but that wasn't like him to make stupid mistakes like that. He'd never locked himself out of his car. *This sorceror has hexed me*, Hamid thought, feeling the fire flicker within him.

Hamid spoke to the parking-lot attendant about his missing vehicle, but the attendant couldn't help. Finally, completely destitute but for an athletic bag and pistol, Hamid gave up, and with his head sunk forward, stumbled down the street, heading for the exit ramp leading to Interstate 84 to hitch a ride he knew not where.

Out on the highway, a red semi pulled over to pick him up. Hamid jogged forward, and when he neared the door, it swung open.

Hamid peered into the vehicle at a ruddy-faced man, balding, with a beer belly, who gave the impression of a man who preferred whores. "I can take you as far as New York," he said.

"New York then," Hamid replied, not knowing what else to say as he climbed up into the passenger's seat, gaining a hightened perspective of the highway as the vehicle started back up.

"Just call me *Buck*," the driver said.

"Hamid. Thanks for the ride."

For a cool, cloudy day, Hamid was sweating profusely. He gazed out the window as they left the city, proving a poor conversational piece for the driver.

Several hours outside of Portland, army vehicles began to whiz all around them. Soon, so many of them were on the road, the traffic congested, and the truck slowed to a crawl.

"What the fuck's up with the military? They're backing up traffic from Timbuktu to Kalamazoo," Buck exclaimed in a fluster.

"It's the aliens," Hamid found himself saying, not knowing why.

"I don't know what the hell it is," Buck said in his crackly voice, "but if this mess don't clear up soon, we'll have to spend the night in Idaho!"

To Hamid's right Mt. Hood loomed in the distance. He longed to reach it. He yearned for it, his heart aching in his breast. His fingers touched the door latch, the sun shining gently onto him, unnaturally bright, strangely bright.

Unearthly.

Buck peered at Hamid from the corner of his eye, his lips a queer grin. "You a Mexican?" He reached over, grasped Hamid's knee, and squeezed.

That was all it took to finish the thought in Hamid's mind. The truck still creeping along, Hamid opened the door and, abandoning his Nike bag, leaped from the vehicle, just making the grassy ditch.

"Hey, where ya going? I was only kidding ya," Buck called out after him.

Hamid landed hard on uneven ground, his left foot twisting to the side. He gasped, clenching his teeth at the pain, then hobbled forward toward Mt. Hood, unbuttoning his shirt to absorb the unnatural light he longed to let touch his sweaty skin.

*   *   *

Beyond civilization, the living and the dead, where paved roads return to gravel, and rocks and earth fade into grass, and grass gives way to forests, and forests hide in the shadow of mountains, he found a secret place, a cave above the treetops. Gazing into the night, careful of Bigfoot and snakes, he cupped his muddy knees, tattered as a werewolf, hunched on stone in ragged Wranglers, his breath hissing warm fog as moonlight sifted down, everything misty, and retreated into himself, finding only the dust.

Suddenly, the thoughts harness slipped over his consciousness in a perfect fit. Hamid leaned forward, alert.

A light, tiny as a firefly, flickered from down the hill, then grew brighter, larger, slowly illuminating the night. From behind a boulder a head popped up, a familiar face, framed in dark honey-blonde hair.

The woman from his dream!

She stepped out from the rock, wearing only her panties. "I've heard stories of prisoners falling in love with their captors," she said with a shy smile.

It's true! Hamid thought. He rose from his kneeling position and started down the hill.

The woman walked down the climb, motioning for Hamid to follow. Lights filled the dark heavens, casting her flesh with prisms of color, making her whole being a single jewel.

Hamid jogged down the slope, feeling a strange joy. Some part of his mind told him the pain in his swollen ankle was excruciating, but he only wanted to laugh.

"It's true! It's true! It's true!" Hamid exclaimed, laughing, flailing his arms, hopping on his bad foot, unaware of the mutation within his genes that had made him chosen for domestication and breeding. He felt happy as a puppy finding a benevolent master, saying goodbye to fleas and worms and hungry nights in cold alleyways.

He ran down the hill toward the ever-increasing illumination. He took the woman's hand, then disappeared into the light.

THE BIG PROLOGUE

By Jasper Grawl
(Tokyo, Japan)
Humor, 1st Place

"Order! Order, please! Would you all take your seats!" shouted the Speaker. He was a prim man, long in the face, whose cheeks swung low off his jaw like gravity-laden chariots. Behind him and above his head was mounted a digital clock, having just passed five minutes on its way to zero. It was the biggest clock anyone had ever seen and as such was the first thing everyone noticed upon entering the chamber.

"Let's get this thing over with. I'm sure that we all have more pressing matters to attend to. Don't make me use the gavel!" threatened the Speaker, waiving his mallet in a cloud of menacing ill-humor. His golf bag propped up yearningly behind the podium, he attempted to usher the other members to their seats. If the indignant scowl on his sagging face did not shout *It's going to take a miracle for me to make my 8:42 tee time,* his plaid knickers and hideous moleskin sweater certainly did. As a licensed golfer the Speaker was required to abide the strictest adherence to the most sprawling, all-encompassing set of archaic bureaucratic regulations outside of those required to order a gyro from an agitated Greek vendor at bar time. Ironically, this didn't prohibit him from dressing like furniture from the 1960s.

"Gentlemen! Gentlemen! Do we have to do this every time?" nagged the Speaker, his face gradually taking the shape of Richard Nixon on a lemon binge. "You there! With the sideburns! Quit squawking about and sit down!"

Dissenting murmurs rippled through the assembly.

"Here we go again."

"I can think of a few places he can stick that gavel."

"We would have been better off with the *real* Nixon . . . well, maybe not—but it's close."

"I am the duly appointed One In Charge, at least for the next few minutes, and I will have ORDER!" The Speaker's gavel—which was really nothing more than an ornament designed to be hung from the rearview mirrors of cars owned by judges who wished to make sure that anyone who missed the black robe *and* the "Oliver Wendell *Who*?!" bumper sticker was reminded that they were driving with someone most likely more important than they were—punctuated the end of the ultimatum with a frenzied succession of inert clonks. This inaudible hammering continued, increasing in exponential fury, until one of the backbencher's bladders—coerced into action through an apoplectic fit of hoots, woops, and snorts—decided that now was as good a time as any to redecorate the inside of its owner's chinos. The resulting trouser puddle—unmistakable, unbecoming, and moist—was the generally accepted signal to finally take a seat and get down to brass tacks. (Mind you, not because everyone was content that they had ruffled a suitable number of feathers and adequately stirred the gumbo—though they most certainly had—but more so due to the fact that the bar had been drunk dry.) This particular parliamentary procedural quirk, originally instituted to be the only "proper" way to conclude a Question Time counter-rebuttal, was just one of the many archaic customs grandfathered in from the long defunct and even less remembered little polity known as the British House of Commons. Though comically ineffective and barbarous by modern standards, pound for pound you'll be hard-pressed to find a body of government anywhere that could turn the allocation and administration of goods and services into more entertaining theater than those limey British hooligans.

"Now that you've all had your fun," sneered the Speaker, glancing longingly at his brand-new, yet-to-be-used driver, "we can finally get down to the business of the day. If there are no objections, I declare this session open."

He paused for a moment, and then began, "Now, on to the little matter concerning the end of my term. As has been tradition and law since the Beginning, the Speaker may only serve one term which, I don't have to remind you all, coincides with the beginning and end of the Universe. Let me just say that it has been an honor serving as the Speaker for this go round, and that I hold you all in the utmost esteem." This bald-faced lie might have been more believable were the Speaker not wearing Richard Nixon's face, but in any event it was the "right and proper" thing to say at The End Of It All.

A smattering of applause and a grumble of acceptance permeated the ranks. The Speaker *had* been a snooty, hoity-toity phlegm bag—*that,* no one would or could deny, but he had been a capable administrator. His Universe had been, for the most part, a better-run affair than any in recent memory. Sure, there had been a few kerfuffles along the way—the dill-pickle scandal, some over-nepotistic appointments here and there, the Nixonian moues—but most of the real hot potatoes, proper nocuous opprobrium, had happened way back when the Universe was still expanding, and was more or less completely forgotten by now. Almost all of the black holes had been re-paved, dark matter had never been more enigmatic, and that whole business about that damned dead cat in the box had finally been put to rest. Definitively.

"Billy, the curtain, if you would," snapped the Speaker.

Behind him the entire front wall of the chamber, previously covered in red velvet, gave way to a panoramic viewing window. The clock above the window had reached ten seconds. 5 . . . 4 . . . 3 . . . 2 . . . and in that final second the Universe, which at that point resembled a deflating, softball-sized garbanzo bean, was observed by all present to collapse harmlessly onto itself with little more than a high pitched "pip" similar to the sound you get when you suck a Mack truck through a straw at eight billion times the speed of light.

The requisite unenthusiastic applause trickled around the room, and everyone turned back to the podium unimpressed, just in time to catch the tail end of the ex-Speaker's golf bag exit the chamber in a blur.

A bespectacled gentleman—ample around the waist, stout above the feet, and clumsy in the tongue—stepped forward. He glanced at his pocket watch, nervously adjusted the microphone and, being one of the more junior members of the assembly, began sweating.

Very few things are more imposing than a room filled with old men. There is just something unsettling about dealing with people who no longer care that their eyebrows have the consistency of a woolly mammoth. Facing them outside, although not advisable, gives you an outside shot; but within the walled confines of a room or chamber, survival is about as likely as having fun on a night out in Salt Lake City. As the youthfully challenged advance in age, they grow impervious to heat, each one turning up the thermostat every time he passes it. The lucky ones melt before the incessant barrages of "Is the heat on?!" and "Somebody better close that window!" cause their heads to implode like defective cinnamon rolls.

The thoroughly stout, amply perspirated gentleman cleared his throat, firing a projectile glottal salvo through the microphone. Percussive feedback yielded him the floor.

"P-P-P-Please, gentlemen. In ac-c-c-c-cordance with procedural by-laws, names w-w-w-will now be accepted into nomination for the new Speaker," stammered the poor fellow, woozy, having already lost six pounds.

The Speaker's office was of the highest prestige, charged with setting policy for and administering the Universe for one whole term—that being from The Bang, however "big" the Speaker had determined to be prudent at the front end, to the inevitable garbanzo bean at the back end. It was a position of unprecedented power and standing, but like most government jobs it was a "promotion" which involved doing boat-loads more work and requiring infinitely larger supplies of aspirin for only slightly more money than the standard job of an MP, which really only involved milling about and getting schlitzed while occasionally voting "yea" or "nay" on assorted motions or omnibus bills. As such, it was a position most people really didn't care to have. Who needed all that hassle when it was much easier to just sit back and guzzle down the bug juice like some freeloading Dead-head vagabond?

To be sure, there was the occasional up-and-comer, too young (comparatively) to realize that hard work and elbow grease were the domain of the lower classes, those who had the unfortunate disposition of having something to prove. These clueless dullards often made fine patsies for the brass to write in when no one was stupid enough to volunteer. And then there were those adept bureaucrats who understood that taking the Universe for a little joy-ride once around the cul-de-sac could really give you a significant leg up on the competition when looking to land that lucrative position in the private sector, no matter how much you had managed to muck everything up.

The previous Speaker, being a penny-pinching, nincompoop ape-brain, had skimped royally on just about every budgetary requirement. His greatest blunder? Convincing himself that the Universe "really didn't need all this dust floating about, especially at this price." (This was in direct contradiction to The Single, Primary, Universal, And Only Accepted Law For Governing The Construction Of A Universe: You had better start with a big-ole bushel of dust, or you can kiss the entire enterprise sayonara.) This blunder has since surpassed coffee-flavored yogurt as the Worst Idea Ever. Needless to say, the whole kit and caboodle got off the ground about as well as asbestos cigarettes. This did not, however, stop the man from procuring a cushy job on the board of directors of the third largest company the minute his Titanic of a term ended. Now he spends his days eating money sandwiches.

"D-d-d-do we have any nominations, g-g-g-gentlemen?"

The silence that strangled the bustling chamber was akin to the one following an F-bomb that has conspicuously squirted out at a nunnery bake sale. Eyeballs ping-ponged this way and that as the members scanned the room for evidence of motion, all the time painstakingly endeavoring not to make any movement which might be considered complicit in indicating that one wished to speak. Nominations are like a high-stakes auction. Inadvertently scratch your nose or flatulate and, before you know it, you are stuck with a costly piece of garage-sale memorabilia that nobody else wanted.

Finally, an elderly statesman near the back stood up. "I think that everyone here knows who should be given the reins this time around."

The right side of the chamber nodded their heads in unison. Their universal grunt signaled acquiescence. The left side grumbled and glowered.

"There is only one man I can think of who has the passion, experience, and expertise to rudder this barge. He has served in the previous eleven administrations in every position of worth with distinction and competence. He's a family man, a company man, a righteous man, the candy man, a man's man, a *lady's* man, *and* a twelve handicap. Trustworthy, honest, above-board; a real straight-shooter. And did I mention he's bona fide?"

The right side became fizzy with excitement in their realization that such a qualified candidate was one of their native sons.

"*And* you will recall his outspoken opposition to that calamitous dust debacle a ways back."

This last statement had everyone, even on the left side, bobbing their heads in agreement.

"I nominate—"

And with that a handsome lion near the front stood up, his hand raised in humble acceptance. This gentleman was perfection, covered in chocolate, wrapped in hyperbole. He was slim and healthy, and he stood with impeccable posture. His tailored conservative black suit emanated none of the stodginess often associated with tailored conservative black suits; it was supplemented by a crisp white shirt with an open button where the necktie should have been. Every hair in his silver mane was present and accounted for. He had the look of a man who knew the menu better than the waiter.

"Hear, hear!" the calls rang out.

"I second the motion!"

"I third!"

"Do we need another second?"

"O-O-O-Order, gentlemen! The nomination is seconded and carried. Are there any other nominations?"

This sent the left side into a delirious flit. There was no one, if left up to any form of coherent discussion, who would be more qualified than such a pro-dust powerhouse. But a challenger was needed, fast, if not just to keep up appearances.

"Going once." The unrest was now palpable. "Going twice." A whole section in the back-left fainted in plenary. "Going three times. Appointed . . . that is unless there are any objections," he added, groping the left side of the chamber with a rummaging gaze. "Anyone who has any objections speak now or forever hold your peace."

The deafening silence that followed was interrupted by a snoring cannonade off the port side.

"Who s-s-s-said that? S-S-S-Speak up, please."

After some shifting around and even more smelling-salts, a man was spatulaed off the floor and propped up against the back wall. He was wearing a coon-skin cap and soiled red full-body long johns, the kind where the bottom flap can be unbuttoned to let the wearer evacuate his bowels without having to go through the arduous process of undressing. The key to this paragon of lavatorial convenience is all in the order: One, open flap. Two, evacuate. By the look and smell of it, and by the flies, it appeared the man had on more than one occasion made his omelet without first cracking the eggs. Although he was not dead, his right arm was. Rigor mortis had clenched his hand around a rusty hip flask, and from a distance the substance on his face could only be accurately described as some permutation of beard and lunch. He spoke only in vowels and with an aroma reserved for outhouses and armpits.

The man next to him, politically savvy as he was, jumped.

"I nominate . . . uh . . . this guy."

"Hear, hear?" sheepishly bleated a man in the fourth row.

"I second the motion?" blurted another as if the statement had been extracted through torture.

"I third?" questioned a third with all the conviction of a ventriloquist's dummy.

"We don't need another second, do we?"

"The m-m-m-motion is seconded and carried. Would the two candidates make their way to the podium for the debate, please."

Any rational being from the planet Earth, employing the principle that objects in nature naturally make informed—and therefore the best—decisions based on rational examination of all possible outcomes and their consequences, and having compared the two candidates side by side, would have inevitably come to the conclusion that any competition between the two would be a complete farce and hence a waste of time, especially considering that the prize was complete control of the Universe. Even more especial with the dust fiasco fresh in everyone's salad. Any inkling of debate would have been prudently bypassed in favor of giving the most obviously over-qualified candidate the keys to the Chevy.

Anyone from anywhere else *besides* Earth would have given himself a mild stroke whooping around like a stoned hyena upon hearing that anyone in the Universe still actually subscribed to such a ludicrous line of thinking. Adam Smith thought like that. So did Karl Marx. They were both dolts—although both are still bestselling humor authors on Klomphithiroo Prime.

"Knock knock."

"Who's there?"

"Bettersit."

"Bettersit who?"

"We had better sit down and think about this before we do something stupid." That one always cracks 'em up.

Farce is the natural state of all things, no matter how much dust there is wafting about. It is the life-blood of existence. Farce dribbles through every particle, anti-particle, quark, and quasitron like a Benny Hill punchline on amphetamines, brazenly tooting its kazoo and stealing rationale's lunch money every chance it gets. Anyone who believes otherwise need only mosey on down to any local, county, state, regional, federal, or cosmic legislature.

Being so, the farce that was the debate for the One In Charge commenced without so much as a wooly eyebrow raised in opposition.

The lion sauntered stately up to the podium to lay out the vision for *his* Universe. The speech that followed was the most eloquent, well-worded, comprehensive, best-structured, oratorical masterpiece ever uttered. Every word he used polled better than free money. Laid out were plans for a whole new manner of Universe, one in which there would be a chicken in every pot, a pot for everyone to piss in, and free pot for anyone who wanted it, all while abolishing pot-holes *and ironing*. The simple beauty of his method twanged the very heart-strings of every politician present. In one ambitious wallop, the ills that had given the Universe hemorrhoids since before gravity had been made mandatory would be amputated from its galactic derriere.

The opus came to its conclusion. Raucous applause erupted from the gallery. Hands were clapped bloody. And when the members on both the right *and* the left had finished mutilating their metacarpi into pulpy red stumps, they sat down, content in knowing that they had just witnessed history in the making. The silver hero gracefully bowed his head and receded to his chair, knowing his chance of winning was better than that of the Globetrotters'.

"O-O-O-Order, Gentlemen! And now for the re-b-b-b-buttal." All the MPs, having completely forgotten about the other speech, returned to their seats, rolling their eyes as if they were just forcefully made to watch the end-credits of a movie.

The challenger stood up, attempted to button his bottom, and managed to lurch in the general direction of the podium. Undaunted by following the most unfollowable of acts—mostly having to do with his having been passed out through its entirety and therefore unaware of the impossibly long odds he faced, or for that matter what his name was or where his left boot had gotten to—he opened his mouth in an attempt at verbal communication.

It is here, if you hear anyone who was there tell it, that this disheveled husk of a deplorable excuse for a life form articulated a counter-argument of political sublimity. Spoken aloud, the remark, so succinct and perfectly devoid of any meaning or relevance while simultaneously conveying the allusion of exactly the opposite, was the great white whale of inane political discourse. It was the gyroball of sound bites. The promised land:

"Fuck taxes!

"Yay puppies!

"This Bud's for you!"

In the subconscious depths of the cosmos, The Kazoo sounded, resonating every quantum particle in the key out-to-lunch in absurd reality.

"HEAR, HEAR!"

"AND HEAR!"

"A-A-A-All those in favor?"

"AYE!"

"Op-p-p-p-posed?"

". . ."

"Th-th-th-the ayes have it. Mr. Speaker, you may begin The Bang at your convenience—once you have finished your drink, of course. This session is c-c-c-closed."

Another bull's-eye. Hear, hear!

Jasper Grawl is the author of The Gates of Valhalla, *a novel of biting satire, social commentary, and outrageous humor. Discover his work at*
http://www.FreshInkGroup.com/authors/jasper-grawl.

FLIGHT OF THE SUPER DUPE

By L.T. Gathings
(Mississippi, USA)
Crimefighter, 1ˢᵗ Place

Carl hated company parties. The primary reason was because every year he wound up the butt of some practical joke. This year proved to be no exception. He'd been given the impression that it was going to be a costume party. Having rented a Superman costume, the thirty-five-year-old African-American arrived on the scene only to discover everyone else in casual attire. Once again, he'd been duped. After enduring a little more than an hour of laughs at his expense, Carl subtly abandoned the social gathering.

Apparently, the joke didn't end with his beguilement. Less than twelve blocks from the party and a little more than fifteen blocks from his home, his blue Dodge Dakota ran out of gas. Having only just filled up earlier it was obvious that someone siphoned virtually every drop. So with his trusty red one-gallon container and donned in the garb of his favorite superhero, Carl was afoot.

En route to the nearest convenience store, which was inconveniently just over a mile away, the red-and-blue-clad pedestrian endured several juvenile remarks from a few passersby. According to the clock on his cell phone, it was 9:32. He'd been hoofing it for nearly twenty minutes, during which those uncomfortable boots were beginning to take a toll on him. Soulja Boy's "Crank That Soulja Boy" suddenly began to play behind him, which had to be another attempt at levity at his expense. Keeping his eyes in front of him with the corrective eyewear on his nose, Carl stayed his course.

The music went down as a sensual female voice called out in its stead, "Hey, you, Superman!"

"Ha-ha, very cute," he mumbled.

"Come on, fella, don't be like that," the sexy voice returned. "I was wondering if you could give us some directions."

Not fully convinced that there wasn't a punch line lying in wait, Carl slowly turned in her direction. Wow. She was a lovely black woman with what his cousin Ray would call the most kissable lips he'd ever seen. So, too,

were the other three in the black GMC Yukon Denali. The one on the passenger's side was a brunette. The woman in the back behind the driver was
definitely black. As for the one on the other side, her face was obscured by
a shadow.

After checking to make sure his tongue wasn't dangling, Carl finally responded. "Sorry. Um, where are you trying to get to?"

"Do you know a guy by the name of, um . . . Luther?"

"Oh, boy, do I." He shook his head disagreeably. "Blond, good looking,
great smile—is that him?"

"Ummmm . . ." She looked at the others, who shook their heads simultaneously. "No. This guy is . . ."

"Black," the one behind the driver concluded. "He's a thick guy, former
NFL and all that. He lives on, ummmm . . . Where do you live?"

"Schuster Drive."

"That's it, Schuster Drive!"

"Wow, you're our hero, Misterrrr . . .?" The laid-back driver raised her
eyebrows.

"Carl. Carl Net." He grinned.

"Would you mind terribly showing us how to get to Schuster Drive?"
The driver smiled in the left corner of her mouth.

"I was just going for some gas. If you don't mind taking me to the convenience store, I'll let you girls follow me home."

The one behind the driver opened her door and stepped out. "Well get
your cute self in here, Clark."

"Uh, it's Carl." He climbed in.

It was quite a nice vehicle with gray leather punctuated by that new-car
smell. Then, there were the passengers; they smelled good as well. Each had
on a party dress made of very little material. Enchanted, Carl wondered if
his truck had died and he'd gone to dumb-luck heaven.

"Allow us to introduce ourselves." The driver looked at him in the rearview mirror. "I'm Josephine."

"I'm Melody," the one in the passenger's seat fell in.

"I'm Valerie," the one on his right added with her eyes on the text that
she was sending.

At last, he could to see her. She was a redhead with pale skin and an
angelic face.

"And I'm Alexandra." The one on his left rounded out the roster with
her hand on his knee.

"It's very nice to meet you all." Carl raised his shoulders, nervous.

"So, Cain, where are you coming from in that spiffy outfit?" Melody looked him over.

"Huh? Oh, I'm coming from a company party. By the way, my name is Carl."

Alexandra relieved him of the crimson container. "Let's just put this in the back."

After about two minutes they drove past the convenience store. Carl watched it carefully as they left it behind.

"Uh, we passed the store," he informed the helmsperson.

"Yeah, we're kinda late. Could you show me how to get there first? That way, we can just go on once you've gassed up. After all, I'm sure you'll have to stop and get more gas."

Carl nodded, agreeing with her logic. "Good point."

"Hey, Jodie!" Alexandra yelled. "Did you lock the windows? Because I can't put mine up! I don't have any curls as it is, witch!"

"I thought she said her name was Josephine." Carl's nervous shoulders remained up.

"It is." Josephine chuckled. "They call me Josie."

"For a minute it sounded like she said Jodie."

"So, Earl, you seemed a little irritated when we rolled up on you." Melody faced him. "What happened? Did Lois Lane leave with the Joker?"

"Actually, it's Carl, and the Joker is a Batman villain, not Superman. But to answer your question, I was just irritated because someone stole my gas and these boots are not really my size. The only way I could even get them on was to wear them with no socks."

"Oh, you poor thing, your feet must be hurting," Melody sympathized with a frown.

Valerie took her eyes off the phone long enough to contribute to the conversation. "Melody is a top-rate masseuse, you know."

Carl cleared his throat. "Um, it's the next left, Josie."

"Gotcha," she replied.

"Is it my imagination or did our little Charles here just try to change the subject?" Alexandra's tone was playful.

"Certainly sounded like that to me." Valeria chuckled.

"No! It's just . . ." Carl's eyes widened. "There is it is; 1938 Schuster on the right. What's your friend's address? I'm sure I can . . ."

"That'll be easy enough to find," Josie interrupted while using his driveway to turn around.

"What about your friend's house?"

"Who?" Josie asked.

"What do you mean who? Lester!" Alexandra kicked the back of the driver's seat. "Keep up with the action, would you, Josie?"

"I thought his name was Luther." Carl turned toward Valerie, who was texting again.

"It is, but we call him Lester just to irritate him, you know?" Alexandra giggled like a school girl.

"That can be kind of irritating, all right." Carl sighed.

"You don't know how much we appreciate you helping us out like this . . ." Josie paused just short of his name.

"Carl," he helped her along.

"Melody, you should give this man one of your famous five-minute foot massages," Josie recommended.

"Sure."

"That's not really, um . . ." Carl verged on stuttering.

Melody turned around again. "Seriously? You'd pass on one of my foot massages?"

"Thanks for the offer, really, but . . ."

"Girls, a little help please." Josie looked in the rearview mirror.

With those words, Alexandra grabbed Carl's left leg by the ankle as Valerie did likewise with his right, and despite his resistance they forced his feet upon the console between the two women up front. Redirecting their strength to his arms, Alexandra and Valerie held the male passenger in place as Melody tugged at the snug footwear.

"Please . . . I'm ticklish." Carl continued to struggle.

After painstaking effort, Melody finally separated the knee-high boots from his feet. She then opened the glove compartment and pulled out a roll of duct tape.

"Ticklish, eh? How ticklish are we talking?" Melody grinned.

"What are you going to do?" Carl asked.

Without a word, the brunette proceeded to wrap Carl's ankles with the gray tape. Once she'd brought the narrow adhesive strip full circle thrice, Melody sadistically tantalized the bottom of Carl's vulnerable feet with her perfectly manicured fingernails. Immediately, he began to laugh and contort his body. Carl begged for mercy, even divulging that prolonged tickling would result in him wetting his pants. With tears streaming down his face, Carl's hysterical belly laughter rendered him oblivious to everything else, inside and outside of the onyx SUV.

"Oh, God . . .!" Carl cried out amid the laughter as he lost control of his bladder.

Though poor Carl hadn't passed out, he was seeing stars. While he was in the process of replenishing his lungs, he heard the lift gate close. That's when he realized that they'd come to a stop. As to how long they'd been parked, he had no idea. He was alone in the SUV. His encumbered hands and feet made it difficult to return to an upright position, but he eventually managed. Though his glasses were on the floor, he could see well enough to recognize his truck driving away.

Obviously, he'd been duped again, but to what end? Who were those women? What were they up to? After all, up until they stole his truck the whole encounter seemed harmless. Even the excruciating tickling episode just seemed like a harmless joke. Perhaps his co-workers had put them up to it. Even if that were the case, what could they possibly want with his Dakota that was only capable of riding three in the cab? Then, there was the question of where did they get the gas?

Struggling against the tape, he could feel some slack, particularly around his ankles. He kicked until his feet were free. Using his toes, Carl picked up his glasses, took them in his hand, and returned them to his face. At least he could see a little better. Like a rat in a red and blue suit, he gnawed at the tape that bound his wrists. Surprisingly, he escaped its grip pretty quickly.

Praying with his fingers and toes crossed, he peeked at the ignition and found the keys dangling. "Yes!"

He climbed into the driver's seat where he felt something flat under his derriere. With his luck, it would be a bomb. Carefully, he reached down and pulled it from under him. Whew! It was a laptop. Why would they leave that behind? Tossing it to the side, Carl started the GMC. He felt something underfoot against the accelerator. Whatever it was; it was cold and hard. Reaching down he pulled up a gun this time. Suddenly unnerved, he took off in the direction that his truck had gone. Par for the course, the black SUV had passed the convenience store when it, too, conked with its gas hand on E.

"Ok. I'll bite. What's next?"

Answering his rhetorical query in swift order, blue lights encompassed the motionless vehicle. The company party was beginning to look pretty good.

A voice called out to him from a megaphone. *"You in the SUV, come out with your hands up!"*

Slowly, he complied as a swarm of uniformed police officers moved in on him and forced him to the ground on his stomach.

*   *   *

It was 10:24, and Carl had been sitting at a table in the small room facing that big mirror for almost an hour. Nervous didn't begin to describe how he felt. Being taken into custody barefoot and wearing a Superman suit with a big pee stain on it conjured up adjectives like "stupid." Finally, the door opened, and in walked two fiftyish white men in suits.

"Mr. Net, I'm Detective Perry. This is Detective White."

"Sir, this is a huge misunderstanding." Carl leaned forward.

"Don't you mean *super?*" White scoffed.

"You're in a lot of trouble, Mr. Net." Perry opened the folder. "Grand theft auto, grand larceny, aggravated assault, and misuse of a computer. There's a lot of jail time here."

Carl's eyes widened. "What . . .? Grand who? I don't know anything about that Denali or that computer. What larceny? What assault? On who?"

"A confession would go a long way right now, son. The way you pulled the job was A-1, but you didn't put much thought into the getaway, did you?"

"Sir, I haven't done anything wrong."

"That why you peed yourself, Superman?" White scowled.

"I told the officers that I was at a company party. That's why I'm dressed like this."

Perry sighed. "Yeah. We checked with your co-workers. They say you eased outta there without anybody noticing, which is pretty good for some-body in that get-up."

"It wasn't a very good party, so I left."

"Really? Because they're all still there." White shook his head. "Maybe you had somewhere else to be, like Olsen's Jewelry."

"Olsen's Jewelry?"

"Okay. We can go the long way if you want." Perry's sigh was more exasperated this time. "About 9:38 p.m. we received a call from Olsen's Jew-elry stating that a black guy in a Superman suit pretended to have car trouble, asked to use the phone, and pulled a gun on the young woman working there."

"But at 9:38 I was . . ."

Perry continued ignoring Carl's effort to explain. "The perpetrator then informed her that the silent alarm and the security cameras had been hacked into and disabled. This perpetrator went into the back where Mr. Jamison Olsen, the proprietor, was doing an inventory on five-million dollars in diamonds that he was brokering for a Solomon Dundee of Australia. Mr. Olsen was hit from behind. The diamonds were taken, and the man in the Superman suit fled."

"Not a lot of people in Superman suits tonight, not even at your boss's party," White insinuated. "Then there's the matter of the GMC Denali that you stole from Ross Auto."

"But I told the officers . . ." Carl was anxious.

"Yeah, yeah, I see it here. Your truck ran out of gas, and four beautiful women picked you up. Why am I never so lucky? Anyway, you gave them directions to your house. Why, I have no idea. Then somehow they managed to subdue you and taped your wrists as well as ankles. Here's my favorite part. The four of them drove away in your truck that you claimed was out of gas. That sound about right?"

"Don't you see? They had to be going back to my house," Carl appealed to the calm-natured cop.

"Why? Was there a kinky orgy scheduled for later at your place? Were they going ahead of you so that they could slip into something more comfortable?" White scoffed with his arms crossed. "I'm curious as to how two women overpowered you."

"There were four of them."

"Oh, come on, two of them would've had to have been in the front, tough guy. So, I'll ask you again; how'd they overpower you?"

Carl cleared his throat. "I'd rather not say."

"Besides, we sent a unit to your house," Perry said, jumping back in. "Your truck is in the driveway with almost half a tank of gas. Oh, and the gas can that you claimed was in the back of the SUV was found in the back of your truck. By the way, there was nothing in the back of the GMC except the rest of your ensemble—namely, your boots. As for your house, nothing seemed disturbed. Your story just doesn't pan out, son. You're in trouble."

With his Miranda rights suddenly coming to mind, Carl reconsidered his position. If every word that he said could be used against him, which seemed to be the way things were headed, and everything that he'd done had been working against him, perhaps he needed an attorney. Of course, he didn't have one.

"I think I'd like to make my phone call now."

White chuckled. "So the *man of pee* wants his lawyer now, is that it?"

"That's my right, isn't it?"

Perry took a cell phone from within his jacket pocket and offered it to Carl. Before he began to make his call, both detectives allowed him a moment of privacy. He dialed his cousin's number and waited anxiously as it rang.

"*Hello.*"

"Ray? Oh, thank God, Ray!"

"*Carl? What's up, Carl?*"

"Ray, listen to me. I've got a situation here . . ."

"*Yeah, I bet you do. That party at your boss's house is boring, isn't it? Didn't I tell you to come hang out with me? You know, I'm getting off in about fifteen . . .*"

"Ray? Ray, are you there?"

"*Hold the phone. You'll never guess what's sitting in gate G4, cousin.*"

"Ray, I really don't have time for . . ."

"*Be still my heart. Carl, I'm looking at a woman with those lips that I love.*"

"Come on, Ray, I don't have time for . . ." Carl hesitated as Ray's words rang in his mind. "Lips. Ray did you say kissable lips? She's at the airport?"

"*I'm looking right at her.*"

"Listen to me, Ray. You have to keep her there. I don't care how you do it, Ray. Just keep her there, okay?" Carl hurriedly hung up the phone and called out. "Detective Perry!"

Perry and White re-entered the room casually.

"I uh . . ." Carl hesitated, swallowing hard. "I'm ready to confess."

Perry took a pen from the pocket of his shirt. "Now we're talking."

"Uh, yeah, but first I want to take you to the diamonds."

"Okay." Perry clicked the pen. "Tell us where they are and we'll send a . . ."

"No! I'll show you myself or the deal is off."

"Deal, what deal? There's no deal." White frowned. "We've got the laptop you used to hack into Olsen's with your prints all over it. Not to mention, the gun used to—"

"I just want to take you to the stuff and get this over, please."

"He's right." Perry nodded to his partner. "Where to, Mr. Net?"

"The airport."

They'd offered Carl a change of clothes, but he was in a hurry. He had no idea when Josie's plane was departing. They'd set him up perfectly, and if he didn't catch Josie before her plane took off, Carl could very easily being going to prison for a crime he didn't commit.

With Perry, the more senior detective, doing the driving, it took the three of them almost twenty minutes to get to the airport. Considering how long it took them to get there, Carl was thankful that the police were at liberty to park at the curb. Again, Carl was the subject of many stares as he walked handcuffed and barefoot between the two detectives, still clad in that stained Superman suit.

"So where are the diamonds, Mr. Net?" Perry asked as they walked through a terminal toward Gate C4.

"She's at Gate C4."

"She?" White shuddered.

"I mean *the* . . ." Carl regrouped. "The bag is in a locker at Gate C . . ."

Now boarding: flight 748 at Gate C 4 departing for Paris, France.

"No!" Carl broke into a mad dash.

"Hey! Hey!" both detectives yelled.

Carl was no athlete and never had been, which was evident by the slow motion of his feet. The cops were closing in on him as he closed in on Gate C4. When they tackled him, the passengers were just beginning to board.

"Wait!" Carl exclaimed. "The real robbers are getting on this plane!"

As Perry and White pulled him off the floor, Carl frantically scanned the group of people who'd halted their course and were now looking at the spectacle that was him. No Josie. Ray was supposed to detain her. Where was he?

"Carl, what's going on?" Ray's voice cried out from behind him.

Carl turned around, and there was his cousin standing next to a beautiful blond with an exasperated expression on her face.

"Oh, Ray, thank God." Carl was out of breath. "Where is she, the woman you told me about on the phone?"

"This is her." Ray frowned.

"No! No! That's not her!"

"What's going on? What is this about?" the angered woman asked Carl. "Who are you? Are you the reason this little security guard dimwit wouldn't let me get on the plane?"

"We're sorry for the inconvenience, ma'am. You can go now." Perry flashed his badge and then turned his attention back to Carl. "All right, Net, that's enough with the games. Where are those diamonds?"

Poor Carl, he'd bet everything on Ray's mystery woman with the kissable lips. He'd been set up but good. Diamonds or no diamonds, things looked bad for him. The statement of the woman at the jewelry store alone was enough to do him in. With no other cards to play, he tried to escape.

"Hey!" The detectives fell in behind him again.

Carl had absolutely no idea what he was doing aside from trying to avoid going to jail—not to mention that he'd already lost one of these foot chases not five minutes ago. His heart pounded as he heard the footfalls of his pursuers getting closer and closer. After footing it only a hundred meters or so, he began to get a stitch, which was the human equivalent to running out of gas. As bad as he hated to admit it, the thing to do was surrender.

A janitor had just finished mopping a spill of some kind outside one of the bathrooms. When Carl tried to put on the brakes, his bare feet combined with the wet floor were a recipe for disaster. His feet went up, and he crashed to the floor, knocking down some hapless soul who couldn't get out of the way fast enough. His head hit hard against the cruel concrete, and for the second time tonight he saw stars as everything slowly faded into darkness.

When consciousness found him again, Carl had a really bad headache and pretty good idea that he was in worse trouble than before. Confirming his suspicions was Detective Perry standing over him with Ray by his side.

"Easy there, son, that's a pretty good bump," Perry cautioned him.

"What happened?" Carl felt the ping pong-ball-sized sized bump on the back of his head, suddenly realizing that his hands were no longer cuffed.

"What are you referring to exactly? How you got that bump? Or did you succeed in closing this case?" Perry smiled.

"Closing the case?"

"Yeah, we got your quartet of pussycats in custody."

"You're a hero, Carl," Ray said with enthusiasm. "There are reporters outside waiting to talk to you right now."

"When? How?"

"You did it. When you recognized your culprit as that black woman coming out of the bathroom, you tackled her before she could fade into the crowd. Her boarding pass said Gate G6, so that's where we found the other three. That was some quick thinking!"

"The diamonds?"

"Were in one of the carry-ons."

"But how'd they get them past security?"

"These ladies were smart. Two of them were travelling as FBI agents extraditing a prisoner while the other was travelling as a naval petty officer returning to duty. Those fake credentials of theirs were really good, too.

That's why they went to your house, to change clothes and catch separate taxis."

"But if they had it all worked out, why try to dupe me?"

"From what we've figured out, you were a diversion. While we were detaining and questioning you, they'd be on their way to Amsterdam. It might've worked, too, if their flight hadn't been delayed, giving you time to nab them. Oh, for the record, we picked up the jewelry-store clerk, too."

"Why?"

"She was their accomplice on the inside. She's the one who actually disabled the alarm and cameras, as well as snuck up behind Mr. Olsen and coldcocked him. The reason she was able to describe you so accurately to the police was because she'd received several texts from one of the others about you."

"Oh, well, I'm glad it all worked out."

"Sure did. You're a hero. We couldn't have caught them without you, Mr. Net."

"You should write a book, Carl," Ray added. "Imagine the women who'd be throwing themselves at your feet."

"No thanks, Ray. I've had enough women at my feet."

Learn more about 1ˢᵗ-place winner and Fresh Ink Group member L.T. Gathings at http://www.FreshInkGroup.com/authors/lt-gathings.

BOBBI LEE

By Maynard
(Oregon, USA)
Regional, 3rd Place

New Glory Hollow, Kentucky, 1922

THE CHURCH

It was called a "reckoning".

The congregation of the Church of The Anointed With Signs Following filled the pews on each side of the sanctuary and stared at the floor, refusing to look at one another; the very air in the little church filled with a sense of guilt and shame. They'd been through this before. Attendance was mandatory. To miss a reckoning was tantamount to being shunned by the congregation.

An aisle ran down the center of the church to the pulpit in front. In the middle of the pulpit stood a podium. Two wooden-railed banisters, one to the left of the podium and one to the right, separated the pulpit from the main sanctuary. Below each bannister was a cushioned altar used for kneeling and praying, and sitting atop each bannister was a Mason jar filled with strychnine. To the right of the pulpit, off to the side, sat a large wooden box with small holes bored into the sides and hinges on top that allowed the box to open out. The box was filled with diamond-back and copperhead rattlesnakes.

For several minutes the congregation sat in silence. Finally, a small door opened from the back of the pulpit and a tall, middle-aged man wearing spectacles, his hair slicked back, entered the pulpit carrying a *Bible*.

Porter Lehman, known as Father Lehman to the members of the congregation, walked up to the podium, laid down the *Bible*, and looked out at the congregation. He remained silent for several moments, staring down the congregation. Finally, he spoke. "I gathered you all here this evening because the Lord came to me in a vision. The congregation has been stained with sin." He stood there for several seconds.

No one made a sound.

"Martha Snow, come forward," he commanded.

A woman in her mid-thirties slowly stood from a pew toward the back of the church. The expression on her face was one of shock and confusion. Passing in front of several people, she inched her way out of the pew into the aisle and stood there. Finally, she made her way up the aisle and headed toward the pulpit. The congregation refused to acknowledge her as she walked past them. Now at the front of the church, the woman stood behind the altar to the left of the podium, with her head hung.

"Martha Snow, where is your husband?" Lehman asked.

She glanced behind her, then back to the pulpit. "Well, Buford's sittin' right back there where we always sit," she said, pointing behind with her thumb.

Lehman's expression didn't change. "That's not your husband, Martha. That's the man you took up with after you *left* your husband. Now, I'll ask you again, where is your husband?"

Martha stood there, motionless, for a moment. Then it finally dawned on her that Father Lehman was talking about Terrance Ballard. She had married the boy when she was fifteen; he was seventeen. But, how could Father Lehman possibly know? It was impossible that anyone, other than her current husband, Buford, could know, and she trusted him with her life. The only other possible explanation was that what Lehman claimed was true and he really did have conversations with God through dreams and visions.

"Martha?"

"I—I don't know where he is," she answered. "We was just kids when we married."

"Then you admit that you do have another husband, is that right?" Lehman prodded.

"Yes," she answered. "But we never came together as man and wife. I just married him to get out of the house. My momma died and it was left up to me to take care of all my brothers and sisters. But, we never—"

"Did you take vows with this man?" Lehman interrupted.

"Yes, but—"

"Then, in God's eyes, you married him, Martha Snow." Lehman opened the *Bible* sitting on the podium in front of him and began to read: "For the woman which hath a husband is bound by the law to her husband so long as he liveth; but if the husband be dead she is loosed from the law of her husband. So then if, while her husband liveth she be married to another man, she shall be called an adulteress. Romans seven: two through three." He closed the *Bible* and stood there, silent.

Martha glanced back at the congregation. "We was just kids!" she pleaded.

The congregation remained silent.

She slowly turned back and faced the podium only to find Lehman glaring down at her.

"The wages of sin is death," Lehman said. "So bury your sin, Martha Snow. Bury your sin and put it behind you. You can die in your sin, or you can test the Spirit. Whether you live or die is up to Him. What's your choice?" he commanded.

She glanced behind her once again, tears streaming down her cheeks.

Again, there was no response from the congregation.

Martha slowly turned, faced the podium again, and pointed to the Mason jar on the left. "I'll drink the poison," she said.

Martha had seen this scenario played out several times before. Sometimes those who drank the poison or got bitten by the serpents would survive. Most of the time, they did not survive

Lehman reached over to the banister on his left and picked up the jar of strychnine. Then he twisted off the lid and handed it to the woman.

Martha stood there for several moments, staring at the jar.

"Live or die, your sins will be forgiven you, Martha Snow," Lehman said.

She took a deep breath, slowly raised the jar to her lips, and took a swallow. Afterwards, she stood there for several seconds, motionless. Then the muscles in her face started twitching. Moments later, the muscles in her legs began to twitch. Finally, she began to sway.

Lehman nodded to two men who were sitting on the front pew to his right.

The men rushed toward the pulpit, one of them carrying a quilt under his arm.

She was losing her balance by the time the ushers reached her.

The two men lowered her to the floor and covered her with the quilt.

Spasms now overtook her body as the men carried her through a side door next to the pulpit.

*   *   *

Lehman took off his spectacles, pulled out a handkerchief, and wiped his eyes. Afterward, he gripped the podium and stared, once again, into the congregation. "Sister Snow has chosen to lay her sins before the Spirit. Live or die, she is forgiven of her sin, and she'll sit at the right hand of God with our Lord, Christ Jesus, in heaven. Now, the Spirit speaks again: Harley Thompson, Hester Bogsley, come forward."

No comment among those in the congregation. They kept silent with their heads bowed.

A few moments later, blond-haired, fifteen-year-old Harley stood. A moment later Hester reluctantly stood and nervously fingered her flowing dark hair. They made their way to the middle aisle and down to the pulpit.

Hester was obviously pregnant, her belly full, round and stretched against the simple white shift she was wearing. She had a small frame for her fourteen years of age.

"Harley Thompson, Hester Bogsley, turn and face the congregation," Lehman said.

The two slowly turned around.

"Look on Harley Thompson and Hester Bogsley," Lehman commanded from the podium.

Those in the congregation raised their heads and looked upon the young couple as they stood there, trembling, with their heads tilted down.

Lehman shook his head and looked, once again, out at the congregation. "Brother and Sister Bogsley, stand and look upon this girl," Lehman commanded once again.

A man dressed in a pair of overalls stood immediately and faced the pulpit. Next to him a woman dressed in a simple black dress hesitantly raised herself to a standing position.

"Is this your daughter?" Lehman asked the man, nodding his head in the direction where the girl stood.

The woman swallowed and kept her head bent to the ground as a single tear ran down her cheek.

"We don't know her," Sherman Bogsley said without raising his head.

"Very well, you may be seated," Lehman replied.

The girl's parents slowly sank to their seats.

Hester stood there for several moments, staring in the direction of her parents.

They did not acknowledge her.

Lehman addressed the congregation on the other side of the aisle. "Brother and Sister Thompson, please stand."

A younger couple in their late thirties stood, keeping their heads bowed.

"Is this your son?" Lehman asked the man.

The man glanced in the direction where the boy was standing, then hung his head once again. "Our son is dead," the man answered. His wife remained silent.

"You may take your seats," Lehman said, watching as the couple sank back into the pew. Then, he addressed the young couple. "Do either of you have anything to say?"

"No," Harley said as Hester shook her head and continued looking at the floor.

"Very well, let it be on your heads." Lehman turned to address the congregation. "Fornication is a grievous sin. Sexual sin not only defiles the body, but the sins of the parents are visited on the children. The two of you have refused to pay for your sins. You have refused to trust the wisdom of the Spirit. You leave me no other choice." Lehman raised his left hand as though he were about to bless the young couple. Then, he shouted, "Let them be anathema!" The rafters in the sanctuary seemed to be vibrating as his voice filled the building. "Go from this place! Don't look back unless the two of you are willing to put your sins before the Spirit."

The congregation sat in silence for several moments.

Hester looked to her right at the wooden box containing the rattlers. "I'll take up the serpents!" she said.

"No!" Harley snapped, turning his head toward Hester.

She glanced, once again, at the box of snakes, and then looked back toward the ground.

Lehman glared down at her from the podium. "He's not your husband, Hester Bogsley. It's your choice to make. Live or die, your sins will be forgiven you. For the wages of sin is death. But, if the Spirit wills, you might live."

She looked, once again, toward Harley.

"That baby's got to have a momma, Hester," he said, staring her down.

She remained silent.

"Very well, you've made your choice, the both of you. Turn and face the congregation," Lehman said without a hint of compassion in his voice.

The couple lifted their heads, their eyes meeting for a moment. They slowly turned to face the back of the sanctuary.

So young and not even big for his age, Harley nevertheless looked defiant as he faced the congregation.

Hester raised her head and looked, once again, in the direction where her mother was sitting. Her eyes were still puffed and red from crying.

The woman refused to look at her.

Hester glanced at Harley, who held out his hand. She took it, and the young couple took several steps down the main aisle toward the back of the sanctuary.

"That child will be cursed if God ever allows it to be born!" Lehman thundered from the podium.

Harley stopped, let go of Hester's hand, and slowly turned to face Lehman, eye to eye. "You go to hell!" he said.

The congregation gasped as Harley took Hester's hand and continued to walk down the aisle toward the back of the sanctuary, their heads held high until they reached the pew where Hester's parents were seated.

Hester paused for a moment, once again looking in the direction where her mother was sitting. Harley tugged at her arm. The two of them were just about to continue down the aisle when all of a sudden Hester screamed, doubled over, and grabbed her stomach.

The mother looked up just in time to see the pains of labor take her daughter.

"Momma," the girl mouthed as water began to drip between her legs, quickly forming a small pool on the floor where she was standing.

Hester's mother impulsively started toward the girl, but she was quickly jerked back into her seat by her husband, who sternly refused to acknowledge his daughter.

The woman stayed in her seat, her head, once again, bent toward the floor.

Harley scooped Hester up into his arms and carried her to the back of the sanctuary.

"I tell you in the name of the Lord that child will be cursed!" Porter Lehman yelled after them as the boy who loved her struggled to open the back door with one hand.

No one dared help him.

Harley stood outside the church with Hester in his arms, his eyes welling with tears. Although they had expected this would eventually happen, now that it had, the reality of the situation overcame them. They couldn't go home. They no longer had a home. They had been banished by the congregation of the Church of The Annointed With Signs Following. For all practical purposes they were dead, not only to the church, but to the small town of New Glory Hollow as well.

"Don't worry. I know a place to go," Harley told her, and just as these words left his mouth the girl screamed, her body writhing in pain as she had her second contraction.

Hester could feel herself slipping away as her vision narrowed to a tunnel. She took several deep breaths in an effort to try to stay conscious, but it was of no use. The tunnel filled with a blinding light as the pain grew more intense, then . . . blackness.

SCHIZOPHRENIA

By Briar Falgoust
(Louisiana, USA)
Suspense, 3rd Place

My mind can be compared to a beautiful work of abstract art—wonderful to observe but ambiguous. Insanity is considered to be madness, or illness, or craziness. It is the hymn of my life, although quite misapplied. I am sane to an extent, yet I am trapped within the solid limestone walls of its dungeon. I have been engulfed in the darkness for almost an eternity; escape is never an option. My permanent residence is here at the Freedom Park Psychiatric Hospital, the year 1952. Oh, the irony! Freedom is forgotten, for the will to live is extracted from each deranged, combusted mind. Every person in here is a victim, a lifeless body pacing the enclosing walls, sentenced to a painful, distorted death. A chance of survival? There is one—let that tick, that insanity, fill the mind. Now beat it out. Stab it out. Drown it out.

Let it slowly bleed out.

My Dementia just wouldn't settle, and now I've been punished for it. My residence, Ward 62, is the "Urgent Care Ward" (known to the wisest patients as the Psycho Ward) and is fit for only the most deranged, hostile patients. My hallucinations have caused me to see the world from a different, demented perspective. Of course it was their fault that I cracked. But who can blame them? Over the years, I've steadily gained their trust and established a solid relationship. Yes, I consider them friends; they guide me to peace. I'm plagued with their eternal presence, so why not show appreciation and gratitude? They give me strength, hope, and courage. See, the neurons in my brain fire at an immeasurable speed. My thought processes can override their capabilities. Therefore, my hallucinations (known to the doctors as my Dementia) control my emotions and allow me to surpass my limits. And when I pass them, I do not stop.

I can elicit the fear from other prisoners' cold, wild eyes. I can feel erratic thoughts emerge through their irritable quivers. I chuckle. I'm not mad, I tell you! It's only my Dementia, my companion keeping me alive. He humors me, keeps me livid. But there are times when he can possess me to be violent. Possess me to cry. Possess me to scream. And it is here where my story takes an ultimate turn. Experience with me the most extreme of my sorrows.

Madness. Pure madness. My legs are chained and my arms, deprived of blood circulation, tightly bind my torso. I awaken to nothing but the glow of black. So this is my reward for listening to my Dementia! My bare, wretched toenails can touch the fore wall. My knees bend into my chest as I align my spine with the back wall.

Thank goodness I'm not claustrophobic!

The floor, made of rubber cushion, strangely irritates me. Even the slightest movement produces a horrid, deafening noise, as if gunshots were fired next to my ear. What have I done to deserve this? My Dementia greets me, grinning with empathy.

"Don't you worry, Andrew. I know you're discreet, and maybe a bit confused. But you're fearless. You know you've kept your sanity. That sweet, luscious sanity. Our savior, is it not? Look at what you've been through. Look at it! And we're locked up, together, you and me. We won't be here much longer, pal. Oh and, Andrew, let me tell you about that wife of yours, that Scarlet."

Scarlet. Her name was all it took for me to fall in love with her. Her auburn hair freely blew with the wind, and her soft lips remained stretched over her glistening smile. Her laugh was so innocent, and her hands so intricate. The last time I held her in my arms, cradling her head with my left hand, was with a bullet lodged into her brain. My hands were bathed in blood, but I still brushed the thin strands of hair out of her face to stare into her dry, crimson eyes. We were together for three years, and this is what it came down to. I smiled at her, and I forced a smile back. Her killer, my M1917 revolver, lay next to my knees. Of course she would never understand my Dementia. I couldn't be with her any longer. She would never realize that this was the only way for us to be together. She could never reside in her bodily presence. I could only be with her by keeping her image alive in my mind, allowing her memory to live for eternity. Besides, my Dementia needed company. Who could blame him? He was lonely. I was sure he would do the same for me.

But Scarlet. Presently I feel her inside of me, breathing with me, speaking with me. Her love colors my veins with vivid immaculacy. I feel reborn. My Dementia is satisfied. I am complete.

I cry. Tears smear on my face as I cringe on the ground. Hours have elapsed, but it feels like days. I grasp my footing and use the back wall to lift myself upwards. Inching closer to the top, my head hits the cushion ceiling;

my space is approximately four feet tall. I fall back to the ground, only to be stabbed with an excruciating pain in my chest. I gasp for air, clinging to my dear life as if I were being pulled into the dark depths of an ocean. My body flails around as if a marionette were empowering my muscles. My Dementia observes closely, dying of laughter as I struggle, alone, against no other force but myself.

That backstabbing son of a bitch. He'd put me through endless pain and suffering, and this is what I'd received in return: a careless demon inside of my soul, controlling me against my own will. He'd filled me with angst and hostility and rage.

But what if he didn't control me? What if I could be freed from all of this madness? What if, in reality, the demon was me?

It was; I just didn't realize it yet.

I scream. I scream louder than imaginable, louder than the subject of an exorcism. The guilt slowly devours me. My Dementia glares at me, looking beyond my soul and into the depths of my mind. He confronts me. He holds his cold hands around my neck onto the wall. I beg and plead for mercy. How could I even think that my Dementia was responsible? He has the power to do as he wishes. I'd instantly die if I doubted him.

"You see, Andrew, you don't have a say in this. You killed her. You blew her brains out with your own two hands. Now you'll pay for that. You'll be damned in Hell forever, where the scorching flames will bury you alive along with your weak little yelps and cries. Do you have anything to say, Andrew? Anything at all before you leave this Earth in complete isolation?"

My head slams against the wall numerous times. I am drenched in perspiration, which is a sign that my body is responding to the rising temperature. I have officially lost my mind, and it is now stranded in an indecipherable dimension. What more could my Dementia need?

Absolute insanity. The only way out of this prison. The only path to freedom.

My heart races; it pulses evenly with my breathing. The deadly silence slices my soul. Quietly closing my eyes, I breathe out and compress my lips. My mouth widens, releasing a blood-curdling, nightmarish scream. I bang my head against the back wall again, cutting my ankles while struggling to free them. I twist and turn my body with unbearable force, but my arms remain locked into place. I begin to feel light-headed and delusional, and the walls of my cell space begin to enclose on me. I stop all movement completely. I can see my Dementia through the blurred semi-consciousness. His grin is scathing and menacing, putting a bullet straight through my head. I can no longer breathe. I fall into a deep coma, fully paralyzed against my will. But then, I see.

A blinding light destroys the darkness. My fears are washed away by the utter purity. A door has been opened, and I proceed to stand up. My legs are freed and my arms are unbound. I can smell the cunning scent of freedom. And as I step forth into the world, it welcomes me with open arms, for I am confined to the realms of my deranged mind no longer.

ENOUGH

By Talya Tate Boerner
(Texas, USA)
Romance, 3rd Place

The best thing about sleeping over at her best friend's house was laughing all night. Side-splitting laughter until tears blurred their eyes. Staying up late, talking for hours about nothing and everything. Best friends are like that. The worst thing about it—her friend's older brother. He made her crazy. Like she-was-gonna-marry-him-someday crazy. Of course he had no idea of this plan. Breathing the same air made butterflies stir deep inside where she lived. But never would she admit this, not even to her best friend, who knew all her secrets.

His bedroom was more like a corridor, a passageway leading to the only tiny bathroom in the home. It was an odd floor plan, as if the bathroom was an afterthought. Walking past his bed and dresser, invading his privacy to brush her teeth at bedtime seemed wrong. What if a middle-of-the-night bathroom break was needed?

The house was hot, a stuffy night in late summer. It would be stifling like this until fall, until the end of September. Maybe until the middle of football season. The air hung heavily, curling the hair that escaped around her loosely tied ponytail. Sleep would never come in this unbearable heat.

Tiptoeing silently with bare feet, small and invisible, she walked through his bedroom, his space, welcoming the darkness. She *was* invisible to him. A faint orange glow from the stereo in the corner was the only light. The floor, smooth from years of wear, vibrated slightly. "*. . . warm smell of colitas, rising up through the air . . .*" What was a colitas? He played that song over and over again.

She closed the bathroom door a bit too loudly, relieved to be unnoticed, like making it to home base during a child's game of hide-n-seek. Safe, until the next game. The door, heavy and off balance, automatically swung shut. Her face was flushed, but the tile felt cool to her toes. *Maybe I should sleep in the bathroom with a cheek on the porcelain floor?* It would be a welcome respite from the heat. Instead, she splashed icy water on her face, shocking and calming simultaneously. It was late, probably after midnight. The light above the sink buzzed like a mosquito zapper.

The toilet flush echoed, bouncing off the walls, embarrassing her. He was so near, on the other side of the wall, hearing her bathroom sounds. Even with the Eagles singing, she knew he heard.

As she cracked open the door leading back through his bedroom, he was visible on the bed against a thin white sheet. "Sorry," she mumbled, closing the bathroom door nervously, careful not to slam it this time. What was she sorry for? Before thinking or breathing or willing her feet across the floor, he stopped her with a touch, patting the side of the bed.

"What?" she whispered back nervously, suddenly aware of his bare chest and her growing fit of giggles. His hand felt hot.

"Shhhhhh," he whispered. She felt his breath on her ear. "Just wanted to say goodnight," he said with that mischievous glint in his eyes visible even in the dark bedroom.

He had never really spoken to her before, not really. "I can't be in here." The beat of the music matched her thumping heart. Could he hear her heart?

"Just for a second." He held her hand to his chest. Strong, muscular, he was one of the best defensive players on the high-school football team. A sound escaped from inside her, a cross between a giggle and a whimper. She felt silly. This was silly. But she had dreamed of this, hadn't she? *"You can check out any time you like, but you can never leave . . ."* The music swelled.

It happened quickly, leaving her unable to prepare, to take a mental picture, to savor it. This kiss, against which all future kisses would be compared, was delicious and warm and tasted of peppermint. And forbidden.

Sleep would never come in this unbearable heat.

*   *   *

The moment replayed in her mind over and over the remainder of the weekend, but the few seconds were blurred and impossible to summon, impossible to recreate. The closer the feeling returned, the further it slipped away. Monday morning at school things would be different. *I would be different; I am different*, she thought, fretting over what to wear, how to act, how to breathe. Never before had she longed for Monday morning. Upon its arrival she was convinced it never happened.

She saw him right off, leaning casually against the wall in the gym with his group of friends, the popular boys, laughing and joking. Wearing torn jeans and a bright blue t-shirt, relaxed and carefree without another thought directed my way, she thought. *Why must he wear that t-shirt, the one that brightens his eyes?* The butterflies multiplied, twisting and knotting inside. He ignored her. She ignored him, yet knew his every move. She felt his energy across the dusty gym floor.

The school bell pealed overhead, jolting everyone into the new week. And then he looked her way. In the chaos, the morning congestion, with books slamming and kids walking toward class, he was smiling. At her. Smiling and pausing to gaze a second longer than was necessary. She smiled back.

It was enough, for now.

THE EGG GATHERING INCIDENT

By Larry Hunter
(North Carolina, USA)
Regional, 1ˢᵗ Place

When I was six years old, I lived with my parents and an older sister and brother on a farm that we worked for the owner, raising tobacco for sale and the usual garden vegetables for us to eat. This made us sharecroppers and therefore quite poor, but I was so happy to be alive and to have the entire farm with its animals and buildings to explore, I thought we were the richest people in the world. It was a paradise until that fateful day when the incident occurred.

"Boy, get to your chores, it's already past seven and we need the eggs for breakfast," my mother yelled as I ran through the kitchen on my way to the outhouse down the hill behind the house.

"Gotta go first, then I'll get the eggs," I yelled as I slammed the screen door behind me. I glanced back and saw her face as she grinned at me and then laughed. I was, after all, the baby; and with that came the special relationship that a youngest boy has with his mom and the privileges attached. I knew she had yesterday's eggs to cook and I could take my time with gathering today's bounty after I took care of business. There was a spring chill in the morning air that told me the outhouse would be quite cold, so I vowed to be quick to finish and get on with my day. Glossy pages from the *Sears Catalogue* made rough but easy work of the cleanup, and I was soon on my way toward the corn crib to get the chickens some corn for breakfast.

My first stop was the big open-sided box that was our corn crib. I got several ears of hard yellow corn and, twisting and rubbing them together, eventually managed to get the kernels to separate and fill the small bucket I used to feed the chickens each morning. By the time I had the ears cleaned, I was surrounded by a flock of hens and one big red rooster whose top-notch flopped as he herded his hens toward me to be fed. I had a history with the rooster, so we stared at each other, both remembering the day he had attacked me and I'd thrown him against the barn wall in terror. Mutual fear had allowed us get along since that occasion.

I spread the corn around my feet and walked a circular path, leaving a spiral path of corn kernels in my wake. As the hens and that old rooster started to eat, I put down my bucket and began to ease toward the hen house where my chores for that morning would be completed.

"Son, how long are you gonna be?" I heard my mama yell.

I called back, "Almost done," and hurried to grab my basket and start gathering the eggs. I entered the dim room, which was lined with boxes attached to the walls at intervals giving each chicken some privacy as she laid her eggs each evening. I could barely reach into each box by standing on tiptoes and stretching my arm over the edge to feel for the eggs and gather all but one, which I was to leave in the nest. My dad had explained to me that the single egg was called a nest egg and it was there to encourage the hens to lay other eggs to join it.

I'd gathered about a dozen or so, and my basket was getting rather heavy, so I set it down and proceeded to the next box. When I stretched my arm over the edge, I felt something unusual and, being the curious boy I was, I raised it up to see what was there. To my horror I held in my hand a black-snake's head. As I tried to open my fingers I thought I saw its mouth open and that long skinny tongue reach out toward me. I dropped the snake. As I turned to run I stepped in the basket of eggs, making quite a mess, but that didn't slow me down as I ran screaming out of the chicken coop toward the house.

"Mama, I picked up a snake. Kill it! Kill it!" I screamed when I opened the kitchen door and ran inside.

My mother just looked at me and with her calm voice said, "Johnny, exactly how did you come to pick up a snake? You know better."

I could see her trying not to laugh at me as I breathlessly explained what had terrified me so much in the chicken house. "It was in the nest with the eggs, and I picked it up. Didn't bite me, but it tried and so I dropped it and ran up here."

"I'll tell your daddy when he gets back from the barn. You go get the rest of the eggs for me. I'm sure the snake is long gone by now. You know they're as afraid of us as we are of them. It'll be okay, Johnny."

"Are you sure he'll be gone, Mama? I'm really afraid."

"Go on, son, he'll be gone."

I went back outside and walked slowly toward the chicken house, dreading entering that room. I was really afraid of snakes, and my mother's assurance wasn't enough to dim my fear. When I went inside the coop the first thing I saw was the snake's head hanging over the side of the nest where I'd dropped it. I turned and sprinted out of the door and didn't stop running until I was sitting at the kitchen table, out of breath, telling Mama that I was never going back into that chicken house again. She was able to hide her amusement mostly, but I could tell she didn't believe the snake was still there and I was just panicked. We sat together, eating biscuits with jelly, and waited for my dad to come home.

When Daddy arrived from the barn and heard about my adventure, he didn't even try to keep from laughing. He was still chuckling at my expense when we walked together toward the chicken house. He fetched a hoe to dispatch the snake on the off chance it was still there. When he entered the chicken coop, I saw him hesitate, then slowly walk toward the back wall where the nests were. I was so scared I couldn't go in. I waited outside for him to return, keeping watch on the ground for evidence of the snake trying to slither away.

After a few minutes I heard my Dad exclaim, "I'll be darned!" He came out the back of the chicken coop. The first thing through the door was that blacksnake hanging over the hoe handle, shaking as the hoe moved, followed by Daddy with a curious look on his face. He dropped the snake, reached down, and pointed out the big knot just behind the snake's head, all the while laughing so loud that my mother soon heard him and came running.

Daddy knelt down by me and said, "Son, you know how I told you about nest eggs and what they're for? Well, yesterday I found an old white glass doorknob and put it in this nest for the nest egg so we could get all the eggs and not leave any. This old snake swallowed that door knob thinking it was an egg, and when he tried to squeeze himself to break it, he choked and suffocated. In all my born days I've never seen anything to beat it."

He and Mom both laughed, knowing they had a real tale to tell at church next Sunday, and I knew all my friends would have fun picking on me about my snake incident.

I just stood up, turned to my parents, and vowed that I'd never put my hands anywhere I couldn't see again.

And to this day I just can't touch a snake.

Learn more about 1ˢᵗ-place winner and Fresh Ink Group member Larry Hunter at http://www.FreshInkGroup.com/authors/larry-hunter.

DEAD FATHER, DEAD SON

By Holly Riordan
(New York, USA)
Crimefighter, 2nd Place

The first time I heard the blast of a gun, I was in single digits. Due to the vile weather, I was perched in the kitchen, playing solitaire with a deck of cards my buddy Bryce got me for the holidays. The patter of raindrops acted as my personal music until sirens swarmed the air.

I rushed to the window and watched a pair of police cars swerve into the cemented driveway across the road—Bryce's driveway. Our houses were parallel, which made for optimum viewing; and it felt like I was in the cinema, watching a film of my neighbors' doppelgangers. When Bryce's father ran outside and into the chaos, they addressed him by a name I'd never heard. Although he seemed distant, his expression showed as much confusion as I felt. He reached into his pocket and extracted his identification. That's when the trigger was pulled. As I watched his body go limp, a slicing scream from Bryce rang out, numbing my ears and piercing the hearts of any observers.

Fifteen years later, after I became an officer myself, the memory resurfaced each time I took out my revolver. I always found it difficult to be reminded of Bryce's father and the family that would never recover from their loss. Both Bryce and his mother were engulfed with such a troubling amount of rage, grief, and disappointment that they could barely function. The incident pressured them to isolate themselves, distrusting the society that betrayed them.

I was off duty, departing from an appointment at a barber shop, when a gun nudged the back of my skull. No creature ever stirred around the barren back street I took to get home; even the plant life was scarce. Therefore, I was unequipped with my own weapon as the criminal dug the barrel deeper into my flesh. The metal chilled the curvature of my head, which was shielded only by a thin layer of hair, as he growled into my ear.

"I heard you joined the traitors. That true?"

The voice caused me to inhale sharply. Fighting to remain calm, I delivered my words in the most soothing tone I could manage. "Hand me the gun, Bryce."

"I'm done trusting you."

"I joined the force to protect as many people as I could," I said, aware that he was in search of an explanation. "What happened to your father was an accident. No one wanted that."

"You were my friend once. You know what they did. But now you're one of them?" He nudged the gun again as he cocked it. "I won't *let* you be one of them."

I twisted my torso to knock the weapon from his hand before scuffling to retrieve it from the pavement. My hand gripped the frame while Bryce tugged at my wrist, grappling in a savage dance of force, pulling the trigger twice as we struggled. One bullet ricocheted off the ground while the other was unseen. Clasping the device in my hand, I switched the safety on as I said, "Listen, I won't tell anyone about this. You won't go to jail, so long as you—"

His blood-soaked shirt froze my tongue. The other bullet had pierced his heart; he died instantly. The twin of Bryce's scream from fifteen years ago escaped my mouth as I ran over to my childhood best friend. Veins protruded from his bony fingers, patches of white frosted his skin, and his crimson blotches mixed with my tears. Bryce was gone—killed by a police officer.

Like father, like son.

ANOMALIES

By Lyndsey Werner
(California, USA)
Science Fiction, 3rd Place

"Morgan! We have to close it!" Raymond shouted.

Morgan slowed, as she realized that her husband wasn't going to see reason. She looked at him, then turned; there was only one way she could stop him from destroying their life's work. Morgan stood before the breach.

"Morgan!" Raymond caught sight of her, and slowed. "Morgan, what are you doing?"

She looked back at him, and smiled.

"Morgan! No!" Raymond yelled, but it was too late.

Morgan jumped into the breach and vanished.

*   *   *

Raymond woke abruptly as an alarm went off—another breach. He stood up and grabbed his keys, walking quickly down the hall in the agency he had helped create, the Temporal Containment Agency. It had been three years since Morgan opened the first breach, and since then breaches had randomly been opening into various eras of Earth's past, only to collapse a few hours later. As the foremost expert on the breaches, Raymond had worked with the government to build the TCA in order to protect the past and present.

Raymond walked into the control room. Zack, a promising young scientist, glanced up at him. "We've got something coming in," Zack said. "I have *never* seen anything like this! It's as if—"

"Enough science," Sgt. Lena Lopez snapped, loading a magazine into her gun and holstering it. "*Where* is it?" Zack looked up, his eyes wide.

"Out there." He pointed out the window overlooking the lobby. "A breach is opening right on our doorstep." The group looked up collectively and started for the stairs, Lena radioing for security as she went. The telltale shimmer preceding a breach rippled across the air, but it did not stabilize into a portal the way it should have. Instead it collapsed, leaving a teenage girl behind. She blinked and looked around, her long hair tied up in a high rope braid that wiped around her head as she took in her new surroundings.

Guns were pulled around her.

Lena took point, gun raised. "Identify yourself!"

"Sgt. Lopez—" Raymond put a hand on Lena's gun. "She probably has no idea where she is, or what just happened."

"What's the date?" the teenager asked.

Lena glanced at Raymond. "Yes, she clearly has *no* idea what's going on," she observed sarcastically.

Raymond stared at the girl. "November 26," he answered. "Who are you?"

"Why are you here?" Lena demanded, adjusting her stance so she was ever so slightly in front of Raymond.

The girl considered them, looking at the guns around her. Then she raised her hands. "My name is Anom Lee, and I'm here to stop Morgan Wendell from making a massive mistake."

*   *   *

Dr. Wendell watched the girl, Anom, in the interview room. He'd known Morgan was alive out there. She'd popped up on the TCA's radar any number of times. Morgan had become unhinged, even going so far as to commit crimes when she returned to the present. Morgan seemed to be gaining money and followers; most of his colleagues at the TCA viewed her as a threat. What did this girl know about Morgan? Could Anom Lee really be from the future? Raymond always suspected it was possible, and from the morbid hints Morgan dropped the last time he'd seen her, Raymond suspected his wife had been there already. But Anom Lee was the first real evidence of the possibility.

"You think she's really from the future?" Raymond looked up at Director Ryan.

"That kind of controlled entry through a breach seems to support the theory," Raymond answered. "The technology involved in manipulation breaches is decades, maybe centuries, beyond anything we have."

"The things she could tell us," Ryan began.

"Director," Raymond said sharply, "preventing temporal contamination is part of our charter. That doesn't just apply to protecting the past from the present." Ryan probably disagreed, but Zack chose that moment to sprint up to them, preventing Ryan from arguing.

"You—not—" Zack panted. "You're not going to believe this." Zack straightened, and held out a file. "We got a match on her DNA."

"So she's not from the future," Ryan said.

"Oh, she's from the future. Probably. I think." Zack stumbled over his explanation. "We actually got two partial matches; it's . . ." Zack trailed off as Raymond opened the folder. His eyes widened and his mouth fell open in shock. He just about stopped breathing. "It's you, Doc," Zack finished lamely. "You and Dr. Morgan, Anom's DNA proves it." Zack glanced at the girl in the interview room. "She's your daughter."

*   *   *

Dr. Wendell and Sgt. Lopez took the seats across from Anom. "You're related to Morgan Wendell," Lena began flatly. She had no love for Morgan.

"Unfortunately," Anom replied, watching them as closely as they watched her. Raymond cleared his throat.

"How did you appear the way you did? You seemed to control the breach." Raymond had fought to be a part of this interrogation, but now he didn't know what to do. He couldn't ask what he really wanted to ask; he didn't even know what he really wanted to ask.

After a moment Anom sighed. "It's not what you think." She leaned against the table. "I have a condition." Anom glanced at Lena. "You know what happened to Morgan." Lena nodded, and Raymond's jaw tightened. "What you may not know is that Morgan was pregnant at the time." Raymond's throat constricted. "Morgan went through quite a number of breaches. All that travel—" Anom paused, searching for the right word. "—affected the embryo."

"You mean, you," Lena clarified.

Anom nodded. "I'm not tethered in time," she explained. "Breaches form around me, or maybe I create them. I don't know." Anom glanced away, leaning back. "All I know is that I can only stay in any given time period for a limited time." Anom crossed her arms. "The longest I've been able to stay in one place on my own was about two months, and I have little to no control of when or where I end up."

"Wait," Raymond spoke. "What do you mean by, 'on my own'? What about your mother?"

Anom looked at him sharply.

*   *   *

Anom had first breached within moments of her birth. Not that she remembered. There was a component of survival instinct connected to her ability to breach that had, somehow, kicked in the minute she was born, breaching her to the one time she could be tethered to, far in the future, where, when, people understood breaches and time travel. The scientists of that era worked out how to hold Anom in their time before she'd breached again. That was where she'd been raised. For twelve years, Anom had been happy, adopted by one of the scientists who'd stabilized her. She had a sister, a brother, and some good friends. Anom's family had always been quite open about who Anom was; it was even in her name, Anom Al Lee, "anomaly".

The timeline, as every schoolchild knew, was more or less set in place. Even killing major scientists in the past would do very little to the present; it was only a short period before someone else achieved their accomplishments. Once the first breach was created, an equation materialized, one that laid out the course of time, taking everything into account. The equation that created the timeline was flexible enough for variations, changes in dates, and deaths, but for all intents and purposes, the timeline was stable.

There were only two anomalies capable of altering the timeline in any meaningful way. They'd be suspended in a breach as the equation was unfolding, as the timeline was settling. Anom and her mother, Morgan, had leapt into the first breach moments after its creation. Because of that, the equation failed to account for them. The scientists who'd helped Anom could loosely track Morgan, and always kept a worried eye on her movements.

Anom had been unconcerned with all of it. She'd been sure that the timeline could withstand anything her biological mother did—until that day, the day things, people, started disappearing as if they'd never existed. No one else even remembered them.

Anom ran up to her mother's office. "Mom!" she cried, bursting in.

Her Uncle Sev, another of the scientists who had saved her, grabbed her shoulders. "Anom, listen to me. We've been tracking your mother."

"Mom?" Anom gasped, panicking. "Did something happen?!"

"Not that mother," Uncle Sev said.

Anom looked at the screens around her. "Morgan?" Anom asked, rubbing her tear-stained face.

"She's two years after the first breach," Sev told the girl, leading her down to the first floor and outside. "Late November, early December."

"I don't understand—where's Mom?" Anom whimpered.

"I just told—" Sev began.

"Not Morgan! Dr. Lita Lee! Your friend!" Sev looked pained, and Anom realized the truth. "She doesn't exist anymore, does she?"

"I'm sorry, I've never heard of her," Sev said in a low voice.

"My brother?" Anom asked. "My sister?"

"You were raised alone," Sev murmured. Anom looked around, trying not to cry. "Listen, Anom, you're going to have to be very strong now." Uncle Sev took her by the *shoulders and looked into her eyes. "You are strong, and I know—" His voice caught. "I know you'll be okay. Promise me. Promise me that you'll be all right."*

Anom started to cry. "Uncle Sev?" She couldn't see his expression, her vision blurred by tears.

Uncle Sev hugged her. "I love you, kid," he told her, his voice thick and shaking as Anom sobbed into his shoulder.

Suddenly Anom fell forward. She looked around. "Uncle Sev?"

The city was vanishing as if it had never been built.

"No."

Ruins dominated the landscape, remains of a long-over war.

"No!"

Anom screamed desperately. She heard something and looked up, hoping to see her mom, Uncle Sev, anybody she knew. Instead, she saw a predator, massive and deformed, ready to pounce.

Anom screamed as the creature leapt, claws outstretched, reaching toward her, catching nothing as Anom breached away to the distant past.

*   *   *

"Morgan doesn't share my condition," Anom answered Dr. Wendell's question, scornfully spitting out Morgan's name. "I never really knew her. It's difficult to stay in one time. Luckily, when I was younger I tended to breach to safer places. I don't really know why." Anom sighed. "Sometimes, with other people's help, I can work out techniques to stay longer. Using things like discipline, meditation, even medication, can buy me a few extra days."

Dr. Wendell appeared unsatisfied with her answer. He opened his mouth to ask more, but Lena cut him off.

"I'm more interested in this mistake Morgan's about to make."

The contempt deepened on Anom's face at her mother's name. "I don't know the details—just the approximate time period and that she's going to do something," Anom said. "Something very bad."

"What exactly?" Lena pressed her. Anom looked at them both.

"Morgan is going to destroy the future."

*   *   *

"That's insane," Ryan snapped. "How can one woman, even one as intelligent and resourceful as Morgan Wendell, destroy the future?"

"It falls in line with what Morgan was talking about last time I saw her,"

Raymond pointed out. "She said she needed to 'remove' that fifteen-year-old because his grandson was interfering with her work." Raymond shrugged. "Since the kid didn't even have a girlfriend, it does hint that she was interested in altering the future."

"I wouldn't put it past her," Lena said. "That woman would do anything to get what she wants." Her eyes flicked to Raymond, then away.

"Morgan probably isn't even in this time zone!" Ryan began, but was interrupted by Zack knocking on the door.

"Um, sir, we just got a report." Zack glanced at Lena. "Morgan's been spotted."

Lena stood up. "Get me the location, now, and you two—" She looked directly at Raymond and Zack. "—Stay here."

*　　*　　*

Anom was waiting for Lena and her team outside. "You can take me with you, or I can find her myself," she said before Lena could speak.

"Fine, you're with me," Lena consented after a moment. "On the way you can tell me how you got out of my holding cell." Anom sat in front while Lena drove.

Lena glanced at the girl. "So, when are you going to stop lying?" Lena asked.

"I'm not lying," Anom said. "I'm not telling you everything, but I'm not lying."

"So you expect me to believe that a girl with no power over where or when she breaches managed to go to our lobby the very day we get our first lead on Morgan in months?" Lena snorted. "Yeah, right."

"I've been trying to reach this day since I was twelve years old. I've tried dozens of different methods of steering myself. I finally found someone who could help me, but it would only work once." Anom stared into the distance. "After this, I'll be stuck wandering again."

*　　*　　*

Anom looked at Zack. This time she'd only missed her target by about twenty years, but Zack thought he could help her. A scar ran down his face. He glanced at her. "I'm aiming for November 20th of that year," Zack said, his voice hoarse from years of hard life. "But there's no way for us to be sure."

"Whether it works or not, thank you." Anom clasped his shoulder.

A smile flickered over Zack's battle-weary face. "You really do remind me of your father sometimes," he told her. "I hope you can change the past."

"I can," Anom assured him, "and I will." She turned to the bulky patchwork machine that should send her back in time to stop Morgan. "Even if this doesn't succeed, I won't stop until I restore the timeline."

"This will only work once; after you've gone, the components will have burned out."

"I understand," Anom said. "The algorithms would be meaningless anyway. I'll have changed everything." Zack walked to the control panel.

"Anom." Anom looked at Zack. "You've told me about the equation, and I know the timeline is your first priority, but I have a request." Zack looked up from the controls. "Please, save your father."

"Zack, you know what I plan to do," Anom replied. "Morgan won't be able to target you, and my father won't die saving you." Anom smiled. "It's why you decided to help me in the first place."

*   *   *

"So?" Lena brought Anom back to the present. "How is Morgan going to destroy the future?"

"Not sure," Anom answered. Lena gave her a suspicious look. "I've been jumping between the past and future for a long time." Anom hastened to explain. "In the future, they can track temporal anomalies. I'm not a very big impact on the timeline because I actively minimize situations where I might mess up the timeline."

"But Morgan doesn't," Lena finished, thoughtful but still wary. Anom nodded.

"While I was in the future, one of the scientists told me that they were tracking a massive temporal event. It was Morgan; something she did caused a cascade." Anom looked out the window quickly, unwilling to let Lena see that her eyes were glistening with tears. "After a few hours, everyone and everything in the time had vanished." Anom took a shuddering breath, getting her emotions back under control. "I knew I had to undo what Morgan had done. I had to restore the timeline and bring back everyone Morgan's actions had erased from existence."

Lena focused on the road. "Heavy burden to bear," she finally said.

Anom felt better. Lena shared her dislike of Morgan; Anom had been worried that she'd have to contend with Raymond and his friends to stop Morgan. Lena's support was reassuring.

"How old are you?" Lena asked abruptly.

"What?"

"You said you've been trying to get here since you were twelve. So how old are you now?" Lena asked again.

"I have no idea."

"You look about seventeen."

"I feel a lot older." There was silence for a minute. "Why do you keep looking at me like that?"

"No, I'm not," Lena tried to protest. "It's just . . ." Lena focused her eyes on the road. "You shouldn't be this old . . . you know?"

Anom gave a little smile. "Time travel," she acknowledged. "It certainly complicates things."

"You know . . ." Lena's eyes were glued to the road now. "The guy in the interrogation room with me, he's your father."

"I know," Anom replied.

"You know?" Lena looked at her, startled, then swiveled her head back to the road. "Why didn't you say anything?"

"Why didn't he?" Anom countered.

Lena lapsed into silence.

Anom glanced at her and sighed. "Honestly, it's better for me not to get too close." Anom stared out the window. "It's already hard for him, suddenly learning he had an adult daughter. If we got close—" Anom paused, fidgeting with her vest. "It would only make it harder when I have to go."

Lena stole another glance at Anom. "You've been through this a lot."

Anom ran her fingers through her hair. "More times than I care to count," she said, effectively ending the conversation.

Lena pulled up to the area Morgan had been sighted. Lena went to the trunk and opened it, surveying her small arsenal. Lena looked up as the passenger-side door opened. "What do you think you're doing?" Lena demanded as Anom closed the door.

Anom glanced around and raised her eyebrow. "Is this a trick question?"

"You're untrained, unarmed, and a minor," Lena snapped, slinging a large gun across her back. "Get back in the car."

"I'm trained in six different martial arts, two of which don't exist yet. We don't know I'm a minor, and—" Anom reached into her pocket and pulled out a small gadget that she briskly unfolded into a gun resembling a rifle. "I'm definitely not unarmed."

"Where'd you get that?" Lena asked, looking somewhat envious.

"Russia, the 22nd century, I think." Anom answered, loading the gun.

Anom looked around as Lena coordinated with the rest of her team.

Something caught Anom's eye, and she smiled. "I know where she's going, if you want to try there," Anom said casually.

"What?" Lena looked up, and she loaded her handgun. "Where?" Anom led Lena to a locked garage, staying low. "What makes you think she's in here?" Lena hissed.

"You see that lock?" Anom nodded at it. "It's got a DNA scanner, not supposed to be produced for another sixty years."

"Can I shoot it off?" Lena asked.

"Not with a nine-mil," Anom answered, promptly blowing the lock—and a small portion of the garage door—away with only a minor crackle of gunfire.

Lena eyed Anom's gun enviously. "You think you can get me one of those?" Anom grinned, and jerked her head. Lena made entry, and Anom followed. They stared around and then Lena summed up her feelings on what they saw in two short words. "Holy shit."

All around them were boards with photographs, surveillance photos, profiles, and even some stuff from the near future. Some of them were heavy hitters, politicians, scientists, etc., some of them they'd never heard of. Dominating the far wall were the words "IT'S THEIR FAULT!" A list of names followed, falling into two categories: "Kill" and "Contain."

"Your name's under kill," Anom observed tightly.

"And Raymond's is under contain," Lena replied. "We are definitely in the right place." Lena heard something and turned in time to avoid a blast from a bizarre handgun. It caught Anom in the shoulder and knocked her off her feet. "Six martial arts, my ass," Lena muttered, ducking behind one of the many boards.

"Lena Lopez." Morgan laughed. "I was so hoping you'd be first." Lena cursed inwardly, and tried to radio for back-up. "If you're waiting for your team, I'm afraid that they're a bit preoccupied at the moment." Lena considered switching to the large gun on her back, but it would be pointless. "Come out, Little Lena," Morgan taunted her. "Or I shoot the girl." Lena took a deep breath. The board wasn't providing any real protection anyway. Lena stepped out and faced Morgan, her gun raised.

"I don't think you should," Lena said coldly. "She's your daughter."

Morgan's eyes narrowed. "I don't know how you found out about that, but my child is gone." Morgan smiled. "And now, so are you."

"Morgan stop!" Raymond stood in the doorway, Zack right behind him. Morgan's gun dipped in hesitation, and that was all that was needed. In an instant, Anom was on her mother, taking her down using a technique no one had ever seen. Morgan was on the floor, Anom standing over her, holding her gun.

"Nice job, Anom!" Lena congratulated her. Anom released the safety on the gun. Lena and Raymond exchanged a glance. "Um, Anom, what are you doing?" Lena asked as Raymond took a few steps into the room, closely followed by Zack.

"Something I've known I'd have to do since I was twelve years old," Anom answered, "when Morgan shattered the timeline."

A volley of protests were raised, but Morgan's rose above them all. "It wasn't me! It was them!" She gestured around the room, encompassing Zack, Lena, Raymond, and all of the people depicted on the boards. "When I found my way back to the future to finish my work, everything had been destroyed!" Morgan glared around at them. "I searched that wasteland to discover who was responsible." She snarled, "Then I came back so I could put a stop to all of you!"

"Wait, a desolate wasteland? You've seen it? Then—" Anom faltered. "Dr. Wendell, how many years has it been since the first breach?"

"What? Um, three. It's been three years." Raymond answered. "Wh—"

"Dammit, Zack!" Anom yelled in aggravation.

Zack started. "Me? What did I do?"

Anom began pacing restlessly. "Not *you*, you," Anom explained. "In twenty years, you designed something to allow me to breach to this time period, but he, you, messed up, sent me a year too late." Anom fired the gun, a warning shot as Morgan reached for Anom's fallen rifle. "Next one goes in your leg," she informed Morgan, then continued as if nothing had happened. "It wasn't his fault, really; we were lucky it worked so well. I'm just frustrated because I really thought that I made it this time."

"But now I know, so in twenty years I can take it into account, right?" Zack pointed out.

"It's a good idea, but I'm immune to changes in the timeline. I'll still end up here, a year too late to stop Morgan." Anom sighed.

"I told you it wasn't me!" Morgan began. "It was them!" She flinched as her daughter pointed a gun at her.

"You really don't understand, do you?" Anom snapped. "There are only two people in all eternity who are capable of changing the timeline like this, and I know that I wasn't responsible, so it *had* to be you." Anom grabbed Morgan by the collar and lifted her up. "And you're going to help me fix it."

"Anom, I need to take her in," Lena said softly.

"I need access to her," Anom replied, not taking her eyes off Morgan's face.

"You'll have it," Lena assured her. "But for now, we need to lock her up." Anom released Morgan and stepped away. Lena grabbed the woman and wrenched her hands behind her back, handcuffing Morgan before she could react.

"Would you have done it?" Raymond approached his daughter as she turned her back on her mother. "Would you have killed her?"

Anom looked away, gathering her thoughts, then looked back at him. "Wouldn't you?" she asked. "If everyone you knew, everyone you loved, was erased from existence, and all that remained was an empty planet, scarred by war. If one woman was responsible for all of that, and more, wouldn't you do whatever was necessary to stop her?"

FARSOOTH

By Anna Cates & Geoff Porter
(Ohio/Ohio, USA)
Fantasy, 1ˢᵗ Place

I'm not sure when he started following me, but I made sure I got a good look at him. He stood about three feet tall. He wore brown trousers, a red shirt, and black leather boots, with a blue pointed hat on his head. Prickly black fur dotted his forearms, and his skin seemed a scaly green more reptilian than human. I picked up my pace, but he stayed about thirty feet behind me, making no moves to hide. I stopped walking and turned to face him, my hand on the hilt of my dirk. His pointy canines protruded from his lips.

He walked right up to me and stopped. "What's your name, boy?"

"I don't talk to strangers."

The little green man said, "But, I'm not a stranger. I'm a troll."

I pulled my dirk just a bit out of its scabbard, so he would know I carried silver. "I'm just trying to get home."

"You live in Farsooth?"

I nodded my head and took a few steps away from the creature.

The troll licked his lips. "There's a wizard near Farsooth who owes me a great debt. We can travel there together."

I ran. I pushed my legs as hard as they would go, pumping away at the ground until my calves burned. The lights from Farsooth dotted the view in front of me like fireflies winking in and out among tree leaves. I paused for only a moment to catch my breath, then walked at a brisk pace in the direction of home.

The troll stepped from around a tree directly in my path. I drew my dirk. The troll did a little three-step dance, and white lightning bolted from his right hand at my blade. The charge made me jump and drop the thing. The troll spoke in a loud, firm voice. "You'll escort me to the wizard in Farsooth."

I fell to my knees and cried, "Why me?"

The troll walked up to me, and I scurried out of his reach, pushing myself along the ground. He reached down and picked up my dirk. He held it out to me hilt-first. "What's your name, kid?"

"Ben."

He tossed the dirk underhanded at me, and it landed at my feet. He said, "My name is Brackfor, and I have urgent business in Farsooth. You know of the ward around the place, yes?"

I let out a little whimper. "The curse, you mean?"

"Curse, ward, magic spell. You know of it?"

"Of course. I'm from there, as I told you before."

The troll's head bobbed up and down. "I need you."

I sheathed my dirk. "Do you have any idea what the wizard will do to me if I lead you there?"

"Do I need to show you how to fear me more than that wizard?"

Tears started streaking down my cheeks. "Why did I ever seek my fortune outside of Farsooth?"

"Take me to the wizard. Right now."

I pushed myself off the ground. "How do I know you don't plan on leading an army there to conquer us?"

"The wizard owes me a debt, boy—an ancient debt, and he concocted the whole curse to keep me from collecting, but now that I've found you, the debt will be paid."

"I could turn around and go the other direction."

"You like the touch of that lightning I showed you? I can hit harder with it. Would you like to see? You are from Farsooth, so you know where the wizard lives. I need you."

"I should never have left home. I wanted to see the world, but the world is a dark place where every place you go they expect coins for every little thing."

The troll smiled. He backed up to a tree and scratched his shoulders on the bark. "I have all night."

I started walking towards town. Brackfor followed me. He rattled on about silly things: Did Farsooth have orchards? A shaded swimming hole? Regular trash collection?

To the last I answered, "A wagon rolls through town every morning, but if you sleep in. . ."

"Ahhh, fair enough. Most towns have both a morning and an afternoon wagon."

We walked for a solid hour, Brackfor babbling cryptic troll jingles. We approached the first structure in town, an inn I was always welcomed at and where my cousin worked. She waved from the porch, and I started to run.

"Jessica! Do you have any food?"

Jessica laughed. "I made stew this morning. There's still half a pot left. Come in and help yourself."

I raced into the house and loaded up a wooden bowl with vegetable mutton stew off the stove. At the table, my stomach protested at first as I ate but soon settled down.

Jessica stepped into the inn. "Slow down, or you'll make yourself sick."

"I haven't eaten in a week! I ran low on coins, and you know the price of good food these days."

"You should never have left Farsooth," she said with a sigh.

I nodded and feasted, savoring a spoon of carrot and potato, rosemary floating in the murky broth.

Brackfor let himself into the house and grinned.

Jessica pointed at the beast. "Who's this?"

The creature with green scales bowed. "I'm but a humble traveler seeking the wizard."

Jessica scowled. "You greasy piece of filth, we should kill you!" She pulled a knife out of her belt and advanced on Brackfor.

"No," I cried, realizing Jessica didn't understand her danger.

Brackfor jumped up in the air, spinning completely around, and pointed his finger at the blade. Lightning arced to the steel, causing Jessica to twitch and drop the dagger with a cry of pain. He turned on me with his finger pointed. "I can hurt you both bad if you want to mess with me. I can hurt you so bad you'll be feeling it for years."

I wanted to run, but I stood my ground. "I'm not afraid of you," I managed to say.

"Take me to the wizard!"

"After supper and a night's rest. I'm famished and fatigued. You don't want me collapsing in the woods along the way or getting lost in the dark?"

"Very well," he replied, his pinhole eyes scrutinizing me suspiciously. "But tomorrow we set out at dawn."

I nodded, knowing I had but one night to devise a plan to escape from my servitude.

That night, downstairs by the fire, he slept, if sleep you could call it. Trolls have a way of slumbering with one eye open, and I knew I'd never slip past him undetected. Upstairs, I tossed and turned the whole night upon my straw mattress, torturing my thoughts for some way out, but nothing came to me. At last I drifted into rest, resigning myself to a new status of temporary lackey to a troll, grinding my teeth at the ignominy of it.

The next morning, just as Brackfor had bid, we set forth at dawn. I carried a sack of biscuits just starting to stale, a gift from Jessica. We paced through the woodland trails, screech owls and ravens noisy in the trees above us, branches heavily laden with moss. I mumbled to myself between gritted teeth as I trod along, hearing Brackfor's rasping breaths hot behind me. How I wished I could club his head off his shoulders and be back to my business right away.

At noon, at the fork in the trail beside the dead oak tree, I turned left, heading for the outskirts of the swamps.

"You better not try any funny stuff," Brackfor said.

"We'll leave the main trail soon," I told him, remembering the familiar landmark of rocks where one turned right down an incline that led to a clearing where lay the wizard's abode. Not that anybody ever ventured down there, but we townspeople knew where he lived. Moments later, we reached the rocks.

"This way," I told him, turning back for a glimpse of his dead, coal eyes. "Are you sure you want to go down there?"

"Lead the way."

We stumbled down the hill, slipping here and there on muddy patches covered with orange leaves, the clean scent of pine needles crisping the air about us.

The wizard's house was built of cobblestones, and a thin trail of smoke snaked from the chimney. *He's home*, I thought, my heart thudding as I estimated how quickly I could run back up the hill before the necromancy began. A troll battling a wizard was not a sight I cared to behold, and I didn't want to choke on any brimstone or get burned, either. I'd heard of people going blind or becoming mute from such exposure. I shuddered, yet kept myself moving forward till I stood in the clearing, facing the cold rocky structure the wizard called home.

"Balshazar, you bastard, come forth," Brackfor cried out. I winced, scurrying over to the edge of the clearing to take cover beside a tree. What terror awaited the woods?

A shutter opened, slamming wood against stone, and a bald head emerged, governed by deep wrinkles. A salt-and-pepper moustache flowed down either side of the wizard's mouth in braids, framing narrow lips and discolored teeth.

"Who dares disturb my peace?" the wizard spoke through a scratchy voice, compromised by centuries of spell-casting.

Brackfor stood boldly with legs spread and arms akimbo. "You've cursed the land. We've had nothing but crop failures for three years, and today is your reckoning."

I could feel my eyes bulging in their sockets, my clammy fingers pressed against the bark. Where Brackfor got his courage from, I could not say!

The wizard disappeared from the window, only to open his front door and present himself, wearing leather boots and pants, but naked from the waist up, his upper body strangely muscled as if a charm were keeping him vigorous beyond his years.

"Idiots!" the wizard said, his eyes rolling in his head as if with impatient anger. "There is no curse. I told the peasants to leave the fields fallow every seven years. Twenty years ago, I finally gave up instructing them." His lips curled into a deceptive grin.

Brackfor stood resolute. "The people have farmed these lands for centuries. Your claim of their stupidity is not convincing. Besides, you owe me a great debt anyway, and I've come to collect."

The wizard twisted his head to the side, his neck wrinkling above his barrel chest. "That again? When will you trolls give up and realize your centuries-old forfeiture is permanent?" He spoke in a mocking tone.

I wasn't expecting the blinding light to hiss from Brackfor's finger so quickly. It landed on the wizard's chest. He gasped, but then seemed to absorb the energy.

"Is that the best you can do?" The wizard raised his arms, forming an arch above him, and a ball of light appeared, smoking in his gnarled grasp. The wizard hurled the ball at Brackfor with an explosion of putrid light.

The scent of something foul burning, like rotten meat, filled the air. The wizard's magic was so dark, so diabolical, it sickened even a mediocre lad like me. I lurched forward, loosing my breakfast on a fallen log.

I stumbled backward, dizzy, gasping, insane dread tearing into me like demonic possession. Nearly blind, I stumbled back toward the hill.

The battle raged for a few moments until the wizard fell to his knees. The troll cackled a hideous high-pitched laugh. "I have you now."

I picked up a smooth rock no bigger than an egg and threw it with all my might at the gloating troll. It hit him right on the back of the skull.

The troll screamed, "Oww!"

I picked up a second rock as the troll turned to face me.

The lightning arced into my body with enough force that I jumped off the ground. I fell to the ground on my back. Pain racked my body as the troll stood above me, raining all kinds of hell on me.

The wizard pushed himself off the ground and began to dance to a silent little tune.

The troll screeched and stopped moving. I could see him struggling in his eyes, but as I watched, the creature turned to stone. The eyes darted around alive, but the rest of him was made of granite.

The wizard walked over to us and helped me to my feet.

I touched the troll. He was cold and stiff. "How long will he stay this way?"

"Until I die," the wizard said. He pointed with his hand, and the stone statue lifted off the ground. "Let me show you something."

We walked a ways. Stepping past a hedgerow, an army of troll statues greeted us. All of them stared with alive eyes at us.

"So many," I said.

"Every few years some fool will decide Farsooth isn't good enough and leave. Every time, they return with a troll. The troll is always stronger than the last, or my powers are slowly waning."

"If you die, they'll conquer Farsooth!"

"Yes, I need to start teaching my magic to a young man."

My eyes opened wide, and my mouth dropped open. "Don't look at me!"

"Farsooth has always been full of cowards."

I sighed. I sat down on the ground cross-legged. "Is it difficult?"

"The hardest thing you'll ever do, but bar wenches tend to like spell-casters," he said with a twinkle in his eye.

I hopped to my feet. "I'll do it!"

Learn more about 1ˢᵗ-place winner and Fresh Ink Group member Anna Cates at http://www.FreshInkGroup.com/authors/anna-cates.

RAINA

By Priscilla Ng
(California, USA)
Short Fiction, 3rd Place

"Where are we going?" I ask. I stop suddenly, trying to catch my breath. Sweat is running down the side of my face, and my braided hair has become all tangled and messy.

"You'll see when we get there," Shen says, smiling down at me. "Come on, Raina, you can't be tired already." I gape at him.

"We've been running for almost two miles now! Who wouldn't be tired?" I reply, but I'm smiling as I say this.

Shen holds out his hand, and I take it. "You won't regret coming here, just trust me." And I do. He's never let me down before, so why would he suddenly do so now? Together we continue to make our way through the quiet forest. Our shoes make close to no sound on the soft green moss covering the ground. Everything here feels healthy and alive. Even the branches and leaves look like they're holding their arms out. At last we reach the entrance to a small cave concealed by a curtain of ivy. Shen gently pushes it aside and I follow him in.

In here, there is a completely different feeling. The cave walls seem blue and feel smooth against my fingers as I run them across them. We silently walk down the mysteriously lit tunnel, passing miniature patches of strange-colored flowers here and there. I look above me and notice a few cracks in the ceiling of the cave, allowing a bit of sunshine to fall through. I shake Shen's hand off in order to peek through one of the holes. My eyes widen in amazement. I can see a beautiful baby doe sipping some water from a tiny pond. It's so close to me that I can almost touch it.

"Let's go, Raina, we're almost there," Shen whispers. I nod. For some reason, the atmosphere around here makes me keep my voice low, too. I feel like I don't want to accidentally wake up an innocent animal.

Finally we've reached the end of the tunnel. I peek over Shen's broad shoulders and gasp in amazement. Stone steps line all the way up the wall, acting as a ladder. They look ancient, with moss and ivy growing all around and over them. Shen carefully steps onto the stone ledge and begins to climb up. I follow closely behind him. As I near the top, Shen, already out, helps me pull myself up, and we sit on the ground, panting from the exertion of the climb.

"Raina, look around you." I look up from my hands and stop breathing as I take in my surroundings. It's the most beautiful place I've ever seen. I spot a magnificent waterfall falling from an enormous purple mountain with lots of animals around it, taking in its pure sparkling water. A large butterfly flutters down from a tree above me and rests on my shoulders. The colors on its wings reflect in the light and start to change from a bright glowing cyan to a crystal clear blue. I squeal in delight as the butterfly takes off and disappears into the sky. Without thinking, I throw myself onto the soft grass and relish the feel of it. Shen chuckles and I am suddenly reminded that I'm not alone in this enchanted wonderland.

"It's beautiful here . . . How did you find such a place?" I ask, not hiding how impressed I am with him.

"I really don't know," he responds. "One day I was exploring, and I just ended up here. Don't you wish you could stay here forever?"

I murmur in agreement and close my eyes, listening to the peaceful sounds of Mother Nature working her magic. I feel like I could almost hear the trees grow.

Shen's hand rests on my cheek. "Raina," he says. My eyes flutter open and I almost jump as I realize the closeness of his face.

"What is it?" I ask.

"What if we really did just stay here . . . and never went home?" Shen asks. His eyes are bright and I can tell he's not kidding when he suggests this.

"But we can't just leave our family like that . . . wouldn't they worry?" I respond. But Shen is already shaking his head.

"It's all right, we'll be safe here, nothing can harm us. Come on, Raina, please? Let's stay here together, forever."

"You're kind of missing my point." Something isn't right. The Shen I knew wouldn't say things like this.

"Raina, look around you! You can't deny that this is the most beautiful place you've ever seen, right?" he says. He almost sounds like he's . . . whining. Like a child. I study his earnest face; something looks different about him. I reach for his face to touch his cheek, but my finger moves right through him. I gasp in surprise.

"What?" he asks questioningly, tilting his head innocently to the side.

"Shen! Your face! My—" I stop when I realize that his body has been blown out of proportion. His mouth continues to move, as if he's trying to tell me something, but I can't hear him. "Shen?" I whisper. "What's going on?" But his body only continues to shrink away. Suddenly I feel someone shaking me and I finally open my eyes.

"You were dreaming, Raina. Are you all right?" It's Shen, the real him. I clamp his cheeks together to make sure of it, and he looks at me funny. "What's the matter?"

"Nothing, just a bad dream," I tell him, hiding a smile. He shrugs and pulls me up. It's still dark outside, but I can see the sun rising from the horizon. "Where are we going today?"

"You'll see," he says, grinning. I get a strange sense of déjà vu. But that was just a dream . . . right? Shen pulls me up and we quietly sneak out of my house, trying not to wake up my sisters. The two of us hop the fence outside and sprint toward the forest nearby. It looks dark and I can hear the howl of a wolf from the distance. We dash through the trees. Branches scratch our skin and tear our clothes, but we ignore it and keep on. Finally we reach a cave, and to my horror, it looks much too similar to the one in my dream. I step back from it.

"What's wrong?" Shen asks.

I shake my head. "I can't go in there."

He laughs, "What do you mean you can't? Come on, you won't regret it." I shake my head again, harder this time. His eyes grow cold. "Raina, you promised you'd come with me."

"No I didn't," I whisper. What is happening to me?

"Raina." Shen's voice sounds dark and he looks at me sternly. "Raina, do as I say."

At this point, I've stepped back so much my back hits a tree and I feel trapped. Shen's hands reach out to me, his fingers forming into menacing claws.

"NOOOOOO!" I close my eyes and scream as loudly as I can. Finally, I collapse onto the floor and begin to sob. It's hopeless; nothing is supposed to be the way it is. I feel like I'm in a dream again, so I clench my hands into fists and start hitting myself as hard as I can.

"Someone stop her!" says a woman. Her voice sounds unfamiliar. Suddenly, I feel huge hands grab my wrists, and I try to wriggle free, but it's no use. I open my eyes wide with fury.

"Let go!" I shout, kicking my legs at the man who is trying to keep me together. But another pair of hands grabs onto my legs, and I'm finally held down. My chest is rising quickly, and I'm breathing heavily. Who are these people? They have no right to do this to me.

"Subject 12 is reacting violently; bring in a sedative. We need to keep her heart rate down. Kevin." The woman motions to one of the men holding me. "Put her on the bed. Use the straps if you need to."

"What did you do with Shen?!" I call out. She looks at me when I mention Shen, and begins to jot down some notes. Then she leaves through a door, and I hear a bolt click behind her.

"Wait! Tell me what's going on!" I yell after her, but the two men strap me down to the hard bed. I am forced to stay put, but I continue to writhe and squirm in place, purposely giving them a hard time. While I'm doing this, I start to take in my surroundings. I'm in a white room. There is nothing in here but my bed and an empty table to the side of me. There's a bright light on the ceiling that hurts when I look straight at it. Where am I? And where was Shen?

The door opens again and a group of people rush in with strange objects. One of them is carrying a sharp-looking needle and walking straight toward me. Before I know it, the needle is forced into my skin and I black out.

"Subject 12 seems to be experiencing hallucinations," I hear someone say. Subject 12? Is that what they're calling me? My eyelids feel heavy, and I slowly try to open them. I'm still in the white room, but this time with more people all wearing masks and gloves. They seem to be studying me, and I can feel some of them probing me with strange utensils.

I try to speak, but my speech sounds slurred. They probably drugged me, I think. Now I'm completely at their hands. I felt so vulnerable and exposed.

"Subject 12, can you hear me?" The same woman from before is on my left, still jotting down notes. "I repeat, can you—"

"Yes . . ." I mutter. "My name—"

"Subject 12 is your name," the woman responds automatically.

"No I . . . My name is—" I clear my throat. "My name is Raina," I finally say.

The woman lifts an eyebrow. "Raina, you say? Hm . . ."

"Shen, he's my friend," I continue. "What did you do to him?" The woman gives me a long look. I take this moment to study her. She looks tired, with dark circles under her eyes. Her skin looks pale, and the white light from the room makes her look sick.

"Raina," she begins, "there is no Shen here. He's not real."

Not . . . real? I simply stare at her, trying to understand. "My family?" I ask. She just shakes her head. What's going on? Is she saying that Shen and my family don't even exist? That I imagined the whole thing? "What . . . Where am I?"

The woman looks unsure about whether or not she should respond. "Where am I?" I repeat sternly. "Tell me."

Finally, she seems to make up her mind and says, "You're being held in a place called Area Nineteen, also known as Sarem. Your memories . . . they're not real because we planted them in your mind. You're here because of an experiment."

"Stop lying! Shen is real and my name is Raina!" Why can't they just believe me? Tears flow quickly out of my eyes. I just want to go back to the real Shen, the one I knew, not the strange one from my dreams. I hear a loud beeping off to the side, and everyone around me starts to move in a panicked haze. They keep saying things like "Keep her heart rate down!" and "Her body temperature is rising too fast." But I don't care. Maybe this is just another dream. I feel a second needle dig into my skin, but I'm out before I know it.

I seem to be floating in a sea of black liquid. I can't breathe. The blackness is too thick, and it's suffocating me. I try to push it away, but it's pointless. Suddenly I hear someone whisper, "Raina . . ." It sounds like Shen . . . Shen. He's here, I knew it. I knew that he wasn't fake. I look around for him, but I don't see anything except a tiny light. It looks so far, but something is telling me to go toward it.

"Subject 12 . . ." I hear that woman's voice again. "Subject 12, come back to us . . ."

No. I will not go back to you. You're nothing but an illusion. I don't want to go back to that scary white place full of people I don't know. I face the tiny light again, and it feels a little closer to me this time. I begin to reach for it, and as I'm stretching my arm out, I can hear Shen's voice getting louder and louder.

"Raina," he's saying, "come on, I want to show you something."

I smile; he always wants to show me something. The light is close enough for me to grab it now, and I reach for it one last time. Everything seems to fade out, and I'm back on the soft grass. Back in the magical wonderland. Back in my world, with Shen next to me.

"I really don't know," I hear him saying. "One day I was exploring, and I just ended up here. Don't you wish you could stay here forever?"

"No," I hear myself say. Was this really happening again?

"Yeah, you're right. I guess we can't leave your sisters alone. Who's gonna take care of them?" Shen ruffles my hair and gazes off into the distance, looking longingly at the stunning waterfall.

"Actually, I change my mind." I start to sit up and wrap my arms tightly around him. "I want to stay here forever."

THE PURPLE SMOKE

By Mikayla Rivera
(Idaho, USA)
Fantasy, 3rd Place

"It's the easiest thing in the world, to die. It gives a freedom from pain that all men crave—why else do you think we all do it?" He set his china teacup down on a limp doily. A slow, rumbling cough emitted from his throat, and he tried to swallow it into his belly until he convulsed and a cloud of purple smoke escaped his mouth. It diffused in lethargic, moaning tendrils until the scent of burning sugar was the only hint it had ever existed.

Sarah sat back and watched the man's sprawling limbs as they curled about his ivory seat. The velvet cushion was worn to a dim fluff of red, but the lacquered ivory caught a sliver of light from the curtained window and cast it into her eyes. She sat back in her mahogany rocking chair and draped one leg over the other.

"Glad to know," she said dully, glancing about her. "So, uh, who are you?"

The man gazed at the window. After a moment, he brought a knobby cigarette to his dried lips and took a long, difficult drag on it. The end simmered like a purple coal.

"You don't know me?" the man asked.

For the first time since she entered the room, the man looked at her. His pupils reflected the burn of the stifled cigarette he smoked, as if he were holding the purple smoke captive inside him.

"No," Sarah said. She frowned to one side as he smirked. "Should I?"

He turned away and looked into the frail, lace curtains shielding the window. "I suppose not."

Sarah leaned forward, out of the insistent rocking of her chair. She found herself bound, suddenly, and looked down. Purple smoke had secured her thighs to the seat of the chair. She looked up.

"What's this?" she asked.

"You don't know what that is, either, Sarah?" the man drawled, ending with a smoky, lavender sigh.

"I don't even remember how I got here." She scowled as her chair rocked. "And could you stop smoking? Or crack open a window, at least? Not all of us want to die of lung cancer."

The man swung his face around and smirked at her. He crushed the cigarette in his trembling hand until violet powder slithered between the thin rivulets of his palm. His whole lanky body seized as his sudden, agonized laughter rattled the moldy corners of the room. The lace curtains curled back against the window, as if to protect themselves from his long trembling guffaw and spidery hands.

"Lung cancer," he repeated. He opened his hand and studied the leftover violet powder. He frowned at it, as if disappointed in its fragility, and coughed as purple smoke tried to escape him. "I'm gonna need another one of these. Will you pass me one?" He picked up his teacup and took a sip. "They're in the box you're holding."

Sarah scoffed. "I'm not holding a box. And I can't get you anything; I'm strapped to this stupid rocking chair, remember?" She closed her eyes and groaned. "Can you undo me or something? This thing won't stop rocking." Sarah opened her eyes and saw him run a finger over the chapped flakes of his lips.

The man shook his head with a gentle smile. "You've always had the box, Sarah."

She sneered. "Oh, so you think you know me? Then how about doing an old pal a favor and undoing me?"

"Undo you?" the man breathed. He faced her, this time with his whole body, and crowded the small table between them with his sharp elbows and overbearing purple smoke. "Undo you. Yes, I'd like to undo you. I've waited a long time for you to arrive."

"Why?" she frowned. "Who are you?"

The purple smoke in his pupils simmered over the parchment-colored roses between them. His elbows adjusted. "Open the box, Sarah."

"I can't." She rolled her eyes. "Your smoke is harassing me. Can you crack a window?"

"It won't bother you if you open the box."

She met his incessant gaze and scowled. "Look, pal, I don't have a box."

"How did you get here, Sarah?" The man leaned back, curling inward, his limbs anchoring to his chest like a dying spider. "When did you last see me?"

She blew a couple of strands of red hair from her face. "I thought we covered this? I never met you before." She coughed. "Seriously, open the window. That stuff's smothering me."

He made no reply. He sipped his tea and slowly sat back against the gleaming ivory of his chair.

She sighed and threw her head against the back of the rocking chair, hearing the clunk, but feeling nothing. "Fine. How did I get here. Let's see— give me a minute."

"I can't give you a minute," the man said. "My clock stopped working when I moved here." He gestured to a large grandfather clock with his white teacup.

"Figure of speech," Sarah grumbled. She watched the face of the grandfather clock. The hands were as still as buried bones beneath the dusty glass. "Well, I think I was at home."

"Who else was home?" he asked as he drew in the violet dust on his palm.

She shrugged. "I don't know. No one?"

He looked at her again. His fingers twitched like the legs of an insect. "Why?"

She met his purple stare. "I don't remember."

"Why was no one there?"

She lifted her shoulders to shrug before pausing. "I'm not married."

He nodded. "But . . . ?"

Sarah looked down at the purple smoke around her thighs. It was coiling about her, squeezing and releasing in rhythm. "Your smoke is getting bigger." Her nose wrinkled.

"Be quiet," he murmured through barely parted lips. "It's not evil." A rumble went through his throat again, but this time he didn't follow it with a cough.

She sighed hard out her nose and looked up. Her frown, dark and deep, marred her lips' supple texture. "Fine. *But* . . . I wasn't always alone. Unfortunately."

He nodded, and let the purple dust bleed through the fingers of one hand into the palm of the other. "Who else did you have?"

Her mouth yanked down on either side. "A son." She looked at the crumbling ceiling tiles. "You should get those repaired."

"I can't." He smirked. "I inherited them. Who was your son?"

"I called him Alex." Sarah looked up and found the man looming above her. He stood in front of her chair, letting her rock on and on, still pouring the dust from one hand to the other. "I'm not sure if that was his name, though."

"Why wasn't he with you?" the man asked. His knuckles popped again when he clenched his hand around the violet dust.

"He died a long time ago, maybe twenty years ago or something. I think he was ten." She looked off to the side, at the curtained window. "Maybe *he* has your box."

"It's not my box," he said. "It's always been your box, Mom."

She frowned. "You keep freaking out over this stupid box. Look, if it's mine, it's mine. You don't need it." She looked up at him, watching the sharp formation of shadows as they cupped the underside of his jaw. "You shouldn't need it. Do you see me going around begging for other people's boxes?" She shook her head and sighed.

The white china exploded against the ground and sent sprays of hot tea over the floor. Sarah watched wave after wave of brown wipe away the gray dust of the wooden floor. The man held the vase of dried, parchment-colored roses and gazed down at the overturned table, his foot still perched on the side. He glared down at Sarah and her rocking chair, letting the violet dust stream through his fingers.

"You never opened your box, and this is what happened. Look." He flung his gangling body into a wild circle, spinning an invisible web that encompassed the room. He pitched the vase to the ground and sent a wave of clear water into the brown puddles. Purple crumbs lingered among the ripples. "Look at my inheritance!"

"You did that yourself," Sarah said. She blew red hair out of her face. "Don't blame me for this dump. Get your own box, Alex."

"Asriel," the man hissed, his joints contracting into him, knuckles popping and shoulders groaning in their sockets. "You named me Asriel."

"But I've always called you Alex," she said. "Why does it matter? You know I'm talking to you."

The man straightened, fingers clenching, spine convulsing. "No, I don't know that. I don't." He turned, toppling his ivory chair, bypassing the frozen clock. He stood with his back to her and his hand on the doorknob. "I waited to see you. But you never changed." He stepped over the threshold and said, "You can crack the window now, Mom."

A COWARD'S BEAT

By Jeptha Storm
(California, USA)
Crimefighter, 3rd Place

Sunlight broke in through my window like a coward and began to vomit morning into my dehydrated ear. 7 AM, and it's hotter than two mice fucking in a wool sock. I stand and greet the day with a routine scratch of the anus and a defeated cough. A brisk and pointless shower is followed by a meticulous inspection of facial hair shape and length. Make sure that mustache is perched right under that nose. Just a hair longer than those lips. Sideburns brought neatly down, cradling the jaw. A quick zip, zip, zip with a number-two buzzer. Keep the neck clean. This is my father's haircut, as it was *his* father's haircut. And now . . . it's mine. It's the haircut of a man with everything to lose. A lawman's haircut. An asshole's haircut.

In the kitchen my breakfast is laid out for me. Eggs, bacon, toast, and coffee. An asshole's breakfast. She sits there with her Sudoku puzzle. I hate that fucking puzzle. I mean . . . what does it give you that a crossword doesn't? But then again I have never fully understood how to do them. And I guess maybe that's why I get so mad at them. We've been married twenty years. I think we probably spoke to each other the first five. Not much after that, though.

The fifteen-minute drive from my house to the office is my only sanctuary, the only salvation I get from this endless circle of banality. My life's not great. But I am safe here. In this Chevy, this beautiful machine of iron and oil and glass. The parking lot is coated in that weird dew Southern California phones in every once in a while. And Scott fucking Vandilier stole my spot . . . again. I wish I could hate him to death.

"What's on the agenda today, Jonesie?" Norville spat at me as he topped off his Styrofoam cup with mud.

"We got a stiff in a parking lot in El Monte." I prop my feet up on the break-room coffee table.

"We got an ID?" Norville asks between slurps.

"Yeah. First name Jane, last name Doe." This is clever. But Norville isn't amused.

"Better get down there, I guess. Get an ID out on her."

"Norville, how do you ID someone who ain't got a head?" This stops him in his tracks.

"Christ, what's the world coming to, Jonesie? When we were kids . . . this . . . it wasn't like this. I read in the papers yesterday about these two kids from Sunland . . . they killed a three-year-old boy. Right there in the school's parking lot. It's like nobody accounts for anything these days. Like people don't care." He was always a good guy. But too sensitive for this line of work. I told him that, too. I was very honest. Told him the sort of thing he'd have to deal with. But he refused to listen. He always tailed me. Even when we were kids. He is good guy . . . but a total follower. He followed me to college, to Vietnam, and to here. But I guess at the end of the day there are worse guys to follow. Not to sound irritating or self-righteous, but it's true. I got him clean and gave him a sense of direction. I guess he doesn't deserve my scorn, my contempt. Why be mad at someone who considers you a positive influence? Right now he needs a talk. I can tell he's shaking.

"We aren't kids anymore, Norville. This is the world we inherited. It's up to us to change it. Or at least dent it, the destruction that happens. Get your coat and let's go meet this dame."

He nods. "I wish you wouldn't talk about the victims like that, Jonesie."

I stand and place a sympathetic hand on his shoulder. "You're right. I'm sorry. Now go get ready." That wasn't my best or most heartfelt speech, but it took the bite out of him.

In the car, I drag on a Marlboro and cruise in slight excess because I can. The radio starts to croak out some CCR. Now on the classic hits station . . . Jesus. It's not long before me and Norville are humming along. And for a minute we are taken back to our teenage days. The summer nights in the vans, the music, the weed, the mysteries, and the dog . . . that fucking dog.

"Jonesie?"

I snub the cigarette in the tray. "Yes?"

"Whatever happened to that van?"

I clear my throat and prep myself to sound unaffected. "My old man made me pawn it . . . crusty old fuck."

We speed down the freeway. And now I'm in a bad mood.

"Detective Jones and Detective Rogers."

"Where's the body?"

"This way, sir. Store manager discovered her this morning behind the shopping carts."

The blacktop has that weird watery look it gets when it is hotter than all fucking hell. It's sectioned off by yellow tape with a host of blues buzzing around her like maggots.

Norville bursts into a slight trot to catch up with the fast-walking deputy and me. "Any parking lot surveillance?" He is readying his pen and little notebook.

"No sir. Not that I am aware of."

We clear the tape and the crowd, and there she lies. Like a headless Fuseli's nightmare. The image is cold enough to stop anyone mid-step. For a second I am concerned to see how this is going to affect Norville. I glance over and see his face awash with disappointment and sorrow. I lean over and examine the corpse. I suggest a few angles to photograph her from. I take full stock of her position before I send an errand boy to get me a cup of coffee.

"This is one twisted fuck," he says. "He put her on display like she's some goddamn—"

"Save it for that novel you've been working on, Norville."

He hangs his head, a tad embarrassed. "It's a novella."

"What's the difference?"

"It's shorter."

"Well, keep a sock in it when we are on the beat. We got to set an example." I bark a few more half-hearted orders, then call for the coroner.

Back in the car Norville fumbles awkwardly with his fingers.

"What's on your mind?"

He looks out the window. "Who do you think she is, Jonesie?"

I kill off my coffee and toss my paper cup in the back seat, which has become a makeshift graveyard for all the others. "Fuck if I know. Why?"

He clears his throat. "Just wondering, I suppose."

Oh shit, here we go. "Look, Norville. Do yourself a favor and don't. Okay? Don't wonder. You'll lose your mind. You can't keep identifying with victims like this. Okay?"

He nods.

"I'm serious, Norville." He looks at me. "I know. I know you are, Jonesie."

I turn the keys and the engine shakes itself into activity. "Okay. Now . . . how about we take Western and see if we can shake down that taco truck."

He chuckles. "Yeah . . . that sounds good."

The car jolts forward, and we make our way out into the unwelcoming street. Just two weary, confused, and defeated nomads in a hostile city ready to break.

IN LOVE AND CHOCOLATE

By Talya Tate Boerner
(Texas, USA)
Regional, 2nd Place

Uncle Rex and Aunt Frances lived in a single-wide at the edge of a cotton field on the home place. It was surrounded by a little stand of pine trees adjacent to Nana and Papa's house. Both of these particulars made the place extra special. Cottonwoods and pecans were plentiful in Mississippi County, but a grove of pine trees was a rare sight.

I often wondered if my uncle planted those trees. Or perhaps they grew from seeds Nana tossed from her back porch much like Jack's enchanted beanstalk. I never thought to ask anyone.

The inside of their home was as special as the outside. The air was altered. Unruffled. Protected. The tiny kitchen often held a freshly baked surprise, gooey brownies, chocolate chip cookies or chocolate pie piled high with meringue.

A massive console stereo spanned the entire living-room wall, anchoring the trailer into the dirt, commanding attention without being obnoxious. Running my index finger softly over the polished wood surface from end to end, I always felt the urge to lower my head and make the sign of the cross, even though I was Southern Baptist. A hidden altar on our farm, it lured us inside the calm inner sanctum, offering a brief respite from mud pies and sweaty games of tag.

It's where I first learned of Patsy Cline.

Their amazing album collection was stacked neatly within the adjoining cabinet, arranged much like the cool display at my favorite record shop on Main Street. My sister and I spent hours thumbing through covers, studying the artists, memorizing lyrics. And we were allowed to play those albums *unattended.* Placing the needle of the record player arm just so, careful not to scratch the vinyl, we listened to "Crazy" over and over until the words burned into our brains like a beloved church hymn. Singing off-key and loudly, we perfected somersaults on the gold shag carpeting in front of the sofa. I was amazed at how such a small home could be spacious enough to accommodate tumbling. It was always spotless. Uncle Rex and Aunt Frances had no children to mess it up—other than my sister and me.

As a kid, I wasn't aware of my uncle's little secret. Later, I learned Uncle Rex was an addict. He was madly hooked on Aunt Frances and *chocolate*. In that order. He was lost without Frances. Adrift. Disoriented. Crazy. Physically ill, as if part of his being had dissolved, the part that kept him happy and focused and stable—the part that made him *him,* that held his chocolate addiction in balance.

Thank God they were rarely apart. But sometimes, it was unavoidable.

One particular summer, Frances willingly agreed to donate a kidney to her ailing sister. To Uncle Rex's dismay, the transplant team wouldn't hear of performing the surgery from their single-wide, *no matter how clean.* A temporary separation was inevitable. It would only be a few days, insurance saw to that, but even so Uncle Rex was anxious.

Sunday morning from the pulpit, scanning the faces of his devoted but sparse congregation, Pastor Brown inquired, "Are there any announcements? Any sick we need to add to the prayer list?" The overhead fans did little to stir the hot air inside the sanctuary. It was a steamy day.

"Please keep praying for my brother-in-law. Doc says there's nothin' more they can do. Hospice is scheduled to come in this week." The members were sympathetic, sadly nodding, a few friends murmuring with heads together, almost touching. The word "hospice" always brought a sense of finality.

"Sister Sue wants us to pray for her brother-in-law," Pastor Brown repeated in his compassionate and commanding preacher voice, making sure everyone heard the plea.

From near the back pew came a high-pitched appeal. "Rebecca had her baby, a little girl, but she's still in NICU over in Memphis. Been there two weeks now."

"Let's everyone pray for Sister Rebecca and her newborn daughter." Pastor Brown added these souls to the growing list, waving his hymnal for emphasis.

"We need to pray for Rex Creecy. Sister Frances is fixin' to give a kidney to her sister. You know he's lost without her. Couldn't even get him to come to church this mornin'," reported a concerned church member from the choir loft. Everyone glanced to the empty place he and Frances always sat each Sunday, *their* pew. The church family nodded in unison. Again, sad low mumbling.

"Yes, everyone be sure to pray for Brother Creecy. He will need strength to make it through Sister Frances's procedure."

And that's how it was. Everyone knew she would be fine. And everyone knew he would worry himself sick in her absence.

*   *   *

By the end of evening prayer meeting, the good southern church ladies had activated the casserole phone tree with the skill and precision of a military operation. A steady stream of china platters and covered crockpots began flowing onto the red Formica kitchen table and spilling over to the countertop and stove. Food of wakes and funerals. Food to sustain and distract Uncle Rex. Food to make the church ladies feel useful. Chicken and dressing, piles of spaghetti with meatballs, macaroni and cheese, buttermilk biscuits with fresh pear preserves, a coconut pie, gallon jugs of sweet tea and green Jell-o salad, the kind with pieces of pecans.

And Sister Lavern made her famous *homemade five-layer triple chocolate cake.*

Uncle Rex never gave a thought to the other church-lady food. Only Sister Lavern's famous *homemade five-layer triple chocolate cake* held his attention. It was moist and creamy with a drizzle of raspberry fudge sauce along the sides and a light-handed dusting of powdered sugar around the top. A tantalizing gastronomical work of art.

As soon as Sister Lavern took her leave on his back stoop, saying, "Okay now, you call if you need anything, anything at all," he slammed the door and hastily peeked inside the cake cover, drawing the chocolate aroma fully into his lungs. Before her dusty Chevrolet backed to the end of the gravel driveway, the kitchen was cloaked in the heavenly smell of warm milk chocolate and vanilla butter cream. And a hint of almond? His acute senses were awakened.

Falling back into the chair, weakened, he allowed himself only a small sliver and a bit of icing. No need for a plate. The first taste was rich and velvety on his tongue. His pulse quickened. Unable to savor the slice, he quickly devoured it. Swathed in euphoria, the sensation lingered.

With great difficulty, he replaced the lid to the Tupperware cake cover, snapping and sealing it shut, then relocated it high above the refrigerator by using a small stepstool. Away—away. He knew to be careful with chocolate.

A better plan would have been to remove it from the trailer altogether.

Sleep wouldn't come. His heart raced, as if beating outside his body, growing quicker and quicker, and louder and louder every instant. As he tossed, his legs became tangled and twisted in the bed sheets.

The television offered no distraction. An old black-and-white movie, combined with the chocolate in his mind, only added to the maddening suspense. He played an old favorite album on his console, but the music was more noisy than soothing.

The cake called.

Weakened, he sat alone at the kitchen table, the trailer shrouded by pine trees throwing odd shadows along the walls. A single dim ray cast from a giant moon gleamed, like the thread of a spider, upon the triple chocolate dessert. Thrusting his finger deep into the frosting, he tasted again. Ummm. Luscious.

Then he began to eat.

He ate. The heady aroma consumed him. A groan of ecstasy escaped from somewhere within him. He ate the *entire cake*. In one sitting.

One decadent bite after another, until the cake plate was empty but for a few moist crumbs. Like the eyes of a mad man, his pale blues rolled back into his head. His heart raced. He collapsed into bed intoxicated. Crazed. Drunk on chocolate.

The clock struck four.

He awoke with excruciating chest pains. Extreme pressure on his rib cage. His breathing was shallow, his arm numb. *I'm having a heart attack. True!—nervous—very, very nervous. I'm being punished for being so pathetic, for having no willpower. It is done.*

Sirens wailed, lights flashed. The faces of neighbors showed as lights swiftly passed across farmhouse windows, their dreams interrupted. Emergency technicians tried to calm him. His sugar levels were strangely and dangerously elevated. He was frenzied and agitated.

Finally, he slept. Dreamless. Black. Sleep.

A bright light. The light drew him up and away from unconsciousness. He followed it. A sense of calm. *I have died. Am I in Heaven?*

"Rex? Can you hear me?" He heard a distant yet familiar voice. *God? Is that You?*

God sounded oddly like Dr. Reggie.

Slowly, through the lingering dark chocolate fog, his physician came into view. He flickered a pen light into his dilated pupils, back and forth, nearly blinding him. "I've never had a patient overdose on chocolate cake." He chuckled heartily.

Rex's head pounded as he remembered his embarrassing night of gluttony. *Homemade five-layer triple chocolate cake . . .*

"Where's Frances?" he asked Dr. Reggie, his mouth dry and swollen, lips chapped. The machinery around him hummed and flashed periodically, the noises magnified in the sterile room.

"They'll be bringing her back from recovery soon. She did great. That'll be her bed over there." He pointed to the empty bed next to him only a few feet away.

Sunlight streamed through the window. Dust motes danced, suspended midair.

He smiled, then dozed. He was where he belonged.

GIFT OF HER OWN

By Dan Dumitru
(New Jersey, USA)
Zombies, Vampires, Lycans, and More, 3rd Place

Eliza dreamed. She was making love to a Greek god, her Apollo, though he never told her his name. In fact, he had never spoken. That was just fine with her. She'd never much appreciated men's conversation. It was mostly hypocrisy, as they only wanted one thing, and their conversation was mating ritual. She always got down to business faster than most men, with a direct-ness some men found more intimidating than arousing.

Still, a hello, an introduction, however perfunctory, was always nice. Part of her was still old-fashioned. A very small part. But not this guy. He simply walked up to her and stopped very close, too close for comfort. He looked into her eyes up close, a smile more in his eyes than on his lips. She rebelled at his obvious self-confidence. She liked to take men down a notch. She had to be in control. Normally, she would have walked away from someone this cocky, let him squirm, embarrass him, no matter how appealing he might have looked. She wanted to turn away, but when she looked into his jet-black eyes she found she couldn't move. As his lips approached hers, she found her resistance turn to desire, and as they touched, to bliss. After a long mo-ment she returned to Earth, awake, and quite wet. She lay there for a while, eyes closed, breathing.

This is how it had been going, the dream, for several weeks now. She did not usually remember her dreams, certainly not in so much detail, and she'd never dreamed the same thing twice—too boring. And now this. She hated this dream. Every time, she'd wake up frustrated, wanting to dominate this man, to possess him, to mount him for God's sake! But not this time. She thought she had finally cracked. This morning she awoke, and all she wanted was to surrender. That was a first, and she contemplated this long-forgotten feeling—the desire to surrender to a man—while her agitated breathing slowed down. She had this feeling of déjà vu about the whole thing, though she couldn't quite explain it.

She could see the moonlight streaming through the large windows of her Beverly Hills mansion. It was still night, which was normal. She was getting on in years, and her sleep was fitful. Thirst or the call of nature might get her to drag her carcass out of bed. Just now, neither was particularly urgent, so she merely rested, contemplating her dream.

She thought it weird to have an erotic dream so late in life. Once, she could have taught Anais Nin a thing or two, she thought with a wry smile. In fact, that's what her friends used to call her, Anais. When she couldn't have lovers anymore, when the boy toys ran away, she paid for it. Shameful, but necessary. She didn't even bother excusing it with "men do it, too." She needed it, and that was that. Later, as time and gravity took their toll, she could no longer stand the look in the eyes of those who serviced her, and she had simply stopped. That had been over a decade ago.

Still abed, she reached over to the nightstand and grabbed her Camels and lighter with a practiced move, without having to look. She lit one up. She thought, When I finish this, I'll fix myself a drink. She always liked a stiff one after sex, pun intended, she thought, inhaling deeply. She held the smoke in, then blew some rings, feeling contented.

"That stuff will kill you," a man's voice said.

She jumped, arthritic joints screaming their age, but managed to hang on to her cigarette. She flicked on the lamp and noticed the man in the chaise longue across the room. She stared. It was her Greek god, in the flesh.

"Who are you?" she said.

"Mario," he said with that arrogant smile she recognized from her dream. She looked at the table, eyeing the phone. Mario followed her gaze, and laughed.

"I am also the man of your dreams, your Greek god, as it were," he said. She stared at him again, dumbfounded. She noticed his dark attire, his waxy complexion. He seemed to be waiting for something. Then she remembered, and opened her mouth to say, *You can read my mind?*

"Yes, Eliza, I can read your mind."

After a pause, wondering what to say, it finally sank in just how futile any mind games would be. She shrugged and said, "Well, now what?"

After a pause, Mario stood up and walked slowly across the room towards her. He was clad in black, including a pair of riding boots that looked straight out of an Errol Flynn movie, the old starlet in her noticed. In fact, the only things not black on him were an oversized silver buckle on his belt and a pendant with something that looked like a ruby, a gem of pure fire in its midst. His long leather coat was undone, and it flapped gently as his long strides brought him closer. She shrank away, a frightened old woman, her dignity and fame forgotten. He stopped in front of her, his gaze unfathomable.

He looked her over. She followed his gaze from her bare feet bloated with diabetes, to the nightgown that barely concealed her sagging body, to her arthritic hands, her wrinkled neck, her old, old face. At least she'd dyed her hair, the aging coquette reminded herself.

She felt shame. It was bad enough to live in that body, to see it every day, but to be examined like this by a handsome young man was humiliating. She remembered when she was the one checking out the men, and how she'd find them wanting. It was power, and now she finally understood what it was like to be at the receiving end. In a different person, it might have been a cause for introspection, but this had never been Eliza's forte. She was just an animal, once stunningly beautiful, capable of passion and cunning, and not much else. That is why those men she liked to conquer and possess, especially the more intellectual ones, found her quite vacuous once the passion cooled off. She always broke it off with a man once he'd lost respect for her. Even though she never got turned off by intellectuals, she never seriously considered reading a book. Her men were prey, something to use and perhaps even to enjoy, not something to emulate.

She interrupted her reminiscing when she saw the man smile. He had the loveliest hair, long and wavy, auburn and soft. His eyes were jet black, like in her dream. She loved his eyes.

"Thank you, Eliza," Mario said.

She remembered her fear and humiliation. Handsome men could be so distracting! She had never been a submissive, not even in play, and she hated being controlled. She had always had a reputation for being a prima donna on set. And if a man ever forgot his place around her, her glare could kill. She was never much for words, but her body language more than made up for it. Presently, she felt anger wash over her, anger at her fear, at her humiliation, at the arrogant man in front of her: anger at her advancing years and at anyone who'd ever used the expression 'aging with grace.'

"Truly, you are perfect! Perhaps too much so, but we shall see," Mario said.

"Enough!" Eliza said, attempting to regain some of her composure. She stood up, sagging breasts flopping about, white hair swirling around her. She tried to ignore the indignity, and drew herself up as straight as she could manage. She barely came up to the middle of his chest.

"Who are you and what do you want?" she demanded in her best smoker's rasp.

Mario just stood there, grinning down at her. Eliza raised her hand to slap him.

"Don't," Mario said, and Eliza felt as if the energy got drained from her arm. It fell by her side, and she just stood there, numb. That voice, that simple baritone, could get her to do anything and she knew it, though she had no idea why. The fear came back, but now there was a note of respect in it. At the risk of sounding cliché, she began to understand that this was not a man to be trifled with.

"You're learning," Mario said, evenly.

As Eliza gradually regained control of her arms, she felt the burning in her fingers. She tore her eyes from him, quickly put out the spent cigarette, and lit up another one. She puffed and inhaled, looking sideways at him. Tall, handsome, calm. Killer, or lover? Maybe both? She didn't know. She did feel interest. An unreadable man was a special challenge, though in her experience that was likely to be just an act; most men were disappointingly simple. The irony of her thinking others simple would never have crossed Eliza's mind.

"May I?" Mario said, gesturing towards the Marlboros.

"Of course," Eliza said after a moment, enjoying the scrap of power his request granted her, but she didn't move to give him the cigarettes. He laughed and came over to the nightstand to help himself, his chest inches from her face. She looked from his chest to his face. "People hate me and envy me because they think that I've had it so good, and I did, and yet fate can be so cruel, you know?" Eliza said softly, and quite rhetorically.

Ever the emotional animal, now she felt vulnerable. She looked away from Mario, no longer afraid, and sat on the edge of the bed, smoking quietly. *Alea iacta est, The dice are cast,* she thought to herself. She still remembered a few Latin quotes from junior high. They were useful at impressing the innocent, or at least those who didn't know her. Then again, these days, who the heck knew Latin anyway?

Mario pulled up a chair and sat in front of her. He put out his half-smoked cigarette, took her hand in his, and began talking. "Quite a man, he was, Mr. Grey, your Latin teacher, wasn't he, Eliza?"

"Yes," she said, blushing, memories flooding back. One had seduced the other, but who? It didn't matter; Eliza liked to remember it as her conquest.

"Now now, there's no need to blush. He taught you the Latin names of all those naughty bits, yours and his, when you were only twelve; yet he wasn't your first one, now, was he?" Mario said, his even voice belying the cruelty of the memories he was dredging out of the depths of her youth.

Eliza sat silently for a moment, trying to comprehend. Then the memory of her uncle came back. She didn't remember the next minute's worth of screaming and clawing at Mario. The next thing she knew her arms were in his grip, and she was shaking and crying. "What? Why do you say these things? Huh? What do you want?"

Mario waited for the storm to subside, then continued talking. "I want you to be serious. This is not a game; I am not one of your lovers, your 'boy toys.' This is important." He waited.

Eliza wanted to spit on him, but somehow she knew it would be a bad idea. She gave herself a moment, then said, "Okay!" Mario let go of her hands. She wiped her eyes and sorted herself out, as best she could. She picked up her fallen cigarette, put it out, and lit yet another one. Mario took her hand again. Eliza suppressed a shudder.

"I mentioned your past so that you will understand just how much I know about you, and how much you are at my mercy. My mercy is going to be very important to you shortly. Tonight, I will make you an offer."

Eliza listened, increasingly mesmerized by his voice as he laid out his intentions. She had to ask.

"Yes, we've met before," Mario said. "Your déjà vu is correct."

"But, I don't remember you, just the feeling . . ."

"Once, you were in the Girl Scouts. You were camping. A girl in your troop was crying that night by the campfire. She had just gotten dumped by her boyfriend for another, a girl who 'puts out', as her boyfriend had explained. Impressed by his equipment, you blurted out to her that she 'didn't know what she's been missing.' When your comment finally registered, it took five other girls to pull her off you, and by then she'd clawed your face off quite viciously. They may have saved your life, but they had no sympathy for you, calling you all sorts of names, so you grabbed your sleeping gear and moved away from the camp, too far away, as it turned out . . ." Mario paused, for effect she was sure, as he lit up.

She knew the rest of the story, but she wanted to hear it from him.

"It was a hot summer night, too hot to be inside your sleeping bag, and so you lay on top of it, hating that girl and her friends who used to be your friends and the boy who cost you those friends—and the rest of humanity for good measure." Mario stopped and watched Eliza.

She looked back, waiting.

"A man came out of the darkness. You were nude, touching yourself lightly, teasing yourself cruelly, not wanting to bring yourself off. He watched you breathe, and you watched him, hating him, wanting him to take you. He stripped in front of you, while you continued to stroke yourself, the moon at his back, his auburn hair glowing in the moonlight, his face in darkness. When he finished taking off his clothes, he took out a dagger and bent down over you."

Eliza remembered the terror of that knife plunging into her breast, and the mad desire to be possessed and be done with it all. Ever after, she would mix fear and excitement whenever she could.

"He raised the knife over you and plunged it into the ground next to your throat. You surrendered to him, and he took you, and as bliss engulfed and penetrated you, you could feel all your hurts, on your body and in your heart, heal and go away. You woke up in the morning, naked and healed and quite unsoiled. You thought it might have been a dream, but the dagger was still next to you."

Somehow, she knew what he was going to say next.

"That was me, Eliza," Mario said.

She stared. "That was nearly seven decades ago! How?"

"I could tell you that I'm a vampire, a creature of the night, but then I'd have to prove it, wouldn't I? So, may I have my dagger back?"

Eliza got her purse and handed him his dagger, the one she'd been carrying all this time. It was her oldest possession.

"This is an enchanted dagger. I always knew where it was, so I could find you and watch you wherever you went. It is also silver, which is highly toxic to us. You didn't know it, but this could always protect you from my kind. Your hand, please," Mario said, reaching for her.

A pang of fear went through her, but she put out her hand anyway. He had broken her and she knew it. Eliza trusted Mario like she had never trusted a human being in her life, though all she knew about him was that he was a monster who had raped her.

He cut across the palm of her hand quickly, leaving a deep gash. Eliza felt a sharp pain and let out a short scream. She tried to pull back her hand, but Mario had her in an iron grip. Blood began to well up. He pulled her hand to his mouth, and to her horror he began to lick her blood.

Wherever his tongue touched her, the pain went away. No, actually it turned to pleasure. She watched in amazement as the lips of the wound began to mesh together. In a minute of gentle licking the bleeding had stopped, and in another her hand was as good as new. Finally, it sank in.

"You really are a vampire!" she said in awe.

"Yes. And now, I'd like to offer this to you, my gift, eternal life."

"So, you won't kill me?" Eliza said.

Mario laughed. "No."

Relief washed over her. A small part of her felt disappointed, too, ever the adrenaline junkie.

"But," Mario continued, "due to the risk of getting caught, the offer is always made just once. If it is refused, there will never be another chance. Attempts to contact the brethren afterwards would be . . . unwelcome."

"Why me, Mario?"

"I've never made another one like me. We're monsters, and most of us become evil. With superhuman powers, with every living thing hating us, with nothing to fear but each other, vampires really do become monsters. I am one of the few who've kept some semblance of civilization . . ."

Eliza squeezed his hand gently and touched his face with her other hand. "You're digressing. Why me, Mario?"

Though she could hardly believe what was happening, she had accepted the situation. Eliza wanted the "gift" more than anything, but didn't want to seem desperate. She was using whatever charm she had left, and hoped to God, or the Devil, that it worked.

Mario smiled. "You don't need to seduce me, Eliza. You did that in a dark forest all those years ago. You are the most purely animal, the most passionate human I have ever met. You gave yourself to me like prey, like an animal, like a goddess to a mortal. I took you then, but I couldn't kill you. I wanted your blood more than anything, but I couldn't fathom a world without you, and I wasn't going to turn you into a monster. So I left my dagger, knowing you'll keep it, and I watched you from afar. And now here you are, closer to death than you realize . . ."

He saw her flinch and hurried to add: "I don't mean me, Eliza, I couldn't hurt you. We see life's ebb and flow in humans, and you are very sick. I don't know how, I'm not a doctor, but if you went to one now, he wouldn't give you long to live." Eliza relaxed, despite the bad news.

"So," Mario continued, "I came here tonight to let you make the decision. Live and die, or be undead."

Mario stopped talking, and waited. Eliza was struggling with unexpected hope, and fear, and perhaps confusion.

"There is so much I don't know, so many questions to ask . . ."

"I will be your mentor, and your friend, and more, if you'll let me. But all that later, for now dawn approaches, and we must hurry. Eliza, do you accept my gift?" Mario said.

"Yes," Eliza said, looking straight into his eyes. "Yes I do. Give it to me!"

Mario looked at her for a moment as if to make sure. Then, seemingly satisfied, he nodded. He put out his cigarette.

She followed suit.

"First, I will have your mortal blood. Then you will have mine."

She felt a moment of fear, but things happened quickly. Mario cupped the back of her head and pulled her closer, gently but firmly. She closed her eyes, and felt his fangs sink into her throat. Surprisingly, it hurt like hell, but only for a moment. Then the pleasure took over, and she could feel her pulse in her neck, pumping her blood into her maker.

Later, she couldn't tell after how long, she began to come to it. She felt blissful and weak, as if she could not move. She was looking up into Mario's loving eyes and realized that he was cradling her.

"I may have drunk too much," he said. "I'll fix that in a moment. You do not have fangs yet, so I'll do the honors." Eliza was too weak to say anything. She merely watched, happy and trusting. He lifted his wrist to his own mouth and bit. As the blood began to flow, he brought his wrist to her mouth. As the first drops touched her lips and her tongue, a second wave of bliss came over her, much stronger than the first. She closed her eyes and rode its crest.

It was different this time. She didn't lose herself. She was, in fact, awake and aware of her surroundings, much more than ever before. She felt powerful, in touch with the world like never before, she was all *there*, in the moment. Her senses were preternatural, her sensations surreal.

Mario took his hand away. She wanted more, obviously, but he told her it's quite enough. She stood up, feeling energized, and noticed that her senses continued to be exquisitely fine-tuned, as if she had never stopped drinking Mario's blood. She looked around her bedroom, admiring every shape, every hue, listening to every night sound. Eventually, when she felt she could not tease herself any longer, she walked quickly, painlessly, across the room and stopped in front of the full-length mirror. She looked at herself.

She had already gained at least an inch in height, and gaining. Grey hair now peppered her white, all of it gradually turning to her original black. Her eyes, her favorite weapons, were clearing up. Under her nightgown, things began to firm up pleasantly.

She saw Mario's reflection in the mirror, turned sideways in his chair, watching her. She smiled to him. In that smile she put a gratitude she'd never experienced before. He smiled back, and they were kindred in that moment. He got up and walked over to her, then stood behind her with his hands across her waist. She liked the way his hands felt on her stomach, and she leaned her head back against his chest. She continued to watch herself.

She had grown back to her original height, a full three inches. Her hair was ebony, her eyes a pair of smoldering coals, jet-black. There was no pain in her body, her healthy body. The wrinkles had smoothed. Mostly. That, her mind resisted, sharp senses be damned. She looked at her face, and her neck, and her hands, and as the horror dawned on her she closed her eyes and focused on her breathing. She didn't dare open her eyes for a long time, knowing that nothing more would change, not now and not ever. She was always going to be a well-maintained seventy-year-old, nothing more. Better than eighty-six, but not exactly eternal *youth*. She continued to breathe, regularly, and knew what she was going to do. She also knew that despite having retired from movies years before, her toughest acting was just ahead of her.

"You've never made another, but you've seen it done, right?" she said. She had to make sure.

"Yes," Mario said, "it is always a miracle, a wonderful transfiguration."

Eliza laughed. "Interesting choice of religious imagery," she said. Then she understood something else. "You cannot read my mind now, is that right?"

"Yes, that is a gift to be used against mortals. But, we don't need that, you and I," Mario said, giving her a light hug.

When she felt her voice steady enough, she added, "I am still weak. Your blood will make me stronger." His face was against the top of her head, and she felt him smile. "Okay, but just a little for now. There will be more tomorrow."

She turned around and opened her eyes. He stiffened for a moment when he saw the look she gave him. She showed only passion and lust in her eyes, not the hatred she kept hidden. She sank her brand-new fangs into his immortal throat and drank. The power that surged into her, she now used to hold him in her embrace, even as he began to struggle, violently at first, more weakly as the minutes went by.

He managed a strangled, "Why?" but she was in no mood for explanations, and did not stop draining him until his heart stopped beating.

At last, she lay him down. Eliza changed clothes, then grabbed her dagger and his brooch. After one last look at Mario's prostrate form, she walked out of her house and out of her life, into the darkness.

THE SORCERESS OF MHUR

By Anna Cates
(Ohio, USA)
Fantasy, 1ˢᵗ Place

We are who we are. We know what we know. Reality is what it is. Brack had always been a level-headed man who didn't chase after fantasies, but fate would have him tested.

He stood in the castle doorway, muddy quicksand on his boots, an odor of earthen decay filling the room, seeming to come from the bubbling cauldron in the fireplace. The air felt dank, stuffy, oppressive, the shutters locked closed. Fatigue filled him. He'd passed through eons of forests full of strange growls, branches hung with moss, and swamplands known as the Wormbog Woods, where slithered through the slime unnamable beasts. At last he'd returned to the strange castle built in a clearing in the woods.

"You're a beautiful woman, Morinda," Brack said, his voice echoing off the candle-lit walls, but he avoided the sorceress's gaze, for in those eyes he saw only death.

Golden bracelets clinking, the Sorceress of Mhur paced over to her lounger, her violet gown trailing the stone floor behind her sandaled feet. Only Morinda's black hair, bound in a loose braid, covered the open back of her gown. She placed herself upon the lounger, leaning against the arm rest, her full breasts compressing into frightening cleavage.

"I knew you'd return," she said, grinning. "You need me."

Brack eyed the skulls lining the castle walls. Had they once been Morinda's favorites before falling victim to her boredom, or was the graveyard just her preference for home décor? Either way, it didn't speak well of her.

A tremor upset Brack's body, sweating beneath leather armor, wracked with mire and blood. "Indeed. Parting your company has been a difficult journey," he said, though his mind fought against the sorceress's charms as he considered Morinda's duplicity.

While a youth, Brack might have more easily succumbed to Morinda's devices. But now, over thirty and an experienced fighter, he'd learned the hard way that women of virtue exceeded those of deceit—that innocence surpasses the ornamental shams of temptresses that coerce through spell and potion. And so, he meditated on Avessa, his lawful wife. Lonely, he had bought her as a slave from the dwarfs of Yurk for companionship. Last in his wishes was to abandon her and become Morinda's hand-man, plaything, toy, prisoner, just a pawn among a harem of masseurs. Yet he suspected that was her desire. *Yes! Avessa*, he mused in silent concentration, teeth clenched, jawbones bulbous.

Brack stood with legs akimbo, his scraggly black hair smelling of swamp water and falling over his broad shoulders, his worn sword tucked in the scabbard at his belt. "I've forded mighty rivers, passed through a thousand fires, been manacled in the deepest dungeons of the earth. I've battled unspeakable foes and slain the ogre hoard of the Caverns of Bazlahan, as you bid, and now I come to claim the Helm of Constitution as my token, which you promised."

But Morinda only laughed. "Stay a while!" She lifted the tip of her braid, placing it to her lips.

"Those are my wishes," Brack said, knowing better than to offend her, "but I cannot. I must return to my king in the east." He tried to keep his thoughts on Avessa, picturing the soft contours of her body and face.

Momentarily, Morinda's smile failed, and the braid fell down like a snake dropping from a tree limb. "Your king will have to wait."

I will not be your chained monkey! Brack thought, his hands forming fists, though he kept silent.

Morinda rose from the sofa. "I must escort you to your bedchamber. I'll send for the slave boys to wait on you. Tonight will be a time of feasting, for you're troubled and weary and need refreshening. I'll prepare a spiced bath for your satisfaction and see that your clothing is laundered. You must be perfumed and pampered," she finished, almost in a mockery.

Brack felt his muscles stiffen with hatred at Morinda's audacity. But, "I'm undeserving of your splendid hospitality," was all he could say, knowing she would not take *no* for an answer, knowing he would have to appease her.

*   *   *

Brack stood naked in the castle bedchamber, wondering what awaited him, a wild excitement brewing inside of him. He knew he was weakening, his resolve failing. Somehow, against his intentions, Morinda had aroused him and now, he feared, he was becoming just a puppet to her whims. *No*, Brack thought. *I won't let her do that to me!* But he knew resistance was futile, and denying the inevitable was only lying to himself.

An eerie silence filled the castle. Where were the masseurs? Where were the slave boys? She couldn't have needed that many innards for spells. Or could she? It seemed to Brack that dark mystery had opened wide its famished jaws and swallowed all of life except for just his own, and that had been spared only for Morinda.

A candle hissed upon the shelf. Brack picked up a strip of fresh linen and toweled off his muscular arms, stubbly face, and hairy chest. In the corner, his bath still steamed with warmth, though swamp sludge and soap scum had dirtied the water.

He pulled back the bed covers, releasing a spicy scent, orange blossoms stashed beneath the blankets. Cinnamon and sassafras. Anise and juniper berry. The aromas vacillated through him, making him tingle. He lodged himself beneath the sheets, sinking into the mattress.

A knock sounded on the door. "Come in," he heard his voice say. *No. Avessa*, he wanted to think, but it was too late. "Morinda," he said, and the door opened.

Wearing a satin robe of crimson and carrying a tray of burning incense, Morinda entered. Not speaking a word, her lips a mocking half grin, she placed the incense on the wooden table. Pink and green smoke, so aromatic Brack could almost taste it, curled through the air with dizzying intoxication, clouding his mind and swirling his thoughts into even deeper desire. His heartbeat rushed, though he fought to stay sober.

Morinda approached the bed, smiling, her fingers loosening the tie of her robe, which she let slip away and fall to the floor. Seeming almost bashful, she draped her unbound hair over one shoulder, forming a partial covering for her nakedness, dancing with shadows.

As she neared the edge of the bed, Brack could smell her intense aroma: safrole, jasmine, and rose. Hardly standing his own excitement, he pulled back the sheets, welcoming Morinda inside the covers. He could do nothing else. He could say nothing else.

Ylang ylang. Tonka bean. Coriander. Myrrh. The incense kept steaming. Caught in a snare of spice, Brack succumbed to Morinda's will, his body entwining with hers. He tasted her soft lips and soon lost himself to the pleasure.

*   *   *

Slosh! Slosh! Slosh! Brack sat on a stool in front of the churn, pumping goat's cream into butter. His hair had been shorn; clean potato sack pants clothed him; and Morinda's apron, hand-sewn with cloth spun from flax by her own fingers, covered his chest and torso. He whistled a merry tune.

The castle seemed so different now, almost like a simple mason's cottage. The open shutters let in fresh air, light, and music from twittering whip-poorwills. Outside the window to his left, sheep and goats frisked about the field spotted with wildflowers—trillium blossoms, red and purple poppies, daisies, buttercups, and foxglove—bumble-bees and butterflies drifting through the warm, scented air. And beyond the fields an apple orchard stretched away to the border of the forest.

Suddenly, Brack stopped churning. *An apple orchard?* He puzzled with wrinkled brow, marveling again at something else he hadn't noticed before. Every day, his world was changing. Not only that, Morinda had removed all of the skulls from the castle walls. He didn't know where she'd stashed or destroyed them, but one day they had just disappeared!

The kettle in the hearth gently bubbled, but without a foul odor. Instead, the aroma of rosemary, mutton, and garden vegetables filled the room, causing his stomach to rumble.

Morinda entered with broom in hand. She placed the broom against the wall and hastened to the hearth to stir the stew with a wooden spoon. Clothed in a modest brown dress, seeming almost virginal, she tucked a lock of dark hair behind one ear, then glanced over at Brack. "Will we have butter for our bread with tonight's supper?"

Brack rose from his stool and walked over to the window, casting him in a stream of sunlight. "Come here." He motioned her forward. Squinting in the sunlight, he gazed outside, then back at Morinda, who crossed the room until she stood beside him before the open window, lambs baaing under blue sky.

"What is it?"

"Tell me," Brack said, pointing outside, "where did that apple orchard come from? It wasn't there yesterday."

Morinda laughed. "It's been there forever!"

Stupefied, he gazed at her rosy-cheeked face. "I swear, I never noticed it before!"

"No?" She looked at him as if she couldn't understand his puzzlement.

"Then we shall have bushels of apples!" Brack said at last, smiling.

"Indeed, we shall."

"And where is your brood of skulls?" Brack gestured toward the walls, his dark eyes twinkling.

"I took them down," she said with gladness in her voice, her eyes shining. "I needed a change." She reached out to smooth a wrinkle in his apron.

"Where are all your masseurs?"

"I told them to go away."

"What about the slave boys?"

"I set them free!" She smiled at him.

"You set them free." He repeated the answer as if the truth of it were marvelous.

"You set me free," she said.

"You set *me* free, Morinda."

She laughed. "You keep calling me by the funny name. That must be a woman you once loved."

Brack looked down, his face tinting. "Yes," he said, lifting again his gaze, "but not anymore. I love only you now. *You* are my wife. Avessa."

"At first I was afraid of you. I didn't know what you wanted me to be."

"*I* wanted to be a hero."

"We are who we are," she said, sunlight from the window cascading over her, igniting her dark hair with flaming highlights.

Brack fell into her gaze. "I see life in your eyes."

"I decided not to kill myself—or you. I decided not to poison the soup."

Brack laughed. "So that's what you were contemplating. I knew there was something dangerous about you, something I feared. Why didn't you?"

"I decided that I liked you, something about you."

"I was hoping you'd come to like me."

"Do you like *me*?"

"*Like* you? I *love* you!"

The breeze stirred the wind chimes dangling in the far window, clinking and jingling their simple song of love and peace.

Love and peace.

Learn more about 1ˢᵗ-place winner and Fresh Ink Group member Anna Cates at http://www.FreshInkGroup.com/authors/anna-cates.

THE HILLBILLY & THE PREDATOR

By Kelly Marino
(New York, USA)
Humor, 3ʳᵈ Place

There is an ancient Native American proverb that says,
"If a pine needle falls in a forest, an eagle will see it,
a deer will hear it, and a bear will smell *it."*

30 years ago, before my husband, Mike, and I had kids (or much common sense, for that matter), we decided to take advantage of his week of shore leave from the US Navy and soak up a little rest and relaxation in my parents' mountain getaway. By "mountain", I mean way out in the boondocks past the high California desert at an altitude of over 7,500 feet, in the middle of NOWHERE. And, by "getaway", I mean a 20-foot trailer, outfitted with the wrap-around deck my family had spent many weekends helping (I mean *watching*) my dad build. The only water supply was a rogue stream that the seller's surveyor hadn't noticed or documented when Dad had placed his paltry bid on the 20-acre lot of "worthless wilderness" (turns out, dad knew about the stream all along—he was a clever man).

First, some quick back-story about Dad. He grew up a poor child in the rough-and-tumble mountains of Alabama. You know, the kind of place where kids had to walk to school barefoot, in the snow, and uphill—both ways.

Dad was cursed (some say blessed) with a semi-typical Southern child-hood that was pepper-sprayed with richly textured yet questionable education. He grew up learning the kinds of things that nobody teaches kids in a structured academic environment: How to skin and prepare a wild critter when you need something to eat while you're lost in the woods for a few days. How to disassemble and then hastily reassemble a tractor motor before its owner comes home. How to steal honey from a beehive without getting yourself flayed alive by your angry momma—who's *worried* about your safety. How to shoot your older brother with a BB gun—just to see if you can—and then successfully hide from your furious daddy. (Incidentally, the best

way to hide from a 6-feet 5-inch, 240-pound maniac who's hell bent on killing you is to crawl under the house and stay there until your older brother
pisses him off so bad that said maniac forgets all about you. I'm just sayin'.)

Despite these crazy everyday occurrences, my dad somehow survived
long enough to drop out of the 9th grade, undergo exhaustive Army Para-
trooper training, and earn an all-expense-paid trip to Korea that lasted 18
months, where he contracted a raging case of TB that should have killed
him. And that was all before the age of 19.

So, it should surprise no one that, after spending my youth pretending
to believe every piece of sage advice he gave me, I secretly shunned all of his
corn-fed wisdom, determined that I would show him how someone with a
"real" education makes her way in the world. Besides, what could a junior-
high-school dropout with a hillbilly accent possibly teach *me?*

When Mike and I initially asked if we could stay at the mountain getaway,
Dad responded with the usual skepticism-laden parental remarks.

"You two couldn't find the place, let alone survive in it." Or, "Kel, you
can't boil water or make ice cubes. You'll both starve." Or, "It's a long way
to the doctor." We had gone camping and off-roading throughout my childhood, and *that* line had always been Dad's favorite.

Well, Mike and I persisted and convinced dear old Dad that we would
be fine. Mike was, after all, a military man who had grown up in New York
City. He was worldly and he would protect me. I wasn't sure exactly WHO
would be protecting him, but the idea of living off the land for a week held
huge appeal. (I never quite figured out what that appeal was, but if I ever do,
I'll let you in on it.)

With great enthusiasm, I packed enough gear to last a month. I assem-
bled some cute outfits with matching sandals, my best make-up bag, and the
all-important ultra-hold hairspray. Mike dropped plenty of dried Italian
meats, cheeses, and olives into the cooler with the eggs, butter, and milk that
my mom had insisted we take. She gave us a can opener and a box of canned
bacon, canned black bread from the Army surplus store, canned shoestring
potato chips, et cetera. You get the idea: durable and shelf-life-friendly stuff
that would keep for weeks, if need be (Mom was pretty clever, too).

With pomp and circumstance, we embarked on the 4-hour drive to our
mountain domain—a domain with no TV, refrigerator, electricity, or running water. We did have the icy-cold stream, though, so we didn't worry our
pretty heads over where to find fresh water.

Our first few hours in paradise were quite fun. As I unpacked everything,

I felt like Eva Gabor on the old TV show *Green Acres* waving my pretty clothes around while Mike solemnly checked out the topography outside.

While we lounged on the deck in our sleeping bag that night and lost ourselves in the natural light show above, I regaled him with clever stories about survival tactics Mom and Dad had taught me over the years. When he voiced concern about rattlesnakes, I assured him that we wouldn't encounter them in the morning because they needed to warm up in the sun for a while before they could move. I then explained that we would definitely spot bear scat on the ground. When he asked how we would identify it, I told him that the gigantic piles of doo-doo imbedded with half-digested wild berries near bear footprints would be a pretty good tip-off.

We woke the next morning to blistering sunshine and oppressive heat, so we decided to take some goodies to the stream and spend the day alternately frolicking in the cool shade, working on our tans, and enjoying the great outdoors. Only mildly concerned for our personal safety—hey, we were stupid kids, so cut us some slack here—we grabbed Dad's shotgun and casually stuffed a couple of shells (shotgun shells, not the mozzarella-oozing Italian variety) into the backpack and headed into the wild blue yonder.

By late afternoon, we'd had our fill of mosquitoes, flies, and prickly leaves; the time had come for us to pack our trash and head back to the trailer. Striking a fierce pose that would have made Uncle Sam cringe, Mike stood proudly with Dad's shotgun, wearing nothing but a Fruit of the Loom wife-beater, his tighty-whities, and a pair of unlaced hunting boots. Armed with bug spray and sporting a yellow string bikini, I fell in line behind Grizzly Adams as he bravely led his trusting damsel through the woods.

We arrived back at the trailer to see the front door dangling in the doorway from one hinge. Alarmed and ready to prove my mad survival skills, I whispered, "Here, give me that," and took the shotgun from Mike's hands. I was, after all, a crack shot, trained in the fine art of putting holes in yellow beer cans that never moved while I aimed at them.

As we crept toward the deck, we glanced around nervously, but didn't see anything out of place except, of course, the door that looked as though its civil rights had been violated. That's when my heart started pounding, and I became truly frightened.

After gathering the remnants of the shredded screen (and his composure), Mike noticed deep claw marks along the edges of the metal door. We tiptoed into the trailer and saw, to our horror, that a bear had plundered the interior, no doubt searching for the pungent cheeses, sausages, and olives that we had foolishly left in the compartment under the bed.

The table was scratched, the cabinet doors were open, and the sleeping bag had been ripped apart. And on the floor, upside down, lay the Tupperware container that Dad had insisted we fill with black pepper and leave on the counter next to the fridge. He had told me that a bear's sense of smell could make a Bloodhound hang his head in shame, and that one good whiff of pepper could make any predator think twice about staying for lunch. When I saw the nasty slick of bear snot splattered all over mom's handmade curtains, it occurred to me that my hillbilly daddy *hadn't* fallen off the turnip truck, as I had long suspected! I also knew it was time for *us* to beat a path out of there, too.

I don't think we've had such a scare since that day, but we've laughed about it over the years and we decided that, if our kids ever pulled anything that stupid, we'd kill them when we found them—and the crawl-space under the house would be the first place we'd look!

CHARMING

By Ruby Fink
(California, USA)
Fantasy, 2nd Place

I steered my horse over the last ridge and reined him to a stop, his chest heaving in exertion. We were so close, I could feel it. My hound whined and circled around us, sniffing furiously, his moist nose digging into the soil. I waited, trusting in his instincts to find me my princess. After a moment, he stiffened, paw pointing toward the darkest part of the forest in front of us. With a bark he bounded forward eagerly. I dug my heels into my mount and we followed.

We raced down the trails at a furious pace, avoiding low-hanging branches and brambles on either side. Ahead of me, the trail opened into the clearing I had seen so many times in my dreams. Several short men clustered in a circle, and with a start, realized they were standing around a glass coffin. I slid to a stop and walked my horse forward, hand resting automatically on my sword hilt. The leader of the dwarves scuttled to my side, bowing and polishing his glasses on his beard, his eyes downcast, face grave.

"You came too late, my Prince," he proclaimed sadly, and his shoulders slumped with grief. "Snow White is dead."

*   *   *

I was born with the expectations of others to be the perfect prince. And, blessed with good looks, intelligence and charm from an early age, I was the Kingdom's pride and joy. I was given everything I could ever want, from a solid gold cradle to my first pony and hunting dog. I was the crown prince, of course; nothing was too good for me.

When I was old enough to leave the nursery, my father had me sent to the best tutors in the land. I was able to excel easily, and when my parents were entertaining royal guests, I was brought out like a trained dog to show what I had learned in my lessons, winning them over with my precociousness.

I never saw my parents when there were no royal ambassadors or kings or dukes to amuse. I was raised by an endless supply of nurses and maids who cooed and coddled me day and night. I played alone in the royal gardens, surrounded by royal guards.

I was seven when I discovered I could slip out of my room and explore the moonlit corridors unfettered by tiresome attendants with their "your highnesses" and "sires." Alone in the darkened halls, I was simply "Charming," a boy who liked making friends with the palace cats. I soon learned every nook and cranny, and discovered hiding places behind many of the tapestries. I grew bolder, and trained myself to eavesdrop on those who thought no one was watching.

I saw servants stealing from the pantries; lords and ladies sneaking into different beds on a whim; my father, the king, snoozing away in the cellars with his favorite page.

The web of intricate secrets was vast, but so was my curiosity. The rest of the secrets traveled as gossip on the tongues of servants or behind the hands of the court. Every single one of the court was a primped, painted doll, a parasite feeding off the misery of each other, betraying each other with a smile. As a member of the court, it was a constant fight for favor, the nighttime supposed to be their release.

During one of my nighttime prowls I discovered a book of witchcraft hidden on a top shelf, something that had been overlooked during the Inquisition. From that night on I sneaked back to the library to read it, looking over the pages. I couldn't read the Latin writing just yet, but I hoped to find someone who could, who could teach me.

This all changed when the Princess Mela came to court. I was fourteen years old.

*   *   *

"Charming," said my father, "allow me to introduce our royal guest, the Princess Mela of Mercia. She and her court will be staying with us for a while. Please make her welcome."

The first thing I saw was a pair of dark eyes staring at me from under a wave of coal-black hair. My knees knocked and I reached my hand out to take her gloved one, pressing my lips to her fingers as I managed to say, "Pleased to meet you."

"Charmed, I'm sure," came the reply, and I caught a quick glimpse of a smile on her pale face. For once, I had no response. My stomach had turned into a host of butterflies, fluttering against my ribcage. I was still speechless as she swept out of the hall on the arms of her escorts, and I decided I needed to learn more about her.

That night as I prowled the darkened halls, avoiding the guards on patrol, I eavesdropped on some of the maids chatting away in the kitchens with the newcomers.

"Oh the princess seems to be a fine young thing," said the cook, and I heard her crunching on a pilfered pastry. "So it's true she's to be married to King Hiram?"

"Her father needs money more then he needs a daughter. Especially since the drought," said another. "Been planning it for years, he has, was only waiting for King Hiram to come back from the war," she finished sadly. The woman speaking appeared to be far more attached to her charge than mine ever were. Perhaps because her father could only afford one to take care of her.

"Pity the prince isn't of age; those two would make a nice couple."

I pricked up my ears in interest.

"Never seen a young boy so besotted," another chuckled.

"You don't know our prince," argued the cook. "Give him a few years, he'll be as bad as his father."

"Perhaps not, he seems like a quiet young thing."

"He's a snob, that's what he is," retorted the cook. "He never liked my food as a child, was always sending it back."

"Oh hush up, Cookie, no one likes your food." There was a burst of giggles from the others and the sound of something being thrown—most likely a rag.

I crept away, but froze at the sound of heavy guard boots in the hallway. I dove behind a hanging tapestry on the left wall just as the boots came around the corner. I flattened myself against the wall. The boots stopped, and I prayed no one had noticed the tapestry swaying ever so slightly, though there was no breeze.

"Do you see her?" one asked, and there was a rumble of noes from the palace guards.

"Keep looking; she hasn't been gone long," said another.

The boots moved on, echoes fading away into the distance, and I breathed a sigh of relief. Someone sneezed.

I would have jumped and yelled loud enough to wake the whole castle, but suddenly a firm hand clamped around my mouth. I twisted, trying to see who was there. But only empty darkness surrounded me. I could feel the warm hand and fingers on my lips, but there was no shape suggesting a person next to me. I was somehow alone.

"Be quiet!" hissed a voice in my ear. "You'll alert the guards." I stopped trying to scream, and the hand relaxed slightly. "I'm going to remove my hand now. Don't scream and stay where you are for the count of ten. Promise?"

I nodded and the hand was gone. Instantly I spun around, straining my eyes in the darkness, but there was no one there. I reached my hands out, feeling the stone wall next to me, but found nothing. "Whoever you are, show yourself!" I whispered loudly.

There was no response, only the tapestry rustling in some slight breeze. I explored the whole area a second time, but again all I found was solid rock wall. Someone had been there; I knew it. Perhaps the person the guards were looking for? Whoever it was knew how to be invisible. Perhaps he or she could teach me. I promised myself I would find out.

I had a hard time dragging myself out of bed the next morning. During breakfast I yawned and almost knocked my goblet over with my elbow, much to the dismay of my parents, who were buttering the princess with compliments.

"I have heard King Hiram's kingdom is especially beautiful this time of year," said my father, putting his hand on hers for much too long. For a second a look of disgust crossed her pretty face. But then the moment passed and she smiled back at my father. He still hadn't removed his hand as a slight ring of crimson wreathed his goblet for a second before winking out. I rubbed my eyes. My father took his hand away and reached for his drink. Without warning it slipped through his fingers as if it had been made of soap. It splashed over his favorite doublet, staining the cloth with purple. Either my lack of sleep was affecting me, or Mela had enchanted the goblet to fall out of his hands.

A week passed, but though I kept careful watch, nothing else unusual happened. One night I was poring over my book again when I saw a white shape flitting outside in the garden. Using utmost care I slipped out the window, landing softly in the dewy grass. The shape was kneeling beside one of the fountains, and for a second I thought my eyes were playing tricks on me again.

"Princess Mela?" I asked, and the figure spun around, startled. It was indeed the princess, hair loose about her shoulders, wearing a white nightgown. A pair of breeches peeked out from under the lacy skirt, covered in grass stains. She looked like a frightened doe for a second.

"My Prince Charming," she said, clutching a small pot in her hand, and she curtsied deeply. "To what do I owe this honor?"

"Why are you not surrounded by your guards?" I blurted, and she came forward, indicating the pot in her hand.

"I prefer to be alone sometimes. Besides, I was merely watering my apple seedlings. They're from my prize tree back home."

She smiled at me, and my heart fluttered in response.

"We'll keep this our secret, won't we?" she asked sweetly.

She was so close at that point, dark eyes looking at me from her pale face. I felt her small hand on my shoulder, and her lips gently brushed my cheek. Then she was gone, out the garden gate. I stood in the garden for a long time before I was able to go back to my room.

*   *   *

I had a hard time sleeping again that night. It was even more difficult to drag myself out of bed and go about my morning routine. I sat on my chamber pot for longer than necessary, headache pounding my temples and visions of Princess Mela in her nightgown dancing before my eyelids.

Standing outside as part of his routine, my favorite manservant Henwas called through the door.

"Is everything all right, Sire?" he asked anxiously. "You are in there for quite some time."

"I am well, Henwas. Proceed with your other duties."

"Yes, Sire. Forgive me, Sire. It was not my place to ask."

I exited the bathroom, and he held out a small bowl of water. I rinsed my hands, and he handed me a towel and a small sheet of parchment.

"Excuse me, my Prince. This was to be delivered to you."

I took them from him, and he went to the wardrobe to bring me my clothes. The parchment was of the best quality, and I knew whom it was from before I even opened it. Heart beating, I read:

Charming. Meet me again, same time, same place. M

That day was a wretched blur for me. It dragged on and on as I waited for nightfall. During the banquet my father was holding for our guests, I accidentally upset my drink on the duchess sitting next to me.

*   *   *

The wine splashed over her ample bosom when she shrieked loudly enough to shake the rafters. Several lords leapt to their feet to eagerly hand her their napkins and assist her. From his spot at the head of the table, my father glared at me over the hubbub. I excused myself and left the dining room, hoping to catch some sleep before meeting the princess. Preparing my bed as I walked in, the maids looked up in alarm when I ordered them loudly out of the room. I flopped down on my bed, but sleep did not come to me.

No moon shined in the garden that night. A cloud cover hung over the sky, obscuring the stars, leaving it pitch black. I brought a candle and carefully hid it under my cloak, giving myself enough light to see, but not enough to alert the guards of my presence.

The Princess was waiting for me by the fountain, as promised. She wore a wool cloak over her nightgown, and I glimpsed her breeches poking out from under her skirt. A tender shoot had its head peeping out of the pot in her hands. She was watering it gently, sprinkling the dark soil with the drops, nurturing it like my nurses used to feed me. She stood as I approached, and curtsied deeply, every inch her title despite her attire.

"You came," she said warmly, and I bowed to her.

"As did you." I wanted so desperately to impress her. "Perhaps you would like to accompany me to the library?"

"I might. Has his highness something there in particular to show me?" Mela's eyes twinkled with amusement. I held out my arm to her and she took it.

"I would prefer to keep it a surprise, Princess." She laughed quietly as I escorted her away, keeping an eye out for the palace guards. We made it to the library without mishap, and I led her to the bookshelf.

"Up we go," I said cheerfully. Mela looked at me as if I had gone mad. "I'll get it by myself then," I amended. I was up and down in a second, landing with the heavy book under one arm. I presented it to her carefully. She examined it, though without much interest.

"It's a book of magic. I thought you would like it."

"And pray, why is that, my prince?" she asked, looking at me with a certain level of coldness in her eyes. Coldness that I wasn't sure I liked.

"Because you know how to use magic. I was hoping you could teach me."

"I? Practice magic? Do I look like I am the sort to consort with the devil?" she asked indignantly. I opened my mouth to explain, but Mela shoved the book back at me, almost toppling me over.

"Good night, your highness," she said haughtily, marching for the exit. This was not how our meeting was supposed to go. I chased after her.

"Wait!" I said, planting myself in front of her. "I know you were hiding behind the tapestry that night, and you also enchanted my father's goblet."

Her eyes narrowed dangerously. "I did no such thing."

"I can bring it before my father. You could be tried for witchcraft, Princess Mela."

The princess gripped my arm in her other hand, and a spark of crimson skipped between us, vanishing into my skin without a trace. "If you tell my secret to anyone, I swear to make your blood boil until you die."

She yanked her hand away and marched off, her head held high. I ran after her, hoping I couldn't be seen in my foolish dash.

"No, wait please!" I pleaded. I got in front of her again, blocking her progress. "All my life I knew I was meant for better things than just filling my duty as crown prince." She tried to go around me but I blocked her. "Teach me!" I begged, and she stopped.

Her eyes studied me as if I had suddenly sprouted a second, less attractive head out of my chest. "I beg your pardon?"

"Teach me your magic," I clarified. "I want to learn how to do everything, I want to—"

"No," she said firmly, walking around me and heading for the library door.

Desperately I followed. Something in me wanted this more than I had desired anything in my whole life. And she was the only one who could teach me. I planted myself in front her for the third time, impulsively and rashly giving her the most valuable offering I had at my disposal.

"Princess Mela of Mercia," I said as formally as I could under the circumstances. "I, Prince Charming, Crown Prince of Bavaria, do swear to you by the powers that bind your secret to my lips, that should you consent to teach me your magic craft, upon the time I am coronated as king, I will ally myself with you and your kingdom in peace and in war as long as I live," I finished breathlessly, waiting. Mela looked back at me, considering, then tried to move around me again. I added hastily, "I also grant you, as well, one request in which you can have anything you desire—as soon as I am coronated king."

There was a moment of silence after my last speech, and she studied me again.

"I will consider your proposition," she said finally. "Await my word."

With that, she swept by me, out of the library, and was gone.

I wasn't able to sleep that night, nor the night after that, nor the night after that. I lay awake, hoping to hear a knock at the door, or find a message of some sort slipped through the window, but there was nothing.

Finally on the fourth night, I found myself drifting off into a dreamless sleep. I was awakened before dawn by a crow cawing outside my window, before I fell asleep again. I woke up much later to find a small piece of rolled parchment on my pillow. The message merely read: "I accept."

*   *   *

It would be too dangerous to meet out in the open where there would be chances to get caught. Instead I showed her an unused room in the dungeons that the hangman used to stay in before executions. I began learning some of the herbs she brought with her: henbane, mandrake, angelica root; and then those that did not come from this area, but were preserved and taken from her homeland: damiana, mullein, mugwart, and bay leaves— among many more. Her mother had been a sorceress before her, and she had taught Mela everything in secret before she died. Mela taught me how each could be used, making potions from the henbane and mandrake, or burning the seeds of the bay leaves. She showed me how to scry, first using an obsidian bowl full of water, then a mirror her mother had given her. It was difficult, in the beginning, to relax to try and see the image she had asked me to. There were very few mirrors in the castle, and none of the size we could use, so I used my hunting dagger as a reflection until I could get the blacksmith to make a small one for me that could fit in my hand.

There were nights when we were unable to meet, but we used our mirrors to talk to each other after everyone had fallen asleep. I also used it to spy on the castle. Now that it was nearing the end of the fall months, fires were being lit to warm the castle, and Mela taught me how to scry using fire as my peephole. I had caught glimpses into the secrets of others before, but now, as long as there was a fire or a candle flame or a mirror or a drop of water, I could be anywhere. In the reflection of a golden goblet, I saw my father's most trusted steward slipping a few coins into his purse from the royal treasury. A puddle beside the stable showed the royal horse trainer beating his young apprentice. A maid cried herself to sleep after one of the guards defiled her by the light of a candle.

I also saw the princess's court would be moving on before the winter months blocked the roads with heavy snow. I began to panic, for once she was gone, there would be no more midnight magic lessons, no more adventures together. With so little time, I voiced an idea that night to Mela about a project I had been thinking about.

"I watch the mirror every day," I began, mentally running over my speech. "I see countless acts of cruelty or transgression all around the palace."

"No person can be as morally strong as you, Charming," the princess said absently, stirring a new concoction, eyes on the recipe in the book before her. "Do not concentrate on the wrongdoings of others; look at some of their virtues."

"There are none!" I burst out. "This whole castle is a stinking hell pit. I have watched them my whole life; no one does anything but lie and steal and push others aside to get what they want."

"And you, Charming," she snapped at me, taking her eyes off the potion, "are the worst of them all. While you complain about the evils of others, you do not seem to realize I am to be married to an old man I have never met before, in order to fulfill my duty to my father. Curses!" she said suddenly, as the potion in front of her suddenly sent up a burst of sparks and began to smoke. I ran to open the small window to clear out the smoke, but I did not give up the subject of our conversation. I wanted to create the perfect human, one without any inclinations of evil, something well out of my experience level by far, which was why I needed her help. She refused.

"If I were to help you create an artificial human, we would need samples of your skin and hair as part of the process. You would be linked to this creature for the rest of your life."

"I understand." I said.

"Do you?" She locked eyes with me. "You would be creating a living, breathing person. What happens if it gets out and everyone sees it? They could find out what we do, and we, my Prince, would be burned at the stake for associating with witchcraft, and not even your father could save you."

That idea had not occurred to me, but I pressed on, determined.

"We could have it live here, in this room," I pointed out. "Have it clean up and help prepare potions."

She laughed, though it was not a cheerful one. "Missing having your servants around, are you, Prince? Very well, I will help you. But you must promise that you will do whatever I say for the spell-casting."

"I promise," I said eagerly, and she smiled at me, this time with more affection.

And that was how we created Dunce, our first creation. Made from my flesh, he looked strange stumping around the room, for we shared the same color hair and build. Dunce was more of an adult child, and wasn't much help with the potions, though he managed to learn to sweep up after us. So after several long discussions with the princess, we created another, and another and another, until we had seven little homunculi shambling around our dungeon room. Smaller than normal humans, they had long beards, and each possessed different characteristics of perfection and imperfection. They were my children, and I loved them like a father.

Sharp had a special place in my heart, though. He was the last of my creations, and had the most intelligence of all of his brothers put together. I made him the leader and taught him what to do when Mela and I were gone for the day: how to put out a fire if someone accidentally started one, even a silencing and invisibility spell so they could hide if someone checked the room. Morpheus was always dozing away on his blanket bed, but he would wake up when hungry, so I made him in charge of cooking for them all. Blithe was the princess's favorite. He was always cheerful and obedient, and unlike me, he didn't grumble and complain about chopping up herbs and roots for potions.

Princess Mela was experimenting more and more these days. She had taught me the basics and explained the rules of magic; now it was up to me to explore the books and learn what I was interested in and where my focus would lie.

I looked up from my books to see Vex, the second youngest homunculus, grumbling as he helped Morpheus cook a small cauldron of porridge for dinner. He'd burned his finger trying to taste some of the porridge while Morpheus was snoozing in his chair. Vex had come into creation cranky, but at least he was a valuable second-in-command. He kept his brothers in order, mostly because they were all slightly apprehensive of him and his various curses he seemed to be born with, and the constant scowl etched on his face.

Unexpectedly, the pot boiled over, hissing as it landed in the fire. Some porridge also scalded Vex's hand. He swore loudly, his cursing awakening Morpheus with a start, who tried to pull the pot off the fire but only managed to burn his hands, as well, in the process. I was laughing so hard during the confusion, Mela had to retrieve the pot herself, wrapping her skirt around her hand to protect it first. She then had Blithe bring over some salves to put on their blistered hands.

"You boys are worse than children," she scolded, and they shuffled their feet and looked at the ground in embarrassment. Mela turned around to reprimand me.

"And you, Charming, for shame! I had to do the work while you stood and laughed like a madman. Where are your manners?" Chastened, I bowed meekly.

"My apologies, Mela."

"Much better," she snapped, returning to her work with vigor.

She never told me what she was working on, and for the most part every time I asked, I only got vague mutterings about it being a secret, or to go back to my own experiments. Our homunculi began to know to hide in a corner when one of us raised a voice. And with good reason, too. A week before, Mela, in a fit of anger, threw a pot, Dunce's shoe, and a partially dissected frog at me. The amphibian had sailed over my head and landed on Runt, one of the sickliest brothers. Runt was always catching one cold or another, so he spent most of his time wrapped in blankets, sneezing into a handful of handkerchiefs. After having frog guts land on his balding head, however, Runt wore a pot as a helmet for protection.

Dawn was approaching when I finally crawled into bed. The hot coals in my bed warmer had long since cooled, and I shivered under my heavy blankets. There was a tap at the entrance to my balcony, so I crawled back out of bed, yawning, wrapping a fur blanket around my shoulders as I opened the door to the outside. A chilly breeze brushed my face, but I couldn't see what had made the noise. A smile crept onto my face. Without turning around, I asked, "Isn't it a bit late for a visit, Mela?"

"Close the door, Charming! The wind is freezing!"

I closed the door and turned around. Mela sat on the edge of the bed, her cloak wrapped around her.

"How did you get up here?" I asked, and Mela held out her cloak. A few scraggly feathers were clinging there.

"I flew," she said simply. I assumed it was one of the new spells she was working on.

"Why are you here, Mela?" I asked, sitting beside her; and she smiled excitedly up at me. I felt as if we had never quarreled at all.

"I've found a way to get out of the marriage and still obey my father's wishes!"

"How?" I asked, and she leaned so close I could feel her warm breath on my face.

"We're going to create a copy of me to send in my place."

The statement would have staggered me if I had been standing.

"Have you lost your reason?" I asked incredulously, "Everyone will suspect it, and we will be burned at the stake like you said!"

"No, we won't," Mela said confidently, grasping my hand in hers. "I've been studying our homunculi for weeks now, reviewing the spells. The key is to not just use skin and hair samples from the sire, but also blood. Have you ever wondered how Sharp was so much more intelligent? You cut your finger when you were preparing the herbs. The single drop made him better than the others."

"Mela, even if we were able to create a more intelligent homunculus, it still wouldn't be your exact copy."

She leaned closer to me then, so close her dark eyes seemed to fill my field of vision. Her lips were barely a hair away from mine, her nose brushing mine lightly. Part of me knew this was her ploy to get me to agree; the rest of me couldn't care in the slightest. If Mela had wanted me to leap off the ends of the Earth at that moment, I would have done so.

"Please say you will help me, Charming," she whispered. "Think of the things we can attain if I stay . . . here . . . forever . . ." I felt my head nodding in agreement, and she smiled back, her lips gently brushing mine for a second.

"You are the most beautiful thing in the world," I whispered as she stood up and went to the door.

"Thank you, my Prince."

The door shut behind her, leaving only a cool breeze and her lingering scent as a memory in its wake.

*   *   *

Upon entering the dungeon that night I was surprised by the saccharine sickly smell emanating from the room. Mela was busy mixing a bowl by the fire, a cloth tied around her nose and mouth, no doubt to breathe less of the odor. I followed her lead and tied my handkerchief to my face, as well. Glancing in the bowl I saw a mix of mashed mandrake and earth, most likely from the garden. Placing the bowl on the table she gestured for me to hand her a small earthenware bowl of gooey white fluid that seemed to be the reason for the smell.

"What is this?" I asked through my mask.

"Copulus interruptus," she answered, a slight color rising in her cheeks. Mela grabbed a second cup that seemed to be partially full of blood. I glanced at her wrist and saw a small bandage. It was her blood.

"I need you to take another sample of blood," she told me, holding out the small dagger she kept by her side. I took the dagger, preparing to make a slight cut on my wrist. She stopped me.

"No, from *me*. I need you to take some heart's blood. I was afraid to do it myself."

She stood before me, opening her bodice enough for me to see her white flesh underneath. It was hard to breathe as I carefully cut into her pale skin, and a drop of blood welled up like a brilliant ruby. I caught the drop in a glass vial and held it out to her. Mela took the vial and added it to the bowl. The mixture began to froth on its own. Dropping in some of her hairs, she quickly took a brush and dabbed the bubbling potion on a clay doll lying ready on the table. This was the humanoid shape we needed the homunculus to become; once the spell took form the doll would grow, hopefully to normal size. Mela grabbed my hand and began speaking the enchantment to bind the creature to her specifications. We had done this ritual many times before; there was no need to worry about anything happening—except something did happen. In the middle of the spell Mela let out a piercing scream. She collapsed onto the floor, writhing in pain. The spell couldn't be stopped now; I had to finish it myself. Grasping Mela's hand in mine, I continued the speech, Latin words feeling heavy on my tongue. On the table, there was a bang of noise, and the sound of a gale in my ears. My other creations huddled in the corner, howling in fear. The room shook as if being held in a giant's hand.

And then, it was gone. The shaking stopped and the noise cleared. Mela lay unconscious on the floor. I let go of her hand and looked at the table. The sight there took my breath away. A child of about seven lay sleeping peacefully on the table, her skin white as snow, hair as black as ebony, lips as red as blood.

I motioned to Sharp and Vex to carry Mela over to their blanket beds, and began to examine the female homunculus carefully. Mela had been right; the added blood seemed to have made a big improvement. Compared to our former creations, who were all somewhat disproportionate, this one looked very human. If I hadn't known better, this girl could have passed for Mela's younger sister. Perhaps if we found an aging potion, there would be a chance we could fool the couriers with this double.

Crossing over to our stack of spell books, I began rifling through them.

"Get off me, you filthy creatures!"

I glanced toward the table, but to my surprise, the girl was still sleeping. Mela struggled up from the blanket beds, striking out at homunculi as they milled around in confusion and fear. Mela pointed an indignant finger at me, her face twisted in fury.

"You! How dare you let me be touched by these monsters!"

She slapped Blithe, who cringed and whimpered, taking refuge in a corner away from his beloved mistress. Something was wrong. She was acting like a completely different person, and I had no idea why. Mela stopped suddenly, wincing and clutching her chest.

"That . . . thing has my heart," she declared venomously. Unsheathing her weapon she moved toward the table, dagger in hand.

I moved to block her path, and she lashed out at me with the dagger. I ducked and grabbed her wrist, forcing it out of her hand. She kicked and scratched me, raving like a madwoman. In the middle of the commotion the girl woke up, sitting up on the table. She saw Mela lunging at her, teeth bared like a wild animal, and screamed.

Mela twisted in my grip, ramming a sharp elbow in my stomach. I maintained a tight grip on her, though I was slightly out of breath.

"She doesn't have your heart," I wheezed as she tried to claw out my eyes. "It's where it should be, in your—" I paused, my hand on her bodice. I could feel no heartbeat. Her free hand came up and slapped my face, cutting me with her signet-ring. I felt a warm trickle of blood roll down my check. I caught her as she tried to lunge around me, and forced her onto her knees.

"How dare you treat me like this!" she screeched. "You—" I ignored the rest of it, concentrating on holding her with one hand, searching for a heartbeat with the other. Again, there was nothing.

I remembered how once I had examined Sharp. He had no heartbeat, either, being a creation of clay and spells. But this did not seem possible. Had the spell gone so wrong as to transfer a living organ from one vessel into another?

"Let me go!" Mela shrieked. "I will kill it! I will rip my heart out of that creature's chest with my hands, if I have to!"

I needed time to figure out a solution, but Mela wasn't giving me the opportunity. Hoping she would forgive me later, I spoke a spell to put her to sleep. Instantly Mela became limp in my arms. Carefully, I laid her on the floor and stood up, catching my breath. I turned and my eyes locked with the girl. She was trembling, holding her bare legs up to her chest. She was as naked as a newborn, her long hair like a shining cloak down her back.

"Please don't let her kill me," were her first words. I handed her one of my spare shirts to clothe herself. I felt more love and pride toward her than I had felt for any of my other creations. There was no way I would let Mela kill her. But did Mela's heart make her human? Reassuring her I would not harm her, I gently put my hand to her chest, and felt the anxious thump of her heartbeat.

Dunce shuffled over from his hiding place, sniffing curiously at the girl's hand. Delighted, she held it out to him, giggling as his beard tickled her fingers. The other six followed suit cautiously, until they were ringed around her, staring at the new arrival curiously, with a hint of awe.

To the girl's credit, she didn't seem frightened or repulsed by them, but perhaps that was part of the innocence of just being created. She simply didn't know any better. An idea began to blossom.

I pulled out my scrying mirror and began to scour the countryside. Finally, I found a place. Over the Seven Mountain Range, I found an abandoned hunter's cottage hidden away where hopefully Mela couldn't find them.

Gathering my creations around me, I knelt before Sharp. Taking his hand, I made a few marks on his palm with a piece of charcoal. The spells flared slightly for a second, and then sank into his skin like water into the ground. It was a simple location spell; it would guide him and the others to the hunter's cabin safely. The road would be clear this time of year, but just in case I covered them each in an illusion cloak. To anyone who passed them by, they would be a party of simple merchants, traveling on the road. I looked Sharp in the eye and gave him my instructions. He was to keep his brothers and the girl in the cabin where they would be safe. I would watch and keep an eye out for them with my mirror, but she would be able to track my magic if I tried anything else; so it was his job was to keep them all from Mela's wrath.

The girl stood in the middle of the commotion, looking around in bewilderment. I knelt before her in order to see more eye to eye.

"Stay with your brothers; you'll be safe," I told her.

"Will the mean lady be able to find me?"

"Not if you stay with them and be careful," I promised. "Listen to the brothers; they will protect you. And make sure Morpheus doesn't burn the food," I added. She nodded solemnly.

Casting an invisibility spell, I led them out of the sleeping castle to the main gate. Watching them go, I felt a pang of remorse tear at my heart.

"I will come back for you one day," I swore. Then I left, returning to the dungeon room. I needed only one look around to tell me the princess was gone. The sleeping spell had worn off. It was daylight as I exited the dungeons. Sneaking back into the castle, I heard the news. Soon after the earthquake, the princess and her court had departed. Apparently the princess had been very afraid of the ground shaking, and urged them all to leave without a moment's notice.

A week passed, and a messenger brought us the news that Princess Mela was now Queen, married to King Hiram. A month passed, and then a year. King Hiram had died and Queen Mela was in charge of the kingdom, wielding her power with a strong arm.

I myself had just turned fifteen and my father had started to groom me as the future king, sending me on ambassador trips throughout the kingdom in order that I might meet the people. At every house I visited, crops were suddenly twice as abundant and the livestock just as prosperous. No one could explain it, but everyone rejoiced at harvest time.

A year before my twenty-first birthday and coronation, I was supposed to be studying, but I managed to sneak down to the dungeons to check my scrying mirror. The homunculi—or dwarves, as they called themselves now—had named their charge Snow White. At thirteen, she was just as beautiful as Mela had been, and I found myself sneaking down to watch her in the mirror more and more. At night, I dreamed of her in the clearing, waiting for me to come back for her.

One day, as I snuck down to look in the mirror, I was surprised that Snow White was nowhere in sight. I called up images of the garden, where she had been helping grow food for winter; her bedroom, where she mended the dwarves' clothes; the kitchen, where she spent hours cooking. I found nothing.

The image before me rippled, and suddenly Mela's face filled the glass. I was surprised by how little she resembled the Mela from my memories. This queen was older, her face was lined, and she wore luxurious, heavy raiment, a delicate crown encrusted with jewels circling her brow. Her eyes were no longer a soft gentle brown, but rather a cold black.

"Hello, Charming. And how is your little princess today?"

"What have you done with her?" I demanded.

"I? Not a thing. Yet." She smiled a nasty smile, taunting me. "I thought I would just pop down there and see how my darling little Snow White was doing. Maybe . . . I don't know, get my heart back? Or I could just kill her outright. I haven't made up my mind yet."

"If you lay one finger on her—"

"So *touchy*, my dear Charming! Is that any way to speak to a lady? Well, as I was saying, before I was *rudely* interrupted, I'm going to go down to visit, but it'll probably take me three days or so to get there. If you can get there first . . . I'll spare her life and never go near her again. Do we have a deal?"

I slammed the scrying mirror down on the table, cracking it. I needed to get to the clearing.

I grabbed a bag filled with basic ingredients for potions and exited the dungeons, leaving my mirror on the table as she continued to laugh. Once I reached the surface, I called for a sack of supplies, a strong horse, and my favorite hunting dog. And then we were gone, down the road in a whirlwind of dust, while everyone stared after us in bafflement. Two days down the road, I ran into a hunched old woman selling apples, who directed me to the forest in the distance.

*   *   *

I slid off my horse, staring at Sharp, who hunched himself over, making himself smaller. Striding through the dwarves I looked into the coffin. Snow White lay there, eyes closed as if asleep, though what the queen had done to her I had no idea.

"We found this by her side," said Vex. He held out an apple to me, a single bite in its crimson flesh. My mind went back to the apple seller I had seen on the road and cursed myself for letting Mela slip through my fingers so easily. She had gotten here first, and I had to save Snow White in order to win this battle.

Placing my fingers on Snow White's neck, I felt the slight fluttering of a pulse. She was still alive, but barely.

Sharp shuffled his feet in guilt.

"We only left her for a couple minutes, my Prince." He blew his nose in a handkerchief and could not continue.

"Snow White was making a special dinner, see. She always has a special celebration around this time because it's when she was first made," Vex continued. "She sent us all out for different things she needed for the dinner. She was so excited about it, we forgot to leave someone behind to watch her." Vex's grumpy face softened for a moment, a slight smile twitching in the corner of his mouth. "We could never refuse our little sister anything."

The other dwarves set up a trumpet of nose blowing, those who didn't have hankies using articles of clothing or their beards as substitute. I tried to concentrate, and leaned over the coffin, searching for a clue to Snow White's sleep. I picked up the apple and examined it from every angle. It seemed like a normal apple; I could not find any coating of poison on it. I smelled it. There was the smell of apple, but something else that made me feel slightly dizzy. I coughed to get the smell out, and suddenly realized what it was.

"Bring me some Chollas mushrooms. You'll find them in the forest by the larger trees. Make sure to bring the roots." The dwarves scattered at once, running toward the forest as fast as they could. I doubted most would know what that fungus actually looked like, but I trusted Vex and Sharp at least to know. My predictions proved correct. They all came hurrying back, some proudly carrying colorful leaves and flowers, which I had them place around the coffin. Sharp and Vex handed me two Chollas mushrooms each, the short roots very much intact.

Going into the cabin, I laid them on the wood table with a mortar and pestle from my bag. Carefully cutting off the roots, I began to gently mash them until I had a fine paste at the bottom of the bowl. Mela had soaked the apple skin in a potion made from the spores of the mushroom. It was a painless poison that attacked the nervous system as the victim fell into a deeper sleep. My only chance was to give Snow White the roots as an antidote before it was too late. If Mela had given her the poison almost a day ago, I had barely a few hours left to save Snow White. Carefully heating the paste, I turned it into a fine powder. Rummaging in my bag, I found a wooden tube and shallow bowl. Running back outside I instructed Sharp to hold Snow White's mouth open long enough for me to get the tube in. Carefully pouring the powder from the bowl into the tube, I blew it as hard as I could down her throat.

The effect was instantaneous. Snow White sat up fast, coughing from the powder in her lungs. Then she slumped down again, exhausted from the effort. Pushing aside the dwarves crowding around the coffin in excitement, I leaned down to tenderly kiss Snow White on the lips. Her eyes fluttered open and she smiled up at me.

"You came," she whispered.

*   *   *

There was much surprise when I came back to court, announcing Snow White to be my bride. The queen would stop at nothing to hurt us now, but at least I could protect Snow White while she lived with me in the palace. We were married a month later.

My coronation was coming up, and Snow White had delivered to us a beautiful baby girl.

She was the most beautiful little baby in the whole world. I was always getting in the way of the nurses and asking to hold her one more time. On the day of the coronation, I had her on my lap as I read over my final speech when there was a knock at the door. It was a servant, announcing loudly that a guest wished to see me in the sitting room. I was about to dismiss the request when the servant placed something on the table; a gift from my mysterious visitor. It was a fresh red apple.

I walked into the sitting room.

"Mela," I said. "To what do I owe the visit?"

"I'm here to collect on a promise you made, my Prince."

My mind flashed back to the night in the library so many years ago.

"You can't have Snow White."

"Who said anything about Snow White? I want your daughter."

She smiled at me, a wolf eyeing its prey. My heart raced in panic and I put my hand on the scabbard of my sword.

"I'd rather die than let you take her."

"So you have decided to go back on our deal?"

There was an explosion of pain in my body, and I was left gasping, clutching at a table for support as spots danced in front of my eyes. My knees almost buckled, and suddenly Mela was in front of me, holding me up effortlessly by the front of my royal robes.

"Feel that, my Prince?" she hissed. "That's just a sample. If you don't give me what I want, I will make the blood of every third child here boil; and there is nothing you can do to stop me. And then, I will link you directly to the tragedy so your father will have no choice but to burn you at the stake. Think of the suffering you will indirectly cause. The lives of a third of the children in this kingdom, gone. Unless . . . you honor your oath and give me your child. You have nothing to fear, my Prince. I swear, I will love her as if she were my own child. You have my word. Choose, Charming. Your child versus the kingdom."

With sinking heart I called the guards to bring me the nursemaids who were looking after my baby. I handed her over, tears running down my cheeks. The bundle stirred slightly, and a tiny pudgy hand waved in the air before disappearing in the blankets again.

"There." The queen smiled. "Now perhaps you will feel a fraction of the pain I felt the day you let someone take my heart." She started to walk out of the hall, carrying my precious bundle, then turned back. "Incidentally, what name did you give your daughter?"

I looked back at her, but my main focus was my last glimpse of my baby girl in her arms.

"Rapunzel." I said. "We named our daughter Rapunzel."

MACHETE

By Jill Clark
(Florida, USA)
Regional, 3rd Place

The town of Sarsaparilla, Florida, used to hound me for naming my dog Machete.

This half-Malamute, half-Siberian Husky prefers her name, though. And I know I am safer for using it.

"Bobby, remember to prop the back door open for The Knife Lady," Dave commanded me. "A little wider, too, than you did last week. I could have sworn I heard her growling as she squeezed her shoulder bags through."

"But Boss," I whined, "the flies flock in after her."

"What do we care? The flies don't go in the kitchen. Her food pouch keeps 'em too busy. And remember—have the leftovers ready for her," Dave insisted. "She prefers steaks for pay, not money—and the boss likes that, too. She likes her meat aged. And get her in and out as quick as possible—with our luck, she'll be here when the health department makes one of their surprise visits."

The Steak Out was known for miles around for their mouth-watering sirloins. Every Friday at noon, the restaurant's sharpened cutlery would be personally delivered through the back porch door. Our manager, Dave, finagled a deal to get our steak knives sharpened on a regular basis—and dirt-cheap. So once a week, a woman known to us only as "The Knife Lady" would rumble into our rear parking lot on a gold, tank-mounted Indian cycle. Fourteen years old at the time, my mind ran to motorcycles. Machete's previous owner claimed to possess the last Indian Chief produced in 1947.

The Knife Lady walked like a linebacker, and slung over each beefy shoulder draped a greasy rawhide pouch. From one pouch she proudly brandished our newly sharpened steak, pruning, and boning knives; in the other pouch, she'd bag the leftover steak scraps the manager tossed her for payment.

Regular as high noon, The Knife Lady screeched into our back lot in a flurry of hot smoke—sporting her usual dun-colored, oil-splotched shoulder bags. Not one for shaving, either, she paraded the longest, wiriest underarm beards I'd ever seen. Her sweaty pits reeked of stagnant pond scum—with gray frizzle contrasting the black-and-orange Halloween mop that matted her head.

That Friday I was in a rush setting tables when I accidentally bumped against one of our lady's grimy pouches. In that same instant, I caught a quick whiff of her sour, onion-scented Brillo pads. Staggering backwards, I tripped and hit the hardwood floor. Struggling to stand, I felt dizzy from the lingering odor of her Grecian Grays. Like Pinocchio free from his strings for the first time, I wobbled up only to get thrust forward by a swift back kick from The Knife Lady. I stumbled and plopped hard on my stomach. Her pouches flung wide as she spun around to face me. Arching my neck, I stared straight up, transfixed by her black-and-white viper-like eyes. I swallowed hard and was about to apologize when her sole two teeth suddenly flashed like daggers—and out from her knife pouch popped a miniature, hand-carved machete. She leaned down and glared into my watery eyes—blinding me with the glint of her flailing scythe.

"Do it again, Shortcakes," she garbled as spit globs slid pendulously from her toothless sneer to my gaping mouth, "and you won't need no haircut never 'gin—know what I *mean?* Don't nobody never get that close to my food pouch and live to tell it." My eyes swelled. A waterfall of sweat pooled beneath my chin. She paused. "But seein' you's such a young runt, maybe I'll letcha go this once—but next time, you're dog meat."

Surprised by my own quick thinking, I managed to eek out a high-pitched, "Cool tattoo!" Suddenly the underside of her left arm flexed with pride and came to life. She raised a forearm covered in steel blue snakes that gyrated toward a bulging bicep. As her other arm slowly lifted toward the ceiling, I found my eyes hypnotized by holographic snake skulls coiling up and down the insides of her arms. I gawked while ivory-colored cobras joined the reptilian dance and wove beguilingly back and forth. Still on the floor, teetering on my elbows with my neck craning up, I felt my body undulate in unison.

"For the love of Pete, boy," Dave bellowed from across the dining room, "what *are* you doing? You look like a rubber-necked chicken staring down an axe. Get up and get to work, *now!*"

I snapped out of my daze long enough to notice the kitchen staff equally drawn in by the bizarre spectacle. The butcher stood paralyzed, his meat cleaver dangling over a slab of prime rib. The baker's face burned beet red as he stared rigor-mortised before an open, steaming kiln. The enticing rhythm of a snake's head finally drew Dave in, too. Mesmerized, he stared at the skeleton of a three-dimensional cobra sleeking through a forest of ashen armpit grass.

The bang of the back screen door slamming shut jolted us back to reality. Two police officers darted into the room, one pointing a Colt automatic straight at the two of us.

"That's it, honey," the first officer shouted, "keep those powerful pits up, high as heaven. Go on, Jerry," he commanded the other officer, "get those bags off her shoulders quick—I'll cover you. Looks like we got here just in time, too. Get up, boy," the officer commanded me, "and ease away— real slow."

I slithered on my stomach toward the cops. I knew how foolish I must have looked, but I could not make myself stand. I remembered how fast she'd pulled that machete on me, and although I hadn't seen it since, I had not seen her put it away, either. I was relieved to have the attention drawn away from me when Jerry wailed, "I can't cuff her, Serge, she'll scalpel me like she done ol' Marv."

"You mean 'scalp,' you idiot, and Marvin was just dumb enough to frisk her." Serge glared at The Knife Lady and added, "Besides, her hands won't get anywhere near her bags, 'cuz if she tries anything I'll shoot 'em off. You might have a point there, though, Jerry—anyone got a shovel or hoe 'round here?"

"Long-handled spatula work?" Dave piped in, finally recovered from the tattoo show.

"Yep, that'll do—even better." Serge nodded. "We just need to flip them bags off her shoulders."

The Knife Lady suddenly jerked around to face Jerry—a vicious snarl meeting his shaky gaze.

Dave lifted the spatula from the wall hook and hurled it to Jerry. He caught the pole in midair with both hands. Jerry skulked toward the now blood-shot, angry-eyed demoness. In bullet speed, he stepped to her side and slid the handle along the back of her shoulder blades, easily hooking both pouches—then jerking them back and into the air. The food pouch plopped like a dead fish inches from my frozen face. I heard a guttural sound and stiffened. But to our surprise, a gamey, wet puppy rolled out. Pushing the sweaty heap with my hand, I scooted the whimpering pup forward as I wriggled toward Serge.

"That's my W-O-L-F—nobody takes my Wolf slab!" The Knife Lady blared. "She'll be good eatin' soon as she fattens. Bites every time she hears her name, too—back off! That's *my* grade-A prime."

At the mention of her name, the pale-eyed whelp lunged toward her master, sinking tiny, razor-sharp teeth into mottled gray-and-black leg hair. The Knife Lady howled and lifted her knee. With her arms still raised, the tattooed, respondent snake bones pulsated in kind. With a swift upper kick, the hanging pup flew from her owner's calf, gripping a jowl of grungy skin and grizzled fur. The baker, who was cradling a warm loaf of rye, looked startled at having caught the canine bundle.

"Ah, go ahead, kid," The Knife Lady jeered down at me, "you can have my Wolf—she might grow to good eatin' size with you—mongrel meat's more tender 'an sirloin. The spirited ones taste best."

"Your dog-eatin' days are over," Serge joined in. "Besides, you won't need to grow your own food where you're goin'. You'll be eatin' compliments of the state."

Nervous laughter shook the room as The Knife Lady sparred, "You mean your trigger-happy days are over." And with that, her machete appeared out of nowhere—spinning from her hand and sinking squarely into the center of Serge's palm. His gun hit the floor with a leaden thud. In lightening speed, he whipped a tablecloth off the nearest table and wrapped it around his bleeding hand.

With gun firmly in holster and spatula still in hand, Jerry stood dumbfounded—his mouth rounded like a singing choir boy's.

Worried about Serge, we momentarily forgot about The Knife Lady. Then, before our astonished eyes, a purplish vapor filled the room—and then vanished. Engulfed by her own coiling brood of swirling snakes, The Knife Lady seemed to have disappeared. Other than the faint stench of rancid meat—nothing of our lady remained.

Wild-eyed, we looked like madmen as we stared each other down in silence—afraid to say what we thought we saw but knew was impossible. Serge's blood-soaked cloth and the unmistakable presence of a now remarkably quiet puppy convinced us otherwise, though.

I guess Dave did not want bad publicity for the restaurant, nor did Serge want to miss his upcoming promotion. As for myself, besides working underage as a busboy, I did not want my slithering snake impersonation blasted as the feature story on the six o'clock news. So we decided to appear sane and report that even though The Knife Lady abandoned her motorcycle, she had escaped as clean as fine dust in a fog cloud. Her beautifully restored Indian relic now serves as an icon of historical Americana, too. The story of how this classic beauty became the centerpiece for the main dining room has grown as legendary as the steaks.

My eerie inauguration into the world of work ended Serge's days on the police force, too—at least as a street cop. But the captain did seem genuinely awed by Serge's hand cut—marveling that, in spite of the fact Serge was firmly holding his gun, The Knife Lady managed to hit her intended target. A desk job as acting captain to a new squad was more agreeable to Serge anyway. The long arm of the law never did stretch quite far enough for Serge. After all, he'd been pursuing The Knife Lady for over twenty years, but she always managed to hover just beyond his reach. Yes, Captain of the Sarsaparilla Canine Unit suited Serge just fine.

It took ten gallons of water and a grove of lemons to scrub that stink from Machete. Yep, I call my mighty mutt Machete because if anyone ever dares call her Wolf, she turns into a growling, slicing, meat-cleaving mongrel. Pedigrees are overrated.

The only time this loyal cur ever gave me a problem was on the anniversary of the disappearance of The Knife Lady. Going to work with me every day, Machete had become a bit of a mascot around the place. But that one night, she would not come when called.

The next afternoon, with dirt balls caked in her fur, Machete limped toward me. As she shambled up to the back door steps, blood dripped from her mouth. When I squatted down to take a closer look, Machete dropped a mass of wiry hair attached to a patch of dirty, blood-soaked skin. When I grabbed a stick to toss her grimy prize into the woods, something flew out.

I rushed over and among the brush I found what looked like a slippery, gooey eight ball.

I didn't tell anyone about the gruesome find for years. But after I did, the Sarsaparilla folks stopped nagging me about naming my dog Machete. And whenever they happened to pass in front of me, they'd lower their heads, say somethin' quick like, "Howdy, Master Machete," and with a wary step, trot on.

But the biggest favor Machete ever did me was when we'd pass by the Sarsaparilla street urchins. They'd stumble back in awe—raising a dusty halo around us—never daring to taunt me like in days past—never once offering me money to crawl on my belly like a reptile.

LONELIES

By Holly Riordan
(New York, USA)
Fantasy, 2nd Place

The needle dug through my skin, pulling a stretch of string with it. An artist weaved navy blue thread through my flesh until a star was designed—the symbol of the independent, the lost, the *lonelies*. The process was like receiving stitches, but left a type of tattoo. I had the same procedure done multiple times, since the result was temporary. After a few months, the thread would dissolve and I would go get the star redone.

Anyone with matching stitching was connected to me by an invisible (and visible) thread that tethered us together. But we never spoke—*what would we say?* We preferred being alone and hated talking about our past. All of the lonelies were children of criminals. We had parents who died from drug overdoses, were sentenced to life imprisonment, or abandoned us without a reason. My parents were drug dealers who murdered a client after he refused to pay. They were placed in prison five years ago, when I was twelve, and I visited them once or twice a year.

When the artist finished my star, I glanced down at it with a feeling of warmth and protection. There were billions of stars blanketing the sky, just as there were billions of people down on Earth. It looked crowded, but each one of us was alone. The thought used to scare me, but I learned to prefer it that way. No one else in my life meant that no one could let me down, betray me, or run off. I was free from pain.

The next week, the government collected anyone with a star design. *Collected.* Not even herded—we were treated worse than animals. We were property, dolls, puppets.

The lonelies who weren't ashamed to declare themselves as such were labeled dangerous. During a rising civil war, our state *needed* dangerous. There were hundreds of us, mostly teens with no future in sight. Why not murder the useless, the abandoned, and the unwanted? Our genes were tainted, after all.

"Lonelies have been called corrupt, diseased, a waste of oxygen," a man in uniform said once we were all gathered together. His jaw was as sharp as a razor, his eyes the color of ink. "You're prohibited from entering college because a degree would be pointless. No good man will hire you because immorality might run in the family."

He threw things at us that we already knew, but hated to hear. He was trying to get us to accept our fate as soldiers and feel honored that we even had permission to be part of the military. By the middle of his speech, I hated him more than the enemy.

"As you know, we are fighting bordering states for control of natural resources. You are the most dangerous weapons we have. Your guardians have lied and cheated. They've killed without mercy or regret. You wear those stars because you are proud of where you came from. Now put that pride to use."

He was expecting applause, but the room hummed with silence. He was just as clueless as the rest of our state. We wore our stars because we were proud of who we were *without* our parents. We were happy that we were able to take care of ourselves and live on our own. The majority of us had no contact with our families anymore. None of us wanted to be anything like them.

Still we were chained to our new beds that night to prevent escaping, and I might as well have been in jail along with them. We were prisoners.

Training began the next day at dawn. Our state thought they scrounged together the ideal collection of people, but they forgot crucial aspects. We hated to work in groups, we had no trust, and we were stubborn. Our army was bound to fail.

The officers started to realize their mistake when we refused to strap on our guns for target practice. Instead, we sat scattered on a stretch of grass while they hovered together, trying to figure out a peaceful solution.

"You know, maybe we should do what they say," a skinny man who looked around my age said. A large group of us glared in unison, causing him to explain in a whisper. "Listen, if we act like we're pledged to them, that we're fighting for them and eager to kill to protect them, they'll give us guns and release us for attack."

"But we can attack *them* instead," I finished. It made sense.

It would be impossible to escape during drills or while we were chained up in our bedrooms. We would have to cooperate, pretending to be loyal while we waited. Then we could turn our guns on them and demand to be freed—even demand our basic rights in society. Even lonelies without stars were unable to live in certain areas, go to college, or have high-paying jobs.

We could change that. We *would* change that.

For months, we trained. Working as a team was difficult, foreign. But in order for everything to work, hundreds of skeptical lonelies would have to trust one another. Doubt was a poison. At first, it hindered us, making it impossible for us to cooperate. It was clear that we could only trust one person at a time. That's when we learned we couldn't treat each other as different people—we were *one*.

The officer who spoke to us on the day we were collected led our troop to its first battle. We stood on the crest of a hill, between our state and the next, waiting for our orders to attack.

"This is it. The day you were born for," the officer said. His lips twisted like a serpent as he tried to hide his grin. "Fight to keep breathing. Not all of you will make it. You never know who is—"

A gunshot rang out and he dropped to the ground, blood gushing from his chest. One of the lonelies, the boy who planned the entire revolt, had lost self-control and shot him. Everyone hated the officers, but we never planned on actually killing any of them. We just wanted to threaten them for our freedom.

Now we would have to fight.

Our army turned around, heading back toward our state to go through with our plan. Citizens and officers were unaware of our intentions, but knew we were dangerous. They whipped out their guns, picked up their knives, and spilled onto the streets. We shot anyone armed. We had to. Otherwise, it would've been suicide.

We barreled through a dozen towns, staining them red. A trail of dead bodies followed us. The towns were surprised, unarmed, and outmatched. Gunshots and screams surrounded me and helicopters flew above. Speakers blared from the sky, commanding us to stop and head back to our headquarters for a discussion.

We knew we had won. Most of the government's weapons were handed over to lonelies across the land. They were forced to listen to us. We would demand our rights or we would continue to kill. They had no choice. We would be free.

I should've been thrilled. I should've been grateful for what we earned. My entire life had been spent fighting to prove my genes had no control of me. I was proud that I was on my own, able to survive without the help of my corrupt parents. But there was a gun in my hand and blood covering the ground.

I was just like them.

FROM THE FILES OF MITT ROMNEY BOUNTY HUNTER

By Eli Hopkins
(Oregon, USA)
Humor, 3rd Place

"Please tell me I'm still your number one man? *78,79,80 . . .*" former vice-presidential candidate Paul Ryan begged his roommate and lover, Mitt Romney, enunciating his words in the clipped, Midwestern twang Mitt had grown to hate. Paul was doing bicep curls in front of the mirror, wearing nothing but high-tops and a backwards Milwaukie Brewers cap—*94, 95, 96*—his favorite funk-rock mixtape blasting full volume on a boombox whose batteries were on the verge of dying. The boombox was the only thing they'd taken with them when fleeing the Salt Lake City Ramada—just moments before Mitt was supposed to appear on the banquet hall stage and deliver his concession speech—climbing out the window of a first-floor bathroom and stealing a Buick LaSabre from the parking lot. *Just keep driving*, Paul had said as Mitt steered the Buick out of the parking lot and onto Route 190. They headed south into the forest with nothing but a portable stereo, half a tank of gas, and a tuna sandwich they'd found in the car, casting their families and careers to the wind in pursuit of something *real*.

Now Mitt was sweating into their room's single bed, watching his lover and only friend run through the excruciating 10-hour-a-day workout routine he'd been maniacally observing since they'd settled in at the *Mucho Motel* in Key West a month and a half ago. "Just say my name over and over while I do pushups. Forever," Paul implored, rubbing his entire body down with prodigious amounts of lavender baby-oil and other exotically scented petroleum distillates. "Listening to the brutal rasp of your voice is like having my scrotum massaged with a wood-file, and I fucking love it. I don't care who knows."

They'd lost the 2012 presidential election by such a dramatic landslide that, in order to maintain already tenuous grasps on sanity, they'd both been obliged to embrace increasingly Buddhist worldviews. They were now totally unencumbered by the feelings of self-consciousness and shame from which all normal people would suffer if the entire population of the *Mucho Motel* and surrounding environs were acutely aware of your most intimate bedroom secrets. That is why they didn't even bother hiding now, lifting weights and audibly making love for hours with the door and window wide open, funk-rock going like crazy.

"You know you're my guy, buddy," Mitt Romney mumbled, flipping through the channels and guzzling his thirteenth *Shasta* of the day.

"I hear the words coming out of your mouth," Paul said, pausing mid squat-thrust to get an eye-full of his lover's new soda-weight, which hung in dense, sinuous folds under Mitt's unbuttoned *Tommy Bahama* shirt. "But for some reason I just don't believe anything you say. Sometimes it's almost like you don't believe yourself. *51,52,53 . . .*"

"I don't know what to tell you, amigo." Mitt sighed, running bloated fingers through his increasingly thin pompadour and viciously clicking the remote.

"The only way I'll believe that you truly love me and only me," Paul said, glancing over his shoulder, flashing the same blue eyes that had gotten Mitt into trouble in the first place, "is if you can pin me thirty consecutive times in traditional Greco-Roman wrestling."

Mitt looked at his one-time running mate and took a deep breath. He was beginning to think that throwing all of his money and belongings into the ocean and eloping to Key West with Paul Ryan was a bad idea. Paul had turned out to be more needy than a dancing horse, and Mitt was just realizing that he didn't even know the dude very well.

Less than two months ago the erstwhile Republican hopeful had been enjoying a life whose absurd opulence could only be compared to the more extravagant Bond villains (he'd always put himself somewhere between Dr. No and Max Zorin, Chrispher Walken's Silicon Valley madman), and now he was cooped up in a dingy motel with the greasiest lunatic he'd ever met, lugging around an extra forty-five pounds of misery weight, and down to his last few dollars. *What the hell happened*, he thought, staring at the ceiling, tears coming to his eyes.

"Baby?" Paul grunted, lifting a barbell over his head and throwing it to the floor with a thunderous crash that would likely result in an angry phone call from the front desk. The local police had already visited the room a number of times for various incidents—and would probably have gone straight from the *Mucho* to the good people at TMZ if it weren't for the fact that the responding officers simply didn't believe their eyes. "I'm still waiting for an answer on the wrestling question," Paul insisted, staring at Mitt's reflection in the strategically placed mirror. Mitt was wheezing uncomfortably and avoiding eye contact. "If this relationship is going to work out for the long haul, we're going to have to be completely honest with each other. So I'm just being honest when I say that I both want and need you to shove me to the ground and forcibly hold me there for at least ten seconds. And I want you to do it thirty times."

Stopping on an infomercial for industrial cleaning solvents, Mitt looked at his lover's glistening, perfectly sculpted body and imagined crushing it with super-strong robotic Dr. No hands. He imagined the sound of Paul's bones succumbing to 3,000 pounds per square inch as they fell under the insane grip of Mitt's shiny black mechanical digits.

It wasn't working and there was nothing else he could do. This wasn't where he wanted to be. Not anymore.

"Where are you going?" Paul protested as Mitt climbed off the bed and slipped into a pair of jean shorts, pulled on his cowboy boots, and grabbed his motorcycle keys off the dresser.

"I'm going out," Mitt said without looking back, closing the door behind him, closing the door to endless hours of cable television and funk-rock, to all-night talks and moonlight skinny-dipping, and to all forms of Greco-Roman wrestling—closing the door to love.

The sun was blazing as Mitt Romney tapped his boots across the parking lot to his neon-green Kawasaki dirt bike, the salty coastal air heavy with southern tang and whistling with some distant Siren's call. It was the ghostly howl of the freelance bounty hunter, and he was ready to howl back. The bike's engine turned over on the first shot, barking to life like a kicked dog, and as Mitt pushed a pair of drugstore aviators over his bloodshot eyes, he knew that this was it. This was for all the chips.

PAST PERSON SINGULAR

By A.H. Furlong
(Arizona, USA)
Zombies, Vampires, Lycans, and More, 2nd Place

All the people from my past appear and disappear in front of me. It is a strange type of soliloquy. They hope that I don't notice them. They even run away, but I see them, I always have. How can they be so foolish? They don't realize that reality isn't mine anymore. I'm different.

When I look at people on the street, I think of them as monsters spreading their vile diseases to my companions and me.

My companions and I are lonely. We watch movies all day, and I tell everyone I meet that I was an artist, and I was, but not anymore. I died and I think I went to heaven, but I didn't stay there. You can't, you have to come back. You have to live on Earth, only you're not a part of it. The things that people do I can no longer experience. My intellect is different; in fact, I don't really understand what people say.

I died two years ago, and I haven't been able to find a job since. Everyone can see that I'm different and they don't want to hire me. I wish that I wasn't sworn to secrecy. All I can say about my condition is that I came back and everyone does. If they go to hell they come back, but not like me. One other thing, if you meet more evil people than good people, you're coming back, but not like me.

There aren't very many like me, and we tend to spread ourselves rather thin. We have no other choice. There are maybe eight people a year who come back like me; the opposition gets the rest.

"So, Miss Cheeno, do you want the job?" the woman asked me.

"I want it, if you want to give it to me."

"If I want?" she repeated. "You're kidding. You're the first person that's come by in a week, I have to give it to you."

I smiled. "This isn't going to be easy," I said to myself. I obviously have a mission here. I need the money, too. My companions tell me that the woman is a demon. They say I'll have to fight her.

My companions panic sometimes. They have more to lose than I do. I have three companions who live with me. They're about eight inches to two feet tall. In real terms: they're dolls. The small one is Monique; she's an antique French doll. The medium one is Rosa; she's a bit matronly. The big one is Thembelina. They are people incarnate. They've been very good in past lives, and so they came back as things, but if they're bad (and they can be) then they'll be destroyed and they'll return as people.

I'm in the first stage; they're in the sixth. If we continue to be good, we'll eventually become something like a river. I want to be a pyramid or a star. But they can be destroyed as well; you really have to be careful.

My companions will help me through this life and I need their help. This is all so new to me. I don't know what got me to heaven, and I'm not supposed to know; if I did I might become hypocritical.

"I think it's a demon coming to challenge you," began Rosa.

"No," I began, "there are so many people to challenge."

"You're wrong," stated Monique. "There are not that many people coming back for the first time."

"She waited for you for a long time, seven days," said Thembelina.

"So what!" I insisted. I couldn't believe that my boss was the devil. She ran a shop and I was her assistant. It was a wholesale dress shop. The dresses weren't that terrific . . . but I couldn't believe that she was a demon.

"Watch," is all they said, and I have to listen, but I have to support them, as well, and I was running out of money. The job was opportune. I start work at nine and finish at six. I hate to leave my companions. I always think about burglars. But the landlord throwing us out would be worse.

So here I sit doing absolutely nothing so that I can earn enough money to keep us going.

My boss invited herself over to my house for dinner tonight. She was talking about a business meeting, and I wish we would just go out. I don't know how to cook, and the fact that I can't taste food didn't make this any easier. I asked her already if we could go Chinese, but she insisted that she wanted solitude.

I arrived home early to tell my companions. There was a stir of activity among them. They were flustered. They didn't like the idea very much. They were very suspicious. I told them it's a business meeting; they looked at me knowingly.

"Well, she's coming at eight," I said, and that's when the doorbell rang. "I'm not expecting anyone," I said as I went downstairs to answer the door. It was my boss. She was early. I hadn't had time to move my companions to the other room. I felt anxious as I followed her up the stairs.

She entered the room before me. I heard the rustle of Thembelina's dress. I asked my boss to sit down. I offered sandwiches. Sandwiches can never be a disaster. She then asked me for some cheese. I went into the kitchen, and that's when it happened.

She touched one of my companions. A little nudge on the leg and the one she touched screamed good and loud. I ran back into the room. My boss was staring at Rosa.

"Did you scream?" I asked.

"I did not!"

"Then what did I hear?"

"It was one of them," she said, pointing at the dolls.

"Don't be silly; dolls don't scream."

"Well it did; I'll show you." And she moved her hand toward Thembelina.

I held my breath but Thembelina didn't scream. My boss looked foolish.

"I found the cheese," I said. She forgot about the dolls and joined me at the table. She kept on saying that we had to talk, but we didn't. All I heard were the syllables of her words. Her voice was strong and mesmerizing. She asked for coffee and I traipsed off once more. She drank the coffee. After that there didn't seem to be room for anything more to say. Naturally she became friendly.

"I have a doll," she said. "I've had it since childhood."

"Really."

"Yes, It's a mammy doll," she added, and I heard a sigh from the other corner.

"Would you like it?" she asked.

"Well," I began, but I didn't get to finish.

"I knew it, it's as good as done, it's yours. I'll bring it around tomorrow." She stood up, making every excuse to leave. We said goodnight and I brushed the crumbs from the table and then took my coffee to the sink. When I came back, my companions were chattering amongst themselves.

"Why did you have to scream?" I asked.

"Because she touched me. She's evil," said Rosa.

"She has a mammy doll," said Thembelina.

"So what?"

"Don't take it," snapped Monique.

"It's a gift."

"Of witchcraft," they said.

"Now really."

"You didn't hear her," winced Thembelina.

"I did. She wants me to have it."

"Not that, she was putting you in a trance."

"She was?"

"Yes, she was. When she was talking to you she was looking at us. She's after something."

"Maybe she's a little odd. Anyway, it was your screaming that set her off."

Then I said how late it was and how I was going to go to sleep. I left them there in the darkness and I went to my room. I couldn't help but spend a restless night thinking about my companions. I knew they were right, but I was scared. I would have to protect them and I was scared of that. I didn't want to be tested.

The next morning was Saturday. There was a ringing from the bell of the front door. I woke from my sleep and got out of bed and hurried downstairs. When I opened the door, my boss handed me a doll and walked away. I closed the door and clutched the doll with my free arm. I went upstairs. I walked into the apartment, and I knew that I shouldn't have brought that doll into the house.

Thembelina, Monique, and Rosa sat paralyzed. They gasped and I just watched the mammy doll fall from my hand.

"She's free!"

"Quick! Grab her!"

But as I went after the mammy, I kicked her under the long sideboard that lined one wall of the sitting room. I kicked her so far that she got stuck way underneath and I knew that I could only get her out by moving the heavy piece of furniture. Maybe I could have done it, but my companions had become hysterical and my attention was divided. I concentrated on them and forgot the mammy.

"Everybody calm down. I'm here, remember?" They were silenced. I sighed. "All right, everyone, we're going to take care of this together. No more arguments."

"That mammy doll is after us."

"I know. I figured it out last night. But I can't get her from under the sideboard by myself, and since it's Saturday, I can't call for help until Monday."

"Monday!"

"What'll we do until Monday?"

"We'll stay in my room."

Thembelina gave a pleasant sigh, and I picked her up—the others, too. I moved them into my room. I locked the door behind us and turned on the television. Thembelina leaned against me and I felt comforted, as if perhaps they had forgiven me for my indecision. I should have thrown that mammy doll into the street, but instead it sat in the other room. Only a hallway separated us and its presence hovered in the back of my mind. We watched a western, and my companions were happy with the story. I was happy with them.

"It's cold in here."

I turned on the heat but there was no difference. We knew that the mammy was trying to make us come out to the other room, if for warmth at least. We knew better. I climbed into the bed and stuffed the covers up under our chins. We kept on watching the television and in time we warmed up. Then the television went dead.

"She's really after us."

"We only have to wait another day," I said.

"Couldn't one of us get to the mains?" asked Rosa.

"It's in the kitchen," said Thembelina.

"Past the mammy doll," I added.

"I'm not brave enough for that," Rosa admitted.

Nobody else said a word. Then Thembelina spoke. "Maybe I am," she said, and we were surprised. She seemed the most timid of us all. She wasn't worldly or wise; she was shy and full of innocence, but with those words she wanted to brave the threat to protect us. We were filled with gratitude. Thembelina descended from the bed and headed out the door and down the corridor to the wicked world beyond. Thembelina was gone for quite a while. We began to pray, and the television came on again. We felt the heater, as well. Finally I heard our secret code being tapped on the bedroom door.

"Thembelina, is that you?" I asked.

"It is," replied a faint voice from the other side.

I opened the door, and in came Thembelina. She was crying very softly. I set her on the bed, and as I turned on the light, I noticed her torn dress and a little bruise forming near her eye and a few more on her soft arms.

"Thembelina," I began, "what's happened?"

"Nothing," she said. Her voice was broken by tears, but I didn't need to know. It was obvious to me that the mammy doll had done the unspeakable.

She had fought with Thembelina. Thembelina had been brave for all of us. I felt ashamed, and then I felt angry. I picked Thembelina up off the ground and placed her in my bed. I kissed her forehead and pulled the covers around her neck. Then I opened my bedroom door and stepped into the hall. I walked down the hall and turned on the light in the sitting room.

The mammy doll was no longer under the bureau. She was sitting where my companions often sat. I moved toward her. She sneered at me. I could see her teeth. I was scared but I moved toward her; I couldn't help myself. I knew that we couldn't be slaves any longer. I moved closer and her teeth became fangs. She seemed scared of me. Then I looked at the French doors that led to the terrace; then I looked back and now I was but a foot away. She dug her fangs into my arm. I wasn't shocked; I knew she would do that. Still the pain was excruciating. I put it out of my mind as I pulled her toward the French door. She pulled me back, and our wills met in the center of the room.

She threw me at the sideboard. My back hit hard against the edge of the wooden piece. I was hurt, but I kept on moving toward the doors. I could see a bit of blood on my arm, but I didn't care about that. I cared about getting rid of the mammy doll. I cared about my friends. Somehow I managed to unlatch the door. She was ferociously holding my wrist in her jaw. As the cold evening air filtered into the room, I felt flushed and strong. I grabbed her with my other hand and flung her body over the banister and onto the street below.

I could hear her screams. As I closed the French doors, I looked down at my wrist; the blood was pouring now. I looked toward the doorway and there were my companions. They smiled and I smiled back.

"Am I going to die?" I asked in a whisper.

"You're going to be a star," said Thembelina.

SNATCHED

By Thomas Joseph Cienki
(Massachusetts, USA)
Say Something, 3rd Place

Amy was always the highlight of my summers. If I were a mountaineer, she would be my Everest. If I were a pirate, she would be an exquisite oak chest teeming with the world's most sought-after jewels. There was never any doubt . . . we were always that close. "As thick as thieves," my mother would grumble as our slender, dirt-caked fingers attempted to capture one of her legendary homemade oatmeal-raisin cookies in one fell swoop. And, every night, when the radiant glow of the scorching summer sun began to fade, my mother would always know where to find me as my father summoned my brother and me to supper. I would either be in Amy's backyard envisioning far-off lands on her expansive swing-set or causing quite the stir throughout our white picket-fence-laden cul-de-sac neighborhood. Sometimes, even though my mother had worked all morning and afternoon to fashion a casserole that would rival Mrs. Jones's award-winning recipe, I would be allowed to eat unwanted Easter chocolate on Amy's monkey bars or split a TV dinner while we waited for Amy's dad to pick her up for the weekend. We didn't talk about it much because my grandmother said it wasn't proper to dabble in the affairs of others, but Amy told me it was because her parents were married too quickly and after she was born, the fights would never end, like gunfire on the battlefields we learned about in our school textbooks. Sometimes it would be about money and other times it would about her father's secretary, Peg, but whatever the cause of dispute didn't matter, because they eventually separated. Divorce was the legal term, but Amy's parents used the term separation because they believed it sounded less traumatizing or something. Sometimes adults forget how perceptive children can be.

Amy was an only child, too, so my mother thought it was a good idea for me to spend so much time with her. Sibling indoctrination, she called it. "You know," my mother said, in between puffs of her cigarette one Sunday evening. "the whole thing is sad, really. Perhaps it would be different if she had a sister, maybe. But either way, things like this never really heal. Every fight, every jarring word, every dark cloud, children witness. Children witness and remember. Parents sometimes think things like divorce seal like zippers or fade away like faint scars. It's more like an open wound, really. Amy's mother or father, or even you can paint over it or bandage it up, but it will still be fresh and vulnerable underneath the superficial surface many, many years later. She might not always remember it's there, but one night, after she's put her children to sleep and she's settling into bed herself, it will burn and sting and force her to fall to her knees just as she's wiping off her mascara, and she'll gather herself and stand in front of the mirror, peering at the reflection in front of her eyes. Except she won't see the image of a forty-year-old woman, mother of two, or even a beloved wife. She'll glance into the mirror and see the distant shadow of an eleven-year-old girl from a broken home. A girl who was snatched up too soon."

Diatribes like this weren't the norm. Mom always kept an above-average poker face. I lived next door to Amy, and encounters with her mother were frequent, whether one was the time Mom had to return the five-dollar bills Amy "borrowed" from her mother's pocket-book to buy my Han Solo action figure, or to send Amy home in a huff after we ripped Mom's tulips from her garden and drowned them in a cheap-as-dirt yellow plastic bowl. Those small acts of mischief couldn't compare, however, to that one Sunday afternoon when my teenage brother, Tad, was supposed to watch us. Dad was out of town and Mom said she would just be at the market for a milk-and-eggs run. I knew she wasn't lying because I had a dentist appointment at four and she wasn't leaving Tad in charge unless she was not away for long. My father said his head was too full of cobwebs and rock-and-roll. I later discovered the medical term for this was called hormones. As soon as Mom rolled out of the driveway in the family Chevy, Amy was getting that look in her eye, that sparkle that told me she was up to no good. She was sizing up the Duffys' fence like it was a stack of pancakes sixteen storeys high.

You see, the Duffys were practically the stuff of neighborhood legend. They lived directly behind us, and there was a rumor that Mr. and Mrs. Duffy were only spotted every third full moon. This wouldn't be anything too abnormal, except the Duffys had a real, live in-ground pool in their backyard. Tad told me he could see it from his window, and every so often he was tempted to run off our roof and jump in cannonball-style. No one had ever tried anything, though. There were rumors that the pool was filled with kid poison or that it was built on the skeletons of eleven-year-old boys that had attempted to relish in its promise of summer solace.

On that day, as soon as my mom rounded the corner of our street, Amy decided to jump the Duffys' fence. I was reluctant for about five seconds, but I would not be a very good friend if I let her die in a pool all by herself. Climbing fences was never my specialty, so by the time I finally made it over to the other side, Amy was already enjoying the Duffys' forbidden oasis, lounging in Mrs. Duffy's pink float!

"Amy!" I cried out in astonishment. "You can't just tramp over someone's belongings like that!"

"Well at least I didn't trample over her garden gnomes scaling the fence," Amy shot back. "It looks like she's got quite the collection."

It was true. In breaking my fall, I had also broken one of Mrs. Duffy's garden gnomes. That was the thing about Amy—she always had a comeback. Since Amy had already made me feel like a first-class criminal, I had no problem enjoying the Duffys' pool. But what if it was filled to the brim with kid poison? Or what if Mr. Duffy were to spontaneously appear with a Remington rifle? I decided it would just be best to dip my face in. We stayed there for what seemed like hours, me thrusting my face into the chilled pool waters and Amy blowing bubbles from atop the pink float. How time seemed to stop just for us in the Duffys' pool. It's amazing how you can be somewhere you know you don't belong and feel the most complete you've ever been. There was something magical about that pool water. It seemed to wipe away who we were and leave us as carefree as those garden gnomes. Eventually we decided to return to my barren backyard. The Duffys would surely find out we had been there and my mom would be returning from the market any minute.

Oh, *my mom!* How I had forgotten about her! No sooner were we over the fence and in my driveway than I saw her racing down the street in our Chevy. That purebred American car looked so menacing that day.

"Quick!" Amy told me. "We can dry off." We spent the next thirty seconds foolishly attempting to mask any presence off our criminal activity, but it was to no avail. Mom had a way of sensing fear. One look and she knew. I don't think we were ever in that much trouble. Amy's parents weren't home, so she had to come to the dentist's with us and that was probably one of the worst punishments Mom could concoct. Part of me still thinks Mom was just jealous that we were the first two to explore the unconquered Duffy territory.

It wasn't often that we were getting into trouble, however. I had an earnest face (according to my Aunt Muriel) and Amy had a toothy smile that could get her out of anything (according to the testimony of our fourth-grade teacher, Miss Donnelly). Instead, our days were filled with amassing an arsenal of scrapes and bruises and dirtying our play clothes in the most efficient manner. Looking back now, there was something so magical about summer days in particular. We were so vibrant then. I remember lying in the miniature toy house that was plopped in the woods at the end of our block, my fingertips gently grazing Amy's sweaty palms, and feeling so alive. Sometimes we would play school or house or bank and pretend like we had any idea what it was like to do any of those things. We would lie for hours in that cheap little house and wish to be just one year older, never really knowing what happens as children age, never really knowing that someday we would forget what it was like to dream without limits and live without inhibition. Somehow I tricked myself into believing that this was a special shelter, our own little world, and no matter what happened we could come back to that one spot and we would be young again, unaware.

One crisp, fall afternoon, just after my twelfth birthday, I was supposed to meet Amy at our house in the woods. She never came. I waited for hours and hours, and she never showed up. I went home that evening just as the sun was beginning to set, and my mom was in tears as my dad paced around the living-room on the telephone. They were looking for her, I heard him say, but she couldn't be found.

I don't remember much of what happened after that. I know posters went up, but they quickly came down as people had their own lives to worry about and their own children to feed. Amy's mother moved out of the neighborhood shortly after that and went to live with Amy's grandparents in Florida. Pretty soon a new family moved next door and there were new kids to play with, but it would never be the same.

Even years later, I would go back to that little house in the woods and, as I lay against the cold, wet earth, sometimes I secretly hoped that this was all just a dream and Amy would come running in, making a joke about why she is late. Even other times, I trace her footstep from years ago in the brown dirt and I look up and see her standing there.

Except it is never her. It's always just a distant shadow.

The shadow of a girl who was snatched up too soon.

Bad Acid At Woodstock

By Beem Weeks
(Michigan, USA)
Humor, 2nd Place

"Holy cow!" Bobby exclaims, peering through our living-room window. "What the hell is *that*?"

"Bobby!" Mama hollers from the kitchen. "I told you about using that kind of talk! You want I should feed you a bar of soap instead of supper?"

Kenny creeps in and sports a gawk of his own. "*Whoa!*" he declares. "I heard they fetched four pairs of 'em back from Vietnam in the sixties. I never did believe it, though."

It's vibrating and hopping up and down on our front lawn like it means to menace only our family. Sometimes it even shakes the whole house.

Todd fearfully says, "I didn't think those things were real."

Too short to see out the window, Nicole tries to pull herself up. She whispers to Bobby, "It's not you-know-what, is it?"

"No, Punkin," he assures her. "It ain't that."

It's curiosity that lures Mama to the living-room with a fresh pot of stuff in her hands. Once her good eye tags that thing, though, she drops the pot and stuff goes all over the floor. Her cry sounds something like, "Why's it in our yard?"

"I ain't sure," Bobby replies. "It just keeps on bouncin' and hummin' and vibratin'."

Nicole offers reassurance. "It's almost like you-know-what, Mama, but it's not."

Just then, Moped, a neighborhood dog, approaches and barks at the thing. But the thing is too loud, and we can't hear Moped's bark. We can only see his mouth move.

"Damn!" Bobby yells. "Did y'all see that?"

We all certainly *did* see it. Poor Moped never stood a chance. All we could do was stand and watch.

I turned my head, unable to view those last few seconds.

"What was that thing grabbed ole Moped?" Kenny wonders aloud.

Mama tells us what she knows. "Hear tell it's called a ligamatrix."

"If it gets too close to the window," Bobby informs us, "my ass is out the back door."

"I once heard you could shoo it away by spraying it with a garden hose," Kenny's remembering, "—but only after it lets down two or three of them reflector thingies."

Todd says, "Might could rust it."

Just then, it bounces smack dab in front of our window. We all jump back. The glass shatters, and we each one of us scampers through the kitchen toward the back door. A ligamatrix creeps in like a wayward snake and snatches the slowest, smallest one of us.

"*Oh! It's got Nicole!*" Mama cries, shooting a parting gawk over her shoulder.

Bobby hollers, "Somebody *grab* her!"

Too late. It sucks her into its gaping maw and begins to hum and whirl, just like it did when it got poor ole Moped.

"Hell, I'm just glad it didn't get *me*," Kenny proclaims outside the back door.

"Yeah," Bobby agrees. "I mean, I like Nicole and all—but hell, better her than us, right?"

"I suppose you boys is right," Mama confirms as we wander back inside our house.

But that thing on our front yard takes to spinning again, awful fast this time. We start for the back again, real quick-like, climbing over each other in our attempted escape.

All of a sudden it stops and stands completely still, like maybe something got broke inside of it. A second maw gapes wide, and vomits the slowest, smallest one of us onto the ground.

Nicole stumbles and staggers, covered in orange ooze that's digested her sunsuit and flip-flops, leaving her naked, dizzy, and laughing.

"That was fun," she giggles.

Mama calls to her. "Well, hurry and get back in here before it grabs ya up again."

"I wanna go again," Nicole protests, pouting as she stomps into the house.

It's gone bored now—or maybe sour in its belly. All that hopping up and down and vibrating just stops, like a show-off who can't get anybody to pay it any mind.

Finally, the thing folds in upon itself and, when it becomes small as a nickel, flies straight up into the sky, vanishing from our neighborhood.

"Whew!" Bobby says. "I'm sure glad *that's* over with."

"Gonna have to get that window fixed," Mama complains. "Third time this month."

We all sit round the kitchen table watching Nicole scrape off orange ooze before it takes to digesting her.

"I'm just glad it wasn't you-know-what," she says, sighing.

And I have to agree with her. I'm also glad it wasn't you-know-what.

Beem Weeks is the author of historical novel Jazz Baby. *Enjoy some of his short stories at* http://www.FreshInkGroup.com/authors/beem-weeks.

IN THE ABSENCE OF MIRRORS

By Anna Midkiff
(Texas, USA)
Zombies, Vampires, Lycans, and More, 1ˢᵗ Place

I awake.

This is not a slow, peaceful awakening, the sort I remember experiencing after a restful sleep. That would happen slowly; I would never consciously open my eyes, but awakening came as gracefully as the sunlight creeping through the third-floor window of our apartment. The best mornings began when I awoke looking at you.

Nor is this the gasping, sheet-clutching awakening that comes after a nightmare. I didn't have many nightmares in the months that I first knew you, and only one brought me reeling awake—the later ones made me too afraid to move. That one time, though, I sat panting and terrified in the darkness for eons, longing for light to chase away the demons, but too afraid to reach across the hell between my bed and the nightstand to my lamp. Then I realized your arms were around me. I hadn't even remembered you were in the bed.

Out of the void I open my eyes, into darkness.

Awakening is barely different than sleep. It is quiet and dark and empty. The only thing that lets me know that I am awake again is the pressure on my back. I am lying on something smooth and flat. I don't remember how I got here.

Eventually, I move my right hand to feel around my body. I only have a few inches of space on either side before I touch wood. I have about six inches above my head. Then I reach up and touch the wood above me.

I am in a coffin.

I scratch at the lid. My nails slide over it; it is too smooth to splinter. I curl my hand into a fist and strike it. The wood trembles, but holds.

How deep have I been buried? Not deep enough. I'm going to get out.

But why am I even here? Did I die? I pause my futile scratching, leaving my hand still pressed to the wood. No one would have buried me if I were alive, but if I were dead, shouldn't I remember dying? The closest things I can find in my memory are the nightmares.

Something heavy is around my neck. I wrap my hands around it: a cross. A heavy metal cross hangs on a chain too thin to support a real necklace rather than a grave accessory. I pull it free, breaking the chain, and holding it like a hammer I begin to pound on the ceiling of my prison.

I will be free, my love, and when I reach the surface, I hope to find you waiting.

Hours pass, maybe days, maybe weeks, as I dig. Once I have broken through the coffin, all I have to do is keep moving through the dirt, tearing free chunks from the space above me, packing it into my new floor, and packing it tightly so I'll still have space to work. My bubble of space moves slowly upward. Once or twice I encounter stones in the ground above me that I pry free carefully with my crucifix, very aware of their weight—I don't want them to hit me when they fall. I never stop.

Eventually, I realize that I should feel tired. I have never been strong, and the effort of this digging should be tearing my shoulders to ribbons. Also, I should have suffocated long ago. I dismiss the second thought from my head almost before it appears. Suffocation is only a concern for those who breathe.

I pause only once, to try to remember how I got here. You would know. You would have been there; we haven't been apart since we met.

Did the nightmares kill me?

I don't mean the jerking, sheet-clutching nightmare. In the last weeks of my life, I was infected with the worse kind: helpless dreams, of monsters sitting on my chest and sucking the life out of me. I could not escape the dreams until prompted by something outside my mind—the bang of our neighbor's door, a dog barking down the street, sunlight.

I must have had at least fifteen of these dreams in the last three weeks. I stopped sleeping in our bed during the second week, moving to the couch to the floor to the orange recliner, trying to find a place where the monster wouldn't follow me. But I could never hide for long.

During the night, it held me prisoner, and in the day I was sick and wretched. I had a job somewhere; I don't remember where—I have images of a pizzeria, of a café, of a boutique—but it doesn't matter. All that matters is that I was too sick to go there, and I was with you in the apartment.

You were out of work. You stayed with me, bringing me massive plates of red meat and slabs of cake that smelled like heaven, but I couldn't touch them. My throat felt like it had caved in.

You're too thin, you told me. You're so pale. You look awful. You have to make yourself eat. Come on, eat. Eateateat.

I can't. I don't look so bad.

How do you know? Can you see yourself?

I just know. I don't need a mirror to know that. We should get a mirror, though . . . the bathroom looks so strange without one . . .

Maybe the sickness killed me in my sleep. My hands twitch towards my dirt ceiling, ready to keep digging, but I stop myself. There is a memory on the edge of my mind. I can't see what it is, but if I can pull it a little closer . . .

It is like trying to remember a dream. The harder I reach, the further it slips away, leaving me with only the vaguest idea of what was in it. Something about your hands . . .

I keep on digging. The dirt is getting damper. I am approaching the surface.

It feels like an eternity passes before I touch something other than the soft, clumping earth. I touch something fibrous: grass roots.

I punch through the last few inches, driving the end of the cross up first, and my hand explodes into the air outside.

I claw my way out like I am drowning. The last layer of dirt caves in on me in my rush, but it doesn't stop me. Nothing can stop me. I burst from my grave, a phoenix out of its ashes, reborn.

I don't know what I expected to see when I got out. Perhaps a graveyard. Isn't that where we are usually buried? But no, I am not in a graveyard. There are no headstones for as far as I can see, only trees.

I have been buried in the wilderness. I could be anywhere. You could be anywhere. I meant to find you as soon as I escaped, but you might be a thousand miles away.

I have nothing else to do, so I walk. It is late evening, the sky is dark grey, and a single star hangs just above the skyline. I walk as fast as I can. My body feels stiff from being shut up so long, and still I am not breathing, but overall I think I am in good condition for someone who might have been dead. I throw the cross into the woods and hear it bounce off a tree.

For the first time, I wonder what I am wearing, and I look down at my body. I am wearing nothing but the blue bathrobe you bought me after you moved in. I used to think it was warm, but now it just sits on my skin, stained and limp. This is the robe I wore during my illness. Did I die in it? Why did you bury me in the wilderness, as if you meant to hide my death? But if you did, why did you give me a coffin? What do I look like now that I have been dead? Why don't we have headstones, my love? Why don't we have mirrors?

I think I know the answer, but I don't remember it. Not yet.

I keep walking. I watch my bare feet skim over the forest floor. My toe-nails are black with dirt or rot. My mottled white skin looks dead, loose and disconnected from the muscles beneath.

The sky has darkened and more stars are out. They sparkle like fine glass-ware, reminding me of your eyes. Your eyes were impossibly beautiful, even though they were almost always lost in shadow: the shadow of a bad memory, that's what you told me.

I asked what light would drive the shadow away. You said—I remember these words more clearly than anything—you said, the light of love. The light you shine on me every moment I am with you.

Beautiful words, I thought, but I knew they were lies.

I wish you would have told me the truth. Why couldn't you realize that I wouldn't care if you couldn't love me like I loved you? For even when most of your time was sunk in memory, the smallest fraction still remained for me, and those fragments of you were better than the entirety of any other.

I'm not walking right. I don't feel tired, but it's hard to balance my body above my legs. I keep lurching to the sides, stumbling against trees and trip-ping. I'm glad to find the footpath cutting through the woods. A faded green sign warns against littering.

I know that sign. I'm in the woods behind our apartment complex. We came here on hikes before I became ill.

I turn right on the path and lurch down it, the bathrobe fluttering behind me. It would be easier to crawl. I'm so thirsty. Grind up some pennies in the blender and have a copper smoothie waiting for me when I get home, please.

I don't know if I see the poor kid coming or not. Was there time to react to me, to even have a chance to see me before I leapt? I don't even remember hearing someone coming.

There's a scream, and the snarl of a hungry monster and something ex-plodes in my mouth, warm, wet, copper-flavored pleasure.

Thanks for the smoothie . . .

It's a long time before I realize what I've done.

Night has fallen when I look up from the body. No one else is out on the trail, only us. I put my hand on the young cheek, now even paler than I.

My Dear: I'm sorry if I told you I was coming home. It's not me any-more. Dying has made me someone else, someone who ambushes innocent teenagers and bites their throats to drink their blood. Love, your lover.

Worst of all is that I can't make myself feel repulsed by what I've done.

It seems the most natural thing in the world. I wipe my mouth with the back of my hand, and my skin rakes against something sharp—my canines.

I pull my hand away and stare at the torn skin. Blood seeps through the cut, but not much, because there's no heartbeat to push it.

And now I remember.

The last night that I have memory of, I lay in bed and watched you undress. I was too feverish to fully appreciate you, but I had to look because I can't look at anything else when you're around. You were looking at the floor, and your hands shook. They were rough, and showed the beginnings of blisters.

I said, What's wrong? and you lied to me again. You said, Nothing.

You said, I'm sorry. You picked your clothes off the floor. They were dirty, sweaty, and torn.

I said, It's okay.

Because by then I knew that you had killed me.

Your clothes were dirty because you'd been digging my grave. The bruises came from assembling my coffin. You already knew it would happen that night, and you couldn't stop it. You lay down beside me and took me in your arms and rocked me back and forth, whispering: I'm sorry, I'm so sorrysorrysorry.

Just do it. At least I won't have nightmares anymore. I know it's been you all along. You're the monster. That's why I can't hide from you. It's why we don't have mirrors. Why I'm so pale and sick. Don't answer. It's okay. I just wish you'd trusted me enough to tell me. Don't you know I'd be glad to give you my blood?

No, you said. It's not me.

I look down at the body by my feet. I don't remember standing. If you'd had your way, I wouldn't be here at all. That's why you gave me a coffin, to be a prison, and why you put the cross around my throat, to keep me from crawling out. But it didn't work, because religion isn't a tool. If there is a God, he punishes the wicked, and that's why the cross didn't work, because I am not the wickedest thing that touched it.

I love you. I would give you anything, my life and my soul afterwards. But my soul is a gift for you and you alone.

And you sold it to the monster.

I leave the body and continue down the path. Soon, I see our apartments. The familiar outline of building eleven is on my left, and I cut through the woods to reach it. I am stronger now that I have eaten. Don't bother with the copper smoothie.

The trees fall away around me. Barefoot, I cross the asphalt parking lot to building eleven. I climb the metal staircase to room three-three-two.

It looks the same as always. I hesitate before trying the knob. What if everything is the same as always? What if I walk in and I see me sitting on the orange recliner with you, our limbs tangled as we watch a movie? What if I'm not really me?

Well, of course I'm not. Not anymore.

I open the door. You always left it unlocked before for the thing. They can't enter uninvited. That's why you had to move in with me, so you could let it in. But I don't need to be invited. This is my home.

I walk in. The TV is on. The rug is wrinkled. I hear the shower running in the bathroom.

I go into the kitchen and find a stainless-steel pan in a drawer, careful not to let it clatter when I open it. I turn it over in my hands, searching for a reflection, and don't find one. Not even the blue bathrobe reflects. I glance at my hands. Under the kitchen lights, they look mottled, and I see that my fingernails really are black with rot.

Maybe this is why we don't reflect—so we don't see how hideous we are.

You weren't one of us, though. We could have had mirrors without them giving you away. Maybe you didn't like mirrors because you couldn't see your reflection without thinking of yourself, and you couldn't think of yourself without knowing how disgusting you really are.

I replace the pan. You never had a job in all the time I knew you; you stayed home and took online classes and you cooked. I came home and you had feasts prepared for me. And you'd send leftover feasts to work with me. Mostly, you fed me on meat.

That's why it didn't kill me the night you moved in, why it waited for a few months. Why go to such a trouble for a hunt, if the prey tastes like McDonald's?

I go back to the living room and sit down in the orange recliner. Then I get up again. I died fighting. You saw it happen; you were still holding me when it came through the door.

I would have died to sustain you, but not for that thing to live. It was a monster. The eyes were lovely, like colored glass or jewels, but they had no business being open. The thing was a corpse. Its skin wasn't rotten like mine is now, but beautifully embalmed, its movements strained like the muscles were disintegrating beneath its milky, polished skin. When it spoke, it spoke like a baby, because all its teeth were gone but the fangs.

It said, I'm sorry that it won't be able to survive another night. It tastes so wonderful. You are brilliant, to make the blood so mouthwatering.

You said nothing. Your arms were rigid on me. I wanted to believe you meant to protect me, but it was just to hold me still. I didn't really believe what was happening until it leaned over me and opened its mouth, the lower jaw dislocating from the upper like a snake's, so it could fit my entire throat inside.

And I realized this had happened before, every time I'd had the nightmare, but I'd been too stupid to see the wounds on my throat. I couldn't let it happen again.

I screamed and ripped my arms free from your embrace. I punched it, breaking its nose, and there was blood everywhere, even before it bit my throat and I knew it was over. I struggled and choked and moaned, and you held me while I died. But the monster was bleeding, too. And while I screamed, some of the blood got in my mouth.

I knew, even then, that its blood would give me its immortality after death. I wasn't just prey anymore. I was destined to be the hunter.

I walk down the hallway, softly. The bathroom door is open and steam billows around its edge. A plastic lid snaps as you open a bottle of shampoo. The scent stings my nostrils.

I step inside the bathroom. The door creaks slightly, but the bathroom rug is thick and my footsteps are nothing. What do you think causes the creak? The force of the steam? Your true lover coming to you with another mission, to inform you that it had found another poor fool you could move in with and feed?

The bathroom is tiny. Only four feet separate me from the blue-and-green shower curtain. It's too thick to see your silhouette. A painting hangs over the sink: you have not forgiven yourself for my murder yet; you still cannot look in a mirror.

I untie the belt from the bathrobe and let the sleeves fall off my shoulders. I glance over my body: white, mottled, naked, dead. Bloodstained. This is what you did.

I take two steps and yank the shower curtain open. Shower rings fly everywhere.

You scream, at first because you're startled, and then because you see me, and then because you recognize me. You take a step back and slip. I grab your shoulders and steady you, and hold on to you as I step into the shower. The water burns my cold skin, but I don't care. The blood's already dried; it will take more than water to wash it off.

You try to pull away. No, no, no, you scream. It wasn't me. Don't you understand? I had to do it. It would have killed me if I hadn't.

You should have died, I say, pulling the shower curtain shut. Water rains around us.

Your hair is sudsy with the shampoo, and now the bubbles are running down your face into your eyes. I don't understand, you say again. I thought you loved me.

Of course I loved you. I never loved anything but you. So how could you take all my trust and faith and use it to feed that demon? Look what you did to me. I'm not alive anymore. I killed someone on the way over here. This is the blood of another soul.

No, you whimper. The shampoo runs over your shoulders and chest. We've made love in this shower before, when I could want love. I don't crave your body like that anymore. I just want your blood, and you know it.

I say, What have you been eating?

Takeout, you say. Fast food. Don't kill me, please, pleasepleaseplease. You slip onto your knees in front of me. There's barely room in the shower for both of us as it is, and even less now.

You treated me like livestock. You fattened me up and sold me to the highest bidder. Do you think I'd be content just to kill you?

You look up at me. Your eyes are red.

I wrap my hand around your throat and pull you to your feet. You come obediently, but I know my touch repels you. Didn't you want me to be this way? I draw you to my corpse and press my lips onto yours, wondering if that will make me human enough to want you. It doesn't. But I keep my lips on yours until you start to whimper.

Then I draw back and look into your beautiful eyes.

Please, you whisper. I'll do anything. Just don't kill me.

I reach past you and twist the shower off.

Would you like something to eat?

I want you to eat.

Eateateat.

THE WHORE

By Anna Cates
(Ohio, USA)
Suspense, 2ⁿᵈ Place

Fatima stepped out of the shower and onto the blue bathroom mat, enjoying its softness beneath her feet. She ran a towel across her naked body, dissolving beads of dew, her burgundy nipples erect at the ends of her goose-pimpled breasts, the triangle of hair above her legs still matted with moisture.

Once dry, Fatima gazed at her reflection in the mirror. She pulled forward two clumps of black hair from either side of her head, analyzing its length. Her hair had grown out again and needed a trim. If she let it get too long, the ends became fine and tapered, which she didn't like. Customarily, she'd let her hair reach halfway down her back, then get a shoulder-length bob at the salon, only to let it grow out again and repeat the cycle. She only needed one haircut a year that way, normally sometime in late spring. Today was May first, about the time to call Sandy's Magic Scissors.

"Maybe I should do something different this time," Fatima said to herself.

Ever since Fatima and her husband, Khaled, had moved to Dayton, Ohio, Sandy had been the only beautician Fatima trusted with her hair, someone one of her Avon customers had recommended to her. Khaled, an Egyptian immigrant, didn't like women with very short hair. Too often, they were the power-hungry women he disrespected, disrespected almost as much as whores. But Fatima had never heard him speak out against women who changed their hair color.

"Maybe that's what I should do," Fatima mused, feeling bored with her appearance. "Color my hair." The idea excited her, sending a spark throughout her body.

Her hair still damp and coiled with a clasp atop her head, Fatima slipped into a pair of jeans and a black long-sleeved t-shirt, then drove her white Subaru across town.

"You want me to bob it as usual?" Sandy asked at the salon, spreading the plastic over Fatima, then running her fingers through her hair, freed from its clasp.

Fatima peered at Sandy in the mirror, noting the chestnut waves reaching her shoulder blades. "I was thinking about enhancing the color."

"You can only go lighter with black hair. Or reddish."

"I don't like red hair. Not for me. How about blonde?"

Sandy's eyebrows rose. "Blonde is very light for a woman with hair as dark as yours, but I can do that, apply stripper first, then the colorant. You want that?" She smiled.

"I think so, yes," Fatima said, her heart racing, feeling unsure, but daring. *Why not?* She folded her fingers in her lap, trying not to tremble.

When Fatima arrived home from the salon, she spent three hours studying herself in the mirror, forgetting everything else on her "to-do list." She liked her platinum blonde bob, but her appearance scared her. She looked so different, more different that she'd expected. "My eyebrows are too dark," she said, her heart pumping wildly, she knew not why. She grabbed her tweezers and attacked each arch, ripping out hairs until she looked like a 1930's movie star, disguising herself even further. "I hope Khaled likes this look," she said, hands clammy.

At 5:30 Khaled arrived home from the contractor he worked for, pulling into the garage with his navy-blue Chevy Cavalier. Fatima stationed herself on the black leather sofa, a modern piece without armrests, and pulled her red scarf over her head.

The back door opened and closed, admitting Khaled whistling a country tune, country the only American music he found barely preferable to silence while driving. He swung into the dining room, seeming in decent spirits, wearing his electrician's uniform, the tight curls at his temples sweaty, a gallon of skim milk hooked under one index finger, a loaf of Aunt Millie's wheat bread, Fatima's favorite, clasped in the other hand. He tossed the bread on the table beside the junk mail.

Fatima let the scarf slide from her head, exposing the new blonde 'do. She knew American women perceived their husbands as inattentive. Would Khaled, now an American, even notice the change?

When Khaled spotted Fatima, poised on the sofa, his whole body flinched as if a wasp had stung him. At first his expression seemed confused; then his light-brown complexion tinted with red; and his eyes, the hue of a cold gray sky, grew even colder.

"What have you done to yourself?" he asked, aghast.

"I let Sandy color my hair," Fatima said, smiling, waiting for some show of approval.

"I thought I'd walked into the wrong house."

"It's me." Fatima laughed, then curled an end of blonde hair around one finger like a French coquette. "You like it?"

Khaled's lips shriveled into his face, his breathing growing laborious. "You look like a whore!" Suddenly, the milk slipped from his finger and fell, bounced, and split open, drenching the brown carpet, much to Khaled's irritation.

"Don't worry, I'll clean that up," Fatima said, rising from her seat.

"Color your hair—and what are you going to do next?" Khaled's hands formed fists. "Augment your breasts like a showgirl?"

Then, as if she'd already committed the said act, Khaled threw himself on Fatima, his whole body a whirl of fists. Fatima raised her arms to ward off the blows, but Khaled quickly flattened her to the sofa, punching her in rapid succession. He ripped the red scarf off her shoulders and threw it onto the carpet.

"I did not marry a whore!" he screamed in her ear. He punched her several more times, then continued screaming, "A whore! A whore! A whore! A whore!" his whole face an open mouth, spittle flying.

Khaled had never hit Fatima before in all their eighteen years of marriage. They'd quarreled badly several times, during which Fatima thought he might strike her, but he never had. Now, like the faintest echo setting off an avalanche, something within Khaled had lost its balance.

He grabbed his wife by a fistful of hair and wrenched her head backward. Her lip had split open, leaking blood; her eyes rolled back into their sockets, her breath coming in rasps.

Khaled had just pulled out one clump of Fatima's hair when their only child, Amal, a senior in high school, walked through the front door, arriving home from basketball practice. He stood in his baggy jeans and sweaty t-shirt, staring at the spectacle on the sofa, a confused expression on his face. "What's going on?" he asked.

"Amal, please, help me," Fatima cried.

"Run back to the bathroom and bring me my electric razor," Khaled said.

Amal hesitated, unsure whom to obey.

"Move it, you stupid bastard!" Khaled said.

Amal hastened down the hallway to the bathroom and returned with the razor. "What do you want me to do with it?" he asked his father. "Is Mom okay? What's wrong with her hair?"

"Plug it in the outlet," Khaled said, wrenching Fatima's arm behind her back, her body a contorted position beneath his knees, her head hanging over the end of the sofa.

"Amal, don't let him hurt me!"

"Plug it in!"

Amal pulled out the lamp chord and inserted the chord for the electric razor.

"You see this whore who's calling you a bastard?" Khaled asked his son, his tone growing calm like a torturer explaining his methods to a lackey. "Let's shave this bleached blonde mess and maybe we'll find your mother hiding someplace beneath.

Nearly suffocating on a throw pillow as Khaled forced her head into position, Fatima heard the buzz of the razor and felt the rotating blades cut their way across her scalp, leaving a bald trail. From the noise of the stainless steel bracelet clanking against the razor, she could tell Amal was shaving her and could feel Khaled's grip boring into her, leaving bruises.

In minutes, like a witch melted down to nothing, all that remained of the "whore" was a pile a bleached blonde hair on the living room carpet.

That night Khaled slept on a mildewed couch in the basement. The next evening, he complained that he'd strained his wrist disciplining Fatima, making his job of installing electrical wiring painfully difficult. And it was Fatima's fault.

Alone in the house, Fatima removed an old hi-jab from her antique cedar chest. She'd never worn it in America, and the wrinkled thing reeked of mothballs. Standing before the bathroom mirror, her lip fat and face bruised, her body aching, her head still dizzy and reeling from a twisted spine, she wrapped the black cloth around her head, concealing her baldness. *Things will never be the same between Khaled and me*, she mused bitterly, imagining herself spiking his iced tea with rat poison.

Several days later, Fatima still felt ill from the attack. Suffering from vertigo, nausea, and dizziness, she called her chiropractor and made an appointment for the same day.

She arrived at Dr. Martin's office wearing her hi-jab and a thick coat of make-up on her face, concealing her injuries.

Fatima lay facedown on Dr. Martin's cushioned table and let him run the massager over her back. He pushed up the top of her hi-jab, ready to measure the alignment of her vertebrae with his pulsar tool.

"What happened to your hair?"

"I'm having a lesbian affair."

Dr. Martin laughed. "That's good. I thought maybe you had cancer."

He switched buttons on his pulsar device and began his adjustment. "You're neck is subluxated. You'll need to come in three times a week for at least six weeks."

"I can't afford that. Maybe twice a week for a month. I'll have to check my bank account."

"Very well." Dr. Martin sighed. "But I can't guarantee that'll be enough."

A week passed. The dining-room carpet stank of sour milk. The whore's blonde hair still rested on the living room floor like a dead cat. Khaled was still sleeping in the basement on the mildewed couch beneath the spider-webs. The housework remained undone, the kitchen trash overflowing with paper plates; plastic cups, forks, and spoons; and Domino's pizza boxes. Fatima missed the next Avon campaign. She found a grocery list in Khaled's handwriting on the kitchen table, his way of telling her to get moving:

Bread

Eggs

Milk

Coffee . . .

Fatima pushed her cart listlessly down the aisle at the Walmart Super-center, gazing at the fruit juices. Someone poked her from behind. She turned around, finding a grinning woman.

"Are you a Catholic nun?"

"I'm a Satanist!" Fatima replied with a snap. She pushed her cart forward toward the eggs. It was the third time that week someone had asked her that question. She felt like the only woman in the world wearing a hi-jab.

Groceries in the trunk, Fatima dropped off some books at the library, then began the drive home, the sky darkening as storm clouds blotted out the sun, a light sprinkle of rain splattering the windshield. *Things can never be the same between Khaled and me*, she thought with a sigh.

She drove on, reflecting, trying not to cry to keep her vision clear. She punched the steering wheel and asked herself, *How can I ever forgive Amal? What kind of young man would take his father's side over his mother's in a life-threatening conflict? He must prefer men to women in general*, Fatima concluded, her spirit dole-ful as a bird with a broken wing. *Amal doesn't like women.* "Amal is a homo-sexual!" Fatima whispered through gritted teeth, her anger attacking her logic.

Fatima knew Amal had lost his faith the year before, studying evolution in biology class. He'd confessed to her in private, "Just like that Brigham Young guy in Utah, Mohammed just made it up, the Koran." He'd asked her not to tell his father that he felt that way, and she'd agreed.

"I kept your dirty secret," Fatima rasped, "and look how you repaid me. You chose your father over me. I begged you for help, and you followed his orders like some trained monkey." Fatima knew her son was already at least as strong as Khaled. He'd inherited the upper body strength of the Turkish fishermen on Fatima's side of the family. He could have overpowered his father and come to her aid, but he hadn't.

Fatima was becoming so angry her lungs had constricted, making breathing difficult. "Things are different now between Khaled and me. And my son, Amal, is a gay atheist!"

She ran a red light, setting off a blare of honking horns, and turned down the next street. *A whore!* Fatima thought. *Me?*

Like a bottom feeder, sinking to the deepest recesses of the abyss to sop up the scum, Fatima's thoughts drifted down the darkest depths of her imaginings. She could picture herself driving to the truck stop outside of town where prostitutes solicited business, dressed in black Spandex and a Dolly Parton wig, her spiked heels clinking under the moonlight. She imagined herself luring home a truck driver, Khaled finding them in bed, her legs wrapped around his beer belly in a pose like Kama Sutra as she laughed at her husband's surprised face.

No! Fatima cast the idea from her head. *I am not a whore.* Her chin tilted upward.

That night, after it seemed like Khaled and Amal had fallen asleep, Fatima lay in bed, listening to the crickets outside the window and the distant drone of semis. Suddenly, the door creaked open, and Khaled, shrouded in shadows, crept into the room.

Fatima's pulse raced. Her heart had become too bitter, her thoughts too dark in her resentment, and now, she feared, Khaled had somehow discovered her. *He's coming to kill me now*, she thought.

Khaled sat on the bed, silent and dignified, looking ahead. He reached out and placed his hand upon her arm. For several minutes, neither of them moved or said anything. Finally, Khaled turned and repositioned himself atop his wife.

Fatima felt the moisture on Khaled's face against hers and could smell the familiar scent of perspiration and Avon's Wild Country. He clasped her head in his hands, then slid his fingers beneath her neck. Fatima felt a tear tickle its way down her face and fall onto the pillow.

Khaled kissed her stubble. He whispered in her ear, "Fatima! Fatima!"

REUNION REDO

By Holly Riordan
(New York, USA)
Humor, 3rd Place

High School: the period of awkward exchanges between naïve teenagers playing the role of adults. The hierarchy was topped with jocks and grounded with geeks; the average nobodies layering the middle. Every day brought along a plethora of golden opportunities to be humiliated. I missed it.

My ten-year reunion was a day away, and I had a profuse amount of personal renovating to do. After skimming through my senior yearbook, I was struck with nostalgia by the four or five faces that I loved, and the 200 I despised. Even with enemies outweighing friends, I was determined to show up. It was my chance for redemption.

"What's the return policy here?" I asked as I piled a sleek dress, clutch, and diamond earrings onto the boutique's checkout counter. I'd be donning the expensive ensemble in less than twenty-four hours, so as long as I could return everything after that time, my plan was faultless.

"You have a week, as long as you provide the receipt and the tags are still intact."

"Great." I grinned as she slid the pricey items across the scanner. "Not that I'd ever return this. I doubt I'll come back. If I do, just kick me out of the store, because I must've gone crazy."

"Wedding?"

"Reunion."

Her eyes rolled as she bagged the products. "Just don't stain anything."

Once the clothes were purchased with four months' worth of salary, I braced myself for my next errand. As I walked down the city streets, the sidewalks sprouted multitudinous men in suits and ties. In a harmless version of Russian roulette, I cornered one to say, "Excuse me. Hi. I was just wondering if I could take a picture with you."

"Oh, no, I'm not George Clooney. Common mistake."

A laugh bolted from my lungs before I explained my peculiar request. "My high school reunion's coming up. I want to go, but I don't want everyone to find out that the prom queen ended up working at a gas station *in*

Queens. I already rented my neighbor's sports car and booked a beauty appointment; all I need is a few snapshots with *the love of my life*. Which is where
you come in."

"You have an engagement ring on."

"That *you* gave me."

Unfazed by the unique situation, he examined the ring as if he were a
potential buyer. "I guess it goes well with your plan. Fake diamonds for a
fake relationship."

My eyes reduced to slits at his uncivil comment. My mother let me bor-
row the ring for the occasion, and the stranger's insults were unwelcome.
How difficult was it to agree to a creepy request from someone you met off
the street? When I was about to scamper off in search of a more consensual
man, he fell to one knee.

"Since I don't know you, I'm hoping you won't follow me home, murder
me, and throw my ashes in the litter box of the dozen cats I'm sure you have.
Instead, will you do me the honor of pretending to be my wife to trick your
classmates into thinking you're not a pathetic mess, desperate for acceptance?"

"You always know exactly what to say."

The stranger wrapped his arm around my neck as I extracted my phone
to snap the first photo. I took a variety of others where we held hands and
stared into the distance. I even coerced him into giving me a convincing kiss
on the cheek.

"Thanks," I said once our makeshift photo shoot was complete. "I know
it's not every day you have to pretend to enjoy some psychotic woman's
company."

"Actually, it is. I have a girlfriend."

The following morning was a blur of preparations. I stumbled from my
house to the hair salon to the school. The event was being held in the lunch-
room. It felt bizarre to see the same tables where I would eat my bagged
lunch, the same ceiling that had been stained by food fights, the same floor
where I had gotten beaten up by 'friends'.

"Oh my gosh! Stacey, is that you?"

Seconds after the question was asked, a swarm of girls surrounded me
like presidential security. All of them began to blabber at once, wondering
how my life was going, where my career had taken me, and if I missed spending time with them.

Instead of attempting to concoct believable answers, I raised my hand to flash the ring. A chorus of girly screams and giggles filled the cafeteria as they congratulated me, admiring the pictures I flipped through on my phone.

"Oh my gosh, I can't believe it!"

"He's so gorgeous!"

"You deserve this, Stace!"

"That's my husband."

As the last comment settled in my ears, all glances traveled to Madge, the owner of the voice. Given her stiletto heels, brunette locks, and flawless skin, it was clear why my *fiancé* had chosen to be with her. Their physical perfection was sickening.

"Do you know how many guys there are in the world?" I asked, my anxiety bubbling. "It's bound for some of them to look . . . identical."

Snatching the phone from my trembling grasp, her features contorted as she said, "No. That's him. That's my husband."

Frozen in an ice block of unmovable lies, I had only one logical explanation to give: the truth.

But instead I said, "*You're* his wife? He promised me he was going to break it off with you."

"*What?* No. There's no way," she said before spinning to wave her husband over. He joined the group, eating a handful of pretzels as she asked, "Do you know Stacey?"

His confusion morphed into amusement when he saw me. "Hey, you. What did I say about stalking me? I better not find you in my bed tonight."

"Oh my gosh, it's true," Madge said as she misjudged our interaction. She grabbed her husband's tie, pulling him toward her as she said, "I saw the pictures. How long has this been going on?"

"Wait, wait, no," he said with a laugh. "It's not like that. At all. She just asked me to take some pictures with her to fool some girls she used to know. I didn't know you'd be one of them."

My polished nails scraped at the skin of my scalp as I said, "Oh, come on, babe. No one's going to believe that."

Madge was torn between who was truly the truth teller, providing me with a possibility to get away with my unlawful lies. But my thread of hope unfurled when her husband posed the question that showered me in embarrassment. With a smug smirk, he asked, "What's my name?"

"Damn."

Mortifying seconds of numbness elapsed until my dress was drenched in Madge's fruit punch. "I'm pregnant, and you almost just broke us up!"

Knowing no words would cleanse the situation, I migrated to the corner where I plopped myself down onto a bar stool.

"What happened to you?" the man beside me asked, his tie and cufflinks unfastened as he gulped down a glass of gin.

"I tried to trick people into liking me," I said. "Didn't work by pretending I cheated with an old friend's husband. Who knew?"

"It could've been worse."

"I'm wearing a fake engagement ring."

He shrugged. "I'm wearing a hairpiece."

"I hired a makeup artist."

"I hired a prostitute. But that was last night."

When my chuckles ceased, I asked, "Hey, want to pretend we're too good for this place and ditch it to go somewhere more fun? Like, I don't know, a jail?"

He grinned. "They won't have alcohol, but at least they'll be more decent people around."

Although our ten-year reunion was a disaster, we went to our 15th together. And that time my engagement was real.

But the diamonds were still fake.

FLIGHT OF THE NIGHTINGALE

By Nicole Conway
(Georgia, USA)
Short Fiction, 1ˢᵗ Place

The windows of Eland Park were lit as the evening drew in thickly around the massive oaks that lined either side of the forward avenue. The sunlight peered over the green hills on the horizon, shining through the wavered glass and draping long shadows over the marble floors. Jane Watford watched the birds flutter through the tops of the trees from the window of her mother's favorite parlor, her dark eyes moving as quickly and lightly as their wings and following their frantic paths across the estate's grand front lawn.

"Jane, dear, come away from there and sing for us," her mother called to her from one of the lavish sofas, peering at her over the rim of a finely painted teacup.

Mr. Longbourne and his son had come to call this evening, bringing with them warm brandy and good humor that Mr. and Mrs. Watford seemed to be enjoying immensely. Their daughter, Jane, however, was less than entertained. The gentlemen stood, chatting idly and pausing only now that Jane's attention had been turned back to the goings-on in the parlor. They offered their willful smiles, appearing silently pleased to see her looking to them now rather than sitting idly at the window.

Young William Longbourne made no mistake about his admirations for the Watford's only daughter and stared at her at length where she sat across the room. He was a pleasant young man, though not handsome enough to capture the wandering eye of an eligible female. Fortunately for him, he had money enough to compensate for any lack of physical charm and the promise of a grand inheritance that would have excused any foulness in his manners. The Watfords couldn't imagine a more appropriate match for their lovely daughter, but she hardly seemed to hear him at all when he spoke to her.

"You play so well." He offered her gentle compliments while he stood beside the pianoforte, looking on while she practiced a delicate melody.

Jane answered him with a soft smile, looking up for only a fleeting second before she returned her gaze back to the yellowed sheet music before her. Her slender fingers brushed the notes from the instrument with careful ease, feeling the weighted presence of the young man who watched her so intently.

"You should sing for us," her mother suggested again, not at all satisfied by Jane's mere playing. Her daughter would not be distracted, and finished the song at length before she stood and dismissed herself for the evening. The night had grown quite late, and it was perfectly excusable for her to leave, though William Longbourne made certain that he expressed that he was sad to see her go. She was careful to say her goodbyes without ever returning that adoring sentiment, and left them in the parlor with a calm, disarming smile.

Jane made quick, quiet speed down the grand staircase to the foyer as the midnight hour passed quietly over the estate. One of the housemaids brought her a long brown coat and a shawl that she wrapped around her narrow frame snuggly before she ventured out into the crisp night air. She bid the maid make carefully certain not to mention to her parents where she had gone, but to tell them simply that she had retired to her quarters for the night. The maid looked distressed, and Jane hated to make the dear woman lie for her, but it couldn't be helped.

The outside smelled of sweet, fresh dew, and the night's soft wind brushed through her long curled hair of deep, coppery red. She walked down the shadowed paths that led into the open rolling hills, stopping short of the estate's grounds and giving way to the wild tangled woods and dark open prairie.

Eland Park rose like a gleaming white fortress behind her, illumed by the candles in the windows and lanterns hung about all the balconies and broad patios. Jane was careful not to look back as she wandered away from the gardens and paved walkways that spanned the formal grounds. No direction or sense of purpose carried her forward as she watched the distant horizon and admired the pale lights of the stars.

She strolled along the borders of her family's estate, and was only satisfied when she had thoroughly muddied the hem of her gown. Her hair was made tousled and wild by the night air, and her fair face was flushed from walking at length. Jane could only praise herself, imagining with pleasure how her mother would have paled and fainted to see her fair daughter in such a splendid mess.

Lights on the distant horizon, tucked up against an outcropping of thick forest, caught her eye, and so she wandered in that general direction. Only when she had finally crossed the few miles towards them did she see the shape of the old farmhouse with a slanted roof against the darkness. A long stone fence marked the boundary of her family's property, and from that point she could see the tiny farm's stables and corrals, the feeding troughs, the oil lamps sitting in the open windows, and the shapes of the little white sheep shuffling about near the stable.

With a huff of effort, Jane pulled herself up and over the stone wall and began across the sloping pasture towards the farm. The sun had just begun to rise again, thrusting the first few shades of daylight into the sky and rousing the birds that nested in the thistle and shrubs. The sound of the crickets humming in the grass began to go silent, always pausing whenever she drew near to them, but now they hid away as the world began to waken.

Jane did not fear for being here, so far from Eland Park where she was absolutely not supposed to be. Her parents were full of fresh compliments and good liquor; they would sleep until late into the afternoon without as much as a stir between them. So she kept her dark eyes upon the farmhouse and followed along the stone fence, letting her hands brush the mossy rocks that were stacked up to waist height, as she admired the simple place from a safe distance.

A voice called to her, hailing her from the open doorway of the farmhouse where someone now stood and waved to her. It made poor Jane's heart hammer sporadically to see that mysterious person beginning to approach, walking deliberately across the pasture in her direction. She paused with her back to the bordering fence, watching the tall shape of a man come gradually into view until he stopped just a few yards short of her.

He looked down at her curiously, a man perhaps only a few years older than she, and put his hands into the deep pockets of long dark coat that was draped over his shoulders. She could see how he was dressed beneath, and it was humble to be sure. The stains on his shirt and tall mud-caked boots marked him to be a farmer without hearing him declare it aloud. He had a tall, broad-shouldered make to him, and lacked nothing in the sturdiness of his structure. She'd seen men of that sort before, working at the docks to load luggage and supplies onto the ships at harbor. But she had only ever observed them through the little glass windows in her mother's favorite carriage. To see one so near made the frail young woman shy back.

"Are you lost?" he asked her with a tone of genuine concern.

Jane looked up to his handsomely crafted face with uncertainty, faltering and stammering over anything she might want to say. "I don't think so."

"My name is Henry Clarke." He inclined his head with a broad smile, his eyes of calm blue meeting hers without the forceful intention of winning her returning smile. "Are you going into town? It's quite a long way for a lady to walk on her own."

"No," she was quick to reply, though she hesitated to give him her name. "No, I was just out for a walk."

"A bit early for a walk, isn't it?" He grinned at her again. If he'd noticed her deliberate lack of introduction, he did not show it at all. "I'll let you to it, then. I offer my apologies if I happened to startle you."

Jane watched him as he gave a small bow before turning back towards the farmhouse. The drab looking structure stood with the door left wide open so that the warm light from the inside bled out into the pale dawn.

"Jane," she called to him then, gathering up the ends of her skirts and wrestling to catch up with him as he crossed the dew-laden grass. "My name is Jane."

At the sound of her voice, Henry stopped to watch and wait for her with a curious arch to his finely crafted brow. "Jane." He repeated the name with a nod of approval. "Are you fond of walking alone so early in the morning, Miss Jane?"

"Yes," she answered quietly. She watched the lax, comically amused expressions cross his face as they walked beside one another, coming to the doorway of the snug little farmhouse and pausing as he shrugged out of his coat and left it on a hook just inside. Jane hesitated on the step, leaning inside to peer about at the simple, humble dwellings.

"You can come in, if you like." He chuckled, stooping at the hearth to place a few more logs on the fire. She watched him stoke the embers, coaxing the fire back to life to fill the main floor with warmth and light.

"Won't your wife mind having a visitor at this hour?" she protested weakly, her fair brow creased with distress.

Henry cast her a bemused smirk, "I haven't a wife. Not even so much as a maid to my name. This is my father's farm, and I keep it on my own, since his passing last April."

"I'm so sorry for your loss." Jane spoke with sympathy, but she needed no more encouragement as she came slowly inside. It smelled of warm, earthy flavors and was only sparsely decorated with the few little sticks of simply crafted furniture positioned about the space. All the windows were pushed ajar to let the cool air move through the house. It made such a peculiar racket, to hear the wind and the soft sounds of the morning birds, that it left Jane feeling confused.

"Can I offer you something to drink?" Henry stood back while the young woman appraised his meager dwellings and moved about as cautiously as a cat.

"No, thank you." Jane sat down in one of his wooden chairs, brushing back her shawl and meeting his quizzical gaze. Already her mind turned over the puzzle of leaving without offending him, though she couldn't say that she had anything pressing that demanded her attention. "I really can't stay; my parents will be expecting me." The lie tasted sour on her lips, and she looked away directly.

"Stay as long as you wish, Miss Jane." He chuckled again. "I've tea and milk enough to drown yourself. There might even be a scrap of cake left, if you should be hungry. You can do as you wish here for as long as you like, though if you stay long enough I might have to put you to a chore or two."

Clearly he was joking, and that much could be told in his light-hearted tone, but something in Jane's fair face seemed to liven at the suggestion. She snapped upright in the chair, watching as he began pouring clean white milk into several large glass bottles and topping each one with a big rubber nipple.

"I can do that for you," she offered in a weak, fragile tone.

He looked back at her over his shoulder. "Do what? Feed the lambs?"

"Yes. Yes! Yes, I can feed the lambs." Jane stood quickly and went to pick up a pair of the large bottles, then stood by waiting for his directions.

Henry was baffled. "You really don't have to do that. It's dirty work, Miss Jane."

"What do you think I am? Look at my dress! I'm not afraid to get dirty," she chastened him with a pouting, determined huff.

Smiling with a broad, crooked grin, Henry resigned to raise his hands in the air and laugh at her. "I stand humbled, Miss Jane. You may be the dirtiest young lady I have ever met. I'm sure the lambs will be pleased to meet you."

He took her to the stable where the tiny lambs were kept, showing her how she might hold the bottles and let the little ones nurse. The air was warm and close inside the stable, smelling of sweet hay and the pleasing musk of animals. Jane smiled and giggled as the lambs suckled and pulled against the bottles, rubbing against her and bleating insistently.

Henry fed the sheep and worked about the farm as the sun began to rise, carrying buckets of grain and filling the water troughs while Jane wandered about. At first she was uncertain, careful, and wary of going anywhere he might not approve of a stranger venturing. But he made no comments or moves to stop her, letting her mill about at her leisure until at last she returned to watch him patching up a section of the barn's roof that had begun to rot through.

Sitting on an upturned bucket and dabbing at the sweat on her brow with her shawl, she started to talk to him. She asked about his family, about his late father and his mother who had gone to live in London with her sister. He told her about his elder sister who was married and living near Bath with her four young children. He spoke about his service in the militia before he had returned here to tend his father's farm, explaining that he'd never cared much to take a place in the clergy and was better pleased with his lot here than he had been living abroad with the militia. He'd been decommissioned after suffering an injury to his leg that, if not for the tender care from his sister, might have caused him to lose it.

He asked about her family, and she told him very little, keeping what she could to herself and giving only what she felt she must, with as much ambiguity as her manners would allow. He liked her stories about her Aunt Fran, the woman who insisted on wearing hats with enormous peacock feathers in them to parties that tickled at her husband's nose whenever she turned around. They gave him terrible sneezing fits that she declared was a symptom of someone talking ill of him, rather than a symptom of her voluminous hats. Those stories made him laugh, and Jane smiled up at him brightly, pleased at the sound of his laugh that came in such a rich tone from where he worked on the roof.

"I really must be going back home now." Jane fidgeted with her shawl anxiously.

Henry peered over the edge of the roof down to her, seeming to share a private bit of worry as well. He amended it quickly with a disarming smile. "You should walk this way again tomorrow."

His suggestion made her face feel hot with embarrassment. It left her speechless and uncertain as to how she should reply or even if she should. She looked at him hesitantly and nibbled at her lower lip, still wrenching her small hands in the fabric of her shawl as she sought desperately for something to say.

He laughed again, waving a hand down to her and shrugging lightly. "I'm only joking, Miss Jane. But I think the lambs would be horribly disappointed if you didn't come again. How am I to explain it to them?"

"I will come back." She smiled at last, leaving him then and beginning the long stroll back to Eland Park with a bit more life to her steps. It gave her energy and greater speed on her journey, and only when she had passed through the threshold back into her family's extravagant home did she feel any hint of fatigue.

It happened just that way every day in the weeks that followed. She would leave in the tiniest hours of the morning, abandoning her mother and father to their lavish parties, and make her way across the vale to the small farm at West End.

Henry kept her only as busy as she wished to be, showing her how she might prepare the bottles of milk for the lambs and gather the eggs from the henhouse. He waited for her by the stone wall that joined the two properties, though Jane took special care in making sure he did not know that she had come from Eland Park. That task was made simple because he never inquired about her origins or even so much as suggested that she volunteer anything about herself.

He would answer her questions readily enough, however, and didn't withhold any detail she might have wanted to hear. Jane imagined the tall, slender woman that he described when she spoke of his sister, giggling at the idea of all four of her young children hanging on to her skirts like chicks around a mother hen.

There was so much warmth in his family, and though she never saw any of them, she could hear the affection in his voice to talk of his mother, sister, cousins, aunts, and uncles. They weren't a wealthy family, not in the same respect that hers was. They had no estates and no large tracts of land. His father had been a clergyman and had tended this little farm for many years when he wasn't at his parsonage. His mother was a scatter-brained lady with a sweet, gentle temper and a delicate disposition. She had married his father at fifteen, and had struggled to bear him any children until much later in her life.

After his father's death and his injury while in military service, a neighbor who had done a poor job of maintaining the property had kept the farm. Henry insisted that he move back as soon as he was able, against the advice of his sister who was determined that he should stay with her in town. But Henry explained that he wouldn't let his father's farm go to ruin, and couldn't imagine selling it away, so he had taken on the work of fixing it up in hopes that he might find a simple job in town to support himself.

"I thought I might inquire at that vast old estate just over the hill there and see if they might hire me as a stable-hand," he mused once, causing Jane's face to flush entirely of color and her heart to flutter with a surge of real panic.

"Oh don't do that." She struggled to keep her own voice even and composed so that she might not solicit a curious look from him. "They are a snobbish lot, I hear. No, I don't think that would suit you at all. They're so terribly rich. Why would you want to be at the call of people like that?"

Jane could see his cheek turn up as evidence that he smiled at her words. "You sound like a snob, Miss Jane," he said to her in jest. "I'm sure they are perfectly respectable people, money and riches aside."

Her daily visits to the farm at West End made Jane feel much more troubled whenever the tenants at Eland Park came up in their conversations. She steered their discussions as deliberately away from that subject as she could without being obvious. But as the months progressed, she felt she could not keep it from him for very much longer.

Mr. and Mrs. Watford began to notice their daughter's strange change in temper and appearance, while not as immediately as they might have. Her mother commented on how many of her dresses had been ruined with mud, and demanded to know what she had done to damage them so. Jane smiled as pleasingly as she knew how, and convinced her mother that she had taken up horseback riding in the early morning for exercise.

Her father noticed that her skin had begun to look much more tanned and weathered, and her hands looked rather rough. Jane shrugged at him and kissed his cheek, telling him the same fabricated tale of morning horseback rides across the prairie for her health.

Such a story allowed her only a few more weeks before she spied a familiar passing carriage on the road, coming up past West End and making for Eland Park. Jane was coming out of the farmhouse with a basket filled with eggs balanced against her hip and looked up to see that carriage and those inside gaping at her. Jane couldn't have hoped to be mistaken for someone else, there was no mistaking the young Watford heiress. She knew her coppery, vibrant red hair stood out rather blatantly. No sooner had she spied the carriage than did the basket slip from her hands and land with a smash on the ground.

Henry was lively with concern, begging her to sit and rest, and insisting that the heat must have caused her to swoon. She could scarcely draw a breath, her hands trembling and dread making her limbs heavy.

He suggested that he might take her back to her home, desiring to see that she would make it back without collapsing again. Jane appeased him with a cup of tea and numerous assurances that she felt fit enough to walk.

But as she left from his farmhouse, her hands still shaking and her head pulsing with alarm, she caught a glimpse of his worried frown as he lingered there in the doorway and watched her depart.

Mr. and Mrs. Watford were in full distress when she returned. Mrs. Newport had come to call in her carriage, arriving in a flurry of breathless excitement that brought the estate into a stir. She felt it well within her right to inform the Watfords that their daughter had been spotted coming from a farmhouse where, by all the common knowledge, a young man with no fortune was the sole tenant.

Mr. Watford was furious, and his wife wept inconsolably, begging her daughter for the truth of the matter as Jane stood in her muddied gown, coat, and shawl with horror plain upon her face.

"Such a scandal! Oh, a scandal!" Mrs. Newport exclaimed, leaving them at the urging of Mr. Watford, who was eager to have a sole audience with his wayward daughter.

"What have you done, Jane?" he asked her coldly.

Jane could not meet his eyes, not for the frantic wailing of her mother who had thrown herself over a sofa in despair. "Nothing, Father. Henry Clarke is my friend, nothing more. He keeps the farm at West End by himself."

Mr. Watford was not satisfied, and he glowered at her punishingly. "You have shamed yourself."

"I have not!" Jane lashed out with a desperate voice, a wild frenzy in her eyes as she held her father's gaze. "Ask him yourself, Father, I have done nothing but to talk to him. He lets me play with the lambs in the stable; that is all!"

"Lambs in the stable," Mrs. Watford snorted and sniffled. "Honestly, Jane? Is that what you expect us to believe?"

"How would you have me prove it to you?" Jane dared to offer.

Mr. Watford was quick to reply. "I have given William Longbourne permission to seek your hand. He's asked us to hold a ball here at Eland where he might ask to court you formally. We will invite Henry Clarke, and you will accept William Longbourne's affections where all can witness it. If it is true what you say, then your dear friend will be overjoyed for your good fortune."

Jane felt instantly sick, but her father did not provide her with enough to counter his offer. He sent her from the room directly and demanded that she remain in her quarters until summoned so that he could try and console her weeping mother. Jane held her own composure well, but only so long as she knew the maids were about making sure that Mr. Watford's orders were followed. Alone in her room, she mourned with bitter tears a fate at the awkward hand of William Longbourne. She grieved to lose Henry's sweet smiles and pleasant laugh. Behind the closed doors and sealed windows, she watched the hours pass in a listless, morose state that could not be comforted.

The days passed swiftly, and it was two weeks before Jane could manage the walk back to the farm. Henry was not waiting for her at the wall as he had before, but she could see that the lights in the farmhouse were bright against the heavy night. The lambs stirred in their corral, bleating to see her familiar presence returning and causing the dark shape of a tall man to fill the open doorway.

Henry met her halfway across the narrow drive, grasping her shoulders and looking down to her with a deep frown of concern. "Jane! I thought something terrible had happened to you! Are you well?"

Tears brimmed in her dark eyes to see him again, to feel the touch of his hands upon her in such a benign and genuinely worried way. With a soft whimper, she let her head fall against the broad surface of his chest, and reached to clench at the back of his jacket.

Standing in the dim light that ebbed from the open door, Henry held her there and let her cry as long as she wished. He asked her nothing else about herself or what had happened, guiding her gently into the house when at last she seemed to calm.

He brought her into the kitchen and sat her down at the table, bringing her a cup of warm tea before he sat down in front of her and watched her carefully. Jane began to compose herself, wiping her eyes on her shawl and looking diligently away from his deeply worried stare.

Her heartbeat stammered as she saw something perched upon the opposite end of the table. A clean white envelope with spidery, swirling penmanship sat upon pile of unopened mail with the red wax seal already broken. It was an invitation to her family's estate asking his presence at the Eland Park ball the following evening.

Henry followed her eyes to where the invitation lay, sitting back in his chair and sighing loudly. "It seems they aren't so snobbish after all," he told her in a softly joking voice.

"Are you going to attend?" she asked him, her own voice lacking any trace of humor.

"It would be rude of me not to." He furrowed his brows deeply as he seemed to grow unusually tense. "But I am sure that the invitation is merely a courtesy. I was hoping to inquire if you meant to attend before I decided if I might go."

Jane flicked a quick, checking glance up to him and reached out to place one of her hands atop his. Such a deliberate gesture took him by surprise, and he looked at her with a flurry of confusion skewing his handsome face, making him hesitant at first, but his confidence grew as he moved to hold her hand.

The young woman had never felt such a sudden and immense relief of pressure before, and Jane quickly found herself smiling at him through her teary eyes. "I would like very much to see you there tomorrow."

Henry was deeply upset that she once again refused his offer to take her back home. But as the sun began to rise, Jane made her way back to Eland Park before her parents even roused. She readied herself, donning a lovely long gown of emerald green silk and sitting quietly while her mother styled her hair, pinning it into place with a beautiful jade comb adorned with the design of a little golden nightingale.

Eland Park was lit in sparkling, clean white light as the night of the ball brought guests from all about the countryside. The marble floors were polished until they shone like pearl, and the doorways were adorned with wreaths of flowers. Couples arrived in intricate carriages drawn by smartly styled horses, greeting the Watfords in the grand foyer with adoring words of praise. They bowed and curtsied, admiring the splendor of the party and offering lavish compliments upon the family.

Jane noticed that everyone regarded her with noticeable care, and it seemed that Mrs. Newport had wasted no time in spreading the news of the girl's frequent visits to a certain small farm in West End. When met with her peers, Jane saw the girls turn and giggle or whisper in hushed voices. The young men seemed equally as amused and eager to scandalize her, though when Mr. Longbourne and his son arrived, their attentions were instantly quieted.

With her face burning freshly with embarrassment, she allowed William Longbourne to kiss her wrist and praise her with compliments that sounded terribly forced. It pleased her parents, who looked on, waiting in silent expectation for another certain young man to pass through the tall, grand doors of the estate and satisfy the stipulations for their peace of mind.

Henry Clarke was let into Eland Park, stepping through the doorway dressed in a black suit and coat that matched his tall frame and fit him handsomely. It was quite plain compared to what the other young men wore, having no lace or finely detailed collar, and drew a clear distinction as to the level of income Henry had come from. But he looked distinguished with his dark hair brushed back and his clear eyes searching the crowds of unfamiliar faces with a hopeful expression. Jane knew exactly who and what he was searching for, and so her stomach churned with dread.

Gradually he made his way to the front of the long line of elaborately garbed folk that stood, waiting for their turn to greet their hosts. No sooner had his turn arrived than Jane met his eyes and watched the wave of realization crash in upon him. He hesitated at first, obviously vexed and confused as he began to piece together what was happening. Finally he did approach, introducing himself with a chilling sense of calm to both of her parents before he finally turned to her.

"You look well, Miss Watford," he said, his eyes speaking more than what passed over his lips. His guarded stare savored strongly of betrayal and hurt, though he managed to keep his countenance amiable enough. The calm in his eyes unnerved her thoroughly, however, and made her tremble as he bent to kiss her wrist.

At the very first moment she could, Jane stole away from her parents to quest through the crowds of guests in search of him. Through the sea of swirling white dresses and finely clad gentlemen, she wandered in search. At last she saw him standing in one of the grand ballrooms where music filled the stuffy, crowded atmosphere even in such a dazzlingly spacious room. He lingered near a white marble staircase with his back to her, a group of three other young gentlemen hovering before him and talking with animated expressions. Among them, William Longbourne stood in such stark contrast to Henry that it was almost silly to watch. William looked sickly and petite compared to the tall, broad-shouldered young man that was Henry. He looked hale and healthy, formidable and strong, even with the other young men sneering up at him like gaunt, hungry coyotes.

When she had come quite close to their group, Jane could hear everything that was being said amongst them. But what she did finally hear caused her to pause short of joining their conversation.

"A farmer, you say?" William jeered, making the other young men laugh with him. "Why on earth would you come here? Surely you realized an invitation like that was merely a formality."

Henry remained calm and even, as though he were distracted and not at all invested in the conversation. His gaze wandered, looking up to the vaulted ceilings and tall windows.

She finally dared to venture forth and speak to him and at that same instant, he bowed away from the conversation and began to walk the crowded rooms of Eland Park. He appeared completely unaware that she followed him, watching him as he gathered peculiar, lengthy stares from the other guests in the halls. Jane haunted his steps with hopeful glances, following him as he finally found his way to the stables where his horse was stabled. It had been brushed and fed, looking out at him with ears pricked as he approached and opened the stall door.

Only when he turned about to lead his horse from the stall did he see her standing there, the hem of her lovely dress stained and tangled with bits of straw from the dirty stable floor.

She felt as thin and frail as wet parchment, looking at him with doe-eyes brimming with fresh tears. "You're leaving," she observed aloud, her voice trembling audibly.

"I cannot stay here, Jane." He met her eyes with calm resolve. She saw nothing of anger or resentment present in his face as she'd expected to. "These gilded doors and painted windows are not for me."

He paused for a difficult amount of time, seeming to falter as a touch of pain caused him to squint his eyes and brought a furrow to his brow. It struck her with the brutal realization of how acutely and selfishly she'd scandalized them both. What small, good opinions there had ever been of him were now perfectly ruined.

"I wondered why you would not tell me more about yourself. I assumed you were simply being cautious. After all, I was hardly more than a stranger to you," he said at last, "but I did come to love you, however foolish and vain that affection may have been. I dared to think, to hope, that some similar affection is what drove you to keep coming to see me."

"Henry," she whimpered helplessly.

"But I am outmatched. There can be no mystery about what I have to offer; you have already seen me for all I am and all I ever care to be." He shook his head and looked to her with such honest amour that it bit furiously at Jane's conscience. "I will not forcefully spring you from a life that promises such lavish comforts."

Jane could not speak. She stood as quietly as a shadow against the wall as Henry led his horse out past the stable doors into the night, unable to say even so much as a word to him. The sound of his horse's hooves clattering on the cobblestones faded away and left her wrapped in cold silence.

The evening passed into the first hours of the morning when the sun had not yet begun to rise and the ball at Eland Park had not slowed, nor had its joyous crowds begun to thin. Music still filled the air along with the sounds of laughter and dancing, but Jane moved through the halls, her face flushed as she wrestled to pull her coat about her. Along her way down to the grand foyer, she felt a snagging hold upon her elbow that snapped her to a halt.

William Longbourne looked upon her with wild-eyed horror and disbelief, gripping her arm fiercely. "You cannot be serious! Him? Are you mad?"

Jane snatched her arm away from him, casting him a fitfully defiant glare. "I am perfectly serious."

"Do not think that I will accept you under any terms after this," William hissed at her, gripping her arm again to yank her forcefully back to face him. "When you leave here, you are resigned to the fate of a wild, hapless peasant. You will poison the shades of your family's estate. You will stain their reputation with lasting shame. No. No, I will not let you do it. Foolish woman, you will come with me back inside right away. I will have what I was promised!"

She could only smile at him the crazed smile of a foolishly reckless young woman and, reaching back to pull the green comb with the little golden nightingale etched upon it from her hair, tucked the trinket into the breast pocket of his coat. She patted it there where she'd nested it before wrenching herself free of his grasp once again.

"That promise was never mine. This is all of me you will have," she whispered, turning then and leaving him there, gaping in the foyer, while she fled into the softly fading night.

Once the doors of Eland Park were opened and left behind her, her feet knew the way as she ran to the small farm at West End. Her long scarlet hair spilled from the pins where Mother had fastened it, and the hem of her green silken gown was tattered by the time she made it to the stone wall that lined her family's property. She called out his name, panting and frantic as she struggled to make her way over the wall in her restrictive clothing. Huffing and puffing, she put her feet upon the free soil on the other side of the stone wall, looking up to see the familiar shape of a man coming towards her from the open door of the farmhouse. Jane Watford smiled, calling his name once again and hearing the distant reply as he answered her.

Winter came and gently faded into spring, bringing with it new lambs and new hungry mouths to feed. The morning dawned early with the sweet smell of dew on the fresh blades of grass, and Jane Clarke carried the large glass bottles from the kitchen out towards the stable, singing merrily all the while. She sang and whistled, a sound that the lambs now regarded with excited affection as it always preceded their morning feeding.

She fed them, humming her sweet tunes to them as they suckled the bottles, and pausing only to look out the open stable door to the distant rolling land beyond. It was only a speck in the distance, but she could just make out the white shape of Eland Park rising above the trees, a clean white palace that she had eagerly forsaken for a house of wood and twigs, but she could only look at it and smile at her good fortune before turning back to the lambs and beginning to sing again.

Learn more about 1ˢᵗ-place winner and Fresh Ink Group member Nicole Conway at http://www.FreshInkGroup.com/authors/nicole-conway.

STARLIGHT

By Grace Lin
(California, USA)
Historical, 3rd Place

The haggard, moth-eaten man huddled in a damp corner of Block 2 with his eyes closed, feeling as though he had single-handedly defeated a great monster of ice and wind, fatigue weighing down his thin frame like dense fog. His body trembled with grief and torture that had long since transcended tears, now only burning ice cold in his heart. Unless they looked carefully, some might think he was sleeping, like his comrades in the despair and gloom that suffocated the death camp. But shutting out all light did nothing to numb his thoughts or erase the silent terror on the face of a young girl from his mind, nor did his wretched hours of slumber. The methodical marching of soldiers outside the compound seemed to mock the recurring screams of children echoing in his head; the eerily beautiful prelude playing during their arrival continued to haunt him. He was undisturbed inside the maze of pain and despair and anger closing his mind. He had lost count of the days since Anastazja had been taken from the block with the other children.

The sound of creaking hinges broke the charged silence and pierced the man's thoughts. He blinked, his eyes readjusting to the sudden burst of harsh white light as brilliant and blinding as he often imagined a star would look up close. A group of fresh arrivals were frog-marched through the door; somewhere, a baby's cry was heard, then silenced. The man fell back into a trance; this group was no different than the last, and they would all die eventually, like Anastazja. They would all be sent to the gas chambers. A slender, elfin figure was thrown roughly to the ground after the rest had passed through. For barely a moment, time slowed to a halt, and the starlight that was cast upon the girl, bloody and sprawled across the floor, looked as though a ray of Heaven had parted the night. With a heaving groan, the heavy door was barred shut, and the room fell into shadows.

The figure lay on the ground, unmoving for a long time, long enough that the man noticed and turned to look at this new curiosity. There was blood in her hair and on her arms and legs, and when she lifted her head, he could see her bright, powerful eyes cutting through the ebony crowding his heart.

Someone carried her away to the back, where the Jewish doctor was. The man heard more commotion, and as if from somewhere far away, he heard a soft voice calling his name. Like an echo it rang upon his ears, faint, yet clear and pure. The sound was foreign; the other prisoners had soon learned to leave him to his vigil, distancing themselves as much as possible in the cramped space.

"Herr Zielinski, sir?" a small voice said hesitantly. He turned to face the source of the sound. She jumped slightly. "That is what the others said your name was. I did not mean to bother you."

He stared at her, unsure of why she was speaking to him. The little girl, now with bandages on her arms and legs, took his silence as acceptance and sat down beside him. For a moment he was angry that she did not respect his obvious desire to be alone, but he swallowed his retort, struck by how much her face looked like Anastazja's. She couldn't be older than eight or nine.

"They said you liked to be left alone, but no one likes to be left alone. That is what my mother told me, when my brother was in school, and often sent me to the school to bring his dinner so he would not have to eat it alone." She paused before continuing. "Do I have your name right, Herr Zielinski?"

He glared at her, then looked away. "Professor Rudolf Zielinski," he said quietly.

"My name is Ruth. Do you believe the Russians will come to free us? The others have been talking about it. They say that they will come soon, that the Soviets have been trying to break through the Eastern borders since July. They have been talking with the British prisoners—"

"No," he said, his reply biting and clipped.

"Why not?" She turned back to him. "They will break through. My brother escaped. He is with the Russian army in the North. He will come."

"No. There is no way for them to come. It is too late," he said bitterly, but even as he spoke, he found himself turning over the child's words in his mind. "No," he continued, an angry edge to his voice now. "They will not come."

"He promised," Ruth said stubbornly.

"That is nothing but a promise waiting to be broken." As he said these words, he couldn't bring himself to look at the child. Overcome with raw and primal suffering as new cuts were drawn across an open wound, he felt the closeness of the crimes and atrocities committed every day a mere block away; he wanted so desperately to believe the girl, to forget the pain that had already come to pass. Lost in thought, he did not speak. He thought of the lands of his childhood, so far away in memory and distance, of the vast, lush lowlands and the majestic mountain peaks. He thought of his father, who raised him in the countryside, where songbirds were the only reminder of time passing, where the harsh and cold winter gave way to forgiving sunlit summers. Life was a simple joy and peace, and he knew now he would not raise his own children there and watch them grow up in peace and happiness, if there was any happiness left in the land, torn apart by the Niemcy, the German bastards.

Zielinski sighed, then spoke again. "I promised Slawomir that I would teach him to fish in the clear-water lakes of the valley, to hunt and trap in the mountains in the South, I promised my Anastazja I would take her to Paris someday." The rekindled light in his heart flickered out. "But all of that, all that could have been, is forever lost."

"My home was nothing like that," Ruth said, "no wide plains and great mountains. We lived in a ghetto in Frankfurt, in the city, where there was always smoke and fog and disease everywhere. Please, tell me more."

"There is no more to tell." He closed his eyes and leaned against the wall.

"Tell me about your daughter. Is she a little girl like me?"

"Yes," he whispered.

"Where is she now? Is she far from here?"

"Yes." She is gone, he finished in his head.

"Tell me about her, please," Ruth said. The man began to cry softly. He saw something about her innocent, unbroken spirit, yet untainted by the burning whip of their German masters, that opened his heart, and words began to form of their own accord on his tongue.

"She was only four years old the night the Germans invaded. I had heard at daybreak on the radio that the Germans invaded Poland, and by nightfall they were upon us. With my children and my brother's two children and my wife, we managed to escape and hide in the home of a German friend in Warsaw. Two years later, we were not careful enough, and they took my family to Auschwitz. Our friend, they killed immediately, in front of my children."

He quavered, and Ruth took his large callused hand in her small, delicate one.

"She was my youngest, yellow hair and bright blue eyes, the color of sapphires." He hesitated and a dry sob shuddered through him. "She didn't cry on the hard road here, not once, not even when they took her away."

"She is not gone. She is with you forever. When they took Mama away, she said she would always look over me, even from Gan Eden. She said she would always love me. Your little girl will, too. She is not gone. She will never be gone."

"Really?"

"Truly." The little girl's eyes shone in the darkness as he locked his tumultuous storm-gray eyes upon her soft jade ones.

They dared not breathe for fear of breaking the fragile moment of heart strings being tugged and connecting, now more often torn apart than joined together.

"Let's tell a story about her. It will make it more real. My papa always told me stories in the winter, ones that he made up himself."

He did not speak.

"You said you are from Poland?" she prompted.

He nodded.

"Perhaps she is somewhere like Poland, with mountains and green valleys and roaring rivers." Her voice broke. "Perhaps, I—I will tell a story, although I can't do it nearly as well as Papa could." She paused, deftly wiping away a teardrop. "Once upon a time, in a land far away . . . I'm sorry, I can't . . ." she cried, tears trickling down to join the first.

Tentatively, he opened his arms to her, wrapping them around her when she didn't respond.

As angry sobs wracked her body and she fought furiously against his comfort, he pulled her close and tight, as he had often held his own daughter.

At last, she fell limp in his arms and the torrent of tears abated, and he pressed a kiss to her hair. "Th-thank you," she stuttered. "Papa . . . it is hard—to remember I may never find him again."

"Let's begin again, shall we?" said the professor soothingly, taking her hands. "Once upon a time," he began slowly, "in a far off land of mountains and lush river valleys, there lived a little yellow-haired, blue-eyed girl and her father. The girl's locks were brighter than gold, and her eyes were the same deep blue as the stormy ocean . . . Her father . . ."

"Her father was tall and handsome," Ruth continued, "with a sharp chin and wide, gentle mouth, and he always wore a kippah of blue upon his head. Sometimes, when she was sleeping, he would come pray over her and bless her sleep."

"For many years," he resumed, "they lived in solitude and peace, and he taught her how to fish for salmon and trap muskrats and hunt elk and how to fight with a sword. He taught her to weave cloth and sew clothes and to keep house, but there came a time in the girl's life when she needed the company and knowledge of another woman. With growing desperation, he searched the nearby villages for a wife, but none were to his liking or willing to come in to the mountains to live with him. Curiosity took hold of the little girl, now nearing her own womanhood, and she begged him to tell her the story of her mother.

"'I shall tell you,' her father told her, 'but first, you must promise not to sacrifice your own life to find her. Do you understand?'

"'I understand,' the yellow-haired girl replied.

"'Very well.' Her father sighed and let her sit on his lap like she did when she was still a little girl.

"'Hardly a few months had passed after you were born when there came from the higher mountains a fiery dragon so fierce it could stare down an Obra water-monster. I had brought your mother home to Zwyciezkow, which was then called Rybaka, and we helped to prepare the defenses around the village as best we could. He approached on a moonlit night, and all the courage of man could not hold against a creature of such strength and size. He entered the town square, thrashing his horned tail to and fro. When he caught sight of your mother through an open window, he stopped to admire her beauty. Your mother began to sing to the monster, and her sorcery entranced him. As I watched, unable to stop her, she continued singing and climbed up onto his back, and he flew off into the mountains. The dragon has not bothered us since, but no one has seen your mother since then, as well.

"'It is because of this victory that the town is now called Zwyciezkow, village of victors. Not long after, I built our house here, halfway up the mountain, as close to her presence as is safe.' He sighed deeply as if reaching far back in his memories. 'And now, alas, you need your mother. I must go search for her. Daughter—'"

"Anastazja," the girl broke in. "Her name is Anastazja," she repeated firmly, eyes glowing, and now he could see the fierce pain they shared, the pain that only made her belief in hope stronger.

"Anastazja," Professor Zielinski said. The word tasted sweet and warm on his tongue, no longer accompanied by the familiar bitter flavor in the back of his mouth. He continued the story. "'Anastazja, you must stay here and keep the house warm for my return. If I do not return in thirty days, pack your things, only the most important ones, and venture down into the river valley to Zwyciezkow and ask to see Babcia the weaver. She is your grandmother.' His eyes began to dart around the room, as if with every word he felt a greater yearning to find his beloved once more. His gaze returning to his daughter before him, his eyes softened and he said, 'I will not leave for another fortnight, dearest. You shall have wood and food aplenty so you will not have to go far.'

"For the next week, her father chopped firewood, smoked game, and mended his cloak in preparation for his long journey. Early on the last morning, he packed a loaf of bread, a flask of water, and other vitals in a linen cloth, then wrapped his cloak around him, carrying his shield across his back and securing his sword in its scabbard around his waist.

"'Anastazja.' He turned to her.

"'Papa, may I not go with you? Must I stay home? Can I not journey with you to find my mother and bring her back?' she pleaded. 'I can fight, I can hunt, I will be useful.'

"'No, my dear Anastazja, you must not. If the dragon catches a mere glimpse of you, he will take you like he took your mother. Promise me you will not venture into the mountains.'

"'I will not let him see me.'

"'Goodbye, Anastazja. I shall return.' He kissed her forehead and started his lonely trek up to the mountaintop, up to the highest cave, the home of the dragon, where only its fiery breath could melt the frosty snow. For thirty days, Anastazja kept the house clean and the hearth swept, and continued preparing for the winter. Each day, as the sun set, she watched the mountainside, hoping to see a silhouette against the darkening sky, or even two figures journeying down the mountain, hand in hand. As night fell on the thirtieth day, his daughter sadly packed her things and made ready to leave the home where she had grown up.

"When dawn broke over the mountain, a graceful figure stood looking over the river valley, bags packed for travel, a broadsword by her side. She took in the valley, hoping to remember the scarlet sunrise illuminating the dark sky with glowing rays of pink and gold, the last facet of beauty to take with her on her journey into the dark depths of the unknown. With a defiant glint lighting her eyes, she turned from the sun and began to climb up the mountain.

"She had traveled for two days when she first encountered a sign of the dragon: a pile of fresh dragon dung. Before long, she saw the dragon for the first time, near a mountain spring. He was a beautiful, magnificent, fiery beast, larger than she could have imagined; with a monstrous, muscular, spiked tail and two horns and a sharp snout. She could see smoke coming out of its nostrils, magnified by the icy mountain air. Hiding behind a rock, she was both terrified and captivated by the beast. She did not have the strength or the means to kill the dragon in an even fight, this she knew. She would not break her promise to her father; she would have to find some other way to defeat the dragon and rescue her mother and father.

"*Sulphur!* she thought.

"Carefully, she climbed out of sight of the dragon and over to the other side of the mountain. There, she wrapped up as much of the foul-smelling rock as she could carry in her cloak, then killed a young mountain goat as an offering. She cut a deep slit down the belly and stuffed the sulphur inside and sewed the cut closed. Under the blanket of a starless night, she crept down beside the spring and laid the goat nearby with a wreath of yarrow upon its head. She scurried back to a safe hiding place and waited for the dragon to descend from his lair.

"Before the first light came, the dragon, snarling and hissing, came down to the mountain spring. After a long drink, it turned and saw the goat, freshly killed. He swallowed it whole, like a snake, just as Anastazja expected. Satisfied by the food, he laid his head on his front paws and drifted into a deep sleep.

"Anastazja stole away before the dragon woke, and continued up the mountain until she came to a dark dragon lair.

"'Anastazja,' whispered a weak voice from the back.

"'Papa!' she cried joyfully.

"'Why are you here? I told you not to come; it is too dangerous. The dragon never leaves his nest for long; he will be back soon.'

"'But I have poisoned the dragon with sulphur, and satiated him with lamb, and put him to sleep with yarrow. Come, you must hurry, before he wakes.' She saw behind him a woman, paler than the moon from years in the cave. 'Mama?' she whispered.

"'Yes,' said her father happily. 'Hurry, we must go.' Her father picked up his sword and instructed Anastazja to lead her mother out. They hurried down the mountain path, Anastazja in front, her mother in the middle, her father guarding the back. They were nearly halfway down the mountain when Anastazja heard a faint sound in the crisp, cold air. She paused, lifting an ear to the wind. In an instant, dark wings blocked out the sun and the mountain was shaken by a deafening roar and burst of flame. Anastazja turned with fright to face the monstrous dragon.

"With another roar, the dragon charged towards them. Anastazja unfroze and hurried forth to help her father parry against the dragon's sharp claws and powerful teeth. For a while, they held their ground, but slowly the dragon forced them into the sharp mountainside where they would have little room to maneuver.

"Her father, in a moment of distraction, was suddenly thrown to the side. Anastazja took this moment to leap onto the dragon's back and slash and stab the dragon's back with all her might, inching slowly up to the unprotected neck. They fought for a very long time, a short gash the only blood wound Anastazja managed to open in the dragon's hide. The dragon was unable to shake off the girl as they fought and fought, Anastazja thinking her limbs would give out. With a screech, the dragon threw her off into a small gully. Anastazja struggled to get up, but when she saw her father lying motionless against a rock, her heart fell, and she felt for the first time what despair truly meant."

Zielinski paused and glanced down at the girl, who seemed to have fallen asleep against his shoulder. He could see a sprinkle of freckles across her nose and a pale pink scar along her hairline that he hadn't noticed before, illuminated by the soft moonlight.

"But there is always hope," little Ruth whispered, eyes closed as if dreaming. "There is always a way to save someone you love, and although she had just found her mother, she already loved her with all her heart. And so, the girl bravely rose up once more, only to be struck down again and again, until she managed to blind one of the dragon's eyes, but at last, her sword had been dulled against the rough dragon hide and she could fight no more. She watched in terror as the dragon closed in on her father."

"But at that moment," Zielinski said, taking over again, "the sulphur began to work its magic, and the dragon felt a wrenching pain in his belly. Frantically, he searched for water, turning away from her wounded father. With renewed strength, Anastazja took up her father's sword and, in one mighty stroke, cut off the dragon's head.

"And together, the reunited family returned to their mountain home, to happily live many long, joyful years together to the end of their days," Zielinski finished softly. With swelling affection in his heart towards the sleeping girl in his arms, he pressed a kiss to her scar and settled himself comfortably, sheltering her from the cold.

And for the first time in many months, he fell into a deep and dreamless sleep.

Epilogue

Several days after this night, Ruth was taken away to be exterminated, but Herr Rudolf Zielinski never forgot the angelic girl or the hope she brought to him. He helped many children of Auschwitz by retelling this tale of enduring courage, finding strength in unlikely places and, above all, unrelenting belief in triumph over evil. Several months later, on January 27, 1945, the remaining prisoners Auschwitz-Birkenau were freed by Soviet troops. Herr Zielinski, who was forced to walk back to Germany on one of the "death marches," was freed soon afterwards. He devoted his life to relocating Polish survivors to Polish communities in America and England, and restoring Polish culture to his native Poland after the fall of the Soviet Union in 1991. Herr Zielinski survived to be ninety-six years old. He never reunited with his beloved daughter, Anastazja, but is survived in memory by the countless children of Polish descent that he was able to reunite with their families.

ONE IN A THOUSAND

By Mark Leigh
(Minnesota, USA)
Science Fiction, 1ˢ Place

My name is Captain Spyridon Tormouli of the Outer Hellene Fleet. I'm going to die on the moon.

I have no regrets. I am a soldier, of a line of soldiers, of a people of soldiers stretching all the way back to the days of the turannoi. My people were once great, and then floundered, but we fought to keep our name, our culture, our tongue, our reasoning, and now we've fought to make ourselves great again. After the Annihilation crippled the major powers, the chaos of the generation-long Remnant War allowed us to strike outwards once again, to re-establish civilization across the fallen and smoldering empires of great Europa all the way to the border with the savage and barbarous Svard in the north, and across Asia Minor and Arabia. Our tongue is spoken on three continents; the Hellene flag now flies over Roma.

And now it flies also on the moon. Other standards abound here as well—the men of Indus have a great industrial complex in Mare Nubium, and the sly Tleca are always busy in Mare Frigoris—but no one else has the vision of Hellas. No one else has the foresight to build a mass driver, a great and endless pair of linear coils converging into distant invisibility, a means to fire spacecraft towards the outer planets that they might soon fly our banner as well. The driver isn't finished yet, nor even started, but the funding is already—

"We're going to die here, you know."

—already in place, the materials gathered and organized on my blue gem of a home, the means to transport them here getting built at this very moment. In less than four months, the first of the cargo hulks will dock at Port Athena and the first of the nanofiber structural segments will roll out over the lunar surface. Two and a half months after that, the first of the superconducting tritanium coils will arrive, and in less than two years from this very moment a spacecraft will erupt away from the moon in vacuum silence, traveling at—

"Captain? We're going to die."

—at over a tenth the speed of light towards the giant amber world of Zeus, there to orbit and gather materials before multiplying and dividing. Another craft, a fleet of crafts, will follow, relying on the presence of the orbital infrastructure built by the first vessel and its copies. In ten years men will be living there.

But I won't be. Because I'm going to die here.

"Captain? Captain!"

"Silence, Aristo." I sigh. Technical Master Aristo Mitropoulos is, sadly, not a soldier, and he's been complaining for the last four hours. As though he thinks I can do anything about our current situation, as though complaining about matters will help to address them.

It's a cramped little space we inhabit, a cluttered volume some two meters by three by four, stuffed mostly with equipment and with little space for two increasingly irritated men. Already my breath is misting before my face, and I've long ago folded arms over my chest, tucking pale and chilled fingers into my armpits for the meager warmth available there.

"We're going to die," continues Aristo mournfully, covering his face with his hands. He is soft, intellectual, clever in his way, but not cut out for service on the moon. "I wish . . . I wish I'd gotten to eat at Koutala's again. Fuck. If I were there now . . . if I were there now, I'd eat until I threw up and they had to carry me out."

Our job was simple enough, almost laughably routine in retrospect. Before the structurals can be placed, there has to be a base; and before there can be a base, the levelers and compactors have to do their jobs; and before they can do their jobs, there has to be a more accurate survey of the lunar equator. *We* are the more accurate survey, we and a hundred others like us. As a soldier, I drive the floater; and as the engineer, Aristo works the survey equipment.

"Eating? No. Eating is . . . eating is too silly, too petty." Aristo rubs a weary hand over his face. "No, what I want is to . . . you know, I've never fucked a Svard girl. That's what I'd do."

I avoid the urge to glare at him. His professionalism is deteriorating even faster than my patience.

The floater is a good vehicle. There are hundreds of them all over Hellene lunar space, and thousands of similar vehicles in the areas claimed by other nations. They're easy to use, cheap to make and maintain, and reliable. Usually reliable. All vital systems are guaranteed mission-critical reliability, with peripheral systems manufactured to a fault-tolerance threshold of one failure per thousand.

Breach foam is considered a peripheral system. I wasn't aware of that until four hours ago. One failure per thousand.

"No, two Svard girls," he muses wistfully. "They'd probably kill me, but I'm already dead anyway, right? You know how pale they are? I bet they're so pale you can see veins in the skin between their tits."

Mare Tranquillitatis is a smooth place, mostly full of powdery regolith, but here and there one can see little craters, tiny little navels fused into rock by the spectacular crashing of some meteorite or other ages ago. Tiny. So tiny they're invisible on maps, invisible a kilometer up, but they're macroscopic here. Not tiny at all on the ground.

I was piloting manually, hovering in after a twenty-minute flight from our last survey location, and dropped it in the center of one of these craters; they're hard, and they make for a decent landing surface, better than the surrounding fluffy regolith. The craters, though, they're brittle. Sometimes they crack. The edge of a crater fragment, apparently, can be sharp.

"Oh, what's the point?" whines Aristo. His voice is getting a little tinny now to my ears, a little shallow. "One girl, two, a thousand? A man could drown in breasts back on Gaea and not find a single worthwhile woman. It's nothing but flesh and perfume and softness, Captain, in a million polities that look like they were all fabricated in the same plant. What's the fucking point of it all? I hate it, you know."

"Silence, Aristo." I cut my eyes toward him. I'm not going to warn him forever.

As the floater fell through the new hole in the crater, it struck something, some odd piece of rock, and it tore. The surface tore. Why? I'm not certain. Maybe I came in too strong, too fast; maybe there's some odd little anomaly buried here, something dense enough to throw off the local gravity just enough to make the vehicle fall when every other time it might have remained happily on the crater surface, just enough to tear a breach when any other time it might just have made a dent and a funny story for later.

Anyway, the surface tore. Air rushed out from the cabin for the few milliseconds it took the breach foam to deploy, but it deployed improperly. Hell, I can see the stuff on the floor from where I stand now, a bulging whipped mass the color of cream, by now hard as diamond but light as feathers. I can't see what's wrong with it, but we're leaking. There are . . . gaps, I suppose, tiny gaps in the foam, not big enough to see, but big enough to let air through in alarming quantities. If the foam had deployed properly, we'd have enough air to last until someone could excavate our floater from this pit of regolith, but that's not how the dice fell. I'm going to die here.

"Fucking hell. Why don't you look for more foam, Captain? They have spare canisters on these things, don't they?"

I eye my companion narrowly. "Do you want me to check the computer again? There aren't any left." The maintenance mechs top our supply off at one spare canister every ten checkups; there's a checkup after each time we return to Port Athena, which we do after every survey flight. We used the spare on flight five; this is flight seven. Usually not having a spare doesn't require a special resupply request, since the main one is supposed to work properly. One failure per thousand.

"Oh, fuck it. We're so screwed." Aristo runs hands through his thinning hair and starts to moan helplessly. "I'm so tired of this, anyway. Metal ships, metal base, grey moon rock . . . I haven't seen the color green in six fucking months. I haven't been with a woman in two years. What's the fucking point? We're going to build shit here and then colonize Zeus, and in a thousand years there'll be a trillion people and none of them are going to be worth the time of day, because they won't *get* it. They won't get that they're all just copies of each other with microscopic variation; they won't get that their troubles are the same as everyone else's have been for a million years and *still* no one's figured out how to make a broken heart not hurt or how to measure love. They won't—"

I draw my sidearm and shoot him in the throat.

Aristo cuts off with a strangled gurgle, with his eyes going wide as he stumbles back against the vehicle's smooth inner wall. At the same time, the weapon in my hand sparks and crackles, emitting a thin streamer of acrid smoke.

After a moment I release the trigger, frowning at the weapon. Then I nod. I recall hearing some warning about how this model has a record of malfunctioning in low-pressure environments.

I can't help but laugh. A pistol that doesn't work in low pressure is deployed to soldiers in space, where low-pressure environments are routine? But then, this is nothing new. People used to try to move cavalry through jungles, and people used to build helicopters that wouldn't fly in sand during an era in which wars were fought primarily in deserts.

Shaking my head, I drop the useless weapon to the floor; the resulting clatter sounds wrong to me, and I wonder how many millibars we're down to now. Six hundred? Five hundred? Stepping over the thing, I stand over the twitching and gasping form of the engineer for a moment before breaking his neck with a barehanded strike.

He didn't want to be here anyway. I'm doing him a favor.

Idly stretching my back, I check the chronometer on the forward display. It's been . . . four hours and twenty minutes since the crash.

I've waited long enough, I suppose. I'm going to die here.

As I punch up the main computer and start keying in my authorization for the self-destruct mechanism, it occurs to me that I'm like the mariners of old. Nameless men all, unremarkable, and their corpses litter the ocean floor next to the rotting remains of biremes and triremes and penteconters. Their sacrifices assured them all anonymous honors and drove the machinery of the early state to daring new heights; the world would not be what it is without them. Progress rests on dead men half-buried in surf and sand and regolith.

A red warning flashes on the display, telling me the self-destruct is armed, needing only manual confirmation before proceeding; this is a holdover from the early days of The War, when electronic attacks would blow ships out of the sky by triggering such things in secret. Folding the console back into place, I climb over Aristo's corpse and a blocky sensor made of heavy grey composite before finally stumbling against the access hatch to the utility closet.

The hatch is locked, of course, but the same code that triggered the self-destruct still pinging away in the forward section allows me entry to the meter-by-meter square room in the back of the ship. It contains little but assorted tools and cables, as well as another secure panel, this one in a bright comical red . . . and below it I spot the telltale yellow of a breach foam canister.

The computer said there wasn't one . . . but here it is. The supply robots shouldn't have put it here, not yet, but if confused they'll provide too many supplies rather than too few. One failure per thousand. If I'd checked earlier, I could've installed it, but now there isn't enough time. I'd suffocate before I could finish.

I find myself laughing as I key in my code to the physical self-destruct mechanism. In moments it starts to beep and flash menacingly, telling me I've succeeded. I'm going to die here.

I have no regrets. I'm a soldier.

Learn more about 1ˢᵗ-place winner and Fresh Ink Group member Mark Leigh at http://www.FreshInkGroup.com/authors/mark-leigh.

WHY I HICCUP

By Jessica Scaggs
(Georgia, USA)
Say Something, 1ˢᵗ Place

I was born with a set of lungs.

I exploded into this world with a screaming gasp of life that reverberated through Arlington, Virginia, for years to come. I sucked in the air, the light, the sounds around me with desperation, afraid that it would all slip through my fingers if I didn't engulf it all immediately. Overwhelmed to the brink of physical pain, I cried. That piercing wail left a sonorous footprint in the sterile white hospital room and in the hearts of my parents, who gazed in loving astonishment at the sonic boom they held in their arms.

"She'll make her voice heard, all right," my father remarked proudly. My mother nervously rearranged my blankets, trying to soothe me.

He was right, for the first few years. I learned to mold that tremendous sound into words at an unusually early age. I spoke not only for myself, but for others, as well: my younger brother, a stuffed animal, a lonely lady on a park bench. But the more I saw, the less I was able to put into words. The world became as foreign to me as it was on the day of my birth. Those few short years of a complacent, illusory understanding ended as it became apparent to me that the world was full of contradictions and indefinable concepts. Words, it seemed, were useless.

The rubber band that had begun to constrict my windpipe turned into a fist, and then a tourniquet. To accommodate my newfound muteness, my other senses strengthened. I recoiled like a touch-me-not under the slightest contact with my sensitive skin, and I became increasingly intolerant of crowds with my amplified hearing. My eyes, perceiving every nuance in my environment while straining to suppress the dormant lung power within me, bulged with the effort and took on an alienesque appearance. Others, repulsed by me, soon ceased interaction.

"Speak up," my teachers continually reminded me when I tried to answer a question.

"I'll have to switch your position if you don't raise your voice," my coaches warned.

"What happened?" my parents asked incredulously.

"You don't have to say a word," she said.

She, a familiar face I had never known. She, who gave me a sketchbook because she knew I'd learned to communicate in other ways. She, who shyly held a poem out to me in a moment of sudden and unexplained trust. I stared down at a single line and drew in a breath as though through a straw: *When faced with the vision of what should be, I know that I will doubtless fail.* We sat alone in our shared existence, among people who could not see our quiet tears. That was the day I first heard the song. It was a faint haunting melody, as painful and familiar as nostalgia. Having become accustomed to a life without respiration, I had forgotten what it felt like to breathe. But the mesmerizing song had the rise and fall of breath, and I was grateful for once that I could experience a beauty unknown to the rest of the room. I knew in an instant that the song came from within her, and that she could not hear it.

One night, a car crash threw me forward with violent force, loosening the tourniquet in the process. The air that had been trapped in my lungs for so long suddenly erupted in a series of tortured screams, the likes of which had never been heard since the day I was born. After eighteen years of restricted respiration, the surge of air ripping viciously through my raw windpipe gave way to excruciating neck pain. I lost consciousness.

Soon after, I realized I had to channel my newfound breath into some form of communication. I knew that words had fallen short in the past. I wished I could sing, but I knew I could not muster up enough air for that yet. I wanted to sing the song back to her, the melody that had haunted me since the first day I heard it. I wanted her to hear it for the first time.

So I spoke not only for myself, but for others, as well.

In the soft white glow of a single burning bulb, it was impossible to distinguish where the ivory keys ended and my pale hands began. The room was dark. She sat in the shadows to my right, waiting patiently.

I exhaled.

I heard there was a secret chord
That David played, and it pleased the Lord.
But you don't really care for music,
Do you?

The tourniquet released its hold on my neck, and my blood turned the room red. It flowed through my fingers, and the keys breathed for me. The notes molded into each other, forming the words I had never been able to find. I realized that the song was not only hers; it was mine.

There was a time that you let me know
What's really going on below
But now you never show that to me, do you?
I remember when I moved in you
And the holy dark was moving too
And every breath we drew was "Hallelujah."

I looked over at her, and saw that she was crying silently, her head finally bowed in submission to the storm that raged within. I had filled her to beyond what she could hold. She, who preferred to fill empty, was full. I had touched the girl in the glass cage. I knew the way inside because I'd been there before. She and I were one and the same.

Maybe there's a God above
But all I've ever learned from love
Is how to shoot somebody who outdrew you.
Well, it's not a cry that you hear at night,
It's not somebody who's seen the light,
It's a cold and it's a broken "Hallelujah."

But that level of freedom could not be sustained. Like the rise and fall of sound waves, it builds gradually to a climax of only a few moments, and then leaves us with the sensation of being touched by the something intangible and all too ephemeral. That fleeting moment slipped into the crevices of time, and it took my breath along with it.

I live for those moments in which I can breathe again.

I live for those moments in which another soul acts as a mirror in which I can see my own.

I live for those moments in which I can finally cry, "Hallelujah."

*   *   *

Song lyrics for "Hallelujah" are by Leonard Cohen.

Learn more about 1ˢᵗ-place winner and Fresh Ink Group member Jessica Scaggs at www.FreshInkGroup.com/authors/jessica-scaggs.

SAND IN HER SHOES

By Joyce E.S. Pyka
(Illinois, USA)
Historical, 2nd Place

Cornflower blue spilled across the April sky, filling the land beneath it with brilliant light. Ordinarily obscured by a chronic yellow haze, rare was a day of such clarity in these parts. It chiseled out the features and illuminated the details of everything that Mattie passed, outlining farmhouses, barns, animals, and scrubby patches of wheat in the fields.

Mattie walked through the front doors of the small Sante Fe train station and up to the center row of the high-back benches, then plopped the worn suitcase down with a sigh. The walk from the Clayton farm had been a long one. Although her feet began aching early on, the beautiful day seemed to fortify her decision, and for whatever reason, gave her courage. Her legs may have been tired and weakened by the journey, but her resolve was not. She would not change her mind. Not again, not this time.

Mattie grabbed the front of her mother's hand-knitted sweater, pulling it closer to her body. She walked over to the clerk, who stood working behind the caged counter. On the wall hung a calendar with large bold bookhand type displaying the number 14, above that in small red letters the month, and beneath that, the year, 1935.

Taking notice of this lone passenger, the clerk pulled out his pocket watch, flipped open the engraved cover, and glanced up at the attractive woman with preoccupied green eyes. Tipping the edge of his visor, he nodded. "5:20," he told her without being asked. "Train might be on time, might not. Never can tell." Then he added, "Ain't likely, though."

Mattie resisted the urge to correct his English and purchased her ticket.

The clerk set to stamping a tower of papers neatly stacked at his side. When she was sure that he was absorbed in his mundane task, Mattie reached down, removing her shoes. She walked over to the trash can and shook the gritty black dust from them. It was not the removal of the sandy dirt that caused her concern—this was customary for almost everyone in the panhandle—but rather the shoes themselves, bright-red high-heeled pumps, utterly impractical for the distance she walked today. They were an extravagance that some of the local inhabitants would not find suitable for the wife of a farmer who was also their children's schoolteacher. Mattie blew the sandy dust away. Taking the cuff of her soft sweater, she rubbed the toes until the red shoe leather shined. Except for the occasional church dance or wedding, where she had been able to brave the stares of disapproval, the pumps lived in a shoebox wrapped in tissue paper on the top shelf of her closet. Five years after the frivolous purchase, they still looked like new.

She slipped the shoes back on and walked over to the window, the heels tapping against the pitted hardwood floor. As she watched the cloudless and fair day fade away, Mattie saw something peculiar. To the north of the train station stood the remains of a dead crabapple tree, ravaged by Oklahoma dusters, bleached by the sun, and as smooth as driftwood. Its branches were holding an entire flock of squawking blackbirds. The chatter was loud enough for the clerk to stop his busy-work and get up from his chair.

"What the heck's all that ruckus about?" he asked Mattie, removing his visor and peering out the window.

Suddenly, the wind picked up, gathering dirt, dust, and stones, pelting the depot like hail. As if by some silent signal, the entire band of birds immediately stopped their prattle and took off for the skies.

The clerk scratched the back of his head. "What the . . .?"

"Look." Mattie pointed at the ground alongside the train station.

Jack-rabbits—dozens of them, racing past the depot as if a coyote were in hot pursuit of his next meal. Alongside the long-ears, tumbleweed rolled with the omnipresent dust, propelled by the gusting wind.

Instinctively, Mattie scanned the horizon; then she saw it: a churning, swirling black mass.

Like a mammoth cyclone turned on its side parallel to ground, it stretched itself across the landscape, spinning end-over-end on its way to the little train station. Within moments, Mattie and the clerk realized that this was no ordinary duster. Blotting out the sky, swelling to a magnitude that seemed a thousand feet high, the black cloud swallowed everything in its path. It picked up speed, steamrolling towards them.

The clerk pushed Mattie back, grabbing the interior shutters. Without a word, she ran to the other side of the room, parroting his actions. Slamming the protective doors closed, she picked up a long piece of thick lumber that lay on the floor beneath the window. Though the heavy beam was difficult to balance, Mattie managed to slide it through an iron bracket at one end and into another on the other side of the window frame. They had just about finished barricading the rest of the place when a group of people rushed into the station. Two of the men immediately turned around, pushing at the doors, struggling against the strong wind. Running across the room, the clerk added his strength to theirs, and all three of them forced the intruder out.

While the wind was kept at bay, failing to gain entrance, Mattie knew that nothing would stop what it carried on its wings, the ever-invasive dust.

Among the storm's refugees was a teenage girl cradling a toddler, his face buried in her protective shoulder while a frail elderly woman clung to her arm. All of them were covered in the storm's sediment, the black-brown dirt clinging to their clothes.

"It's the end!" cried out the old woman hysterically. The dark dust cracked on her face, revealing the wrinkles on her weathered skin, making the whites of her fearful eyes glow.

"Imogene, are we gonna die?" the little boy said. As he pulled away from his sister, the curls on his head shook like a dust mop, his face the only part not covered by the powder.

"Hush, Grandma, you're scaring Bobby," the young girl scolded the woman as they walked to the benches. "Don't cry, Bobby, it's just another windstorm." But by the look of concern on her face, Mattie knew that the young girl also realized that this duster was far from the usual variety.

One of the men removed his hat. Dirt poured from the brim as he beat it against his trousers. "Car broke down, back a ways," he said, feeling the need to explain their appearance. "Just couldn't get it started again." Pulling a red kerchief from his side pocket, wiping the grime from his lips first, and then the rest of his face, he added, "We were luckier than some folks, though. Static from the storm caused a lot of cars to stall out there; at least we got this far."

Suddenly the lights flickered, dimmed, and went out. Darkness doused the depot, stunning them into silence.

Bam! A thud reverberated through the building, shaking its foundation. For a full fifteen minutes, the black blizzard picked up object after object, smashing them against the walls of the station. Since they could not see, with only the sound of things to identify what was being hurled at them by the unstoppable wind, size was about the only thing they could determine. Louder sounds meant larger objects. A tree branch? A rain barrel? Unfortunate livestock?

Convinced she was about to meet her maker, the old woman began singing, "Ama . . . zee . . . ing Grace . . ." Rocking back and forth to the rhythm of the prayerful hymn, she prepared for her demise.

Something slammed into one of the windows, shattering the outside glass. The little boy cried out in fear. The noise of storm was so deafening that Mattie thought the train was on time, after all, had jumped the tracks, and was about to rip right through the depot.

Finally, the storm started to run out of breath. Taking the worst of itself off, it whipped its way across the plains, leaving behind a howling gale, a lingering reminder of its ferocity.

Blackness gave way to the dim light filtering through the shutters and cracks of the doorframes. Mattie looked around the room with expectation for the lingering effect of the storm. It sifted down from the ceiling rafters, creating puddles that rippled across the floorboards. If it was anything like at home, it would also seep through crevices, slip around windows, snake its way down stove pipes, cling to food, and funnel down the chimney shaft to settle anywhere and anyplace it damn well felt like.

There were a few things that women did, in attempting to keep the intrusive dust away. And over the years, inefficient as they were, Mattie had also given them a try. But, not anymore. Never again would she hang wet sheets at her windows, hoping to collect the dust before it invaded her home, or cover her dinner with towels to prevent the wind from salting it with sand. Never again would she seal up her house like a tomb. Even though she had already made up her mind, Mattie felt as though this black Palm Sunday blizzard was providential. It was an affirmation of her decision.

"I've seen my share of dusters before," said the man sitting next to the young girl, "but this was something else . . . worse than all of 'em put together."

The little boy began to cough, ejecting brown spittle from his lungs.

"Pa, you got something for Bobby?" asked the teenager.

Remembering that the man used his handkerchief on himself earlier, Mattie opened her purse, pulled out a piece of lace-trimmed linen, and walked over to them.

"Here you go, Bobby," she said, handing it to his older sibling.

Imogene looked at Mattie with hesitating eyes. Bobby's coughing fit started up again. Trying to prevent her brother from spraying Mattie's dress, she grabbed the neatly folded triangle, fluffed it open, and quickly covered Bobby's mouth.

"It's okay, Bobby." The father reached over, gently tapping the toddler's back, hoping to help his son purge the poison. "Get it all out."

The words echoed in Mattie's ears. Get it all out—as if he really could. As long as that child remains here . . .

Mattie walked quietly back to where she'd been sitting. She watched the teenage girl, mature beyond her years, soothe her brother as she took on the role of his mother, who was in all likelihood dead. Dead, of what could also end up killing the boy.

Mattie was all too familiar with that cursed ailment. She had seen friends and neighbors succumb to it, as well as children in her classroom, but worst of all . . .

Oh, how she hated it here! How she wanted to leave and never come back to this drab, joyless land. She was not made of the same stoic stock that some of these people were. But more than that, she did not understand the fervent bond that tied these generations of farmers to their land. How could she feel what she did not understand?

"Hallelujah, Imogene!" the elderly woman shouted. Then turning to the girl, she added, "God in heaven be praised, the devil is done whisperin' in our ears."

"Sure does sound like the wind is calming down, Grandma." She patted the old woman's hand. "Pa, what are we going to do about the car?" she asked her father.

"Whatever needs to be done."

His answer was straightforward and direct, with the resignation of one who endures whatever life tosses in his path. To Mattie he appeared to be the kind of man that didn't ponder on the reasons why such things happened to him or his family. Beaten down by the hazards of life, it was better not to question fate, best to use his energy instead on *fixin' what needs fixin'*, whatever it took to survive.

Mattie envied his simple philosophy, though for her it was different. She could not live the rest of her life in such benevolent acceptance. The wind had carried her dreams away with the dust. It had robbed her of her ability to endeavor. If she stayed, it would also rob her of her spirit.

*   *   *

In spite of everything, Mattie did not blame herself or her husband for their failed venture. Lured by advertisements that promised prosperity in the panhandle, they had been seduced by slick slogans of getting rich by farming. Was it greed? Perhaps so, she had to admit to herself, but not entirely. It was also the potential of succeeding at farming, of being rewarded in good measure for the backbreaking work that farmers do. It propelled them into taking a chance. So, Mattie left a teaching job in her small hometown, and Jim left his father's Wisconsin farm to his brothers for a chance to strike it rich with the prospect of mining acres of golden wheat on the Oklahoma grasslands.

At first it was just as they had hoped; the early years were prosperous. Jim had spent long hours plowing up sod and planting seed. Though the grasslands' climate, and indeed even the soil itself, were different from home, Jim turned and prepared the earth in much the same way as he had learned on his father's place, a Midwestern farm that held beans, corn, and wheat, and was rich in rainfall and abundantly thick with topsoil.

As a result of helping the US meet almost half of the world's needs to make their daily bread, the Claytons and their neighboring farmers' plentiful harvests brought in sizeable profits. By the mid-twenties, Jim told Mattie it was time to expand. In order to do this, they would need a bigger, heavier, more modern, and of course more expensive plow—perhaps a new tractor, too.

"Really, Jim," Mattie said, sliding her finger down the column of their budget ledger. "We're doing okay; the last two years we've been able to save. If we take on another loan in addition to the mortgage, we'd have little next to nothing left over at the end of the month."

Until then, Mattie's practical feet-firmly-planted-on-the-ground common sense was always a good counterpart to Jim's visionary-but-often-impractical plans. On this matter, however, their complementary personalities were firmly at odds. It was as though Jim became obsessed by his plan to expand; he was infected by some kind of wheat-fever like so many other farmers on the Great Plains.

"You just can't see it," and "You think too small," or "You've got to spend money to make it," he told her, defending his idea.

They fought for nearly a week, followed by another of stubborn silence. No longer able to the bear the agitation between them, Mattie came up with a feasible compromise. He could take out a loan for the farming equipment, but only if she could take a teaching job to help meet the payments.

Mattie hadn't realized how much she missed her profession. To her, it didn't matter if the children were really eager to learn, or just plain happy to leave their farm chores. Whatever their reasons, she was determined to see the light of revelation flicker in their eyes when they finally understood a difficult problem or had learned something new. She felt fulfilled in educating young minds. It was the same feeling, she sensed, that her husband experienced after a season of laboring on the land when he harvested the fruition of his efforts.

For the next few years, they had both reaped the rewards of their hard work.

*   *   *

"Let's take a look and see what's happened," the clerk announced, taking Mattie from her memories.

Mattie shook her head. She knew that he knew quite well what was out there: a sight all too familiar to Oklahomans. Whatever lay beyond those doors would be smothered by dust. Her thoughts trailed off again, to a Saturday breakfast of scrambled eggs, bacon, and oven-fresh blueberry muffins slathered in white sweet butter.

*   *   *

"What's the occasion?" Jim asked Mattie as he sat down at the table, the restless night still lingering in his eyes. Blueberry muffins were made only on holidays and for special celebrations.

Grabbing a potholder, Mattie wrapped it around the handle of blue metal coffee pot. She poured the brew into Jim's cup and smiled. "Have your coffee first."

Rubbing the back of his head, he yawned, took a sip, set the cup back down, and said, "Okay, I drank some. Now, tell me what's going on."

She had hoped he'd down the entire meal so he'd be fully awake and alert. But he was too anxious to hear what she had to say, and for that matter, she had a difficult time holding back her news.

"You, my dear man," she said unable to wait, "are going to be a father."

Jim looked into her eyes. His glistened with happiness, making them shine like polished emeralds. She knew he wanted to ask, "Are you sure?" There had been false hope before. Instead, he spoke to her with an expression and a gesture. The dimples in his cheeks deepened as a smile slowly crossed his lips. He rose from his chair, walked over to Mattie, and gently grabbing her hand pulled her toward him. They held on to the moment, embracing in joyful silence, all three of them.

Mattie had worked nearly to the end of her pregnancy, until it became too difficult for her to travel to the schoolhouse. She said goodbye to her pupils in March, and her baby was born in the month for which she was named, April.

Jim would not hear of Mattie returning to teaching, and though she felt guilty, she was glad of it. How would they be able to meet the payments on the farming machinery? But, she could not bring herself to leave April in the care of anyone else.

"We'll manage, Mattie. You'll see, the price of wheat will pick up again," Jim reassured her, for it had fallen considerably the year before. "If it doesn't, I'll just plow up the north quarter and plant a few more acres; that'll make up the difference."

But the price did not rise, and planting more of it did not make up the difference because nobody could afford to buy it. The effect of the Great Depression had reached the panhandle. A vicious cycle had been set into motion, and to Mattie it seemed that the Great Plains got the worst of it. In addition to their economic woes, the following years also brought drought, wind, and dust storms that sucked the land dry. It swept the shallow topsoil of the grasslands away, taking with it Jim's ability to farm the land. The stolen soil turned to dust that suffocated the cattle and, most horrible of all, invaded the lungs of their three-year-old daughter, giving her dust pneumonia, ultimately taking her young life.

Devastated, trying desperately to distract herself in order to fend off her grief, Mattie returned to teaching. It didn't matter that the county was broke like the rest of the country and couldn't pay her except in worthless warrants. Working was the only way she could escape her emotional pain.

Jim was determined to wage war on the neverending wind. He would fight for his farm, fight until he would drop. And, for the next few years Mattie would be a partner right at his side. She valiantly dug back a six-foot drift of sand that nearly swallowed her hen house, helped to repair the wind-beaten roof, shoveled and reshoveled the dust storm dirt, trying her best to keep their house a home. Over time, though, this lifestyle of a losing battle had eroded her soul as it did the farmland. With Jim unable to plant wheat on acreage covered in stagnant waves of sand, the farm machinery and mortgage payments overdue, and no extra money coming in from her teaching job, Mattie Clayton felt as lifeless as the landscape that surrounded her.

Then, she found that she was pregnant again.

Just as she had done before, she prepared a big breakfast with all the trimmings—an extravagance, considering their budget—eggs scrambled, bread toasted, and the plump muffins popped hot from the tin.

Jim came downstairs, smelling the scent of bacon and fresh blueberries. Pulling one of the straps of his overalls over his shoulder, he asked, "Mattie, what's up?"

She walked over to the hot stove, took the corner of her apron to the handle of the coffee pot, and poured the dark brew into his cup. "Nothing," she said with soft bluntness. "Just thought you'd like a hearty Sunday breakfast."

Jim dug into the fluffy yellow mound and crunchy translucent strips of fried brown pork fat. Savoring over the aroma of the muffin, he took a bite of it, butter drizzling down his chin. Mattie reached over, dabbing it away with a napkin, her eye catching the edge of a suitcase peeking out from between the cupboard doors beneath the kitchen sink. Jim was so absorbed by the unexpected sumptuous breakfast that he didn't notice the corner of the case, or that Mattie was wearing her infamous red shoes.

His mind is already out in the fields, Mattie thought to herself. It would do no good to ask him again. He was compulsive, he was obsessed, and above all, he was passionate about his land—this tired, worn, barren wasteland that offered nothing and took everything. She would never feel the way he did about this farm, but she could not bring herself to give him an ultimatum to leave the plains. Mattie knew that if Jim conceded, he would resent her forever.

*   *   *

"This is the most god-awful duster I've seen yet," said the clerk, bringing Mattie from her kitchen back into the depot. "I'm sure the train had to detour around that blizzard some, but it'll eventually make it through. Could be a while, though."

"That's okay. I don't mind waiting." She reached for her suitcase and, bracing it at her side, leaned against it, placing her head on it like a pillow. The walk and the stress of the storm had taken its toll. She reminded herself that she needed her rest. Now, more than ever, she had to be careful.

Closing her eyes, Mattie was soon drifting off to sleep. In the twilight moments of consciousness she thought of her parents' home with wide-open windows, friendly breezes tugging at calico curtains, apple orchards filled with lush trees ripe with fruit, and cool green, green grass.

The corners of her mouth rose, and with a quiet sigh she whispered to herself, "Perhaps I will buy a red dress to go with my shoes."

THE TRAINS LAMENT

By Talya Tate Boerner
(Texas, USA)
Say Something, 2nd Place

Pulling the feather duvet over her head to block the day, she considered never leaving the comfortable bed. The sunlight was already bright in the room, streaming through the windows overlooking the grounds to the swimming pool beyond. She would prefer avoiding the day, but the maid was coming to clean. She could not be in bed when the maid arrived. In the distance she heard the train whistle, a familiar sound that now seemed to underscore her loneliness.

She had dreaded this day since she heard the rumor through *supposed* friends—the rumor that turned out to be devastating. And true. Today was her husband's wedding day, technically her ex-husband. He was getting re-married. *He will always be my husband*, she thought.

Less than six months ago he returned from a New York business trip distracted. She had known something was wrong by the way he went straight upstairs without checking the stack of mail on the credenza. His quickened pace, his distant gaze, his tie loosened at the neck. Stone-faced and pre-occupied, he wouldn't look at her. He was different. After twenty-five years she recognized different.

"What's wrong?" she asked.

"We need to talk." She knew.

Now she felt old and tired and divorced. She missed the smell of his aftershave, his robe in the bathroom, the black one bought in Aspen years ago. The house even missed him. It was already bigger with the kids off to college; now it had taken on an echo.

Her reflection was unrecognizable in the bathroom mirror. Dark circles and lines shadowed her hazel eyes where none existed before. Even her favorite eye cream from Nordstrom's didn't camouflage the last six months. Since the "talk," everything required effort—effort to shower, effort to apply that expensive eye cream, to plaster a fake smile on her face, to pretend everything was back to normal. Nothing would ever be normal again.

There were always signs. She had watched enough Lifetime television to know. Even so, she was totally unprepared. When the children were young, she began adding to the ever-growing list in her head of projects she intended to do and places she planned to visit *when she had time*. She needed that list but it vanished along with her husband, her future. She could not recall a single item or project or trip that did not involve her kids or husband. She could not remember herself. She could not think.

Everyone said the art class at SMU was a good first step, a fresh start, time to herself to enjoy her interests. Pretended excitement was exhausting. In truth, she enjoyed being the wife of an important man, planning events and hosting parties in their home, her home now. Her empty home. She was lost, a fraud. Untethered.

The hole-in-the-wall café by the railroad track provided her only relief. She was unknown there. It was not the type of place she had visited *before*. But now it became her refuge. She sat and drank white wine each afternoon until the 6:00 train passed by, until it was respectable to return home, until she had accomplished something that day, left the house at least. She stared at the wine label, studied it, thinking about trips to Napa and Sonoma with friends from her husband's business. She didn't know that much about wines and remembered laughing when a vintner described his Chenin Blanc as "sprightly and beguiling." These words stuck with her all these years. She was sprightly and beguiling once, in college, another lifetime, when they first met.

"You want something to eat, ma'am?" The waitress stared at her. She had not heard her walk up to the table.

She checked her iPhone. It was 5:45. "No, I have somewhere to be soon." The waitress, a child really, was beautiful and still hopeful. She wore a thin gold wedding band. So young.

She almost blurted out to her, *"Do you know what happens when your husband walks out with his robe and his aftershave and your life?"* But she didn't, afraid it would sound like the opening line to a bad joke. Instead she smiled. Sometimes she did eat chicken salad there—she always intended to ask for the recipe but never had. It was made with walnuts and dried cherries and something she couldn't quite make out—maybe dill? She sat and experienced the wine, feeling numb. Numb was better.

Leaving a generous tip under the saltshaker, she walked to her new Lexus, concentrating on walking straight, hoping her stride appeared effortless. *I never got the car tags in the mail*, she thought. Even with the car window lowered a bit, the inside was steamy, the steering wheel hot to the touch.

Texas was too hot. She re-applied lip gloss, checking the mirror to make sure there was none on her teeth. She hated to be without lipstick. She noted the time again.

Leaving the parking lot she heard the train whistle only a few blocks away, slow but building, like the symphony orchestra warming up, a bit off-key, not quite in tune. As the train neared, the sound of the whistle became steady and louder, in tune, vibrating the ground with its power. It altered the air. She just had time to make it.

Story Contests
Fresh Ink Group

Short Stories, Novels, Memoirs, All Genres

NO ENTRY FEES

The Members of FIG
invite you to submit
your most impressive writing.

We recognize and publish
The BEST so
YOU grow your loyal fan-base.

Varying contests run year-round.

Submission guidelines:
FreshInkGroup.com/Contests

The Fresh Ink Group

Publishing
Memberships
Share & Read Free Stories, Essays, Articles
Free-Story Newsletter
Writing Contests

Books
E-books
Amazon Bookstore

Authors
Editors
Artists
Professionals
Publishing Services
Publisher Resources

Members' Websites
Members' Blogs
Social Media

www.FreshInkGroup.com

Email: info@FreshInkGroup.com

Twitter: @FreshInkGroup

Google+: Fresh Ink Group

Facebook.com/FreshInkGroup

LinkedIn: Fresh Ink Group

About.me/FreshInkGroup

More Books by Stephen Geez

General Fiction
Dance of the Lights
What Sara Saw
Papala Skies
How It Turns Out

Media Thriller
Fantasy Patch

Mystical Adventure Series
Rich Mr. Fixx: *Crystal Clear* #1
Rich Mr. Fixx: *Spider-Boxed* #2
Rich Mr. Fixx: *Hot Doggies* #3
Rich Mr. Fixx Graphic Flashback #1: *Shell Game*

Science Fiction
Invigilator
Zhasou Pure

Essay Collection
Been There, Noted That

GeezWriter How-to
E-book Series for Writers

JAZZ BABY

By Beem Weeks

While all Mississippi bakes in the scorching summer of 1925, a sudden orphanhood casts its icy shadow across Emily Ann Teegarten, a pretty young teen.

Taken in by an aunt bent on ridding herself of this unexpected burden, "Baby" Teegarten plots her escape using the only means at her disposal: a voice that makes church ladies cry and angels take notice. "I'm gonna sing jazz up to New York City," she brags to anybody who'll listen. 'Cept that Big Apple—well, it's an awful long way from that dry patch of earth she used to call home.

So when the smoky stages of New Orleans speakeasies give a whistle, offering all kinda shortcuts, Emily soon learns it's the whorehouses and drug joints promising to tickle more than just a young girl's fancy that can dim a spotlight . . . and knowing the wrong people can snuff it out.

Jazz Baby just wants to sing—not fight to stay alive.

www.FreshInkGroup.com
ISBN: 978-1-936442-10-2

THE GATES OF VALHALLA

By Jasper Grawl

From the very beginning of the Universe, to primitive man's invention of Time, through the distant future when countless souls populate vast swaths of empty space, *Valhalla* shows us what really becomes of mankind when we let the politicians run the show.

In an age where farce is the Universe's only unifying principle, where the only requirement for faster-than-light travel is proper footwear, where a cheap catchphrase and an orange brochure constitute what passes for religion, Stan has the audacity to resurrect his failing church business by turning the place into a bar and giving his customers what they really want. Stan's is the only church with the recipe for Salvation. They sell it on tap.

Meanwhile, crotchety curmudgeon Gumballs finds himself trying to navigate the mind-numbing bureaucracy of the afterlife, his sin-surance policy wholly inadequate, the specter of eternal Hell looming every bit as wretched as an afternoon on C-SPAN.

The Gates of Valhalla offers a hilarious yet biting satire on the foibles and fallibilities of everyday people, what they believe, and how they somehow manage to govern their daily lives. It dares to tackle such trivialities as life and death, heaven and hell, sin and redemption, Earth's corned beef claim to galactic fame, and the very survival of mankind. Jasper Grawl's side-splitting novel leads you straight to the gates and dares you to step through.

www.FreshInkGroup.com
ISBN: 978-1-936442-18-8

Fantasy Patch

By Stephen Geez

Picture This!

Danté Roenik creates ad campaigns, reveling in the fine art of rendering his concepts on million-dollar canvasses financed by big-budget clients. Intoxicated by the sheer power of directing public opinion, he dares wage war against the conglomerate behind a worldwide antidepressant increasingly associated with sporadic violence. To juxtapose his images with reality, he enlists a mixed palette of business tycoons, his fiancée/attorney, a team of corporate-spy soldiers of fortune, one resurgent news anchor, and the best TV-production crew in Chicago.

But the sharp lines dividing perception from truth begin to blur when the darker motives shaping mass media come to light. Forced to re-examine the ethics of designer pharmacology, Danté is painted into a corner, his future about to be erased as patients die, clients lie, and unhealthy doses of murder prove too hard to swallow. Too late to whitewash the stain of deceit, Danté must decide who deserves to appear in his picture, the true subject an unfinished self-portrait way past its own deadline. It's not what you see, not what you get . . .

But all you could ever imagine. Let Danté show you how . . .

With a Fantasy Patch!

www.FreshInkGroup.com
ISBN: 978-1-936442-06-5

PAPALA SKIES

By Stephen Geez

Chicago native Rochelle DuFortier likes to imagine the future, her world a series of picture postcards so vivid they sometimes seem real. When a foolish mistake at thirteen causes her mother's death, she's sent to a secluded Hawaiian valley, an outsider "haole-girl" among pidgin-speaking boys who hurl flaming papala spears under the full moon to summon her mother's spirit. After boarding school and a prestigious university back east, the ambitious young woman is torn between chasing new career opportunities, discovering her mother's heritage in a remote French village, and meeting obligations pulling her back to Hawaii.

On this island steeped in ancient mythology and modern superstition, Rochelle tests the possibility of sharing pieces of her life with those whose beliefs she barely understands and never intends to embrace. She dives the depths of a pristine coral lagoon, conceals bodies in a subterranean lava tube, and challenges the eruptions of a living volcano, even as she deciphers the truth about her mother's death and struggles to satisfy new debts born of old betrayals.

Papala Skies is the story of a young woman who makes all the right choices, only to find herself living an unexpected life. It is about the need to belong, and seeking one's own version of truth amid such differing cultures' responses to wrenching loss and abiding grief. It is about yearning for a sense of place, yet having to confront new ways to honor the love of family and friends.

Will Rochelle lose what matters most, or might she learn what the smart octopus already knows?

www.FreshInkGroup.com

ISBN: 978-1-936442-07-2

BEEN THERE, NOTED THAT:

Essays In Tribute To Life

Observations, Inspiration, Remembrance, & Noteworthies To Share

By Stephen Geez

The simple lives of everyday people in a mundane world prove extraordinary in this collection of 54 personal-experience essays by novelist Stephen Geez. The eclectic mix of memoir, commentary, humor, and appreciation covers a wide range of topics, each beautifully illustrated by artists and photographers from the Fresh Ink Group. Geez catches what many of us miss, then considers how we might all share the most poignant of lessons. *Been There, Noted That* aims to reveal who we are, examine where we've been, and discover what we dare strive to become.

www.FreshInkGroup.com
ISBN: 978-1-936442-05-8